THE GHOST RIDERS OF ORDEBEC

Also by Fred Vargas

The Chalk Circle Man
Have Mercy on Us All
Seeking Whom He May Devour
The Three Evangelists
Wash This Blood Clean From My Hand
This Night's Foul Work
An Uncertain Place

Fred Vargas

The Ghost Riders
of Ordebec

*Translated from the French by
Siân Reynolds*

Harvill *Secker*

LONDON

Published by Harvill Secker 2013

2 4 6 8 10 9 7 5 3 1

First published with the title *L'armée furieuse* in 2011
by Éditions Viviane Hamy, Paris

First published in Great Britain in 2013 by
HARVILL SECKER
Random House
20 Vauxhall Bridge Road
London SW1V 2SA

www.vintage-books.co.uk

Addresses for companies within The Random House Group Limited can be found at:
www.randomhouse.co.uk/offices.htm

The Random House Group Limited Reg. No. 954009

A CIP catalogue record for this book is available from the British Library

ISBN 9781846557361 (hardback)
ISBN 9781846554452 (trade paperback)

This book is supported by the Institut français as part of the Burgess programme.

MIX
Paper from
responsible sources
FSC
www.fsc.org
FSC® C016897

Typeset in Minion by Palimpsest Book Production Limited,
Falkirk, Stirlingshire

Printed and bound in Great Britain by
Clays Ltd, St Ives plc

THE GHOST RIDERS OF ORDEBEC

I

A TRAIL OF TINY BREADCRUMBS LED FROM THE KITCHEN INTO THE bedroom, as far as the spotless sheets where the old woman lay dead, her mouth open. Commissaire Adamsberg looked down at the crumbs in silence, pacing slowly to and fro, and wondering what kind of Tom Thumb – or what ogre in this case – might have dropped them there. He was in a small, dark, ground-floor apartment, with just three rooms, in the eighteenth arrondissement, in northern Paris.

The old woman was lying in the bedroom. Her husband was in the dining room. He showed neither impatience nor emotion as he waited, just looked longingly at his newspaper, folded open at the page with the crossword puzzle, which he didn't dare try to solve while the police were there. He had told them his brief life story. He and his wife had met at work, in an insurance company: she was a secretary, he an accountant. They had married in their careless youth, not knowing it was destined to last fifty-nine years. Then his wife had died in the night. Heart attack, according to the local commissaire, who was ill in bed and had called on Adamsberg to replace him. Just do me a favour, it won't take more than an hour, a routine morning call.

One more time, Adamsberg walked the trail of crumbs. The flat was impeccably kept: the armchairs had antimacassars, the Formica surfaces were gleaming, the windows were spotless and the dishes washed. He went over to the bread bin, which contained part of a baguette, and a large half-loaf, wrapped in a clean tea towel and hollowed out in the middle.

He returned to the husband sitting in his armchair, and pulled up another chair alongside.

'No good news this morning,' the old man said, lifting his eyes from the paper. 'And it's so hot, the ink is smudged. Still, here we're on the ground floor, it's a bit cooler. That's why I leave the shutters closed. And you have to drink plenty, that's what they tell you.'

'You didn't notice anything?'

'She seemed all right when I went to bed. I always checked, because she had heart trouble. It was only this morning that I realised she'd gone.'

'There are breadcrumbs in her bed.'

'Yes, she liked to nibble some bread or perhaps a *biscotte* last thing before going to sleep.'

'I would have thought she'd clean the crumbs up afterwards.'

'Oh yes, indeed. She cleaned things from morning to night, you'd think her life depended on it. It wasn't so bad at first, but over the years it got to be an obsession. She'd even make things dirty, just for the pleasure of washing them. You should have seen her. Still, poor woman, it gave her something to do.'

'But what about this bread? She didn't sweep it up last night?'

'No, because it was me that brought it her. She was too weak to get up. She *did* tell me to clear the crumbs away, but I couldn't be bothered. She'd have done it in the morning. She turned the sheets every day. What for, I couldn't tell you.'

'So, you brought her some bread, then you put the rest back in the bread bin?'

'No, I threw it in the *pedal* bin. It was too hard, she couldn't manage it. I brought her a *biscotte* instead.'

'But the loaf isn't in the pedal bin, it's in the bread bin.'

'Yes, I know.'

'And there's nothing inside the loaf. She ate all the heart of it?'

'No, good heavens, commissaire. Why would she just eat the inside of it – and stale at that? You *are* a commissaire, aren't you?'

'Yes, Jean-Baptiste Adamsberg, Serious Crime Squad.'

'Why didn't the local police come?'

'This district's commissaire's in bed. Summer flu. And his team isn't available.'

'Have they all got the flu?'

'No, there was a disturbance last night. Two dead, four injured. All because of a stolen scooter.'

'What's the world coming to? Still, this heat, it gets to people. My name is Tuilot, monsieur. Tuilot, first name Julien, accountant, retired, for the insurance company ALLB.'

'Yes, I've got a note of that.'

'She always nagged me about my name, Tuilot, she thought her maiden name was nicer, Kosquer. She was right, I suppose. I thought you must be a commissaire to ask questions about the breadcrumbs. Your colleague up here, he's not like that.'

'You think I'm making too much fuss about the crumbs?'

'Oh, you just do whatever you want, monsieur. It's for your report, you have to have something to write on the report. I understand, that's all I ever did at ALLB, accounts and reports. Not that the reports were strictly honest. Think about it. The boss had this motto, he brought it out all the time: an insurance company shouldn't pay, even if it ought to pay. Fifty years cheating like that doesn't do your brain any good. I used to say to my wife, if you could just wash out my head instead of the curtains, you'd be doing something really useful.'

Monsieur Tuilot, Julien, gave a little laugh at his joke.

'It's just that I don't understand what you're telling me about the half-loaf over there.'

'Ah, to understand, you have to be logical, commissaire, logical and cunning. That's me, Tuilot, Julien, I've won sixteen top-level crossword championships in thirty-two years. One every other year on average. Just with my brain. Logical and cunning. It brings in good money at that level. This one,' he said, pointing to his newspaper, 'is just kids' stuff. But you have to sharpen your pencils and it leaves shavings. Oh, she was always on at me, because of the shavings too. So what bothers you about the bread?'

'Well. It's *not* in the pedal bin, it doesn't seem all that stale to me, and I don't understand why the crust has been hollowed out.'

'Aha. A domestic mystery!' said Tuilot, who seemed to be enjoying himself. 'Well, I have two little tenants, Toni and Marie, a sweet little couple, who love each other dearly. But they're not at all to my wife's taste, believe me. One shouldn't speak ill of the dead, but she did all she could to kill them. I've been one step ahead of her for three years. Logic and cunning, that's my secret. My poor Lucette, you'll never beat a cross-word champion, I used to tell her. No, we're a little gang of three, these two and me, they know they can count on me, and I can count on them. A little visit every night. They're crafty and careful, they never come until Lucette's in bed. They know I'll be waiting for them, you see. Toni always arrives first, he's bigger and stronger.'

'And they ate all the crumbs? While the bread was in the *pedal bin*?'

'They love doing that.'

Adamsberg glanced at the crossword, which didn't look as simple as all that to him, then pushed the paper aside.

'So who are "they", Monsieur Tuilot?'

'I don't like to say, people disapprove. People are very narrow-minded.'

'Animals? Dogs, cats?'

'Rats. Toni's darker than Marie. They're so fond of each other they can be in the middle of their meal, and they stop to stroke each other's head with their paws. If people weren't so prejudiced, they'd see sights like that. Marie's the lively one. After eating, she climbs on my shoulder and puts her paws in my hair. She's combing it, sort of. Her way of saying thank you. Or perhaps she just likes me. Who knows? It's comforting. Then after we've said nice things to each other, we say goodbye till next evening. They go back to the cellar, through a hole behind the drainpipe. One day Lucette cemented it up. Poor Lucette. She had no idea how to mix cement.'

'I see,' said Adamsberg.

The old man reminded him of a certain Félix, who used to prune his vines, eight hundred and eighty-eight kilometres from Paris. He had tamed a grass snake that he used to feed with milk. One day a neighbour killed the snake. So Félix killed the neighbour. Adamsberg went back to the bedroom where Lieutenant Justin was keeping watch over the dead woman, while waiting for the doctor to arrive.

'Look inside her mouth,' he said. 'Just take a look and see if you can see some white residue that could be breadcrumbs.'

'I really don't want to do that.'

'Just do it. I think the old man could have choked her by stuffing bread down her throat. Then he took it out and chucked it away.'

'You mean the inside of the loaf?'

'Yes.'

Adamsberg opened the bedroom window and shutters. He looked out at the little courtyard, strewn with birds' feathers, and partly transformed into a junkyard. In the centre, a grid covered the drain. It was still wet, although there had been no rain.

'After that, go and lift up the grid. I think he chucked the bread down there and emptied a bucket of water after it.'

'This is nuts,' muttered Justin, as he shone a torch inside the old woman's mouth. 'If he did that, why didn't he throw away the crust, or clean up the crumbs?'

'To throw away the crust, he would have had to go to the dustbins on the street, and that would mean going out on the pavement at night. There's a cafe terrace next door, and these warm nights plenty of people about. He'd have been seen. He's invented a good story about the crust and the crumbs. So original that it seems plausible. He's a crossword champion, he has his own way of linking ideas.'

Adamsberg, feeling rather regretful and yet slightly admiring, came back to Tuilot.

'When Marie and Toni turned up, you took the bread out of the pedal bin?'

'No, they know how it works, they like it. Toni sits on the pedal, the lid goes up and Marie gets out anything they want. They're great, aren't they? Really smart, got to hand it to them.'

'So Marie got the bread out. Then they ate it up. While making little loving gestures?'

'That's right.'

'*All* the inside of the loaf?'

'They're big rats, commissaire, they need to eat a lot.'

5

'So what about those crumbs on the floor, why didn't they eat those?'

'Commissaire, are you here to take care of Lucette or the rats?'

'Well, I still don't understand why you wrapped up the remains of the loaf after the rats had eaten out its inside. Whereas before that, you'd put it in the pedal bin.'

The old man filled in a couple of crossword clues.

'You're probably no good at crosswords, commissaire. If I'd thrown the empty loaf into the pedal bin, Lucette would have realised that Toni and Marie had been here.'

'You could have put it in the dustbin outside.'

'The door squeaks like a pig being slaughtered. You must have noticed.'

'Yes, I did.'

'So I just wrapped it in a tea towel to avoid a scene in the morning. Because believe me, there are scenes all day long. Fifty years or more she's been yelling at me and wiping up under my glass, under my feet, under my bum. You wouldn't think I had the right to walk about or sit down. If you'd been living like that, you'd have hidden the loaf too.'

'She wouldn't have seen it in the bread bin?'

'No, no. In the morning she eats *biscottes* with raisins. She must do it on purpose, because they make plenty of crumbs. Then she can busy herself for hours afterwards cleaning them up. See?'

Justin came into the room and nodded briefly to Adamsberg.

'But yesterday,' Adamsberg said, with a slightly heavy heart, 'that's not what happened. You hollowed out the loaf, two big fistfuls of solid bread, and you crammed them into her mouth. When she stopped breathing, you pulled it all out and put it down the drain in the courtyard. I'm amazed that you chose this method of killing her. I've never come across a case of someone being choked with bread.'

'Yes, it's inventive,' Tuilot agreed calmly.

'As you will know, Monsieur Tuilot, we'll find your wife's saliva on the bread. And since you are logical and cunning, we'll also find signs of the rats' teeth on the hollowed-out loaf. You let them eat the remains, to bolster your story.'

'They like nothing better than burrowing inside a loaf, it's a pleasure

6

to watch them. We spent a good evening here last night, really. I had a couple of drinks, while Marie combed my hair. Then I washed and dried my glass to avoid a row. When she was already dead.'

'When you had just killed her.'

'Yes,' said the man, sighing casually as he filled in a few blanks in his crossword. 'The doctor'd been round the day before, he told me she could last months. Dozens of Tuesdays having to eat sausage rolls for supper, endless recriminations, thousands of little wipes with a duster. At eighty-six, a man's got the right to live a little. There are nights like that. When a man just gets up and takes some action.'

Tuilot got up and opened the shutters in the dining room, letting in the stifling heat of these early-August days.

'She didn't like having the windows open either. But I won't say all that, commissaire. I'll say I killed her to put an end to her suffering. With bread-crumbs, because she liked that, a final little treat. I've got it all worked out in here,' he said, tapping his forehead. 'There's no evidence I didn't do it as a mercy killing. Eh? An act of kindness. I'll be acquitted, and in a couple of months, I'll be back here, I'll be able to put my glass on the table without a coaster and the three of us will be happy together, Toni, Marie and me.'

'Yes, I can believe it,' said Adamsberg, getting up quietly. 'But it might turn out, Monsieur Tuilot, that you won't dare put your glass down directly on the tabletop. You'll fetch a coaster. And you'll clean up the breadcrumbs.'

'Why would I do that?'

Adamsberg shrugged. 'Just that I've seen cases like this. It's often the way.'

'Don't you worry about me, monsieur. I'm cunning.'

'That's very true, Monsieur Tuilot.'

Outside, the heat was forcing people to walk in the shade, hugging the walls and breathing hard. Adamsberg decided to walk on the empty pavement exposed to the sun and to head south. A long hike to rid himself of the contented and, yes, cunning face of the crossword champion. Who might, one Tuesday soon, be buying sausage rolls for his supper.

II

HE WAS BACK AT HEADQUARTERS AN HOUR AND A HALF LATER, HIS black T-shirt dripping with sweat and his thoughts back in order. It was rare for an impression, good or bad, to haunt Adamsberg's mind for very long. So much so that you wondered if he had a mind at all, as his mother had often remarked. He dictated his report for the colleague with the flu, and went to collect any messages from reception. Brigadier Gardon, who was manning the switchboard, was bending his head low to catch the breeze from a little electric fan on the floor. His fine hair was floating in the cool draught, as if under a hairdryer.

'Lieutenant Veyrenc is waiting for you in the cafe, commissaire,' he said without moving.

'In the cafe or the brasserie?'

'The cafe, the Dice Shaker.'

'Veyrenc isn't a lieutenant any more, Gardon. We won't know till this evening whether he's going to rejoin the force.'

Adamsberg looked for a moment at Gardon, wondering whether Gardon had a mind and, if so, what he kept in it.

He sat down at Veyrenc's table and the two men greeted each other with warm smiles and a long handshake. The memory of Veyrenc's providential appearance in Serbia during his last case still sent a shiver down Adamsberg's spine. He ordered a salad, and ate it slowly while telling at some length the story of Madame Tuilot, Lucette; Monsieur Tuilot, Julien; Toni; Marie; their love, the half-eaten loaf, the pedal bin, the closed shutters and the sausage rolls on Tuesdays. Now and then he glanced at the cafe window. Tuilot, Lucette, would surely have made a better job of cleaning it.

Veyrenc ordered two coffees from the proprietor, a large man whose normally grumpy mood got worse in the heat. His wife, a silent little Corsican, went to and fro delivering the food like a dark fairy.

'One day,' said Adamsberg, gesturing towards her, 'she'll choke him with a couple of handfuls of bread.'

'Quite possibly,' Veyrenc agreed.

'She's still waiting on the pavement,' said Adamsberg, looking out at the street again. 'She's been there getting on for an hour in this blazing sun. She doesn't know what to do, she hasn't decided.'

Veyrenc followed Adamsberg's gaze, and examined the thin little woman, neatly dressed in a flowered overall, the kind you don't find in Paris shops.

'You can't be sure she wants to see *you*. She's not standing by the offices, she's coming and going about ten metres away. She must be waiting for someone who hasn't turned up.'

'No, it's for me, Louis, I'm sure of it. Who'd arrange a rendezvous in this street? She looks scared. That's what bothers me.'

'That's because she's not from Paris.'

'Maybe it's the first time she's come here. So she must have some serious problem. But that doesn't help us with yours, Veyrenc. You've had months to paddle your feet in the stream and think, and you still haven't decided.'

'You could extend the deadline.'

'I've already done that once. You have to sign, or not sign, by six o'clock tonight. You have to decide if you're going to be a cop again. Four and a half hours,' said Adamsberg consulting his watch, or rather the two watches he always wore for reasons no one could quite fathom.

'Plenty of time,' said Veyrenc, stirring his coffee.

Commissaire Adamsberg and ex-Lieutenant Louis Veyrenc de Bilhc, from two neighbouring villages in the Pyrenees, had in common a sort of detached tranquillity, which was rather disconcerting. In Adamsberg, it came across as a rather shocking air of inattention and indifference. In Veyrenc, this detachment generated unexplained absences, a stubborn obstinacy, sometimes silent and massive, sometimes punctuated by outbreaks of rage. 'It's the old mountain's fault,' Adamsberg would say, without looking for further justification. 'The old mountain was never going to produce frivolous, light-hearted grasses, like the ones that wave in the wind on rolling meadows.'

'Let's go,' said Adamsberg brusquely, paying the bill, 'the little woman looks like she's leaving. See, she's discouraged, hesitation is winning out.'

'I'm hesitating too,' said Veyrenc, swallowing the rest of his coffee in a gulp, 'but you're not helping me.'

'No.'

'OK. *Thus the waverer wanders, amid thickets of doubt / With no one to help him find the way to get out.*'

'People have always made their minds up before they take a decision. From the start. So there's no point asking advice. Except that I can tell you your verses irritate Commandant Danglard. He doesn't like to see poetry massacred.'

Adamsberg bade farewell to the cafe proprietor with a discreet wave. No point saying anything, the big man didn't like it, or rather he didn't like being 'nice'. He was like his cafe, lacking in comfort, aggressively proletarian and almost hostile to his customers. There was near-open warfare between this proud little bistro and the opulent brasserie across the road. The more the Brasserie des Philosophes accentuated its bourgeois pretensions, the more the Dice Shaker exaggerated the poverty of its decor, both of them engaged in a ruthless class struggle. 'One day,' Danglard would mutter, 'there's going to be a death.' Not counting the little Corsican woman who might stuff bread down her husband's throat.

Leaving the cafe, Adamsberg blew out his cheeks as the burning heat hit him, and cautiously approached the little woman who was still standing a few steps away from the squad's offices. There was a pigeon in front of the door to the building, and he thought that if he made the pigeon fly away as he walked past, the woman would fly away too, in imitation. As if she were light and airy and might vanish like a straw in the wind. Seen from close up, she looked about sixty-five. She had taken the trouble to visit the hairdresser before coming to the capital: there were blonde streaks in her grey hair. When Adamsberg spoke to her, the pigeon didn't budge and the woman turned a frightened face towards him. Adamsberg spoke slowly, asking her if she needed any help.

'No, thank you,' the woman said, dropping her gaze.

'You don't want to go inside?' asked Adamsberg, pointing to the old building where the Serious Crime Squad worked. 'To speak to a policeman or something? Because in this street there isn't a whole lot else to do.'

'But if the police don't listen to you? Then there's no point going to them,' she said, taking a few steps back. 'They don't believe you, you know, the police.'

'But that's where you *were* going? To this station?'

The woman lowered her eyelashes; they were almost transparent.

'Is this the first time you've been in Paris?'

'Oh goodness, yes. And I have to get back by tonight, they mustn't find out.'

'So you did come to see a policeman?'

'Yes. Well, maybe.'

'I'm a policeman. I work in there.'

The woman looked at Adamsberg's casual clothing and seemed disappointed or sceptical.

'So you must know them, the people in there?'

'Yes.'

'All of them?'

'Yes.'

The woman opened a large, shabby, brown leather handbag, and took out a piece of paper which she carefully unfolded.

'"Monsieur le Commissaire Adamsberg",' she read out painstakingly. 'You know him?'

'Yes. Have you come a long way to see him?'

'From Ordebec,' she replied, as if the confession cost her something.

'I don't know where that is.'

'Near Lisieux.'

Ah, Normandy, thought Adamsberg, that could explain her reluctance to talk. He had met several Normans in his time, taciturn people who had taken days to loosen up. As if saying a few words were the equivalent of giving away a gold sovereign, without feeling it was deserved. Adamsberg started walking, encouraging the woman to accompany him.

'There are plenty of police stations in Lisieux,' he said. 'And even in Ordebec, I dare say. You have your local gendarmes, don't you?'

'They wouldn't listen to me. But the curate in Lisieux knows the priest in Mesnil-Beauchamp and *he* said this commissaire here might listen to me. It cost a lot of money to come.'

'Is this about something serious?'

'Yes, of course it's serious.'

'A murder?' Adamsberg pressed.

'Maybe. Or maybe not. People are going to die. I ought to tell the police, shouldn't I?'

'People are going to *die*? Have they had death threats?'

This man reassured her a little. Paris was a scary place and her decision to come even more so. Leaving stealthily, lying to her children. What if the train didn't get her back in time? What if she missed the bus? This policeman had a soft voice, almost as if he were singing. Certainly not anyone from her area. No, he was a little man from southern France, with his dark complexion and drawn features. She would have told him the whole story, but the priest had made it very clear. She should speak to Commissaire Adamsberg and nobody else. And the priest wasn't just anyone, he was a cousin of the former chief prosecutor in Rouen who knew a lot about the police. He had only given her Adamsberg's name reluctantly, advising her preferably not to say anything, and looking as if he didn't expect her to make the trip. But she couldn't stay back home when these *things* were happening. What if any harm came to her children?

'I can only talk to the commissaire.'

'I *am* the commissaire.'

The little woman seemed on the point of arguing, frail though she looked.

'Why didn't you say so right away, then?'

'Well, I don't know who you are either.'

'Oh, no. You tell someone your name and next thing everyone can repeat it.'

'What does that matter?'

'It would bring trouble. Nobody must know.'

A busybody, a troublemaker, Adamsberg thought. Who would end up one day with bread stuffed down her throat. But a troublemaker who was scared stiff about something precise, which still preoccupied him. *People are going to die.*

They had turned back and were now walking towards the station.

'I only wanted to help you. I'd been watching you for a while.'

'And that man over there? He's with you? Was he watching me too?'

'Which man?'

'The one with funny hair, orange stripes in it, is he with you?'

Adamsberg looked up and saw Veyrenc a few metres away, leaning against the doorway of the building. He hadn't gone in, but was waiting, alongside the pigeon, which hadn't moved either.

'Ah,' said Adamsberg, 'that man, when he was a kid someone attacked him with a knife, and where he had scars, the hair grew back ginger like that. I advise you not to mention it.'

'I didn't mean any harm. I'm not good with words. I hardly ever say anything in Ordebec.'

'Never mind, no harm done.'

'But my children talk a lot.'

'Right.'

'What the devil's the matter with the pigeon anyway?' muttered Adamsberg to himself. 'Why doesn't it fly away?'

Weary of the little woman's indecision, Adamsberg left her and headed towards the pigeon, which was standing still, while Veyrenc came to meet him with his heavy tread. Fine, Veyrenc could take care of this woman, if it was worth bothering about. He could handle it perfectly well. Veyrenc's solid face was convincing, persuasive, and had the great advantage of a charming smile that made his top lip lift to the side. An advantage Adamsberg had once hated, and which had pitted them against each other as fierce rivals. Each of them was now trying to efface the last traces of their enmity. As Adamsberg lifted the pigeon up, cupped in his hands, Veyrenc came unhurriedly towards him, followed by the transparent little woman, who was breathing fast. In fact she was so slight that Adamsberg might not have noticed her at all if it weren't for the flowered overall that gave her body a shape. Perhaps she would be completely invisible if it weren't for the overall.

'Some nasty little kid has tied its feet together,' he said to Veyrenc, looking at the bird, which was filthy.

'Do you look after pigeons too?' asked the woman without a trace of irony. 'I've seen a whole lot of pigeons here, it's not hygienic –'

'Well, this one,' Adamsberg interrupted her, 'isn't a whole lot, it's just the one, one solitary pigeon. Makes all the difference.'

'Yes, of course,' said the woman.

So, she was understanding and, after all, doing no harm. Perhaps he was wrong and she wouldn't end up choked to death with bread. Perhaps she wasn't a troublemaker, but really had something serious to report.

'Do you like pigeons?' she asked him now. Adamsberg looked up absent-mindedly.

'No,' he said. 'But I don't like some sadistic kid tying their feet together either.'

'No, of course not.'

'I don't know if this kind of thing goes on where you live, but in Paris it happens. They catch a bird, tie its feet together with a bit of string. Then it can only take tiny steps and can't fly at all. It dies slowly from hunger and thirst. Just a game. But I hate it, and I intend to catch the kid who thought it was funny.'

Adamsberg went in through the large entrance to the squad's offices, leaving the woman and Veyrenc outside on the pavement. The woman was gazing spellbound at Veyrenc's hair, with its conspicuous ginger stripes.

14

'Will he really try to take care of that bird?' she asked, puzzled. 'It's too late, you know. Your commissaire had fleas jumping all over his arms. That means the pigeon hasn't got the strength to look after itself any more.'

Adamsberg took the bird to the squad's giantess, Lieutenant Violette Retancourt, whom he trusted blindly to care for it. If Retancourt couldn't save the pigeon, nobody could. Retancourt, an impressively tall and well-built woman, pulled a face: not a good sign. The bird was in a bad way. The skin of its feet had been pierced by its efforts to peck off the string, which was now embedded in its flesh. It was hungry and dehydrated, but she finally said she'd see what she could do. Adamsberg nodded, pinching his lips together, as he did whenever he encountered cruelty. Which that bit of string represented.

Following Veyrenc in, the little woman walked past the imposing Violette Retancourt with instinctive deference. The lieutenant was deftly wrapping the pigeon in a damp cloth. She'd tackle its claws later, she told Veyrenc, to try and get the string off. Held in her large hands, the pigeon did not attempt to move. It allowed her to handle it, as anyone would, anxious but impressed.

The little woman, seeming somewhat calmer, sat down in Adamsberg's office. She was so thin that she took up only half a chair. Veyrenc stood in a corner of the room, examining the surroundings that had once been so familiar to him. He had three and a half hours in which to make up his mind. It was, according to Adamsberg, already made up, but Veyrenc didn't know that yet. As he had walked through the large communal office, he had met the hostile gaze of Commandant Danglard, who was rummaging through a filing cabinet. It wasn't only Veyrenc's verses that Danglard disliked, it was the man himself.

III

THE WOMAN HAD FINALLY AGREED TO GIVE HER NAME AND ADAMSBERG was noting it down on a scrap of paper – a sign of negligence that worried her. Perhaps this commissaire really had no intention of listening to her.

'Valentine Vendermot, with an o and a t,' he repeated, since he always had difficulty with new words, especially proper names. 'And you're from Ardebec?'

'Ordebec. It's in the Calvados.'

'And you have children?'

'Four. Three sons and a daughter. I'm a widow.'

'So what happened, Madame Vendermot?'

The woman fished about again in her big bag and took out a local newspaper. She unfolded it, with slightly trembling hands, and put it on the table.

'It's this man. He's disappeared.'

'And what's his name?'

'Michel Herbier.'

'A friend of yours? A relative?'

'No, no. Quite the opposite.'

'What do you mean?'

Adamsberg waited patiently for the answer, which seemed difficult to put into words.

'I can't stand him.'

'Oh, OK,' he said, picking up the paper.

While Adamsberg was concentrating on the short news report, the woman kept glancing around anxiously at the walls, looking first left then right, though Adamsberg couldn't imagine why she was inspecting them. Something else was frightening her. She was scared of everything: of the big city, of other people, of gossip, and of him. Nor did he understand why she had come all this way to tell him about this Michel Herbier, if she hated him. The man in question, a pensioner, and a keen hunter, had disappeared from his home, on his moped. After he had been missing for a week, the gendarmes had entered his house to make a security check. They had found the contents of his two freezers – which had been packed with every kind of game – scattered all over the floor. And that was all.

'I can't get mixed up in this,' Adamsberg said apologetically, handing her back the newspaper. 'If this man's disappeared, the local gendarmes are in charge, you must understand that. And if you know anything about it, it's them you should go and see.'

'That's impossible, monsieur le commissaire.'

'Perhaps you don't get on with your local gendarmes?'

'That's right. That's why the priest gave me your name. That's why I made the trip here.'

'But to tell me what, Madame Vendermot?'

The woman smoothed down her flowered overall, and lowered her head. She spoke more readily if one didn't look at her.

'What has happened to him. Or what *will* happen to him. He's either dead already, or he'll die soon if nobody does anything.'

'It looks as if this man just took off, since his moped is missing too. Do we know if he took any baggage?'

'No, he just took his shotgun. He owns a lot of guns.'

'Well then, he'll no doubt be back sooner or later, Madame Vendermot. You know quite well that we've no right to launch a search for an adult, just because he hasn't been seen for a few days.'

'He won't be back, monsieur. The moped doesn't mean anything. It isn't there because someone wants there *not* to be a search for him.'

'Are you saying that because he's received threats?'

'Yes.'

'He has an enemy?'

'Holy Mother of god, he has the most terrible of enemies, commissaire.'

'Do you know his name?'

'Oh no, Lord alive, we mustn't speak it.'

Adamsberg gave a sigh, feeling sorrier for her than for himself.

'And according to you, this Michel Herbier has run away?'

'No, because he doesn't know about it. He must surely be dead. He was *seized*, you see.'

Adamsberg stood up and walked around the room for a few moments, hands in pockets.

'Madame Vendermot, I'm willing to listen to you, and perfectly willing to contact the gendarmerie in Ordebec. But I can't do anything if I don't understand. Give me a second.'

He left the office and went to see Commandant Danglard, who was still consulting the filing cabinet with a grumpy expression. Among the many billions of pieces of information Danglard held in his head were the names of the chiefs and deputy chiefs of the gendarmeries and central police stations throughout France.

'Danglard, the capitaine of gendarmes of Ordebec, can you do that?'

'In the Calvados?'

'Yes, that's it.'

'Émeri. Louis Nicolas Émeri, he was named Louis Nicolas after one of his ancestors on the wrong side of the blanket, one of Napoleon's marshals, Louis Nicolas Davout, commander of the third corps of the Grande Armée. Davout fought at Ulm, Austerlitz, Eylau and Wagram, and he was given the titles of Duke of Auerstadt and Prince of Eckmühl, after one of his famous victories.'

'Danglard, it's just the one who's around now that interests me, the head man in Ordebec.'

'That's what I'm saying. He's very keen on his ancestry, doesn't let you forget it. So he can be rather arrogant, proud, military. Apart from all the Napoleonic stuff, though, he's quite agreeable, a clued-up policeman, rather cautious – perhaps a bit too cautious. He's about forty. He didn't distinguish himself in his previous posting, somewhere near Lyon, I think. In Ordebec, he has a pretty quiet life. They don't get up to much there.'

Adamsberg returned to his office where the woman had once more continued her careful inspection of the walls.

'It's not easy, I know, commissaire. Because as a rule, you're not supposed to talk about it. It could bring terrible trouble. Tell me, are your shelves fixed on properly? Because you've put all the heavy boxes on the top ones and lighter things lower down. They could fall on top of a person, you know. You should always put heavier things at the bottom.'

Scared of the police, and scared of collapsing bookshelves.

'This Michel Herbier, why do you hate him so much?'

'*Everyone* hates him, commissaire. He's a brute, he's a horrible man, and he's always been like that. Nobody talks to him.'

'Well, that might explain why he's left Ordebec.'

Adamsberg picked up the newspaper again.

'He isn't married, he's retired, he's sixty-four. He might have decided to go and make a new start somewhere else. Does he have relations anywhere?'

'He *was* married. He's a widower.'

'How long since he was widowed?'

'Oh, fifteen years or more.'

'And you see him around now and then?'

'No, never. He lives a bit outside the village, so it's easy to keep out of his way. And that suits everyone.'

'But some neighbours are concerned about him?'

'Yes, the Hébrards. They're honest folk. They saw him go off at about six in the evening – they live across the lane, you see. And he lives about fifty yards further on, in the Bigard woods, near the old rubbish dump. It's very damp down there.'

'So why were they worried, if they saw him go off on the moped?'

'Because usually, when he goes away, he gives them the key to his mailbox. But he didn't, this time. And they didn't hear him come back. And there was post for him, sticking out of the box. So they thought Herbier only meant to go out for a short while, but something stopped him coming back. The gendarmes checked the hospitals, and he isn't there.'

'And when they went into his house, they found all the food from the freezers scattered on the floor?'

'Yes.'

'Why did he have all that meat? Does he have dogs?'

'He's a hunter, he puts his game in the freezers. He kills a lot of animals, and he never gives any to anyone else.'

The woman shivered.

'One of the gendarmes, Blériot, he's nice to me, not like Capitaine Émeri, he told me what it was like in there. Horrible, he said. There was half a carcass of a doe, with its head still on, and some sides of venison. Other female animals too, hares, wild boar, partridges. All chucked about any old how, monsieur. It had been rotting for days when the gendarmes went in. In this heat, all that rotting meat, it's a health hazard.'

Scared of bookshelves and scared of germs. Adamsberg glanced at the two huge stag antlers gathering dust, still lying on the floor of his office. They had been the generous gift from a Norman, as it happened.

'*Female* hares and whatnot? Your gendarme is observant – or perhaps he's a hunter too.'

'No, no, he says that because everyone knows what Herbier is like. He's a disgusting hunter, a wicked man. He only kills females and young animals and sometimes whole litters. He's been known to shoot at pregnant does.'

'How do you know that?'

'Everyone knows, monsieur. Herbier was had up once for killing a wild sow with some sucklings. Fawns too. Oh, it's unbelievable. But since he does it at night, Émeri can't catch him. What I can tell you is no other hunter will go out with him, and they haven't for years now. Even the other people who shoot game won't have him. He's been expelled from the Ordebec hunters' league.'

'Well, he seems to have dozens of enemies, Madame Vendermot!'

'Nobody wants to go near him, no.'

'So you think some other hunters might have killed him? Is that it? Or maybe *anti*-hunting campaigners?'

'No, no, commissaire. It was something else, something quite different.'

After being quite talkative for a few minutes, the woman was having difficulty speaking again. She still looked frightened, but this time it wasn't the bookshelves. It was a deeper, more persistent fear, still holding Adamsberg's attention in spite of himself, although the Herbier case did not apparently warrant making a trip all the way from Normandy.

'If you don't know anything,' he said wearily, 'and if you can't talk about it, I don't see how I can help you.'

Commandant Danglard had appeared in the doorway and was making urgent signals to him. A report had just come in with news about the little girl of eight who had run away in the Forest of Versailles, after breaking a fruit-juice bottle over the head of her great-uncle. The uncle had managed to reach a telephone before passing out. Adamsberg gave both Danglard and the woman to understand that her interview was coming to an end. It was the start of the summer holidays, and in three days a third of the staff would be off on annual leave, so current cases had to be dealt with quickly. The woman understood that there wasn't much time left. In Paris, you can't hang about all day, the priest had warned her, even if this little police chief had been patient and kind to her.

'It's Lina, my daughter,' she said hurriedly, 'she *saw* him, Herbier. She saw him two weeks and two days before he disappeared. She told her boss, and in the end all Ordebec knew about it.'

Danglard was back sorting out his files, a frown wrinkling his wide brow. He had seen Veyrenc in Adamsberg's office. What the hell was *he* doing there? Was he going to sign up, join the force again? The decision was due that evening. Danglard stopped near the photocopier and caressed the big cat lying on top of it, seeking comfort from its soft fur. The reason for his antipathy to Veyrenc was not easily confessed. It was a persistent and nagging jealousy, almost like that of a woman, the need to keep Veyrenc away from Adamsberg.

'We have to be quick, Madame Vendermot. Your daughter saw him, and something made her think he was going to be killed?'

'Yes, he was shrieking. And there were three others with him. At night.'

'There was a fight? Because of these does and fawns? A meeting, a hunting supper?'

'No, no.'

'Well, look, just come back tomorrow,' Adamsberg decided, moving towards the door, 'when you feel able to talk.'

Danglard was waiting for him, standing up and looking cross, leaning on the desk.

'Have they found this little girl?'

'The searchers found her hiding up a tree. She'd climbed very high, like a wild cat. And she was holding this gerbil in her hands, she didn't want to let it go. But the gerbil seems to be OK.'

'A what, Danglard? A gerbil?'

'It's a little mouse thing. Kids love them as pets.'

'And the child? What state is she in?'

'She's like your pigeon. She's starving hungry, and thirsty and tired. She's been taken to hospital. One of the nurses won't go in because of the gerbil – it's hiding under the bed.'

'And can the little girl tell us what this is all about?'

'No.'

Danglard was only giving his information out with some reluctance, still preoccupied with his own thoughts. It wasn't a day for chatting.

'She knows her great-uncle has survived?'

'Yes. She seemed both relieved and disappointed. She'd been living with him, just the two of them, for goodness knows how long, never set foot in school. And we're not at all sure now that he's actually a great-uncle.'

'Right, tell the Versailles police to follow it up. But tell whoever is in charge not to kill the gerbil. Have them catch it, put it in a cage and feed it.'

'Is that so urgent?'

'Obviously, Danglard, because it may be the only thing in the world this child has. One second.'

Adamsberg hurried over to Retancourt's office. She was getting ready to swab the pigeon's feet.

'Have you disinfected it, lieutenant?'

'Just a minute,' said Retancourt, 'we had to rehydrate it first.'

'Good, don't throw the string away, I want it analysed. Justin's got hold of the technician, he's on his way.'

'Damn bird just crapped on my hand,' said Retancourt coolly. 'What does that little woman want?' she asked, pointing to his office.

'To tell me something she can't tell me. Indecision personified. Either she'll leave of her own accord, or they'll have to chuck her out at closing time.'

Retancourt shrugged a little disdainfully. Indecision was something foreign to her way of life. Hence her powers of propulsion, far exceeding that of the twenty-seven other members of the squad.

'And what about Veyrenc? Is he still undecided too?'

'Veyrenc made his mind up long ago. Cop or schoolteacher, which would you choose? Teaching is a virtue that brings bitterness, police work is a vice that brings pride. And since it's easier to give up a virtue than a vice, he has no choice. I'm off to see this so-called great-uncle in hospital at Versailles.'

'What shall we do with this pigeon? I can't have it at home, my brother's allergic to feathers.'

'Your brother's staying with you?'

'Just for now. He lost his job, he nicked a case of bolts and some oil cans from the garage.'

'Can you drop him off at my place tonight then? The bird, I mean.'

'I suppose so,' Retancourt grumbled.

'Watch out, we have cats patrolling our garden.'

The little woman's hand was placed timidly on his shoulder. Adamsberg turned round.

'That night,' she said slowly, 'Lina saw the Furious Army.'

'The what?'

'The Furious Army,' the woman repeated, in a whisper. 'And Herbier was with them. And he was screaming. And three others with him.'

'Is it a club? Something to do with hunting?'

Madame Vendermot was staring at Adamsberg in disbelief.

'The Furious Army,' she whispered again. 'The Great Hunt. The Ghost Riders. Haven't you heard of them?'

'No,' said Adamsberg, staring back at her stupefied gaze. 'Come back some other time and you can tell me all about it.'

'But you don't even recognise the name? Hellequin's Horde,' she whispered.

'Look, I'm very sorry,' said Adamsberg, taking her back into his office. 'Veyrenc, do you know anything about some curious army?' he asked, pocketing his keys and his mobile.

'Not curious, *Furious*,' the woman corrected him.

'Yes. Madame Vendermot's daughter saw the missing man riding with it.'

'And some other people,' she insisted. 'Jean Glayeux, and Michel Mortembot. But my daughter didn't recognise the fourth.'

An expression of astonishment appeared on Veyrenc's face, then he smiled slightly with that raised lip. Like a man who has just been offered an unexpected treat.

'Your daughter really saw all this?' he asked.

'Yes, of course.'

'Where?'

'The usual place where people see it. On a road near Ordebec, the Chemin de Bonneval, in the Forest of Alance. It's always passed that way.'

'Is that near where she lives?'

'No, we live a few kilometres away.'

'And she went to try and see it?'

'No, no, certainly not. Lina's a very sensible girl, very down to earth. She just happened to be there, that's all.'

'At night?'

'It's only ever seen at night.'

Adamsberg was leading the little woman out of the office and asking her again to come back the next day, or to telephone him another time, when she'd sorted it all out more clearly in her mind. Veyrenc held him back discreetly, chewing on a pen.

'Jean-Baptiste,' he said, 'do you really not know what she's talking about? The Furious Army? The Ghost Riders?'

Adamsberg shook his head, rapidly combing his hair with his fingers.

'Well, ask Danglard,' Veyrenc insisted. 'It'll interest him a lot.'

24

'Why?'

'Because, as far as I know, if anyone sees them, it foretells disaster. Perhaps some big disaster.'

Veyrenc smiled again, and as if the intrusion of the Furious Army had made up his mind for him, he signed up to re-enlist.

IV

WHEN ADAMSBERG ARRIVED HOME, LATER THAN HE INTENDED, SINCE the great-uncle had turned out to be complicated, his neighbour, the elderly Spaniard Lucio, was pissing noisily against a tree in the little garden, in the warm evening.

'*Salud, hombre,*' said the old man, without interrupting what he was doing, 'one of your lieutenants is waiting for you. This big fat woman, tall as a house. Your boy let her in.'

'She's not a big fat woman, Lucio, she's a goddess, a polyvalent goddess.'

'Oh, that one?' said Lucio, buttoning his trousers. 'The one you're always going on about?'

'That's the one. The goddess. So naturally she doesn't look just like everyone else. Have you ever heard of something called the Curious Army? Mean anything to you?'

'No, *hombre.*'

Sitting in his kitchen were Lieutenant Retancourt and Adamsberg's grown-up son, known to him as 'Zerk'. (The commissaire couldn't get used to his given name, Armel, having been aware of his son's existence for only seven weeks: the nickname had its origin in the previous case, which had brought them together.) Cigarettes dangling from mouths, the pair were both peering into a basket lined with cotton wool. They didn't look up when Adamsberg came in.

'Have you got that?' Retancourt was asking the young man sternly. 'What you do is, you dip little bits of *biscotte* in water and you feed him gently with them. And a little water using the dropper, not too much at first. And you add one drop of the stuff in this bottle, it's a tonic.'

'Still alive?' Adamsberg asked, feeling himself oddly a stranger in his own kitchen, which had been invaded by this large woman and his previously unsuspected son aged twenty-eight.

Retancourt stood up, hands on hips. 'I don't know if he'll survive the night. Story so far: it took over an hour to peel the string off his legs, it's cut right down to the bone, he must have been pecking at it for days. But it didn't break. I've disinfected the wounds, and you'll have to change the dressing every morning. There's some gauze in here,' she went on, tapping a little box on the table. 'And he's been treated with flea powder, should take care of that problem.'

'Thanks, Retancourt. Did the young lad from forensics take the string?'

'Yes, after a bit of fuss, because the lab isn't paid to analyse string from pigeons. This one's a male by the way. Voisenet identified it.'

Lieutenant Voisenet had missed his vocation as a zoologist, because his father had high-handedly decided he should join the police. Voisenet was really a specialist on fish, saltwater, and especially freshwater, and ichthyological journals were always strewn around his desk. But he knew a lot about other fauna, from insects to bats, by way of gnus, and his scientific interests sometimes distracted him from his duties. The chief superintendent, Divisionnaire Brézillon, who was well aware of this, had sent him a warning, as he already had to Mercadet, who suffered from narcolepsy. But then, Adamsberg wondered, who in his squad didn't have some peculiarity? Apart from Retancourt, but then her capacities and energy were also a major deviation from the norm.

After she had left, Zerk stayed standing, arms dangling, and staring at the door.

'Impressive, isn't she?' said Adamsberg. 'It gets everyone that way the first time they meet her. And every other time as well.'

'She's really, really beautiful,' said Zerk.

Adamsberg looked at his son in surprise, for beauty wasn't the first thing that came to mind on meeting Violette Retancourt. Or grace, subtlety or indeed affability. In every way she was the opposite of the charming and fragile delicacy of her first name. Although she had fine features, they were framed by broad cheeks and powerful jaws, mounted on a neck like a bull's.

'If you say so,' Adamsberg agreed, not wishing to argue about the tastes of this young man he didn't really know yet.

He wasn't even sure about his son's level of intelligence. High? Low? One thing reassured the commissaire. Most people, including himself, were still undecided about his own level of intelligence. He didn't query his own intellectual capacity, so why start worrying about Zerk's? Veyrenc had assured him that the young man was talented, but Adamsberg had yet to discover at what.

'The Curious Army. Mean anything to you?' asked Adamsberg, as he carefully placed the basket holding the pigeon on the sideboard.

'The what?' said Zerk, who was laying the table, putting forks on the right, knives on the left, just like his father.

'Never mind. We'll ask Danglard. It's like I told your little brother when he was seven months old. And I'd have told you the same, if I'd known you at that age. There are three rules you have to remember, Zerk, and you'll always get by. When you can't find your way through to the end of something, ask Veyrenc. When you can't manage to do something, ask Retancourt. And when you don't know something, ask Danglard. Just bear those three things in mind. But Danglard is going to be very grumpy tonight, so I don't know if he'll tell us. Veyrenc's rejoining the squad and he won't like that. Danglard is an exotic plant and like all rare objects he's fragile.'

Adamsberg called his oldest deputy while Zerk was serving up dinner. Steamed tuna with courgettes, tomatoes and rice, followed by fruit. Zerk had asked if he could stay with his new father for a while, and the agreement was that he would look after the evening meal. It was an undemanding arrangement, since Adamsberg was fairly indifferent to what he ate and could have gone on forever swallowing identical platefuls of pasta, just as he always dressed in an identical manner, wearing a black canvas jacket and trousers, whatever the weather.

'Does Danglard really know everything?' the young man asked, frowning in a way that brought his eyebrows together: thick, like his father's, they made a sort of thatch over his vague expression.

'No, there are plenty of things he doesn't know. He has no idea how to find a woman, although, just now, he's had this lady friend for two months, which is an exceptional event. He can't divine water, but he's good at sniffing out white wine. He can't control his anxiety or forget the mass of questions that he keeps circling around, like a rat in a maze. He's no good at running, he doesn't know how to sit and watch the rain fall or the river flow, he has no idea how to ignore the cares of life and, worse still, he manufactures them ahead of time so that they won't take him by surprise. But he knows absolutely everything that doesn't look useful at first sight. All the libraries in the world have found their way inside Danglard's head and there's still plenty of room. It's something colossal, unprecedented, and I can't describe it to you.'

'But what's the point, if it isn't useful at first sight?'

'Well, obviously, it does become useful at second or sixth sight.'

'OK,' said Zerk, apparently satisfied with the answer. 'I don't know what *I* know. What do you think I know?'

'Same as me?'

'And what's that?'

'No idea, Zerk.'

Adamsberg raised a hand to indicate that he had finally got through to Danglard.

'Danglard? Everyone asleep at your place now? Can you pop over here?'

'If it's for that pigeon, forget it. It's covered in fleas and I have very bad memories of fleas. Plus I don't like their expression under the microscope.'

Zerk consulted his father's two watches to find out the time. Violette had ordered him to give the pigeon something to eat and drink every hour. He soaked a few fragments of *biscotte*, filled the water dropper, including the drop of tonic, and set about his task. The bird's eyes were closed but it accepted the food the young man put into its beak. Zerk lifted the pigeon up gently as Violette had shown him. This woman had given him a shock. He would never have imagined that such a creature could exist. He could still see her large hands deftly dealing with the pigeon, and the blonde curls falling on the golden feathery down that covered her strong neck, as she lean over the table.

'Zerk's taking care of the pigeon. Anyway, it doesn't have fleas any more, Retancourt's sorted it.'

'So, what do you want?'

'Something's bothering me, Danglard. That little woman in the flowery overall who was in the office today, did you notice her?'

'I suppose so. Strangely inconsistent, physically evanescent. If you blew on her she'd fly away like the achenes of a dandelion clock.'

'The *what*, Danglard?'

'You know, dandelion seeds, with fluffy parachutes. Didn't you blow on them when you were little?'

'Yes of course, everyone does, but I didn't know they were called achenes.'

'Well, they are.'

'Anyway, apart from her fluffy parachute, this woman was paralysed with fear.'

'Didn't notice that.'

'Yes, she was, Danglard. Pure terror, terror from deep inside some well of horror.'

'Did she tell you why?'

'It was as if she wasn't allowed to say. On pain of death perhaps. But she whispered something to me. Her daughter had seen the Curious Army go past. Do you know what she meant?'

'No.'

Adamsberg was bitterly disappointed, almost humiliated, as if he had just carried out a failed experiment in front of his son, and not lived up to the promise he had just made. Meeting Zerk's anxious expression, he signalled to him that the demonstration wasn't over yet.

'Veyrenc seemed to know something about it,' Adamsberg went on. 'He suggested I consult you.'

'Oh, he did, did he?' said Danglard more sharply, as the name of Veyrenc seemed to operate on him like the buzzing of a hornet. 'And what did he hear her say, exactly?'

'That her daughter saw this Curious Army go past in the night, and among this band of people, the daughter – Lina, her name is – saw this hunter and three other men. And since then the hunter has been missing for over a week, and the little woman thinks he's dead.'

'Where? Where did she see this?'

'On some road near where they live, somewhere near Ordebec, in Normandy.'

'Ah,' said Danglard, now really animated, as always when his knowledge was requested, and as ever when he could plunge into his vast reservoir of information and bask in it. 'Ah. You mean the *Furious* Army, not the Curious Army.'

'Sorry. Furious, yes.'

'That was what she said? Hellequin's Horde?'

'Yes, she did say some name like that.'

'The Ghost Riders? The Great Hunt?'

'Yes, that too,' said Adamsberg with a triumphant wink at Zerk, like someone who has just managed to land a huge swordfish.

'And this Lina, she saw the hunter with this troop?'

'Correct. He was shrieking, apparently. So were the others. The group was apparently alarming in some way, the little woman with the dandelion parachute seems to think these men are under threat.'

'Alarming,' said Danglard, allowing himself a brief laugh. 'That's hardly the word for it, commissaire.'

'That was what Veyrenc said too. That this wretched band was somehow indicating some kind of disaster.'

Adamsberg had mentioned Veyrenc once more deliberately, not with the intention of wounding Danglard, but to try and get him used to the idea that the lieutenant with the ginger stripes in his hair would be back in the squad, to vaccinate him so to speak, by injecting Veyrenc's name in gentle repeated doses into his conversation.

'Just some kind of internal disaster,' said Danglard, more evenly. 'Nothing urgent.'

'Veyrenc couldn't tell me anything else. Come round and have a drink, Zerk's been laying in stocks for you.'

Danglard didn't like to agree immediately to Adamsberg's summonses, quite simply because he always accepted, and this lack of willpower humiliated him. He put up some muttered resistance for a few minutes, while Adamsberg, well used to the commandant's reluctance, went on insisting.

'Off you go, son,' said Adamsberg, putting the phone down. 'Go and get some white wine from the corner shop. Don't mess about, get the best, we can't serve any old plonk to Danglard.'

'Can I have a drink with you?' Zerk asked.

Adamsberg looked at his son without knowing what to say. Zerk hardly knew him, he was twenty-eight years old, he didn't have to ask anyone's permission, least of all Adamsberg's.

'Of course,' he said automatically. 'As long as you don't knock it back like Danglard,' he added, and the paternalism of this remark surprised him. 'There's some money on the sideboard.'

They both looked across at the basket. A maxi-punnet for strawberries, which Zerk had emptied to make a cosy bed for the pigeon.

'How does he seem?' Adamsberg asked.

'He's shivering, but he's alive,' his son replied cautiously.

Surreptitiously, the young man stroked the bird's feathers with a finger on his way out. Well, he's good at that, at least, thought Adamsberg, watching his son go, he's got a talent for stroking birds, even one as ordinary, dirty and unprepossessing as this one.

V

'IT'LL GO QUICKLY,' SAID DANGLARD, AND ADAMSBERG DIDN'T KNOW at first whether he was talking about the Furious Army or the wine, since his son had brought only one bottle back from the shop.

Adamsberg took a cigarette from Zerk's packet, a gesture which irresistibly reminded him of how they had first met, during a particularly gruesome case. Since that time, he had been smoking again, usually Zerk's cigarettes. Danglard was attacking his first glass.

'I presume the dandelion woman didn't want to talk to the capitaine of gendarmes in Ordebec?'

'She refuses to consider it.'

'Doesn't surprise me, he wouldn't appreciate it. And you, commissaire, you'll be able to forget it all afterwards too. Do we know anything about this hunter who's disappeared?'

'He's a brutal hunter of game, and worse, he mostly kills females and young animals. The local hunting league has expelled him, and nobody wants to go out shooting with him now.'

'Bad guy then? Violent? A killer?' asked Danglard, taking a mouthful of wine.

'Looks like it.'

'That fits. This Lina, she lives in Ordebec then?'

'Yes, I think so.'

'Have you really never heard of this little place, Ordebec? A great composer lived there for a while.'

'That's irrelevant, commandant.'

'But at least it's a positive note. The rest is more disquieting. This army. Did it go past on the Chemin de Bonneval?'

'Yes, that was the name she mentioned,' Adamsberg replied in surprise. 'Did you hear her say that?'

'No, but it's a well-known *grimweld*, it goes through the Forest of Alance. You can be sure anyone who lives in Ordebec will be well aware of it, and that they often talk about this story, even if they'd prefer to forget it.'

'I don't know what that means, Danglard: *grimweld*.'

'It's the name they give a road where Hellequin's Horde goes past – the Furious Army if you prefer, or they sometimes call it the Great Hunt, or the Ghost Riders. Only a very few men or women have ever seen it. One man is quite well known. He saw it going to Bonneval, like your Lina. Gauchelin, his name was, a priest.'

Danglard swallowed another two large mouthfuls of wine and smiled. Adamsberg tapped his cigarette ash into the cold fireplace and waited. The slightly provocative smile creasing the commandant's jowly cheeks was not a good sign, except that it meant Danglard was now completely at ease.

'It happened in early January in the year 1091. Good choice of wine, Armel, but there won't be enough for three of us.'

'In the year what?' said Zerk, moving his stool closer to the fireplace and preparing, elbows on knees, and glass in hand, to pay close attention to the commandant.

'The end of the eleventh century. Five years before the First Crusade.'

'Oh, for god's sake,' said Adamsberg to himself, suddenly having the unpleasant impression that this little woman from Ordebec, fragile dandelion clock or not, had been leading him on a wild goose chase.

'Yes indeed,' said Danglard. 'A lot of fuss about nothing, commissaire. But you do still want to know why she was afraid, don't you?'

'Maybe.'

'In that case, you ought to know the story about Gauchelin. But we'll need another bottle,' he repeated. 'There are three of us.'

Zerk jumped up. 'I'll go back to the shop,' he said.

Before he went out, Adamsberg saw him pass a finger lightly over the pigeon's feathers. And Adamsberg repeated mechanically, like a father: 'There's some money on the sideboard.'

Seven minutes later, Danglard, reassured by the presence of a second bottle, poured himself another glass, and began to tell Gauchelin's story, then broke off, frowning up at the low ceiling.

'But maybe it would be clearer if I told you about Hélinand de Froidmond, from the early thirteenth century,' he wondered. 'Give me a minute to remember it, it's not a text I look at every day.'

'Whatever you like,' said Adamsberg, now completely lost. Since learning that they were off into the mists of the Middle Ages, abandoning Michel Herbier to his fate, the story of the little woman and her panic now seemed of little consequence to him.

He stood up, poured himself a little wine, and took a look at the pigeon. The Furious Army didn't concern him, and he had obviously been mistaken about the evanescent Madame Vendermot. She didn't need his help. She was simply an inoffensive woman with mental problems, who was afraid bookshelves might fall on her head, even those of the eleventh century.

'It was his uncle Hellebaud who told the tale,' Danglard went on, now addressing the young man only.

'Hélinand de Froidmond's uncle?' asked Zerk, concentrating hard.

'Precisely, his paternal uncle. And this was what he said: "*When towards midday we approached this forest, my servant, who was ahead of me, riding fast to make the lodgings ready for my arrival, heard a great tumult in the woods, like the whinnying of many horses, the clash of arms and the shouts of men on the attack. He and his horse being terrified, he came back towards me, and when I asked him why he had turned round, he said, My horse would by no means go forward even when I whipped or spurred him, and I was so frightened myself, I was unable to move. I have heard and seen the most astounding things.*"'

Danglard held out his glass towards the young man.

'Armel,' he said – since Danglard absolutely refused to call the young man by his nickname, Zerk, and regularly criticised Adamsberg for using it – 'Armel, please refill my glass and I'll tell you what this young woman Lina saw. Then you'll know why she suffers these night terrors.'

Zerk poured the wine, with the eagerness of a child who's afraid he won't hear the end of the story, and sat back down again alongside Danglard. He had grown up without a father, nobody had ever told him stories. His mother had worked nights as a cleaner in a fish-gutting factory.

'Thanks, Armel. So the servant went on: "*The forest is full of dead souls and demons. I heard them talking and shouting: We have caught the Provost of Arques, and now we shall capture the Archbishop of Reims. And I replied, Let us make the sign of the cross on our foreheads and go forward in safety."*'

'That was the uncle talking, was it?'

'The last bit, that's right. And Hellebaud says: "*When we advanced and came to the forest, it was getting dark and yet I could hear voices and the sound of armour and horses neighing, but I could neither see the shades nor understand the voices. After reaching home, we found the archbishop at his last extremity and he did not survive fourteen days after we heard those voices. People said he had been taken by spirits. They had been heard saying they were going to seize him."*'

'Well, that doesn't correspond to what Lina's mother said,' Adamsberg interrupted gruffly. 'She didn't say her daughter had heard voices, or horses, or seen shades. She simply saw this Michel Herbier and three other men, with the Riders in the Army.'

'That's because the mother didn't dare tell you the whole story. And because in Ordebec there's no need to explain. Up there, when someone says, "I've seen the Furious Army go past", everyone knows perfectly well what it means. I need to tell you a bit more about the horsemen Lina saw, to explain why she probably doesn't sleep at night. And if there's one thing that's sure, commissaire, it's that her life in Ordebec will have become very tough. People will certainly be avoiding her like the plague. I think the mother came to talk to you above all to get some protection for her daughter.'

'What did she see?' asked Zerk, his cigarette hanging unsmoked from his lips.

'Armel, this ancient cavalcade causing havoc in the countryside is damaged. The horses and their riders have no flesh and many of their limbs are missing. It's an army of the dead, of the putrefied dead, an army of ghostly riders, wild-eyed and screaming, unable to get to heaven. Imagine that.'

'Yeah, right,' said Zerk, pouring himself some more wine. 'Can you excuse me a minute, commandant? It's ten o'clock, I have to see to the pigeon. Instructions.'

'From whom?'

'Violette Retancourt.'

'Well, you'd better do it then.'

Zerk set conscientiously to work with the wet crumbs, the water dropper and the bottle of tonic. He was getting used to it now, but when he sat down, he looked anxious.

'He's no better,' he said sadly to his father. 'That horrible kid.'

'I'll catch him, believe me,' said Adamsberg serenely.

'Are you really going to investigate some kid who's been torturing a pigeon?' asked Danglard, looking mildly surprised.

'Absolutely, Danglard,' said Adamsberg. 'Why not?'

Danglard waited until he had Zerk's full attention to continue the tale about the ghostly army. He was increasingly struck by the resemblance between this father and son, their expressions were so similar: vague, without sharpness or movement, their eyes shadowy and withdrawn. Except that in Adamsberg's case there was sometimes a sudden flash of light like the sun illuminating strands of seaweed at low tide.

'The Ghost Riders always carry along some living men or women, who are heard shrieking and lamenting in suffering and flames. They're the ones the witness recognises. Just as Lina recognised this hunter and the three other individuals. The living people beg some good soul to atone for their terrible sins, so as to save them from torment. That's what Gauchelin says.'

'Stop, Danglard,' Adamsberg begged him, 'that's enough about Gauchelin, we get the general idea.'

'Well, it was you who asked me in the first place to come over and explain about the army,' said Danglard in some irritation.

Adamsberg shrugged. Stories like this sent him to sleep and he would have preferred Danglard to keep it short. But he knew how happy it made his commandant to wallow in the telling, as if swimming in a lake of the finest white wine in the world. Especially when he had the admiring and excited attention of Zerk. Well, at least this excursion had wiped out Danglard's fit of the sulks, since he seemed much more at ease with life now.

'What Gauchelin actually wrote,' Danglard went on with a smile, fully aware of Adamsberg's weariness, 'was: "*Now behold an immense army of men on foot began to pass. They bore on their necks and shoulders cattle, clothing, objects of all kinds and diverse utensils which brigands habitually carry with them.*" Great text, isn't it?' he said to Adamsberg with a deliberate smile.

'Yeah, great,' Adamsberg replied without thinking.

'Sobriety and grace, it's all there. Rather different from Veyrenc's verses, eh, which are clumping doggerel.'

'Not his fault, you know that. His grandmother knew Racine by heart, and she recited it to him all day, just lines and lines of Racine's plays. Because she had rescued them from a fire at her school.'

'She would have done better to rescue some books on manners and politeness and then teach her grandson about that.'

Adamsberg remained silent, without taking his eyes off Danglard. It was going to take some time for this problem to resolve itself. At present, it looked as if there was going to be a duel between the two men, or more precisely – because this was one of its causes – between the two intellectual heavyweights in the squad.

'So, moving on,' said Danglard, '"*All were lamenting and exhorting each other to move faster. The priest recognised in this throng several of his neighbours who had recently died and he heard them crying out about the great torment they were suffering because of their sins.*" He also saw, and here we're getting closer to your Lina, he saw also a certain Landri. "*In court sessions and cases, this man gave judgment according only to his whims,*" and according to witnesses, if he received gifts, he modified his sentences. "*He was at the service of cupidity and deception rather than of justice.*" And that is why Landri, Vicomte d'Ordebec, was seized by the Furious Army. To be a corrupt magistrate in those days was as serious as to commit bloodshed. Whereas nowadays, nobody cares.'

'Yeah, right,' breathed Zerk, who was uncritically in awe of the commandant.

'Well, whatever the efforts of the witness when he goes home after seeing this terrifying vision, and however many Masses are said, the living persons he's seen riding with the army die in the week following the vision. Or within three weeks at the outside. And that's something you should remember about the little woman's story, commissaire. All those who are "seized" by the Riders are certainly bastards beneath contempt, real villains, exploiters, corrupt judges or murderers. But their crime is not generally known to their contemporaries. They've remained unpunished. That's why the army gets hold of them. When exactly did Lina see them go by?'

'Over three weeks ago.'

'In that case, there's no doubt about it,' Danglard said calmly, looking at his glass. 'Yes, the man's dead. Carried off by Hellequin's Horde.'

'His what?' asked Zerk.

'His horde, his servants if you like. Hellequin's their overlord.'

Adamsberg approached the fireplace again, curious to hear a little more, and leaned against the brick hearth. The fact that the Riders singled out unpunished villains interested him. He suddenly realised that the other people whose names Lina had revealed would not be going about their lives very cheerfully in Ordebec. Everyone else would be watching them, asking themselves questions, wondering what crime these marked men had committed. You can tell yourself you don't believe this kind of thing, but it's difficult not to believe it. The pernicious idea digs a deep channel. It silently infiltrates the unavowed corridors of the mind, penetrates, and trickles through. You suppress the idea, it lies dormant for a while, then it returns.

'How do they die, these people who are "seized"?' he asked.

'It depends. A sudden fever, or murder. If it isn't some galloping disease or an accident, an earthly being may execute the implacable will of the Riders. So it's murder, but one commanded by Lord Hellequin. You see?'

The two glasses of wine he had drunk – something he did only rarely – had softened Adamsberg's bad mood. Now it seemed, on the contrary, that meeting a woman who was able to see the ghostly cavalcade would be an unusual and distracting experience. And that the real-life consequences of a vision like that might indeed be frightening. He allowed himself another half-glass, and stole a cigarette from his son's packet.

'Is this legend peculiar to Ordebec?' he asked.

Danglard shook his head. 'No, Hellequin's Horde is known throughout Northern Europe. In Scandinavia, in Flanders, all of France, and England. But it always travels along the same paths, and it's been using the one through Bonneval for a thousand years or so.'

Adamsberg drew up a chair and sat down, stretching his legs, completing the little circle of three men around the hearth.

'All the same,' he began – and his sentence stopped there, for want of an exact thought to take it further.

Danglard had never got used to the cloudy vagueness of the commissaire's mental processes, his lack of logical, overarching reason.

'All the same –' Danglard picked up his expression to complete it – 'it's just the story of some unfortunate young woman who is disturbed enough to have visions. And of a mother sufficiently frightened to believe in them and ask the police for help.'

'All the same, it's also the story of a woman who foretells several deaths. What if Michel Herbier hasn't just gone off somewhere, and they find his body?'

'Then your Lina would be in a very awkward spot. Who's to say she didn't kill Herbier herself? And then go round telling this story to confuse people?'

'What do you mean "confuse" them?' said Adamsberg, smiling. 'Do you really believe that the horsemen in the Furious Army are credible suspects for the police? Do you think Lina is being Machiavellian, by pointing to a culprit who's been riding round the area for a thousand years? Who are they going to arrest? Capitaine Hennequin?'

'Hellequin. He's a nobleman. Maybe a descendant of Odin.'

Danglard refilled his glass with a steady hand.

'Just forget it, commissaire. Leave the limbless horsemen be, and this Lina person too.'

Adamsberg nodded his agreement and Danglard drank off the glass. When he had left, Adamsberg paced round the room with a blank expression.

'Do you remember,' he said to Zerk, 'the first time you came here, there wasn't a bulb in the overhead light?'

'There still isn't.'

'Shall we replace it?'

'You said it didn't bother you whether there was a bulb working or not.'

'That's right. But there comes a time when you have to take action. A time when you tell yourself to replace the light bulb, and decide to call the captain of the Ordebec gendarmes tomorrow. And then you just have to do it.'

'But Commandant Danglard's quite right. That woman's crazy. What are you going to do about her Furious Army?'

'It's not these ghosts riding round the countryside that bother me, Zerk. It's that I don't like people coming and warning me about some impending violent deaths, however they do it.'

'Yes, I see. OK, I'll look after the light bulb.'

'Are you going to wait till eleven to feed the bird?'

'I'll stay down here tonight to feed it every hour. I'll just take a nap in the armchair.'

Zerk touched the pigeon with the back of his fingers.

'He doesn't feel very warm, in spite of the heat.'

VI

AT 6.15 NEXT MORNING ADAMSBERG FELT SOMEONE SHAKING HIM.

'He's opened his eyes! Come and see. Quick!'

Zerk still didn't know what to call Adamsberg. Father? Too formal. Papa? He was rather old to do that. Jean-Baptiste? That might seem too familiar and inappropriate. So for the time being, he didn't call him anything, and this absence caused embarrassing gaps in his sentences. Hollow spaces. But those hollow spaces perfectly summed up his twenty-eight years of absence.

The two men went downstairs and peered into the strawberry basket. Yes, things certainly looked better. Zerk took the dressings off the bird's feet and applied antiseptic, while Adamsberg filtered the coffee.

'What are we going to call him?' asked Zerk as he wound bandages round the bird's legs. 'If he survives, we'll have to give him a name. We can't keep on saying "the pigeon". Shall we call him Violette after your beautiful lieutenant?'

'Not suitable. Nobody would ever be able to catch Retancourt and tie her ankles together.'

'OK, let's call him Hellebaud, like the guy in Danglard's story. Do you think he revised his texts before he came over?'

'Yes, he must have read them again.'

'Yeah, but even so, how could he remember them like that, word for word?'

'Don't ask, Zerk. If you and I could really see inside Danglard's head and take a walk round it, it would be more terrifying than any hullabaloo from the ghostly cavalcade.'

As soon as he arrived at the office, Adamsberg consulted the lists and called Capitaine Louis Nicolas Émeri at the Ordebec gendarmerie. He introduced himself, and sensed a certain hesitancy at the end of the line. Sounds reached him of murmured questions, answers being given, grunts, and chairs being moved round. The intrusion of Adamsberg into a gendarmerie often produced this immediate unease, as people wondered whether they should take his call or find some excuse not to. Louis Nicolas Émeri finally came back on the line.

'What can I do for you, commissaire?' he said distrustfully.

'Capitaine Émeri, it's about this missing man, whose freezer was emptied.'

'Herbier?'

'Yes. Any news of him?'

'No, nothing. We visited his home and all the outbuildings. No sign of him.'

A pleasant voice, a little mannered, clear and courteous intonation.

'Are you taking some interest in this case?' the capitaine asked. 'I would be amazed if you had been asked to look into a very ordinary missing-person matter.'

'No, I haven't been asked to look into it. I was simply wondering what you were thinking of doing about it.'

'Applying the law, commissaire. Nobody has been in to ask us to launch a search, so this individual isn't officially listed as missing. He went off on his moped, and I don't have any authority to try and trace him. He's got a perfect right to his freedom,' Émeri insisted, rather stiffly. 'We've followed regulations and run checks, no reports of a road accident and his moped hasn't been sighted anywhere.'

'What do you think about his going off like that, capitaine?'

'Not all that surprising. They don't like him round here, and some people absolutely hate him. What the freezer might perhaps indicate is that some individual successfully threatened him, because of his nasty hunting habits, which you may know about?'

'Yes, females and young animals.'

'It's possible Herbier was intimidated, took fright and left without hanging about for more. Or maybe he had some sort of crisis of remorse, emptied the freezer himself and scarpered.'

'Yes, why not?'

'In any case, he has no relatives or friends in the district. That could be a reason to start again somewhere else. The house isn't his, he rents it, and since he'd retired, he was getting a bit behind with the rent. Unless the landlord complains, my hands are tied. If you ask me, I think he's done a moonlight flit.'

Émeri was open, cooperative, as Danglard had suggested, though he seemed to consider Adamsberg's call some kind of distant entertainment.

'That's all quite possible, capitaine. Is there a Chemin de Bonneval in your district?'

'Yes. Why?'

'Where does it run?'

'From a hamlet called Les Illiers about three kilometres from here, through part of the Forest of Alance. After the Croix de Bois, it changes its name.'

'Do many people go there?'

'In the daytime, yes. But people don't go there at night as a rule. There are a lot of old wives' tales about it, you know the kind of thing.'

'And you haven't taken a look there, by any chance?'

'If that's a suggestion, Commissaire Adamsberg, I have one for you too. I suggest you have received a visit from someone who lives in Ordebec. Am I right?'

'Quite right, capitaine.'

'Who?'

'I can't tell you that. Someone who was worried.'

'And I can well imagine what she told you. About some damned phantom army seen by Lina Vendermot, if you can call it "seeing". And in among them, she saw this Herbier.'

'Spot on,' Adamsberg admitted.

'You're surely not going to get involved in this, are you, commissaire? Do you know why Lina saw Herbier with this blasted so-called army?'

'No, why?'

'Because she hates him. He's an old friend of her father's, probably the only one Vendermot had. Take my advice, commissaire, and forget you ever heard of it. That girl's been completely crazy since she was a child, as everyone round here knows. And everyone gives her a wide berth, and the whole family, they've all got something odd about them. Though it's not their fault. In fact, they're more to be pitied than anything.'

'And everyone knows she saw these Riders?'

'Of course. Lina told her family and her boss.'

'Who's her boss?'

'She works as a junior in the local solicitors', Deschamps and Poulain.'

'And who spread the word around?'

'Oh, everyone. They've been talking about nothing else here for the past three weeks. Sensible people laugh about it, but fainter souls are frightened. Believe me, we can do without Lina having fun terrorising the local population. I bet you anything you like that nobody's gone near the Chemin de Bonneval since then. Not even those who don't believe a word of it. Myself included.'

'Why not, capitaine?'

'Don't imagine *I'm* afraid of anything,' – and here Adamsberg seemed to hear something of the Napoleonic marshal – 'but I have no wish for people to go thinking Capitaine Émeri believes this stuff about the Furious Army and goes looking. And the same would go for you, so take my advice. This whole affair needs a lid put on it. But if your business ever brings you to Ordebec, I would of course always be very happy to see you.'

An ambiguous and slightly uneasy exchange, Adamsberg thought as he put down the phone. Émeri had been politely mocking him. He had let him get started, when he already knew all about the visit by a local resident. His unwillingness to be drawn was understandable. Having someone who saw visions on your patch was not a gift from heaven.

Gradually the office was filling up. Adamsberg usually got there early. The large figure of Retancourt briefly blocked the light from the door, and Adamsberg watched as she moved heavily towards her desk.

'The pigeon opened its eyes this morning,' he said. 'Zerk fed it through the night.'

'That's good,' said Retancourt calmly. She wasn't given to showing emotion.

'If he lives, he's going to be called Hellebaud.'

'Elbow? Funny name.'

'No, Hellebaud, with an h. It's some old name. An uncle or a nephew, of someone or other.'

'Fine,' the lieutenant said, switching on her computer. 'Justin and Noël want to see you. Apparently Momo, our local pyromaniac, is at it again, but this time it's serious. The car was completely burnt out as usual, but someone was asleep inside. According to the scene-of-crime people, an elderly man. Involuntary manslaughter at least – he won't get away with six months this time. They've launched the investigation, but they would appreciate – what shall I say? – some *guidance* from you.'

Retancourt stressed the word 'guidance' with apparent irony. Because for one thing, she didn't consider Adamsberg capable of giving any, and for another she generally disapproved of the way the commissaire allowed himself to float with the flow of inquiries. This contradiction in their approach had been latent since the beginning and neither she nor Adamsberg had tried to resolve it. Which didn't prevent Adamsberg having the instinctive affection for Retancourt that a pagan would have for the tallest tree in the forest. The only one that offers real refuge.

The commissaire went over to the desk where Justin and Noël were noting down the latest information about the burnt-out vehicle with the man inside. Momo the firebug had just torched his eleventh car.

'We've left Mercadet and Lamarre stationed by the flats where Momo's pad is, Cité des Buttes,' Noël explained. 'Car was in the fifth arrondissement, rue Henri-Barbusse. Top-of-the-range Mercedes, as per usual.'

'This man who died, do they know who he was?'

'Not yet. Nothing left of his ID, or the number plates. The lads are working on the motor. Attack on a toff, it's got Momo written all over it. He never tries anything outside the fifth.'

'No,' said Adamsberg, shaking his head. 'This one's not Momo. We'd be wasting our time.'

In itself, wasting time didn't bother Adamsberg. He was impervious to impatience and didn't rush to follow the usually hasty rhythms of his colleagues, just as his colleagues couldn't follow his slower meanderings. Adamsberg didn't have a method, still less a theory, but it seemed to him that as far as time was concerned it was in the almost imperceptible interstices of an inquiry that the choicest pearls were sometimes to be found. Like the little shells that slip into cracks in the rock, far from the crashing breakers of the open sea. At any rate, it was there that he tended to come across them.

'Go on, it's classic Momo,' Noël was insisting. 'The old geezer must have been waiting for someone in the car. It was dark, and he must have dropped off. Best-case scenario, Momo didn't notice him. Worst-case, he set fire to the car, passenger and all.'

'No, it can't be Momo.'

Adamsberg visualised quite clearly the face of the young man in question, obstinate and intelligent, rather delicate under his shock of dark curly hair. He didn't know why he hadn't forgotten Momo, or why he liked him. While listening to his colleagues, he was simultaneously phoning about train times to Ordebec, since his car was in the garage for repairs. The little woman hadn't appeared again and the commissaire presumed that since she had failed in her mission, she had gone back to Normandy. The commissaire's ignorance about the Furious Army must have overwhelmed the last shreds of her courage. Because it must have taken courage to come and tell a cop about a horde of thousand-year-old demons.

'Commissaire, he's already torched ten cars, he's famous for it. They all admire him on his estate. He's moving up, he wants to go big time. For him there's not much difference between a Merc and the guy inside it, they're both class enemies.'

'There's all the world of difference, Noël, and he won't make the jump.

I know this lad, he's been in youth custody twice before. But Momo would never torch a car without checking if there was someone in it.'

There was no station at Ordebec, it seemed; you had to get off at Cérenay and take a bus. He wouldn't be there until five o'clock, which was rather a long excursion for a short walk. But it would be light enough in the summer evening to give him time to cover the five kilometres known as the Chemin de Bonneval. If a murderer had wanted to exploit the Lina girl's madness, or fantasies, this was where, perhaps, he might have left the body. This escape to the forest was no longer a half-formed duty he felt vaguely obliged to fulfil for the little woman, but a healthy break. He could already imagine the smell of the path, the shadows, the carpet of leaves under his feet. He could easily have sent one of his juniors, or even persuaded Capitaine Émeri to go there. But the idea of exploring it for himself had made its way in his head that morning, gradually, inexplicably, though with the obscure feeling that certain inhabitants of Ordebec were in deep trouble. He switched off his mobile and turned his attention to the two lieutenants.

'Find out everything you can about this old man who was burnt,' he said. 'Momo's got a reputation in this part of the fifth arrondissement, and it would be easy to frame him for murder by using his MO, which isn't complicated. All the killer would need would be some petrol and a short fuse. He gets the man to wait in the car, comes back under cover of darkness, and sets it alight. Find out about the victim, whether he could see and hear properly. And find out who was driving the car, whether it was someone the old man would have felt perfectly safe with. It shouldn't take you long.'

'Shall we check Momo's alibi all the same?'

'Yes. But get the remains of the petrol analysed – octane level and so on. Momo uses two-stroke, mixed with oil. Check the formula, it should be on file. But don't try to reach me during the afternoon, I'm out now until this evening.'

'Where?' Justin's enquiring glance said silently.

'I'm going to look for some ancient riders in a forest. I won't be long. Tell the others. Where's Danglard?'

'At the coffee machine,' said Justin, pointing to the first floor. 'He went to carry the cat to its feeding bowl, it was his turn.'

'And Veyrenc?'

'At the other end of the building,' said Noël with a malicious smile.

Adamsberg found Veyrenc in the office furthest from the large shared central office, leaning against a wall.

'I'm immersing myself,' he said, pointing to a pile of folders. 'I'm looking at what you've been up to in my absence. My impression is that the cat's put on weight, and so has Danglard. He looks better.'

'Well, of course he's put on weight! He spends the entire day next to Retancourt, lying on the photocopier.'

'You mean the cat? If people didn't carry him to his feeding bowl, he might make up his mind to walk for himself.'

'We did try, Louis. He just didn't eat, and we stopped the experiment after four days. He can walk perfectly well. When Retancourt goes away, he's quite capable of jumping down from his perch and sitting on her chair. But if you meant Danglard, he's got a new girlfriend: he met her at the London conference.'

'That explains it. Still, when he met me this morning he seemed to be bristling with irritation. Did you ask him about the Riders?'

'Yes. Very ancient, he said.'

'Yes, very,' said Veyrenc with a smile. '*In the oldest of haunts lie the powers of the dead / Seek not for these secrets, buried deep under dread.*'

'I'm not seeking them, I'm just going for a stroll along the Chemin de Bonneval.'

'Is that a *grimweld*?'

'Yes, the one near Ordebec.'

'And did you tell Danglard about your little expedition?'

Veyrenc was tapping into his computer.

'Yes, and like you say, he was bristling with irritation. He loved telling me about the Riders, but he doesn't like me going after them.'

'Did he tell you about people being "seized"?'

'Yes.'

'Well, you should know, if this is what you're after, that it's very rare for the bodies of those seized to be abandoned in a *grimweld*. You usually find them simply in their homes, or on a duelling ground, or down a well, or near some deconsecrated church. Because you know that abandoned churches attract the devil. As soon as the righteous leave it, the Evil One comes in, and those who are seized by the Riders are returning to the devil, that's all.'

'Logical.'

'Look,' said Veyrenc, pointing at his computer screen. 'This is a map of the Forest of Alance.'

'Here it is,' said Adamsberg, following a path with his finger, 'this must be it.'

'And here you have the Chapel of St Antony of Alance. And there, in the other direction, south, a calvary. Those are the places you should visit. Take a cross with you for protection.'

'I've got a pebble from the river back home in my pocket.'

'That should do the trick.'

VII

IN NORMANDY, THE TEMPERATURE WAS ABOUT SIX DEGREES COOLER than in Paris, and as soon as he was standing on the forecourt of the almost-deserted bus station, Adamsberg turned his head to catch the fresh breeze, allowing it to run over his neck and ears, in an almost animal gesture, like a horse shaking off flies. He walked round the north side of the small town of Ordebec and half an hour later set off down the Chemin de Bonneval, to which he was directed by an ancient, hand-painted wooden signpost. Contrary to what he had expected, it was a narrow bridlepath: no doubt the idea of hundreds of armed men riding along it had made him imagine a broad and imposing avenue, under a canopy of tall beech trees. This path was much more modest, made of two long rutted tracks with grass growing between them, and on either side were ditches full of brambles, elm saplings and hazel bushes. Many blackberries were already ripe, well ahead of time, because of the abnormal heat, and Adamsberg picked some as he went along the path. He walked slowly, looking carefully at the ditches, and leisurely eating the fruit in his hand. He was surrounded by flies buzzing round his face as if anxious to taste his sweat.

Every few minutes, he stopped to pick a fresh handful of blackberries, tearing his old black shirt on the thorns. Halfway along, he stopped suddenly, remembering he hadn't left any message for Zerk. He was so used to living alone that letting people know when he would be away took some effort. He called his son on his mobile.

'Hellebaud has stood up,' reported the young man. 'He ate some seeds all by himself. Then he crapped on the table.'

'That's what happens if you come back to life. Put a plastic sheet on the table for now. There are some in the attic. I won't be back till tonight, Zerk, I'm on the Chemin de Bonneval.'

'Have you seen them?'

'No, it's still too light. But I'm looking for the body of the hunter. Nobody's been here for three weeks, there are brambles everywhere, they're fruiting early. If Violette phones, don't tell her where I am, she wouldn't like it.'

'No, of course not,' said Zerk, and Adamsberg told himself his son was perhaps sharper than he looked. Crumb by crumb, he was amassing information about him.

'I've changed the light bulb in the kitchen,' Zerk added. 'And the one on the stairs needs changing too, shall I go ahead?'

'Yes, OK, but don't put in too strong a bulb. I don't like it when you can see everything.'

'If you meet the Ghost Riders, call me!'

'I don't think I'll be able to, Zerk. I dare say if they go past that'll knock out the signal. The shock of two different eras.'

'Could be,' agreed the young man and rang off.

Adamsberg advanced another few hundred metres, probing the sides of the path. Because Herbier *was* dead, he was quite sure of that. It was the only point on which he agreed with Madame Vendermot, the woman who would fly away if you blew on her. At this point, Adamsberg realised he had already forgotten the name for the little seeds of the dandelion clock.

There was a silhouette on the path and Adamsberg, narrowing his eyes, went forward more cautiously. A very long silhouette, sitting on a tree trunk, and so old and bent that he was afraid he might scare it.

'*Ello*,' said the old woman, in English, as she saw him approach.

'*Hello*,' Adamsberg replied in surprise, pronouncing the H. Following a recent visit to London, '*hello*' was one of the few words of English he knew, along with '*yes*' and '*no*'.

'You took your time getting here from the station,' she said.

'I was picking blackberries,' Adamsberg explained, wondering how such a confident voice could come out of this skeletal figure. Skeletal but intense. 'You know who I am then?'

'Not exactly. Lionel saw you get off the Paris train and on to the bus. Then Bernard told me, and what with one thing and another, here you are. Seeing what's going on at the moment, the chances are you're a policeman from Paris. There's a bad atmosphere in these parts. Incidentally, Michel Herbier is no great loss.'

The old woman sniffed loudly and wiped a drop off the end of her very long nose with her hand.

'And you were waiting for me?'

'Not at all, young man, I'm waiting for my dog. He's besotted with the bitch on that farm, just over there. If I don't bring him over to cover her now and again, he's impossible. Renoux, the farmer, is furious, he says he doesn't want his yard full of little mongrels. But what can you do? Nothing. And I've had a summer cold, and haven't been able to bring him out for ten days.'

'Aren't you afraid, all alone on this path?'

'What of?'

'The Furious Army?' Adamsberg suggested tentatively.

'Oh don't worry,' said the old woman with a shake of her head. 'In the first place it isn't dark, and in any case, I don't see them. It isn't given to everyone.'

Adamsberg could see a huge blackberry above the old woman's head but he didn't dare disturb her to reach it. It was strange, he reflected, how instinctively the urge to pick berries returns to humans the minute they go into a forest. That would have pleased his friend, the prehistoric scholar Mathias. Because when you think about it, it's the act of gathering that's bewitching. Blackberries in themselves aren't all that marvellous a fruit.

'My name's Léone,' said the woman, wiping another drop from her large nose. 'Usually known as Léo.'

'Jean-Baptiste Adamsberg, commissaire from the Serious Crime Squad in Paris. Glad to have met you,' he added politely. 'And now I'll be on my way.'

'If it's Herbier you're after, you won't find him along there. He's lying in a pool of dried blood, up by St Antony's Chapel.'

'Dead?'

'Yes, and he's been dead for some time. Not that anyone will grieve for him, but it's not a pretty sight. Whoever did it didn't mess about, you can't even see his face.'

'Was it the gendarmes who found him?'

'No, young man, it was me. I often take flowers to the chapel, I don't like to leave St Antony all alone. St Antony protects animals. Do you have an animal?'

'I've got a sick pigeon.'

'There you are then. When you go to the chapel, you need to make a request. He helps people find things that are lost as well. As I get older, I lose lots of things.'

'You weren't upset? By finding a corpse up there?'

'It's not the same if you're expecting it. I knew he'd been killed.'

'Because of the Ghost Riders?'

'Because of my age, young man. Hereabouts, a bird can't lay an egg without my knowing about it or feeling it in my bones. So for instance, last night you can be sure a fox took a chicken from Deveneux's farm. He only has three legs and no tail.'

'The farmer?'

'The fox. I've seen his droppings. But believe me, he's quicker than you'd think. Last year this coal tit took a fancy to him. First time I've ever seen anything like it. It would perch on his back and he never snapped at it. Just that one, no other bird, mark you. The world's full of details, have you noticed? And since no detail is ever repeated in exactly the same shape and always sets off other details, there's no end to it. If Herbier'd still been alive, he'd have finished up killing that fox, and while he was at it, the coal tit as well. That would have led to a lot of trouble during the local elections. But I don't know whether the coal tit has come back this year. Out of luck.'

'And have the gendarmes come? You've told them?'

'Now, how could I do that? I had to wait for my dog. So if you're in a hurry, you can just call them yourself.'

'I'm not sure that's a good idea,' said Adamsberg after a moment. 'The gendarmes don't like Paris cops coming and sticking their noses in.'

'So why are you here then?'

'Because a woman from Ordebec came to see me. So I thought I'd take a look.'

'Mother Vendermot? She's frightened for her brood. And she'd certainly have done better to keep her mouth shut. But this business has upset her so much she couldn't resist going for help.'

A large beige dog with long floppy ears emerged suddenly from the bushes with a yap, and came to lay its head on its mistress's long thin legs, closing its eyes as if to offer thanks.

'*Ello*, Fleg!' she said, wiping her nose, while the dog wiped its own snout on her grey skirt. 'See how happy he looks.'

Léo took a sugar lump from her pocket and pushed it into the dog's mouth. Fleg paced round Adamsberg, full of curiosity.

'Good boy,' said Adamsberg, patting his neck.

'His name's Fleg, short for "Flegmatic". Ever since he was a pup he's just flopped about, lazy as can be. Look at his ears. Other people say that apart from wanting to chase all the bitches in the neighbourhood, he's a waste of space. I say at least that's better than going round biting people.'

The old woman stood up, unfolding her long stooped frame, and leaned on two sticks.

'If you're going back home to call the gendarmes,' said Adamsberg, 'would it be all right if I accompany you?'

'No need to ask. I love company. But I can't go very fast, it'll take about half an hour if we go through the wood. Before, when Ernest was alive, I did bed and breakfast at our farm. There were plenty of people about all the time, young ones too. Lots of folk, coming and going. I had to give up twelve years ago, and it's a bit lonely now. So when I come across a bit of company I don't refuse it. Talking to yourself isn't much fun.'

'They say Normans don't like to talk very much,' said Adamsberg, chancing the remark, as he fell into step behind the old woman, who gave off a slight fragrance of woodsmoke.

'It's not so much that they don't like talking, but they don't like answering questions. It's not the same thing.'

'So how do you go about asking questions?'

'We find ways. Are you going to follow me all the way back to the house? My dog's hungry now.'

'I'll walk with you. What time does the evening train go?'

'The evening train, young man, went a good quarter of an hour ago. There's one from Lisieux, but the last bus goes in ten minutes, and you won't catch that.'

Adamsberg hadn't foreseen spending the night in Normandy: all he had with him was his ID card, keys and some money. The Ghost Riders were pinning him down in this place. Without seeming perturbed, the old woman walked quite briskly through the trees, using her sticks. She looked rather like a grasshopper jumping over roots.

'Is there a hotel in Ordebec?'

'It's not a hotel, it's a rabbit hutch,' pronounced the old women in her booming tones. 'But anyway, it's closed for repairs. You have friends you can stay with, I suppose.'

Adamsberg recalled the reticence he had found among Normans about asking direct questions, something that had already caused him difficulties in the village of Haroncourt on a previous case. Like Léone, the men in Haroncourt got round the obstacle by making a statement, whatever it might be, and waiting for an answer.

'You'll be counting on finding somewhere to sleep,' Léo said again. 'Come on, Fleg. He insists on peeing against every tree.'

'I've got a neighbour like that,' said Adamsberg, thinking of Lucio. 'No, I don't know anybody here.'

'You could sleep in a haystack of course. The weather's hotter than normal now, but there's still dew in the morning. You'll be from some other part of the country, I suppose.'

'From the Béarn.'

'That would be in the east.'

'No, south-west, near Spain.'

'And you've already been in these parts, I suppose.'

'I have some friends at the cafe in Haroncourt.'

'Haroncourt in the Eure *département*? The cafe near the market hall?'

'That's right, I have some friends there, especially one called Robert.'

Léo stopped suddenly and Fleg took advantage to choose a new tree. Then she set off again, muttering to herself for about fifty metres.

'Well, Robert is a *petit cousin*, a relative of mine,' she said finally, still overcome with surprise. 'One I'm fond of.'

'He gave me two antlers from a stag. They're sitting in my office.'

'Oh! If he did that, he must have thought well of you. You don't give antlers to just anybody.'

'Well, I would hope not.'

'We *are* talking about Robert Binet?'

'Yes.'

Adamsberg walked another hundred metres or so in the old woman's wake. A road was now visible through the trees.

'Well, if you're a friend of Robert's, that's different. You could sleep Chez Léo, if that isn't too different from what you were intending. Chez Léo is my place, it was the name of my guest house.'

Without having made up his mind, Adamsberg could clearly detect an appeal from the old woman, who was lonely and bored. But as he had told Veyrenc, decisions are taken before you announce them. He had nowhere to stay, and he had rather taken to this outspoken old woman. Even if he felt a bit trapped, as if Léo had organised it all in advance.

Five minutes later, he could see Chez Léo, an old longhouse of a single storey, which had somehow survived with its ancient wooden beams for at least two centuries. Inside, nothing seemed to have changed for decades.

'Sit down on the bench,' said Léo, 'and we'll call Émeri. He's not a bad sort, quite the contrary. He gives himself airs and graces from time to time, because some ancestor was one of Napoléon's marshals. But on the whole people like him. On the other hand, his job's not good for his character. If you have to suspect everyone, if you're always punishing people, you can't improve yourself, can you? I dare say you're the same.'

'Yes, probably.'

Léo dragged a stool up to the telephone.

'Well,' she said with a sigh, as she dialled the number, 'I suppose the police are a necessary evil. During the war, an evil full stop. I should think quite a few of them went off with the Riders. We'll have a nice blaze, now it's cooling down. You know how to lay a fire, I suppose. The log pile's just outside on the left. *Ello*, Louis, this is Léo.'

When Adamsberg came back with an armful of wood, Léo was in full flow. Clearly Émeri was getting the worst of it. Léo passed the old-fashioned earpiece to the commissaire.

'Well, it was because I always take flowers to St Antony, you know that, come on. Tell me, Louis, you're not going to make trouble for me now, just because I came across a corpse, are you? If you'd bothered to stir your stumps, you'd have found him yourself, and saved me a deal of bother.'

'Don't get ratty, Léo, I believe you.'

'His moped's there too, it's been pushed into some hazel bushes. What I think happened is someone arranged to meet him there, and he hid his bike so nobody could take it.'

'Léo, I'm going up there right now, and then I'm coming round to see you. If I come at eight, you won't have gone to bed?'

'At eight, I'm still eating my supper, and I don't like being disturbed when I'm eating.'

'Eight thirty then.'

'No, it's not convenient, I've got a cousin visiting from Haroncourt. Having the gendarmes call the evening you arrive isn't polite. And I'm tired. Trotting round the forest is tiring at my age.'

'That was why I asked what you were doing, trotting all the way to the chapel.'

'And I already told you. Taking some flowers.'

'You never let on the quarter of what you know.'

'The rest wouldn't interest you. You'd do better to go over there, before he gets eaten by wild animals. And if you want to see me, make it tomorrow.'

Adamsberg put down the earpiece and set about lighting the fire.

'Louis Nicolas can't do anything to me,' explained Léo, 'because I saved his life when he was knee-high to a grasshopper. The silly boy had fallen into the Jeanlin pond, and I hauled him out by the seat of his pants. He can't go playing marshals of France with me.'

'He's local?'

'He was born here.'

'But how did he get posted here then? Policemen aren't usually appointed to their home ground.'

'I know that, young man. But he had moved away from Ordebec when he was only eleven, and his parents didn't have many contacts round here. He was a long time near Toulon, then Lyon, then he got a special dispensation. But he doesn't really know the people round here. And he's protected by the count, so no problem.'

'The count?'

'Rémy, Comte d'Ordebec. You'll have some soup, I suppose.'

'Thank you,' said Adamsberg, passing his plate.

'Carrot. After this there's some veal in bean sauce.'

'Émeri told me that Lina is completely insane.'

'No, that's not right,' said Léo, thrusting a large spoon into her small mouth. 'She's a bright enough girl and reliable. And she wasn't wrong. Herbier is certainly dead. So Louis Nicolas will be after *her* now, you can count on that.'

Adamsberg mopped up his soup with bread, as Léo did, and fetched the dish of veal and beans, breathing in the atmosphere of woodsmoke.

'And since she's not much liked, not her and not her brothers either,' Léo went on, serving out the food rather haphazardly, 'there'll be hell to pay. Don't go thinking they're bad people, but folk are always afraid of what they don't understand. And what with her gift, and her brothers who aren't quite normal, they haven't got a good reputation.'

'Because of the Ghost Riders?'

'That and other things. People say they have the devil in that house. It's like anywhere else, round here, there are plenty of folk with heads so empty they fill them full of rubbish, most of it bad. That's what everyone prefers, something nasty. Otherwise it's boring.'

Léo gave a satisfied nod of her chin and swallowed a large mouthful of meat.

'I suppose you have your own ideas about the Riders,' said Adamsberg, using Léo's way of asking a question.

'Depends how you look at them. In Ordebec, there are some who think Lord Hellequin is a servant of the devil. I don't really believe that, but if some people can survive because they're saints, like St Antony, why shouldn't others survive because they're wicked? Because this Horde, they're all wicked, you know that?'

'Yes.'

'That's why they get seized. But other people think Lina has visions, that she's sick in the head. She's been seen by doctors but they couldn't find anything wrong. And others again say her brother puts poisonous mushrooms in their omelettes, and that's what gives her hallucinations. devil's fungus. You know what that looks like, I suppose, red-footed fungus.'

'Yes.'

'Oh, you do, do you?' said Léone, rather disappointed.

'All it does is give you a serious bellyache.'

Léone took the plates into her dark little kitchen and washed them up in silence, concentrating on her task. Adamsberg dried the dishes as she went along.

'You know, it's all the same to me,' said Léone, drying her large hands. 'It's just that Lina sees the Riders, that's for sure. Whether the Riders are real or not, I couldn't say. But now that Herbier's dead, there'll be people who'll have it in for her. And in fact, that's why you're here.'

The old woman picked up her sticks and returned to the table. She took a large cigar box out of a drawer, passed a cigar under her nose, licked the end and lit it carefully, then pushed the open box towards Adamsberg.

'A friend sends me these, he gets them from Cuba. I spent two years in Cuba, four in Scotland, three in Argentina and five in Madagascar. Ernest and me, we opened restaurants pretty well everywhere, so we saw the world. We offered Normandy cuisine à la crème. Would you be good enough to get out the Calvados from the bottom of that cupboard and pour us a little glass each? You will have a drink with me, I imagine.'

Adamsberg did as he was asked. He was beginning to feel quite at home in this dimly lit little room, with the cigar, the glass of Calvados, the fire, lanky old Léone, who looked like a broomstick in clothes, and her dog snoozing on the floor.

'So why am I here, Léo? If I may call you Léo?'

'To protect Lina and her brothers. I don't have any children, and she's after being a sort of daughter to me. And if there are any more deaths, I mean if the other men she saw with the Riders should die too, then things are going to turn nasty. The same sort of thing happened in Ordebec in the eighteenth century, before the Revolution. There was this man, François-Benjamin, who saw four local villains being seized by the Horde. But he could only identify three of them. Just like Lina. And two of the named men died eleven days later. People were so terrified – because of the fourth *unnamed* person – that they thought they could put an end to these deaths by killing the man who saw them. The villagers went for François-Benjamin with pitchforks and then burnt him at the stake in the marketplace.'

'And the third man didn't die?'

'Yes, he did. And so did a fourth, in exactly the order he had said. So they didn't get anywhere by killing poor old François-Benjamin with their pitchforks.'

Léone took a mouthful of Calvados, swilled it round her mouth, swallowed it noisily and with satisfaction, and took a long draw on the cigar.

'And I don't want anything like that to happen to Lina. People say times have changed. That just means they've got more discreet. Not pitchforks and fire, but some other method. Anyone round here now with some shameful act on their conscience will be scared to death, depend on it. They're terrified of being seized, and terrified of anyone finding out.'

'Do you mean some serious crime, like a murder?'

'Not necessarily. It could be spreading malicious rumours or doing someone out of an inheritance, or some other injustice. They'd like to put an end to Lina and her loose talk. Because that would cut the connection to the Riders, you see. That's what they say. Calm things down, just like in the old days. Times haven't really changed, commissaire.'

'Is Lina the first person to have seen the Riders since François-Benjamin?'

'No, of course not, commissaire,' Léo said in her hoarse voice, through a cloud of smoke as if she were scolding some disappointing pupil. 'This is Ordebec. There's at least one medium every generation. The medium is the one who sees the sight, who forms the connection between the living and the army of the dead. Before Lina was born, it was Gilbert. Apparently he laid hands on her head when she was a baby, over the font in the church, and that way he passed on his destiny to her. And when you've been marked by destiny, it's no use running away, because the Riders will always take you back to the *grinveld*, or *grimweld* as they say in eastern Normandy.'

'But nobody killed this Gilbert?'

'No,' agreed Léone, blowing out a large smoke ring. 'But the difference is that this time, Lina did the same as François-Benjamin, she saw four, but she could only name three: Herbier, Glayeux and Mortembot. And she hasn't named the fourth. So of course if Glayeux and Mortembot were to die too, the whole town will be scared to death. If you don't know who's next, nobody will feel safe. And the fact that she named Glayeux and Mortembot has already caused a deal of trouble.'

'Why?'

'Because there's been talk about both of them for a long time. They're both nasty pieces of work.'

'What do they do?'

'Glayeux makes stained-glass windows for all the churches in the region. He's very talented with his hands, but not at all a nice man. He thinks himself above all the yokels round here and doesn't hesitate to tell them so. Yet his own father was only a blacksmith in Le Charmeuil-Othon! And if the yokels didn't go to Mass, he wouldn't have any call for his stained-glass windows. Mortembot has a garden centre on the road to Livarot, and he keeps himself to himself. Of course, since these rumours started, their businesses have fallen off. Customers aren't going to the garden centre any more, people are avoiding both of them. And when the news gets out that Herbier's dead, it'll be worse. That's why I think Lina would have done better to keep quiet. But that's the problem with the mediums. They feel obliged to speak out, to give a chance to the people who were seized. You know what I mean by "seized", I suppose.'

'Yes.'

'The medium speaks out and sometimes the seized person gets to redeem himself. Well, anyway, Lina *is* in some danger, and you can protect her.'

'I can't do anything, Léo, the investigation will be in Émeri's hands.'

'But Émeri won't bother himself about Lina. All this stuff about the Furious Army annoys and disgusts him. He thinks times have changed and that people these days are reasonable.'

'Well, first of all, they'll want to find out who killed Herbier. And the other two people are still alive. So Lina isn't in any danger at the moment.'

'Maybe,' said Léo, puffing on the remains of her cigar.

Getting to his bedroom meant going outside, since each room communicated only through an external door, which squeaked, reminding Adamsberg of Tuilot, Julien, and the creaking door which would have allowed him to avoid arrest if he had dared to open it. Léo pointed out Adamsberg's room to him with one of her sticks.

'You have to give the door a bit of a lift to make less of a noise. Goodnight.'

'I don't know your last name, Léo.'

'Police, they always want to know that. What about yours?' asked Léo, spitting out a few strands of tobacco stuck to her tongue.

'Jean-Baptiste Adamsberg, I told you before.'

'Make yourself at home. In your bedroom there's a whole stack of nineteenth-century pornography. Inherited from a friend, whose family wanted rid of it. Read it if you like, but be careful turning the pages, they're old and the paper's fragile.'

VIII

IN THE MORNING, ADAMSBERG PULLED ON HIS TROUSERS AND WENT quietly outside, treading barefoot on the wet grass. It was six thirty and the dew was still heavy. He had slept soundly on an old woollen mattress with a hollow in the middle, into which he had curled like a bird in a nest. He walked round the meadow for a few minutes, before finding what he was looking for: a supple twig, so as to turn the end into a makeshift toothbrush. He was peeling the end of his twig when Léo poked her head out of the window.

'*Ello*' – in English as usual – 'Capitaine Émeri has telephoned to ask for you, and he doesn't sound too pleased. Come in, the coffee's hot. You'll catch cold outside with no shoes on.'

'How did he know I was here?' asked Adamsberg when he was back inside.

'I suppose he didn't buy the story of the cousin, and he put two and two together with reports of a Parisian getting off the bus yesterday. He said he didn't like having some cop looking over his shoulder, and that I'd kept it from him. You'd think we'd been plotting, like in wartime. He might make trouble for you, you know.'

'I'll tell him the truth. I came to see what a *grimweld* looked like,' said Adamsberg, helping himself to a large piece of buttered bread.

'Exactly. And there was no hotel.'

'You see.'

'If you've been summoned to the gendarmerie, you won't be able to catch the 8.50 train from Lisieux. You'll have to get the next one, the 14.15 from Cérenay. But be careful. It takes at least half an hour by bus. Now, when you go out of here, you turn right, then right again and go straight ahead, about eight hundred metres towards the town centre. The gendarmerie is just behind the main square. Leave your bowl, I'll clear up here.'

Adamsberg walked through the fields to the gendarmerie, which, oddly enough, had been painted bright yellow as if it were a holiday home.

'Commissaire Jean-Baptiste Adamsberg,' he said to the portly officer on the reception desk. 'Your capitaine's expecting me.'

'Yeah, he is,' said the officer, looking at him with an apprehensive air, as if he wouldn't like to be in his boots. 'Down the corridor, sir, office at the end. The door's open.'

Adamsberg stopped in the doorway and for a few seconds observed Capitaine Émeri, who was pacing up and down in his office, looking on edge and tense, but very elegant in a close-fitting uniform. A handsome man, the wrong side of forty, with regular features, a full head of hair that was still blond, and cutting a slim figure in his military jacket with epaulettes.

'What do you want?' Émeri asked as he turned and saw Adamsberg. 'Who told you you could come in here?'

'You yourself, capitaine. You summoned me first thing this morning.'

'Adamsberg?' said Émeri, quickly eyeing the commissaire, who not only wore his usual casual clothes, but had not been able to shave or comb his hair.

'Apologies for being unshaven,' said Adamsberg, shaking hands. 'But I wasn't expecting to stay the night in Ordebec.'

'Sit down, commissaire,' said Émeri, still unable to take his eyes off Adamsberg.

He was having difficulty reconciling Adamsberg's reputation, good or bad, with such a small man, and such a modest appearance: with his dark complexion and black clothes he appeared out of place, unclassifiable or at any rate nonconformist. Émeri looked for the right expression without really finding it, finally settling on a smile which was as pleasant as it was distant. The aggressive speech he had been thinking of delivering had somehow got lost in his perplexity, as if coming up not so much against a wall as against an absence of obstacles. And he couldn't see how to attack or even get to grips with an absence of obstacle. So it was Adamsberg who broke the silence.

'Léone told me you were displeased, capitaine,' he said, choosing his words. 'But I think there's been a misunderstanding. In Paris yesterday it was thirty-six degrees, and I had just arrested an old man who had killed his wife by choking her with bread.'

'With bread?'

'By pushing a couple of handfuls down her throat. And the idea of being able to take a walk in the cool of a *grimweld* appealed to me. Perhaps you can understand.'

'Perhaps.'

'I was picking blackberries and eating them.' Adamsberg noticed that his hands still bore the stains. 'I hadn't expected to come across Léone. She was waiting for her dog and sitting by the path. And *she* hadn't expected to find Herbier's body by the chapel. Out of respect from one professional for another, I didn't go to the crime scene. And since the last train had gone, she offered me hospitality for the night. I wasn't expecting to find myself smoking a Havana cigar and drinking some excellent Calvados by her fire, but that's how the evening ended. She's a splendid woman, as she might say of someone else, but more than that.'

'Do you know how this splendid woman comes to be smoking genuine Cuban cigars?' said Émeri, smiling for the first time. 'Did she tell you her full name?'

'No, she didn't.'

'That doesn't surprise me. Léo's full name is Léone Marie de Valleray, Comtesse d'Ordebec. Some coffee, commissaire?'

'Yes, please.'

Léo, the Comtesse d'Ordebec. Living in a tumbledown old farmhouse, having kept it as an inn, slurping down her soup and spitting out strands of tobacco. Capitaine Émeri came back with two cups, smiling broadly now, allowing the good-natured and hospitable side of his character described by Léo to appear up front.

'You're surprised?'

'Yes, rather. She doesn't seem well off. And Léo told me the Comte d'Ordebec was very rich.'

'She's the count's first wife, but it goes back sixty years. They were young, they were carried away. But the marriage caused such a scandal in the count's family that heavy pressure was exerted and there was a divorce two years later. People say they went on seeing each other for a long time. But then they saw reason and went their separate ways. That's enough about Léo,' said Émeri, ceasing to smile. 'When you arrived on that path yesterday, you didn't know anything? What I mean is: when you spoke to me on the phone from Paris in the morning, you didn't know Herbier was lying dead by the chapel?'

'No.'

'All right. Do you often do that, leave your squad to go walking in a forest at the first opportunity?'

'Yes, often.'

Émeri took a mouthful of coffee and looked up. 'Really?'

'Yes. And there'd been all that bread in the morning.'

'What do your officers have to say about that?'

'Among my officers, I have a hypersomniac who goes to sleep without warning, a zoologist whose speciality is fish, freshwater fish in particular, a woman with bulimia who keeps disappearing in search of food, an old heron who knows a lot of myths and legends, a walking encyclopaedia who drinks white wine non-stop – and the rest to match. They can't allow themselves to stand on ceremony with me.'

'And that lot get some work done, do they?'

'Yes, plenty.'

'What did Léo say when you met her?'

'She just said "Ello", that way she does. And she already knew I was a cop and just off the train from Paris.'

'Not surprising – she's more gifted at sniffing out information than her dog. She'd be shocked, though, at my calling it a gift. She has her own theory about the combined effect of details on each other. She's always quoting this story about the movement of a butterfly's wing in New York leading to an explosion in Bangkok. I don't know where that comes from.'

Adamsberg shook his head, being equally ignorant.

'Léo goes on about the butterfly's wing,' Émeri continued. 'She says the important thing is to spot the moment it moves. Not when everything explodes later. And I have to say, she's pretty good at it. Lina sees these Riders go past. That's the butterfly's wing. Lina's boss tells other people, Léo hears about it, Lina's mother takes fright, some priest gives her your name – I'm right, aren't I? – she gets the train to Paris, her story intrigues you, the temperature in Paris is thirty-six degrees, the woman gets killed with a mouthful of bread, the cool walk in the *grimweld* tempts you, Léo is waiting on the path, and here you are sitting in front of me.'

'That isn't exactly an explosion.'

'But Herbier's death is. That's when Lina's dream explodes into reality. As if the dream made a wolf come out of the woods.'

'Lord Hellequin designates the victims, and someone thinks he's had the go-ahead to kill them? Is that what you think? That Lina's vision has pushed a murderer to act?'

'It isn't just a vision, it's a legend that's been current in Ordebec for a thousand years. You can bet that more than three-quarters of the people here are terrified of this parade of dead horsemen. They'd all be panic-stricken if their name was announced by Hellequin. But they wouldn't say so. I can assure you that people tend to keep well away from the *grimweld* at night, except for a few lads who dare each other to go there. Spending a night on the Chemin de Bonneval is a sort of initiation rite, to prove you're a man. A kind of medieval ritual. But there's a big difference between all that and someone believing in it enough to assassinate someone at Hellequin's bidding. No. But I do admit one thing. It's fear of the Riders that's behind Herbier's death. Note that I said *death*, not murder.'

'Léo said this man had been shot.'

Émeri nodded. Now that his plans for confrontation had melted away his bearing and face had lost their pomposity. The change was striking and Adamsberg thought again about the dandelion. When it's closed at night, it's nondescript, with just a hint of yellow, but in the daytime it's a rich, attractive, bright flower. Still, unlike Madame Vendermot, Capitaine Émeri was anything but a fragile flower. Adamsberg was still trying to remember the name for the little parachutes, so he missed the beginning of Émeri's reply.

'. . . it was his gun, yes, a sawn-off shotgun, a Darne. Herbier was a brutal hunter, he liked to scatter the pellets and kill a female and her young with one shot. From the impact, which was at very close quarters, it's quite possible he held it in front of him with the barrel pointing at his forehead and pulled the trigger.'

'But why would he do that?'

'For the reasons people have said. Because of the appearance of the Ghost Riders. You can guess the chain of events. Herbier hears about the prediction. He's a bad character and he knows it. He takes fright and something clicks in his head. He empties out his freezers himself, as if to deny all his hunting atrocities, and he kills himself. Because they say that someone who enacts justice on himself won't go to hell with Hellequin's army.'

'Why did you say he had the barrel pointing at his forehead, but not touching it?'

'The shot was fired from at least ten centimetres.'

'It would have been more logical to put the muzzle directly against his forehead.'

'Not necessarily. It depends what he wanted to see. The muzzle pointing at him. So far we've found only his own prints on the gun.'

'But you could equally well suppose that someone else thought they would take advantage of Lina's prediction to get rid of Herbier, disguising it as suicide.'

'But you can't seriously imagine someone would go to the lengths of emptying his freezers? Round here there are more hunters than animal rights campaigners. And wild boar are a damned pest, they cause terrible damage. No, Adamsberg, a gesture like that must be some sort of penance for his crimes, an expiation.'

'What about the moped? Why would he hide it in the hazel bushes?'

'It wasn't hidden, just pushed in under the bushes out of the way, a sort of reflex, I suppose.'

'And why would he have gone to the chapel to kill himself?'

'That bit makes perfect sense. In the legend, the people who are seized are often found near some abandoned religious site. You know what "seized" means?'

'Yes,' Adamsberg repeated.

'So, they go to some site which is cursed, in Hellequin's domain. Herbier kills himself there, he's anticipating his destiny, and he'll escape punishment because of his contrition.'

Adamsberg had been sitting too long on his chair and his legs were itching with impatience.

'Is it all right if I walk around a bit in here? I can't sit still too long.'

An expression of total sympathy appeared on the capitaine's face. 'Nor can I!' he exclaimed, with the intense happiness of someone who finds another person shares their own torment. 'It makes my stomach clench, I get nervous electricity in little bubbles bouncing round inside me. Apparently my ancestor, Napoleon's marshal, Davout, was a man of great nervous energy too. I have to walk at least a couple of hours a day to get rid of it. Let's go for a walk through the streets. Ordebec's a pretty place, you'll see.'

The capitaine proceeded to drag his colleague through the town's narrow passageways, between ancient wattle-and-daub walls, low houses with exposed beams, abandoned barns and gnarled apple trees.

'Léo didn't agree,' Adamsberg was saying. 'She seemed convinced that Herbier had been killed.'

'Does she say why?'

Adamsberg shrugged. 'No, she seems to know it because she knows it, that's all.'

'That's the trouble with her. She's so quick-witted that as the years go by she thinks she's always right. If she were to be decapitated, Ordebec would lose a lot of its brains, that's true. But the older she gets, the less explanation she gives. She likes her reputation and she fosters it. She really didn't tell you any details?'

'No. She said Herbier was no great loss. That she wasn't shocked when she came across him, because she already knew he was dead. She told me more about some fox and a little bird than about what she'd seen up at the chapel.'

'The coal tit that fell in love with the three-legged fox?'

'That's right. And she talked about her dog and the bitch on the farm, about St Antony, about her guest house, about Lina and her family, and about how she pulled you out of a pond.'

'That's quite true,' said Émeri with a smile. 'I owe her my life and it's my earliest memory. They call her my "water mother" because she gave me a new lease of life after pulling me out of the Jeanlin pond, like Venus from the waves. My parents idolised Léo after that, and I was ordered never to touch a hair of her head. It was in winter, and Léo came out of the water carrying me, chilled to the bone. They say she took three days to get warm again, and then she developed pleurisy and nearly died.'

'She didn't tell me about the chill. Or that she was married to the count.'

'She never shows off, she's just happy quietly imposing her views and that's already quite enough. No lad from hereabouts would dare shoot at her three-legged fox. Except Herbier. The fox lost his paw and tail in one of Herbier's wretched traps. But he never managed to finish him off.'

'Because Léo killed him before he could kill the fox?'

'She'd be quite capable of it,' said Émeri with a grin.

'Are you going to keep a watch on the next person who's supposed to be seized? The glazier?'

'He's not a glazier, he makes stained-glass windows.'

'Yes, Léo said he was very gifted.'

'Glayeux's a hard bastard, not afraid of anyone. Not the sort to worry about the Furious Army. But if by some chance he did take fright, we can't do anything about that. You can't stop someone killing himself if he's determined.'

'But what if you're wrong, capitaine? What if someone did kill Herbier? That someone might kill Glayeux too. That's what I mean.'

'You're very obstinate, Adamsberg.'

'So are you, capitaine. Because you haven't got any other answers. Suicide would be a handy solution.'

Émeri slowed down, then stopped and took out his cigarettes.

'Explain what you mean, commissaire.'

'Herbier's disappearance was reported over a week ago. And except for going and checking his house, you haven't done anything.'

'That's the law, Adamsberg. If Herbier decided to take off without telling anyone, I had no right to go chasing after him.'

'Even after the sighting of the Riders?'

'That kind of idiocy has no place in a police investigation.'

'Yes, it does. You said yourself that the Riders are behind all this. Whether someone else killed him or whether he killed himself. You knew he'd been named by Lina, and you didn't do anything. And then when they find the body, it's a bit late to start looking for clues.'

'You think I'm going to get into trouble, do you?'

'Yes, I do.'

Émeri pulled deeply on his cigarette, let out the smoke in a sigh, and leaned against the old wall along the side of the road.

'All right,' he admitted. 'Perhaps I will get into trouble. Or maybe not. You can't be held responsible for a suicide.'

'That's why you want to hang on to the idea. It's less likely to be called negligent. But if it is a murder, then you're in it up to your neck.'

'There's nothing to indicate murder.'

'Why didn't you try and find Herbier?'

'OK, I'll tell you. Because of the Vendermot family. Because of Lina. And her degenerate brothers. We don't get on, and I didn't want to play their little game. I stand for order, they stand for anarchy. It won't work. I've had to tell Martin off several times, for poaching. And the oldest brother, Hippolyte. He trained a gun on a group of hunters, he made them take off their clothes, he took away their shotguns and threw the lot in the river. He couldn't pay the fine, so he was jailed for twenty days. They'd all love to see me go down in flames. That's why I didn't take it any further. So as not to fall into their trap.'

'What trap?'

'It's quite simple. Lina Vendermot pretends to have a vision, and Herbier disappears. They're all in it together. I start searching for Herbier, and they immediately complain to the authorities that I'm exceeding my powers and infringing their liberty. Lina's studied law, she knows the rules. So let's suppose I persist and go on looking for Herbier. The complaint goes up to the top. One fine day Herbier turns up again, right as rain; he adds his voice to theirs, and also lodges a complaint against me. I get a reprimand or a transfer.'

'But in that case, why would Lina mention the names of the army's two other hostages?'

'To add credibility. She's as cunning as a weasel, although she makes out she's just a simple country girl. The Riders often seize several people, she knows all that. By naming a few others, she muddies the waters. That's what I *thought*, anyway. And I was absolutely sure of it.'

'But it's not what happened.'

'No.'

Émeri stubbed out his cigarette against the wall, and dropped the fag end between two stones.

'That's enough now,' he said. 'Instead of that, he topped himself.'

'I don't think so.'

'Bloody hell!' exclaimed Émeri in exasperation, and moving to address Adamsberg familiarly as 'tu'. 'What have you got against me? You don't know anything about this case, you don't know the people around here, you waltz down from your capital city without warning and start giving orders.'

'Not *my* capital city. I'm from the Béarn.'

'I don't give a damn where you're from.'

'And they weren't orders.'

'I'll tell you what's going to happen next, Adamsberg. You're going to get back on the train, I'm going to file this as suicide, and it will be forgotten in a few days. Unless of course you're determined to ruin my career with your suspicions of murder. Something you've conjured out of thin air.'

Thin air: his mother had always said that a current of thin air went through Adamsberg's head, from one ear to the other. With that kind of wind blowing through, no idea can remain in place for a moment, let alone become fixed. Adamsberg knew that, and distrusted himself.

'I have absolutely no intention of ruining your career, Émeri. All I'm saying is that if I were you, I'd get some protection for the next one on the list. The glazier.'

'The stained-glass man.'

'Right. Put him under protection.'

'If I did that, Adamsberg, I'd be walking off a cliff. You still don't understand? It would mean I didn't believe in Herbier's suicide. Which I *do* believe in. If you want my opinion, Lina had every reason to drive that guy to suicide. And maybe she did it quite deliberately. And there, yes, I could open an inquiry. Driving someone to suicide. The Vendermot kids have very good reasons for wanting Herbier to rot in hell. Their father and Herbier were such a pair of villains it was a moot point which one was worse.'

Émeri had started walking again, hands in pockets, spoiling the cut of his uniform.

'They were friends, you said?'

'Like that,' Émeri replied, showing two crossed fingers. 'They say Vendermot *père* had an Algerian bullet lodged in his skull and that explained his outbursts of violence. But when he was with his pal, the sadist Herbier, they egged each other on, no question. So trying to terrorise Herbier and drive him to suicide would be a sweet revenge for Lina. Like I said, she's cunning. Her brothers are too, though they're all damaged in some way.'

They had arrived at the highest point in Ordebec, from where one could see the little town and its fields. The capitaine pointed to the east.

'The Vendermot house,' he said. 'The shutters are open, they must be up and doing. Léo's statement can wait, I'm going over to talk to them. When Lina isn't there, it's easier to get the brothers to talk. Especially the one made of clay.'

'Made of clay?'

'You heard. Crumbly clay. Believe me, just get on the train and forget them. If there's one thing that's true about the Chemin de Bonneval, it's that it can drive people nuts.'

IX

ON THE HILL OVERLOOKING ORDEBEC, ADAMSBERG FOUND A WALL in the sun, and sat down on it cross-legged. He took his shoes and socks off, and gazed at the pale green rolling hills, the cows standing like statues in the fields as if they were landmarks. It was perfectly possible that Émeri was right, quite on the cards that Herbier had shot himself in the head, having been terrified by the arrival of the dark horsemen. True, aiming a shotgun at yourself from several centimetres away didn't make a lot of sense. It would be more sure and more natural to put the barrel in your mouth. Unless, that is, as Émeri had suggested, Herbier wanted to make some kind of expiatory gesture. Killing himself like he did the animals, shooting himself full in the face. But was that man capable of remorse, of a guilty conscience? Above all, was he someone who could be scared by the Riders to the point of suicide? Well, yes. The black cavalcade with its mutilated and stinking corpses had been roaming the region of Ordebec for centuries. It had dug deep pits into which anyone, even the most sensible, might suddenly tumble and remain captive.

A message from Zerk told him that Hellebaud was now drinking water without help. Adamsberg took a few seconds to recall that that was the name of the pigeon. There were also several messages from the squad: analysis had confirmed the presence of breadcrumbs in the throat of the victim, Tuilot, Lucette, but none in her stomach. It was a clear-cut case of murder. The little girl with the gerbil was recovering in the hospital in Versailles, and the so-called great-uncle had regained consciousness and was now under guard. Retancourt had sent a more alarming text message, in capital letters: *MOMO QUESTIONED, CHARGES IMMINENT, WE HAVE ID OLD MAN IN CAR, BIG SCANDAL, CALL BACK SOONEST.*

Adamsberg felt a prickling at the back of his neck, a feeling of irritation, perhaps one of the little bubbles of electricity Émeri had talked about. He rubbed his neck as he called Danglard's number. It was 11 a.m. and the commandant ought to be at his desk. A bit early for him to be operational, but he ought to be there.

'What are you still doing out in the sticks?' Danglard asked in his usual grumpy morning voice.

'They found the hunter's body yesterday.'

'Yes, I saw about that. And it's none of our business. Get out of that goddam *grimweld* before it swallows you up. There's trouble here. Émeri can manage perfectly well without us.'

'He'd certainly like to. He's OK, not uncooperative, but he wants me back on the next train. He thinks it's suicide.'

'That would be good news for him. Best outcome really.'

'Yes. But this old woman Léo, whose house I stayed in, was convinced it was murder. She is to the town of Ordebec what a sponge is to water. She's been absorbing everything for eighty-eight years.'

'And when you squeeze her, she tells you?'

'Squeeze her?'

'Like a sponge.'

'No, she's careful, not a gossip, Danglard. She takes seriously the butterfly wing that moves in New York and causes an explosion in Bangkok.'

'Did she say that?'

'No, that was Émeri.'

'Well, he's wrong. It's in Brazil that the butterfly moves its wing, and it causes a hurricane in Texas.'

'Does that make any difference, Danglard?'

'Yes. Because once you get away from the original words, the purest of theories just become rumours. Then we don't know anything. From one approximation to another inaccuracy, the truth unravels and obscurantism takes over.'

Danglard's mood was improving, as it did every time he had a chance to give a lecture, or better still to contradict someone with his knowledge. The commandant wasn't a chatterbox, but silence wasn't good for him either, because it offered too much room for his melancholy to take over. Sometimes it just took a few exchanges to hoist Danglard out of his despondency. Adamsberg was putting off the moment of mentioning Momo the local fire-raiser, and so was Danglard, which was not a good sign.

'There must be several versions of the butterfly story.'

'No,' said Danglard firmly. 'It's not a fable, it's a scientific theory about predictability. It was formulated by Edward Lorenz in 1972 in the version I gave you. The butterfly's in Brazil and the hurricane's in Texas, you can't go altering that.'

'All right, Danglard, let's leave it alone. So what the heck is Momo being questioned for?'

'He was picked up this morning. The petrol corresponds to the kind he uses.'

'Exactly?'

'No, not as much oil. But it certainly was two-stroke, the kind you put in a moped. And Momo has no alibi for the night of the fire, nobody saw him. He claims some guy arranged to meet him in some park to talk to him about his brother. Momo says he waited two hours and when no one turned up he went home.'

'That's not enough grounds to arrest him, Danglard. Who took the decision?'

'Retancourt.'

'Without your permission?'

'With. There were footprints all round the car from trainers with petrol on the soles. And this morning we found the shoes showing traces of petrol in a plastic bag at Momo's place. No arguing with that, commissaire. Momo just keeps stupidly saying they're not his. His defence is completely hopeless.'

'Are his prints on the bag and the shoes?'

'We're waiting for the analysis. Momo says they will be, because he'd handled them. Because he found the bag in his cupboard and looked to see what was in it. Or so he says.'

'Right size?'

'Yes, 43.'

'That doesn't mean anything, average size.'

Adamsberg rubbed the back of his neck again to try and catch the bubble of electricity wandering about there.

'It gets worse,' Danglard went on. 'The old man hadn't slipped down in the seat, he wasn't asleep. He was sitting upright in the passenger seat when the fire began. So the arsonist must have seen him. We're moving away from a manslaughter charge.'

'Were they brand new?' Adamsberg asked.

'Were what brand new?'

'The shoes.'

'Yes, but why?'

'Tell me, commandant, why would Momo have set fire to a car and at the same time made a mess of his new shoes, and if he did, why didn't he get rid of them? Did you look at his hands? Were there traces of petrol on them?'

'Forensics are expected any minute now. We've had instructions to move fast. Look, when you hear the name you'll know why we had to get a move on. The old man who died was Antoine Clermont-Brasseur.'

'No less,' said Adamsberg after a silence.

'You've got it,' said Danglard gravely.

'And Momo just came across him by chance?'

'What kind of chance would that be? If he killed Clermont-Brasseur, he'd be striking a blow at the heart of capitalism. Perhaps that's what he wanted.'

Adamsberg let Danglard go on talking for a few moments, while putting his socks and shoes back on with his other hand.

'Has the examining magistrate been informed?'

'We're just waiting for the results of the tests on Momo's hands.'

'Danglard, whatever the result, don't ask for the charges to be lodged yet. Wait for me.'

'I don't see how we can. If the judge finds out we've dragged our feet, with a name like Clermont-Brasseur, the minister will be down on us within the hour. The prefect's chief of staff has already called for information. He wants the murderer under lock and key within twenty-four hours.'

'Who's in charge of the Clermont industrial group now?'

'The father was still holding two-thirds of the shares. His two sons have the rest between them. That's putting it simply. In fact the father had two-thirds of the building and metal industry. One of the sons has the majority in the IT sector and the other handles the property development. But overall, the old man was in charge, and he didn't want his sons running it on their own. There'd been rumours over the last year that Antoine had started to make some blunders, and that the older son, Christian, was thinking of getting power of attorney in order to protect the group. The old man was furious and had made up his mind to marry his housekeeper next month: she's from Ivory Coast, forty years younger than him, and she's been looking after him and sharing his bed for the last ten years. She's got two children, a son and daughter, and old Antoine was planning to adopt them. It may have been pure provocation perhaps, but the determination of an old man can be a hundred times more implacable than the passion of a young one.'

'And you checked the alibis of the sons?'

'Total veto,' said Danglard between clenched teeth. 'They're too shocked to talk to the police, we've been asked to wait.'

'Danglard, which technician is the lab sending us?'

'Enzo Lalonde. He's good. Don't go there, commissaire. The ground under our feet is already starting to smoulder.'

'Don't go where?'

'Anywhere.'

Adamsberg ended the call, rubbed his neck, and flung out his arm towards the hills to throw the bubble of electricity into the landscape. It seemed to work. He walked quite quickly through the little streets of Ordebec, his laces trailing, heading straight for a telephone box he had noticed on the way from Léo's house to the town centre. A cabin that was not overlooked at all, surrounded by giant hogweed plants. He called the lab and asked to speak to Enzo Lalonde.

'Don't worry, commissaire,' said Lalonde at once, apologetically. 'I'll be over there in forty-five minutes. I'm on my way now.'

'No, that's just it, I don't want you to be on your way. You've been held up at the lab, then your car won't start, you've got stuck in traffic, if possible an accident, something like a headlight against a lamp post would be ideal. Or a bumper. I'll let you improvise, I gather you're a bright lad.'

'Something wrong, commissaire?'

'I need time. Do the analysis as late as you can, then say that some accidental contamination has ruined it and you'll have to start again tomorrow.'

'Commissaire,' said Lalonde after a silence, 'do you realise what you're asking me to do?'

'Just a few hours, no more. On the orders of your superior and in the interests of the investigation. The man under arrest is going to prison in any case. But you can just give him an extra day.'

'I don't know, commissaire.'

'Never mind, Lalonde, no offence taken. Put Dr Roman on and forget this conversation. Roman will do it.'

'Look, all right, commissaire,' said Lalonde after another silence. 'But to ask a favour in return, I was the one who picked up this business with the string round the pigeon's feet. Can you give me some extra time too? I've got a lot on my plate.'

'As much as you like. Just find some way.'

'There are scraps of skin on the string. The kid must have scraped his fingers on it, maybe even grazed them. So you need to find someone with a barely visible lesion in the fold of the index finger. But the string might tell you more. It's unusual.'

'Good, good,' Adamsberg congratulated him, sensing that the young Enzo Lalonde was trying to make him forget his earlier reluctance. 'Now, whatever you do, don't call me on my mobile or at the squad HQ.'

'Understood, sir. But one more thing. I can hold back the results till tomorrow. But I will never falsify the results of an analysis. Please don't ask me to do that. If the guy's had his chips, I can't help it.'

'No, no. No question of falsifying anything. You're sure to find traces of petrol on his fingers, whatever happens. And it'll be the same as on the shoes, because he's handled them and the same too as was found at the scene of the fire. He's going to be banged up, no matter what.'

And then everyone will be happy, thought Adamsberg, hanging up and wiping his prints off the receiver with his shirt tail. And young Momo will see his destiny ahead of him, signed, sealed and delivered.

Léone's farmhouse was now visible in the distance and Adamsberg suddenly stood still, listening. The clear air carried to his ears a long whining sound, the cry of a dog in distress. Adamsberg started running down the road.

X

THE DINING-ROOM DOOR WAS WIDE OPEN. SWEATING, ADAMSBERG stepped into the dark little room, then stopped short. Léone's long thin body was stretched out on the stone flags, her head in a pool of blood. At her side, Fleg was lying down, whining, one large paw on the old woman's waist. Adamsberg felt as if a wall was falling inside him from his head to his stomach and crumbling into his legs.

Kneeling by Léone, he put his hand to her neck and wrists, but couldn't feel the slightest pulse. It wasn't a simple fall, someone had killed her, having banged her head savagely against the stone floor. Pounding his fist on the ground, he felt himself groan aloud with the dog. The body was warm, the attack could have been carried out only a few minutes before. Perhaps he had even disturbed the killer with the sound of his steps on the pebbles in the path. He opened the back door, looked quickly over the deserted surroundings and ran to the neighbours to get the number of the gendarmerie.

Adamsberg waited for the cops to arrive, sitting cross-legged alongside Léo. Like the dog, he put one hand on her body.

'Where's Émeri?' he asked the officer who came in, accompanied by a woman who had to be the police doctor.

'He'd gone to see the crazies. He's on his way.'

'Ambulance,' the doctor ordered urgently into her phone. 'She's still alive. But maybe only for a few minutes. She's in a coma.'

Adamsberg looked up. 'I couldn't feel a pulse,' he said.

'It's very weak,' said the doctor, a woman of about forty, attractive and brisk in manner.

'When did it happen?' asked the gendarme, waiting for his boss to arrive.

'Only a few minutes before you reported it,' said the doctor. 'No more than five perhaps. She must have hit her head when she fell.'

'No,' said Adamsberg, 'someone banged her head on the floor.'

'Did you move her?' asked the woman. 'Who are you anyway?'

'No, I didn't move her, I'm a cop myself. Look at the dog, doctor, he can't stand up. He was defending Léo and the killer must have hit him.'

'I looked at the dog, I know Fleg, he's not hurt. When he doesn't want to get up, there's nothing to be done with him. He won't leave here until they take his mistress away. If then.'

'She must have fainted,' said the fat gendarme unhelpfully, 'or perhaps tripped over a chair. And fallen.'

Adamsberg shook his head, refusing to discuss it. Léone had been hit because of the butterfly in Brazil whose wing she had seen move. But which detail had she seen? And where? The little town of Ordebec itself could offer thousands of details a day, thousands of beats of the butterfly's wings. And as many linked events. Including the murder of Michel Herbier. And somewhere among this mass of fluttering wings, one had vibrated in front of Léone's eyes, and she had had the faculty of seeing or hearing it. But which one? Finding a butterfly's wing in a settlement of two thousand inhabitants was trickier than the proverbial needle in the haystack. Something which had never seemed insurmountable to Adamsberg: all you had to do was burn down the haystack and you'd find the needle.

The ambulance had drawn up in front of the house and its doors clanged open. Adamsberg stood up and went out. He waited until the paramedics had cautiously slid the stretcher into the vehicle, and gently touched the old woman's hair with the back of his hand.

'I'll be back, Léo,' he said to her. 'Brigadier, please ask Capitaine Émeri to have her guarded day and night, twenty-four-hour watch.'

'Right you are, commissaire.'

'Nobody must get into her room.'

'Right you are, commissaire.'

'Waste of effort,' said the doctor coolly, as she got into the ambulance. 'She's unlikely to live beyond nightfall.'

Walking even more slowly than usual, Adamsberg went back into the house which the fat brigadier was now guarding. He ran water over his hands, washing off Léo's blood, and wiped them with the towel he had used the previous evening to dry the dishes, then draped it neatly over the back of a chair. A blue-and-white tea towel with a pattern of bees on it.

Despite his mistress's departure, the dog hadn't moved. He was still whining quietly, with every breath.

'Take care of him, will you?' Adamsberg said to the gendarme. 'Give him some sugar, and don't leave him here.'

In the train, mud and leaves dried on the soles of his shoes and flaked off in a number of dark clumps, attracting disapproving glances from the woman sitting opposite. Adamsberg picked up a fragment, moulded to the pattern of his boot, and slipped it into his shirt pocket. The woman couldn't know, he reflected, that she was sitting alongside the sacred remains from the Chemin de Bonneval, trampled by the hooves of the Ghost Riders. Lord Hellequin would be back to strike at Ordebec – he still had three living souls to capture.

XI

IT HAD BEEN TWO YEARS SINCE ADAMSBERG HAD SEEN MOMO, THE
youth who liked torching fancy cars. He would be about twenty-three
now, too old to be still playing with matches, too young to have given up
his campaign. There was a shadow of stubble on his cheeks, but the new
attempt to look manly didn't make him look any more impressive.

The young man had been put in the interview room, which had no
natural daylight or ventilation. Adamsberg observed him through the
two-way mirror, and saw him slumped in his chair, staring at the floor.
Lieutenants Noël and Morel were questioning him. Noël was pacing
around, playing carelessly with the yo-yo he had confiscated from the
young man. Momo had won championships with it.

'Who put Noël on the job?' Adamsberg asked.

'He's only just taken over,' explained Danglard, looking uneasy.

The questioning had been going on since morning and Danglard had
not yet ordered a halt. Momo had been sticking to the same version of
events for hours: he had been waiting on his own in this park in the
Fresnay district, he had found these brand-new trainers in his cupboard
at home, and had taken them out of the bag. If there was petrol on his
hands, it must have come from the shoes. He had no idea who Antoine
Clermont-Brasseur was, never heard of him.

'Has he had anything to eat?' Adamsberg asked, over the intercom.

'Yes.'

'And to drink?'

'Two Cokes. Good grief, commissaire, what are you imagining? We're not torturing him.'

'The prefect called up in person,' Danglard intervened. 'We've got to get a confession out of him by tonight. Straight from the top, Ministry of the Interior.'

'And where are these famous trainers?'

'Here,' said Danglard, pointing to a desk. 'They still reek of petrol.'

Adamsberg looked them over without touching them and nodded.

'Yes, soaked to the ends of the laces,' he agreed.

Brigadier Estalère hurried in, followed by Mercadet, holding a telephone. Without the unexplained protection of Adamsberg, young Estalère would long ago have left the squad for some little police station in the provinces. All his colleagues more or less thought that Estalère wasn't up to the job, or indeed that he was completely stupid. His big green eyes were always wide open, as if he were trying to take in everything in the world around him, but he failed to register the most obvious things. The commissaire treated him as if he were a promising youngster, and assured everyone that he would realise his potential one day. And every day the young officer made scrupulous efforts to learn and understand. But over the two years he had been with them, nobody had yet seen this famous promise come to anything much. Estalère followed in Adamsberg's footsteps like a traveller setting his compass, without any critical spirit; and at the same time he idolised Lieutenant Retancourt. The clash between the procedural methods of his two role models caused him the greatest perplexity, since Adamsberg journeyed by roundabout paths, while Retancourt moved in a straight line towards her objective, with the realistic reflexes of a buffalo heading for a waterhole. So the young brigadier often stopped at the fork in the road, unable to decide which way to go. At such moments of crisis, he went off and fetched coffee for everyone in the squad. This task he carried out to perfection, since he had memorised all the preferences, however minor, of all his colleagues.

'Commissaire,' Estalère now said breathlessly, 'there's been a disaster in the lab.' He stopped to check his notes. 'The samples taken from Momo are non-viable. An incident of contamination took place where they were stored.'

'In other words,' Mercadet interrupted – being on this occasion wide awake – 'one of the technicians spilt a cup of coffee on the slides.'

'Tea, actually,' Estalère corrected. 'Enzo Lalonde will be back to take more samples, but we won't get the results before tomorrow.'

'Annoying,' Adamsberg murmured.

'But since the traces of petrol might be getting fainter, the prefect has ordered us to see Momo's hands are tied so that he can't touch other surfaces.'

'The prefect has already been told about the contamination?'

'He calls the lab every hour,' said Mercadet. 'The guy with the cup of coffee got an earful.'

'Tea, the guy with the cup of tea.'

'Same thing, Estalère,' said Adamsberg. 'Danglard, call the prefect and tell him he needn't bawl out the technician, we'll have a confession from Momo by ten this evening.'

Adamsberg went into the interview suite, carrying the trainers by his fingertips, and with a nod of his head sent Noël out. Momo gave a smile of relief when he recognised him, but the commissaire shook his head.

'No, Momo. Your days as leader of the gang are over. Do you understand who you set light to this time? Know who it was?'

'Yeah, they told me, guy's got a building firm and metal factories. Clermont.'

'And who sells his products, Mo. All over the world.'

'All right, he sells them.'

'In other words, you burnt to death one of the pillars of French manu-facturing, no less. You understand?'

'It wasn't me, commissaire.'

'That's not what I'm asking you. I'm asking if you understand.'

'Yes.'

'You understand what?'

'That he was a pillar of the French economy.' There was a trace of a sob in Momo's voice.

'In other words you've set fire to the whole fucking country. As we speak, the Clermont-Brasseur company is in chaos and stock exchanges all over Europe are nervous. Get it now? No, don't start telling me stories about mystery rendezvous, parks and strange trainers. What I want to know is whether you were aiming deliberately at Clermont-Brasseur, or whether you got him by chance. Involuntary or premeditated homicide in other words. It makes a big difference.'

'Commissaire, I dunno what you're getting at.'

'Don't move your hands. Was he your *target*? Did you want to go down in the history books? If so, you're on the right track. Put on these gloves and these trainers. Or just one, that'll be enough.'

'They're not mine.'

'Just put one *on*,' said Adamsberg, raising his voice.

Noël, who was listening from behind the glasses, shrugged with annoyance.

'Now he's driving this kid to tears, hard as he can. And I'll get the blame, because they all think *I'm* the vicious bastard round here.'

'Give it a rest, Noël,' said Mercadet. 'We've got our orders. The fire that kid lit has gone right up to the Palais de Justice, we need a confession.'

'And since when has our commissaire been so keen to obey orders?'

'Since his head's been on the block. Normal, isn't it, to want to save your own skin?'

'Of course it's normal,' said Noël, walking away. 'But not from him. In fact, it disappoints me.'

Adamsberg came out of the interview room and handed the trainers to Estalère. He met the confused looks of his colleagues, especially Commandant Danglard.

'You carry on, Mercadet, I've got this Normandy business. Now that Mo's lost confidence in me, he'll soon go to pieces. Put a ventilator in there, his hands will sweat less. And as soon as the technician gets the second set of results, send them to me.'

'I thought you were opposed to charges being brought,' said Danglard, rather precisely.

'But since then, I've seen his eyes. He did it, Danglard. Sad, but true. Whether it was deliberate murder or not, we don't know yet.'

If there was one thing about Adamsberg that Danglard disapproved of more than anything else, it was his habit of considering his hunches as solid fact. Adamsberg regularly replied that hunches *were* facts, material elements as valuable as a lab test. That the brain was a mega-laboratory quite capable of sorting and analysing any given data, such as for example the expression on someone's face, and deriving virtually cast-iron results from it. This false logic infuriated Danglard.

'It's not a matter of seeing or not seeing, but of knowing.'

'And we *do* know, Danglard. Mo sacrificed this old man on the altar of his political convictions. Today in Ordebec, someone smashed the skull of an old lady like throwing a glass on the floor. I'm in no mood to be lenient towards murderers.'

'This morning, you thought Momo had fallen into a trap. This morning, you said he'd surely have got rid of his shoes instead of keeping them in his cupboard like a gift for the prosecution.'

'Mo thought he was being too clever by half. By buying some new shoes and getting us to think they were a plant. But he was the planter.'

'You think that because of the way he looks at you?'

'For example.'

'And what evidence did you find in his eyes?'

'Arrogance, cruelty, and now a blue funk.'

'So you've taken samples of all those things and analysed them?'

'Danglard,' said Adamsberg, with slightly menacing gentleness, 'I told you I was in no mood to argue the case.'

'I'm appalled,' Danglard muttered.

Adamsberg took out his phone to call the hospital in Ordebec. He made a sign with his hand to Danglard, a sort of sweeping aside of objections.

'Go home, commandant, that's the best thing for you to do right now.'

Around them, seven colleagues had appeared to listen to the exchange. Estalère looked shattered.

'And that goes for the rest of you too, if you think you can't take what's coming. I just need two men here with Mo, Mercadet and Estalère.'

The group, having been given its marching orders, dispersed in silence, puzzled and disapproving. Danglard, trembling with rage, had stalked off as fast as his awkward gait would let him, on his long legs which always looked as useless as melting candles. He went down the spiral stairs to the cellar, took out a bottle of white wine that he kept behind the boiler, and took a few rapid swigs. It was a pity, he told himself, that for once he had managed to hold out until 7 p.m. without touching a drop. He sat on the packing case he used as a bench, forcing himself to take deep breaths to calm down and above all to tame the pain of disappointment inside him. He felt a kind of panic, he who had been so fond of Adamsberg, who had counted on the seductive meanders of his mind, on his detachment and, yes, on his gentle nature, a rather simple and usually unvarying one. But time had passed and repeated success must have corrupted Adamsberg's original character. Certainty and self-assurance must have seeped into his consciousness, bringing with them new elements, ambition, arrogance, rigidity. Adamsberg's celebrated nonchalance was tilting and beginning to show its darker side.

Danglard put the bottle back in its hiding place, inconsolable. He heard the door of the office slam shut as the others obeyed orders and one by one left the building, hoping that tomorrow would bring better things. The obedient Estalère would be staying on guard with Momo, accompanied by Lieutenant Mercadet, who would probably nod off. Mercadet's cycles of sleep and wakefulness were about three and a half hours. Being ashamed of this weakness, the lieutenant wasn't in a position to challenge the commissaire.

Danglard got to his feet listlessly, thinking ahead to the evening meal with his five children, to dispel the echoes of the quarrel. His five children, he thought with fierce tenderness, as he gripped the handrail up from the basement. His real life was there, not with Adamsberg. He could resign, and why not? Go over to London and see the woman he loved but saw so little of. This near-resolution brought him a feeling of pride, injecting a little energy into his troubled mind.

Adamsberg, locked in his office, heard the door bang several times as his disconcerted colleagues left the building, a site now infected with unease and resentment. He had done what he had to do, and had nothing to reproach himself with. He'd been a bit crude in going about it, but the pressing urgency of the case left him little choice. Danglard's angry outburst had surprised him. It was odd that his old friend hadn't backed him up and followed him as he almost always did. Especially since Danglard was convinced Mo was guilty. His keen intelligence had been caught napping. But the waves of anxiety that often engulfed the commandant also prevented him seeing simple realities, distorting everything as they flooded over him and closing his eyes to the obvious. Never for very long.

At about 8 p.m. he heard Mercadet's slow footsteps, bringing Mo to his office. In an hour, the lot of the young arsonist would be sealed and tomorrow he would have to face his colleagues' reactions. The only one he really dreaded was Retancourt's. But this was no time to hesitate. Whatever Retancourt or Danglard might think, he had looked into Mo's eyes and read them clearly, and that made his next steps inevitable. He stood up to open the door, pocketing his phone. Léo was still clinging on to life, back in Ordebec.

'Sit down,' he said to Mo, who shuffled in head down, to hide his eyes. Adamsberg had heard him sobbing, his defences were dropping.

'He hasn't admitted anything,' said Mercadet in a neutral tone.

'Won't be long now,' said Adamsberg, pressing the young man's shoulder to make him sit down. 'Mercadet, will you cuff him please, and then go and get a bit of rest upstairs?'

He meant, go to the room with the drinks dispensers and the cat's feeding bowl, where Mercadet had installed cushions on the floor for his cyclical siestas. He had got in the habit of using the breaks to carry the cat up to its bowl and then they both had a nap. According to Retancourt, since the cat and the lieutenant had formed this bond, Mercadet's sleep was more productive and his siestas shorter.

XII

CAPITAINE ÉMERI'S TELEPHONE RANG WHEN HE WAS IN THE MIDDLE
of dinner. He picked it up irritably. Dinner time was for him a luxurious
and beneficial interlude which he protected in a near-obsessive manner,
within a comparatively modest lifestyle. In his official lodgings, the largest
of his three rooms had become his dining room, and there was always a
crisp white tablecloth laid. On the cloth sat two sparkling pieces of silver-
ware inherited from Marshal Davout: a fruit bowl and a bonbonnière,
both stamped with the imperial eagle and his ancestor's initials. Émeri's
housekeeper was in the habit of discreetly turning the cloth if it was soiled,
to save on laundry, since she felt no respect for the long-dead Prince of
Eckmühl.

Émeri wasn't stupid. He knew that this homage to his ancestor was a
form of compensation for a life which he himself regarded as humdrum,
and a character showing none of the marshal's famous audacity. Lacking
sufficient courage, he had ducked out of a military career like his father's,
opting instead for the *gendarmerie nationale*, while his conquests were
restricted to the opposite sex. He judged himself harshly, except at the
sacred hour devoted to dinner, when he countenanced a self-indulgent
escape. Sitting at table, he thought of himself as having personality and
authority, and this daily dose of narcissism gave him renewed energy. His
staff knew that he was not to be interrupted during the meal. So Brigadier
Blériot's voice was hesitant.

'Very sorry, sir, but I thought I should inform you.'

'Is it news about Léo?'

'No, it's the dog. Dr Chazy, she said he was OK, but Commissaire Adamsberg was right about him in the end.'

'Get to the point, Blériot,' said Émeri impatiently. 'My supper's getting cold.'

'The dog, he couldn't get up, sir, and this evening he coughed blood, so I took him up to the vet. Vet says he's got internal injuries. He says Fleg must have been kicked in the belly. Looks like Adamsberg was right after all. Léo must have been attacked.'

'Oh, give me a break from Adams-bloody-berg! We're quite capable of drawing our own conclusions.'

'Sorry, sir, just he said so from the start.'

'And the vet's sure?'

'Yessir. Ready to sign a statement.'

'Get him to come in first thing tomorrow. And what's the news about Léo?'

'Still in a coma. Dr Turbot, he's counting on the internal bruises getting absorbed, he says.'

'Really counting on it?'

'Well, no, capitaine. Not at all.'

'Have you eaten, Blériot?'

'Yessir.'

'Come and see me in half an hour.'

Émeri banged the mobile on to the white cloth and sat in front of his plate with a deep frown. He had a paradoxical relationship with his subordinate, Blériot, who was in fact older than him. Émeri despised him, taking no account of his opinions. Blériot was a simple-minded, uneducated, lumpish brigadier. But at the same time his easy-going temperament – soft-headed, according to Émeri – his patience, which was easily confused with stupidity, and his discretion made him a useful and safe confidant. Émeri treated him by turns like a dog or like a friend, a friend with the special function of listening to him, comforting him and encouraging him. They had been working together for six years.

'This is a bad business, Blériot,' he said to his junior as he opened the front door to him.

'Bad for Madame Léone?' asked Blériot, taking a seat on his usual Empire chair.

'For us, for me. I've fucked this case up, from the start.'

Since Marshal Davout was reputed for his salty language, supposedly inherited from his revolutionary years, Émeri didn't bother to censor his tongue either.

'If Léo was attacked, Blériot, it means Herbier was murdered too, not suicide.'

'What's the connection, sir?'

'Everyone will connect them. Think about it.'

'What'll they say?'

'That she knew about Herbier's death, because Léo always knows everything about everyone.'

'She doesn't gossip.'

'No, but she's very sharp, and she has a good memory. Unfortunately, she didn't tell me anything. It might have saved her life if she had.'

Émeri opened the bonbonnière, filled with sugared almonds, and pushed it across to Blériot.

'We're in deep shit now, Blériot. Someone who knocks down an old lady is not to be messed with. A brute. And I've let him run around for days. What are they saying about it in the town?'

'I told you, sir, I don't know.'

'Oh yes you do, Blériot. What are they saying about me? That I haven't done my job properly, is that it?'

'It'll blow over, sir. People gossip, then they forget.'

'No, Blériot, they're right. It's eleven days since Herbier disappeared, and nine days since I was alerted about it. I decided to ignore the whole thing because I thought the Vendermots were laying a trap for me, you know that. I was covering myself. And then when his body turned up, I decided he must have killed himself, because that was convenient for me. I went on persuading myself, I was pig-headed about it and I didn't lift a finger. If they say I'm responsible for Léo's death, they'll be right. When

Herbier's murder was still fresh, there might have been some chance of getting a trail.'

'We weren't to know that.'

'*You* weren't, no. But I was. And now there are no clues at all. Always the way. It's when you try to protect yourself that you make yourself most vulnerable. Remember that.'

Émeri offered the brigadier a cigarette and the two men smoked in silence.

'What's so serious, capitaine? What can happen?'

'A reprimand from the General Inspection of Gendarmes, that's what!'

'For you?'

'Obviously. You needn't worry, you're not responsible.'

'Get some help, capitaine. You can't win with one hand behind your back.'

'Where from?'

'The count. He's got a long arm. He can pull strings in Paris. And with the General Inspection.'

'Get out the cards, Blériot. We'll play a couple of hands, it'll do us good.'

Blériot dealt the cards with the heavy manner in which he did everything and Émeri felt a bit better.

'The count is very attached to Léo,' Émeri objected, as he fanned out his hand.

'Ah, well, they do say he never loved anyone else.'

'And he'd be entitled to think I'm responsible for what happened to her. So *he*'ll wish me to the devil.'

'Don't say that name, sir.'

'Why not?' said Émeri with a short laugh. 'You believe the devil's here in Ordebec?'

'Well . . . Lord Hellequin has been seen.'

'Oh, my poor Blériot, if you believe that . . .'

'You never know, capitaine.'

Émeri smiled and put down a card. Blériot put an 8 on top of it.

'You're not concentrating.'

'No, sir . . .'

XIII

'COMMISSAIRE,' MO WAS BEGGING.

'Just shut up!' Adamsberg cut him off. 'Your head's on the block, and time's running out.'

'But I don't kill people, man, I don't kill anyone, all I ever kill is cockroaches in my flat.'

'Will you, for Pete's sake, shut up!' said Adamsberg, making an imperious gesture.

Mo fell silent in surprise. Something about the commissaire had clearly changed.

'That's better,' said Adamsberg. 'You heard me just now. I'm not in the mood to let murderers run around free.'

An image of Léo passed in front of his eyes, triggering a pain at the back of his neck. He rubbed it with his hand, to expel the bubble of electricity to the ground. Mo looked at him, thinking he must have caught some invisible insect. Instinctively he did the same, putting a hand to his neck.

'You got a bubble there too?' asked Adamsberg.

'A bubble?'

'Electricity. You've got good reason.'

Mo shook his head, failing to understand.

'In your case, Mo, we're dealing with a cynical, calculating and very powerful killer. The opposite of the frantic and impulsive murderer we've got in Ordebec.'

'I dunno what you mean,' murmured Mo.

'Never mind. Someone eliminated Antoine Clermont-Brasseur. I won't bother explaining *why* this rich old man was blocking someone's light, we don't have time, and it's not your problem. What you've got to realise is that you're going to take the rap for it. That was planned from the start. You might get out for good conduct in twenty-two years, that's if you don't set fire to your cell.'

'*Twenty-two years?*'

'This is a Clermont-Brasseur who was killed, not some two-bit cafe owner. Justice isn't blind.'

'But if you know I didn't do it, you can tell them, so I won't go to prison.'

'In your dreams, lad. The Clermont-Brasseur clan won't allow one of their own members to come under suspicion. We can't even get near them for some simple questioning. Whatever happened the other night, our leaders are going to protect the clan. So when I say neither you nor I count for anything, it's an understatement. You're *nothing*, they're every-thing. If one can put it that way. And you've been chosen as the fall guy.'

'But there isn't any *evidence*,' Mo whispered. 'How can they charge me without any evidence?'

'Of course they can, Mo. Stop wasting time. I'm offering you a deal: two years' prison instead of twenty-two. Are you up for it?'

'What do you mean?'

'You escape from here and you go into hiding. But you have to under-stand that when they find you gone tomorrow, I'm going to have some explaining to do.'

'Ye-ah?'

'What you've done is this: you've taken Mercadet's gun and phone – Mercadet's the lieutenant with a side parting and small hands who brought you here – because he fell asleep in the interview room. He's always drop-ping off.'

'But he *didn't* drop off, commissaire.'

'Don't argue with me. He fell asleep, you took his gun. And his mobile. You hid them in your pocket. Mercadet didn't notice a thing.'

'What if he swears he's had his gun on him all the time?'

'He'll be wrong, because I'm just now going to take it from him, and his mobile as well. The idea is, you've used the phone to call a pal and got him to wait for you outside. Now I've come in, you pull out the gun, you hold it to my head, and force me to take off your handcuffs, and put him on myself. Then I open the back door of the station. Listen carefully. There are two men on duty in the street, one each side of the door. You come out, holding the gun to my head with a determined expression. So determined they don't try to intervene. Think you can do all that?'

'Oh . . . I can try.'

'Right. So I tell the lads outside to take it easy, not to move. You've got to look tough, ready for anything. Agreed?'

'What if I don't look tough enough?'

'In that case, it's your own neck you're risking. Just do it. At the corner of the street, there's a no-parking sign. You walk me that far, we turn right, you punch me on the jaw, and I fall to the ground. Then you run straight down that road. You'll see a car parked there in front of the butcher's shop, about thirty metres along; it'll flash its lights once. You chuck away the gun, and you jump in.'

'And the mobile?'

'You leave that here. I'll destroy it.'

Mo looked at Adamsberg, thunderstruck, raising his heavy eyelids in surprise.

'Why are you doing this? They'll say you couldn't even deal with a yob from an estate.'

'What they say will be my business.'

'They'll suspect you.'

'Not if you do what you have to do convincingly.'

'This isn't a trap, is it?'

'Two years' prison, or eight months if you keep your nose clean inside. Best-case scenario, I get my hands on the real killer, but you'll still be charged with an armed attack on the commissaire, plus evading arrest. So is it on?'

'Yes,' breathed Mo.

'OK. Now pay attention. It may be that they build a wall so high around this inquiry that I *never* get to catch the murderer. In which case you'll have to run a long way, maybe overseas.'

Adamsberg looked at his watch. If Mercadet was subject to his usual cycle, he ought to be fast asleep by now. Adamsberg opened the door and called Estalère.

'Keep an eye on this so-and-so for me, I'll be back in a minute.'

'Has he said anything?'

'Getting close. I'm counting on you, don't take your eyes off him.'

Estalère smiled. He liked it when Adamsberg referred to his eyes. The commissaire had told him one day that he had excellent eyesight, capable of spotting anything.

Adamsberg slipped upstairs quietly, remembering to miss the ninth step, which always tripped everyone up. Lamarre and Morel were on duty in reception, and he didn't want to attract their attention. In the room with the coffee machine, Mercadet was in situ, fast asleep on the cushions, with the cat stretched out on his legs. The lieutenant had unfastened his holster so the gun was easy to reach. Adamsberg patted the cat's head and lifted the Magnum without making a sound. It was trickier to extract the mobile from Mercadet's trouser pocket. Two minutes later, he sent Estalère away again, and locked himself in with Mo.

'Where am I to hide?' Mo asked.

'Somewhere the police will never look. In a cop's house.'

'Where?'

'My place.'

'No shit.'

'That's how it is, we have to improvise. I haven't had time to arrange anything else.'

Adamsberg had sent a quick message to Zerk, who reported that Hellebaud had spread his wings, and looked ready to fly.

'It's time now,' said Adamsberg, getting up.

Handcuffs on his wrists, Mo pressing the gun to the back of his neck, Adamsberg opened the two barred doors on to the large courtyard where the squad's cars were parked. As they approached the back entrance, Mo put his hand on Adamsberg's shoulder.

'Commissaire, I . . . I dunno what to say.'

'Save it for later, concentrate.'

'My first-born son, I'll call him after you, I swear to god.'

'Just keep moving, for god's sake,' said Adamsberg angrily. 'And look tough.'

'Commissaire, just one thing.'

'What? Your yo-yo?'

'No, my mother.'

'She'll be informed.'

XIV

DANGLARD HAD DONE THE WASHING-UP AND WAS LYING ON HIS old brown sofa with a glass of white wine to hand, while his children finished their homework. Five children, all growing up, five children who would leave home one day and he didn't want even to think about that this evening. The youngest, who was not actually his son, and continually presented the enigma of his blue eyes inherited from an unknown father, was the only one now still a small child rather than a teenager, and Danglard was trying to keep him that way. He had been unable to hide his depression during the evening, and the older of the boy twins had shown insistent concern about it. Danglard had not offered much resistance before telling him about the confrontation with the commissaire, about Adamsberg's harsh tone and how he supposed his boss was declining into mediocrity. The twin gave a doubtful grimace, as did his brother, and their double expression now haunted Danglard's saddened mind.

He overheard one of his twin daughters reciting her homework about Voltaire, the man who laughs at the way people are taken in by illusions and lies. And he suddenly sat up, leaning on one elbow. It had been a sham, that was what he had witnessed. A lie, an illusion. He felt his mind start ticking over in a higher gear, finding itself back on track again. He stood up, pushing aside the glass. Unless he was mistaken, Adamsberg would be needing him, and now.

Twenty minutes later, he hurried into the squad office, out of breath. Nothing was untoward, it seemed. The night-duty officers were nodding off under the fans rotating on the ceiling. He went quickly into Adamsberg's empty office, then saw the gate open into the courtyard and ran, if you could call it running in Danglard's case, to the back entrance of the building. The two guards were helping Adamsberg back along the darkened street. The commissaire seemed dazed, and was leaning on their shoulders to walk. Danglard took over from them.

'Just get that little bastard back for me,' Adamsberg was telling the officers. 'I think he had a getaway car. I'll send you reinforcements.'

Danglard helped Adamsberg back into his office without a word, having shut the gates behind them. The commissaire refused to sit on a chair, and let himself collapse to the floor, between his precious deer's antlers, leaning his head against the wall.

'Doctor?' asked Danglard drily.

Adamsberg signalled no.

'Some water then. That's what you need if you've had a knock.'

Danglard went out to instruct the reinforcements, and ordered a top-level alert on roads, stations and airports, before coming back with a glass of water, an empty glass and his bottle of white wine.

'So how did he manage to do this to you?' he asked, offering the glass, then uncorking the bottle.

'He'd taken Mercadet's gun. Couldn't do a thing,' said Adamsberg, drinking off the water then holding out the empty glass towards the bottle.

'Not a good idea to drink wine, in your condition.'

'Nor in yours, Danglard.'

'So what it adds up to, you let yourself be hoodwinked, like a raw recruit?'

'That's what it adds up to, yes.'

One of the uniformed officers knocked and came in without waiting. Holding the Magnum by his little finger, he offered it to the commissaire.

'Found it in the gutter,' he said.

'And the mobile?'

'No, sir. The butcher was in his shop doing his accounts, and he says this car took off at speed. It had been parked for about five minutes in front of his shop. And a man jumped into it.'

'Mo, presumably,' said Danglard, with a sigh.

'Yes, sir,' the officer said. 'Description fits.'

'Didn't get the number, did he?' asked Adamsberg, without betraying any tension.

'No, sir. He didn't come out of the shop. What shall we do?'

'The usual. A report. Always the right answer.'

The door closed and Danglard poured half a glass of wine for the commissaire.

'In your state of shock,' he went on, in pompous tones, 'I can't allow you any more.'

Adamsberg felt in his shirt pocket and took out a bent cigarette, one he'd nicked from Zerk. He lit it slowly, trying to avoid Danglard's gaze, which seemed to be boring into his head like a long fine needle. What the hell was Danglard doing here at this time of night, anyway? Mo really had hurt him with the punch to the jaw, and he rubbed his chin, which was aching and probably bruised. Very good. He felt a graze and a little blood on his fingers. Excellent, everything going as planned. Except for Danglard and his long fine needle, and that was what he had been afraid of. The commandant didn't usually take long to put two and two together.

'Tell me about it,' said Danglard.

'Nothing to tell. He just jumped up like a mad thing, took me by surprise, put the gun to the back of my head, what could I do? He went down the street on the right.'

'How did he manage to get an accomplice to help?'

'He'd got hold of Mercadet's phone too. He texted some pal while I was sitting there. So what shall we say in this report? To avoid letting on that Mercadet had gone to sleep?'

'Yes, good question, what indeed shall we say in our report?' said Danglard, articulating each word clearly.

'We'll cheat a bit about the time. We'll say Mo was still in the interview room at 9 p.m. If an officer nods off when he's doing overtime, it's not so bad. I think the colleagues will show solidarity.'

'Who with?' asked Danglard. 'Mercadet or you?'

'Well, what do you suggest I should have done, Danglard? Got myself shot?'

'Go on, it wouldn't have reached that stage.'

'Yes it would, Mo was like a man possessed.'

'Oh yeah,' said Danglard, taking another mouthful of wine.

And Adamsberg read his defeat in his deputy's clear-eyed gaze.

'All right,' he admitted.

'All right,' Danglard confirmed.

'But you're too late. You got here too late, show's over. I was afraid you'd catch on earlier. You took your time, actually,' he added, sounding disappointed.

'True. You had me going there for three hours.'

'Exactly what I needed.'

'Adamsberg, you are completely crazy.'

Adamsberg took another sip of his half-glass and swilled it around his mouth.

'Doesn't bother me,' he said, swallowing.

'And you'll drag me down with you.'

'No. You're not obliged to have understood what happened. You still have a chance to look like an unsuspecting idiot, commandant. Make your choice. Go or stay.'

'I'll stay, if you have a single thing to dispose me in his favour. Not counting "the way his eyes look".'

'Nope. If you stay, no strings.'

'And if not?'

'If not, life won't have much interest any more.'

Danglard suppressed a movement of protest, as he gripped his glass. His anger now was much less painful, he reflected, than when he had imagined Adamsberg was becoming despicable. He took some time to think in silence. It was a formality and he knew it.

'Right,' he said.

It was the briefest expression he could find to express his surrender.

'Remember the trainers?' Adamsberg asked. 'The laces?'

'Mo's exact size. What about them?'

'I'm talking about the laces, Danglard. The ends had soaked up petrol for several centimetres.'

'So?'

'They're those high-sided trainers teenagers wear, with really long laces.'

'Yeah, my kids have them too.'

'And how do your kids do them up? Think about it, Danglard.'

'They take them once round the ankle and tie them in front.'

'There you are. It used to be the fashion to leave the laces undone. Now the fashion is to have very long laces and take them round the back before tying them. So they don't drag on the ground, do they? Only some older guy would put them on without knowing what you're supposed to do.'

'Shit.'

'My feelings exactly. This older guy, Mr Not-so-cool, fifty or sixty years old, let's say one of the Clermont-Brasseur sons, buys some teenage trainers. And he just ties the laces in front, like he would have done in his time, so the ends trail into the petrol. I asked Mo to put them on, remember?'

'Yes.'

'And he tied them like you said, round the back and in front. If Mo had really torched the car, there'd have been some petrol on the soles, yes, but not on the laces.'

Danglard filled up the glass he had just emptied.

'And that's your evidence?'

'Yes, and it's worth its weight in gold.'

'Right. But you started this play-acting before that. You knew before.'

'Mo's not a *killer*. I never had any intention of letting him fall into their clutches.'

'So which of the Clermont sons do you suspect?'

'Christian. He's been a calculating bastard since he was twenty.'

'You won't get away with it. They'll catch Mo, wherever he is. That's their only hope. Who picked him up in the car?'

Adamsberg finished his glass without replying.

'Ah. Like father, like son,' said Danglard, standing up heavily.

'We've already got one lame pigeon, might as well have another.'

'You won't be able to keep him long at your place.'

'Don't intend to.'

'Good. But what next?'

'The usual,' said Adamsberg, extracting himself from between the stags' antlers. 'A report. We'll write a report. That's what you're good at, Danglard.' His mobile rang just then, with an unknown number. Adamsberg consulted his two watches. Five past ten. He frowned. Danglard was already tackling the falsified report, with his unshakeable devotion to the commissaire, considering the extremities in which they now found themselves.

'Adamsberg speaking,' the commissaire said cautiously.

'Louis Nicolas Émeri,' said the capitaine in a hollow voice. 'Did I wake you up?'

'No, one of my suspects has just got away.'

'Right,' said Émeri, not understanding.

'Is it about Léo? Has she died?'

'No, still holding out. *I'm* not though, I'm being taken off the case, Adamsberg.'

'Officially?'

'No, not yet. But a colleague from the IGN tipped me off in advance. Tomorrow. They're jackals, those s.o.b.s.'

'We did guess it might happen, Émeri. Is it a suspension or a transfer?'

'Just a temporary suspension, while they do a report.'

'Ah, always a report.'

'Jackals, sons of bitches,' Émeri said again.

'So why are you calling me?'

'I'd rather die than see the capitaine from Lisieux take over the investigation. St Teresa of Lisieux herself would pack him off with Hellequin's lot, no bother.'

'One second, Émeri.'

Adamsberg covered the phone.

'Danglard, what's the name of the capitaine in the Lisieux gendarmerie?'

'Dominique Barrefond, bastard of the worst kind.'

'So what is it you want, Émeri?' said Adamsberg into the phone.

'I want you to take the case. It's yours anyway.'

'Mine? Since when?'

'From the start, before it became a case at all. When you took a walk on the Chemin de Bonneval without knowing anything about it.'

'I was just taking the air. And eating blackberries.'

'Don't give me that. It's your case,' Émeri stated. 'But if you're in charge, I can help you unofficially, and you won't kick me out of the way. Whereas that bastard in Lisieux wants my guts for garters.'

'That's the reason?'

'That and the fact that the case has picked you out and nobody else. It's your destiny to deal with the ghostly army.'

'Oh, come off it, Émeri!'

'That's the way it is. He's galloping towards you.'

'Who?'

'Lord Hellequin.'

'You don't believe that for a second, you just want to save your skin!'

'Quite right.'

'Look. I'm sorry, Émeri, but you know I can't get this assigned to me, I've got no pretext at all for getting involved.'

'I'm not talking about pretexts, I'm talking about pulling strings. I can get the Comte d'Ordebec to wangle something. See what you can do your end.'

'Why should I do this, Émeri? I don't want any aggro from the Lisieux gendarmes. I've got enough trouble on my hands right here.'

'But you're not up *against* it.'

'What do you know about that? Like I just told you, one of my suspects has got clean away. From my own office, using a gun he'd taken from one of my own juniors.'

'Good reason to pick up some credit somewhere else.'

Not wrong, thought Adamsberg. But who could tackle the leader of the Furious Army?

'Is your escaped suspect involved in the Clermont-Brasseur affair, by any chance?' Émeri was asking.

'Correct. So you see, there's going to be hell to pay, and I'll have to face the music myself.'

'The Clermont sons, you're interested in them?'

'Naturally. But we can't get near them.'

'The Comte d'Ordebec can. He sold his steelworks to their father,

Antoine. They went on safari in Africa together in the fifties. The count was a friend of his. When Léo pulled me out of the duck pond, she was still married to him.'

'Forget the Clermonts. We know who started the fire.'

'Glad to hear it. It's just that, sometimes, you feel like cleaning up around the edges to get a clearer picture. Just a matter of professional hygiene, of no great consequence.'

Adamsberg moved the phone from his ear and folded his arms. His fingers came across the little piece of earth he had slipped into his shirt pocket. Only at noon that day.

'Let me think about it,' he said.

'Yes, but get a move on.'

'I never think quickly, Émeri.'

No, sometimes you don't think at all, thought Danglard, without voicing it. This whole business of Mo's escape was utter madness.

'Off to Ordebec then?' the commandant asked out loud. 'As soon as it's light you'll have the entire government against you, and now you want to take on the Furious Army as well?'

'The great-great-grandson of Marshal Davout has just surrendered. The fortress is there to be stormed. Quite a swashbuckling mission, wouldn't you say?'

'Since when have you been into swashbuckling?'

Adamsberg collected his things in silence. 'Since I promised Léo I'd be back.'

'She's in a coma, she can't possibly care one way or the other, and she won't even remember you.'

'But I remember her.'

And after all, thought Adamsberg as he walked home, perhaps Émeri was right. It *was* his case. He made a detour along the Seine and threw Mercadet's mobile phone into the water.

XV

BY 2 A.M., DANGLARD HAD FINISHED WRITING THE REPORT. AT 6.30 a.m., Adamsberg took a call at home from the secretary general at the prefecture of police, followed by one from the director of the same, then the minister's secretary, and finally from the Minister of the Interior himself at 9.15. At that moment, Mo walked into his kitchen, wearing a T-shirt of Zerk's that was too big for him, and timidly looking for something to eat. Zerk, with the pigeon perched on his arm, got up to reheat some coffee. The shutters on the garden side were still closed and Zerk had pinned a garish length of chintz across the glass pane of the garden door – because of the heat, he had told Lucio. Mo had been ordered not to go near any of the upstairs windows. With a couple of gestures, Adamsberg signalled to the two young men to keep quiet and leave the room.

'No, monsieur le ministre, he won't get away. Yes, all the gendarmeries have been on the alert since 9.40 last night. Yes, the frontier posts too. No, I don't think that's necessary, monsieur le ministre, it wasn't Lieutenant Mercadet's fault.'

'Heads are going to roll, and so they bloody well should, Commissaire Adamsberg, as you must well know. The Clermont-Brasseur family is appalled at the laid-back attitude apparent in your squad. And so am I. It's come to my attention that you've kept a sick man on your staff, in what's supposed to be a crack outfit.'

'A sick man, sir?'

'A narcoleptic, a hypersomniac. A man so incompetent that he allowed his weapon to be taken from him. Going to sleep while guarding a suspect – you call that normal? I call it a dereliction of duty, Adamsberg, nothing less.'

'Monsieur le ministre, perhaps you haven't been fully briefed. Lieutenant Mercadet is one of the best men in the team. But he had had only two hours' sleep the night before and was doing overtime. It was almost thirty-four degrees in the interview room.'

'And who else was on guard?'

'Brigadier Estalère.'

'Reliable?'

'Excellent.'

'Then why did *he* leave the room. The report doesn't say.'

'To fetch some cold drinks.'

'Total dereliction of duty, heads will roll! Cold drinks for the suspect, Mohamed Issam Benatmane, not the best way to get him to talk.'

'The refreshments were just for the officers, monsieur le ministre.'

'Well, he should have asked a colleague to do it. A grave professional error. An officer should never be left alone with a suspect. And that goes for you too, commissaire, when you had him in your office for questioning, without any backup. And then you didn't even manage to disarm a twenty-year-old street gangster. It was incalculable negligence.'

'Yes, monsieur le ministre. It was.'

Adamsberg was absent-mindedly drawing lines in the drops of coffee on the plastic sheeting, tracing routes between the deposits made by Hellebaud. He pondered for a moment on the extreme resistance bird droppings offer to washing. That was a chemical enigma which Danglard would be unable to solve, he wasn't much good at science.

'Christian Clermont-Brasseur has called for you to be dismissed with immediate effect, and your two incompetent officers as well, and I'm tempted to agree with him. But for some reason, the thinking over here is that you could still be useful. So you've got a week, Adamsberg, not a day more.'

Adamsberg called the entire team together in the big meeting space to which Danglard had given the erudite name of chapter room. Before leaving home, he had aggravated the injury to his chin by rubbing it with a dish scrubber, making more red scratches on his face. Very good, Zerk had said appreciatively, as he dabbed scarlet Mercurochrome on the bruise to make it more obvious.

It was not something he enjoyed doing, sending his agents off on a wild goose chase after Mo, when he knew him to be sitting at his own kitchen table, but the situation left him no choice. He assigned tasks and the officers all looked at their instructions in silence. He took in the expressions of the nineteen colleagues present: they all seemed stunned by the new turn of events. Only Retancourt looked secretly amused, which caused him some anxiety. Mercadet's expression of total consternation reawakened the sharp feeling at the back of his neck. He had caught this bubble of electricity from Capitaine Émeri, and it would have to be returned to him sooner or later.

'A week?' repeated Lamarre. 'What's the point of that? If he's run off into the woods somewhere, we could be a month or more trying to find him.'

'The week's for me,' said Adamsberg, without mentioning the precarious status of Mercadet and Estalère. 'If I can't deliver, Danglard will probably have to take over the leadership of the squad and the work will continue.'

'I really don't remember dropping off in the interview room,' Mercadet said, his voice choking with guilt. 'It's all my fault. But I don't remember it. If I've started falling asleep without realising it, I'd better give up the job.'

'We were all at fault, Mercadet. You went to sleep, Estalère left the room, we didn't search Mo, and I took him into my office alone.'

'Even if we find him in a week, they'll probably sack you to make an example,' said Noël.

'Quite possible, Noël. But we've got a window of opportunity. And if not, well, I'll be happy enough in my mountains. So, it's not a catastrophe. The first thing is, you'd better be prepared for an unannounced inspection of our office sometime today. So everything has got to be absolutely impeccable. Mercadet, go and have forty winks now, you'll have to look wide awake when they arrive. And get rid of the cushions. Voisenet, put away your fish magazines. Froissy, not a crumb of food must be left in any cupboard, and your watercolours must be out of sight too. Danglard, your stashes of wine will disappear. Retancourt, please take the cat and its dishes out to one of the cars. We've got to pay attention to every detail.'

'What about the string?' asked Morel.

'What string?'

'The one from the pigeon's feet. The lab sent it back, it's on the sample table with the other forensic results. If they ask, it might not be the moment to tell them about the bird.'

'I'll handle the string,' said Adamsberg, noting as he spoke Froissy's distress at the idea of getting rid of her hidden rations. 'But there's one piece of good news. For once, Divisionnaire Brézillon is on our side. We won't get any trouble from him.'

'Why not?' asked Mordent.

'The Clermont-Brasseur combine ruined his father's firm, which was importing Bolivian minerals. It was a stock-market raid, he's never forgiven them. He just wants one thing, "to see those bastards squirming in the hot seat", those were his words.'

'There's no hot seat waiting,' said Retancourt. 'It wasn't the Clermont family that burnt the car.'

'I was just giving you an idea of the divisionnaire's state of mind.'

Retancourt's gaze once more registered some irony, if he was not mistaken.

'Right, off you go,' said Adamsberg, standing up and throwing his bubble of electricity to the ground at the same time. 'Clean up the place. Mercadet, can you come with me for a moment?'

Sitting opposite Adamsberg, Mercadet was twisting his tiny hands round each other. He was an honest, scrupulous but also fragile person, whom Adamsberg was pushing to the edge of depression and self-hate.

'I'd rather be sacked right away,' said Mercadet with dignity, rubbing the dark rings under his eyes. 'That kid could have killed you. If I'm capable of dropping off without realising it, it's time to quit my job. I was pretty unreliable before but now I'm dangerous, unable to control myself.'

'Lieutenant,' said Adamsberg, leaning across the table. 'I said you had fallen asleep. But you didn't. Mo didn't take your gun.'

'Commissaire, it's kind of you to try and help me. But when I woke up upstairs, I didn't have my gun or my phone. And Mo had them.'

'He had them because I gave them to him. I gave them to him because I took them from you. Upstairs, in the coffee room. Do you get it?'

'No!' said Mercadet, looking up in consternation.

'It was me, Mercadet. I had to get Mo out of there before he was put into a detention centre. Mo has never killed anyone. I didn't have any other way to do it, and I landed you in the shit.'

'Mo didn't threaten you?'

'No.'

'You opened the gates?'

'Yes.'

'Wow.'

Leaning back, Adamsberg waited for Mercadet to digest the information, something he usually did quite quickly.

'OK,' said Mercadet, looking up again. 'I much prefer that to the idea that I dropped off in the interview room. And if you're sure Mo didn't kill the old man, it was the only thing to do.'

'And to keep quiet about, Mercadet. Danglard is the only one who's got an inkling about it. But you, me and Estalère, we could probably all be in big trouble within a week. And I didn't consult you about it.'

'It was the only thing to do,' repeated Mercadet. 'Well, at least my sleeping turned out useful for once.'

'That's true. If you hadn't been there, I don't think I would have been able to come up with anything.'

The butterfly's wing. Mercadet blinks his eyes in Brazil and Mo escapes to Texas.

'Is that why you kept me back doing overtime yesterday?'

'Yes.'

'Good. I thought you had it in for me.'

'We're both in for it now, lieutenant.'

'Unless you can pin it on one of the Clermont sons.'

'Is that how you see it?' asked Adamsberg.

'Could be. A youngster like Mo would have tied his laces front and back. I didn't understand why his laces were soaked with petrol.'

'Bravo.'

'You saw it too?'

'Yes. But why did you immediately think of the old man's sons?'

'Well, think of the fallout if the father went ahead and married his housekeeper and adopted her children. People say his sons don't have old Antoine's diabolical business savvy. They've taken a few dodgy decisions. Especially Christian. He's a hothead, likes to live it up, known to spend the daily output of an oil well in twenty-four hours.' Mercadet shook his head with a sigh. 'But we don't even know if it was him driving the car,' he said, getting to his feet.

'Lieutenant,' said Adamsberg, 'we need absolute secrecy about this, and that means this secret is never to be revealed. To anyone.'

'It's OK, sir. I live on my own.'

When Mercadet had gone, Adamsberg paced around his office and replaced the antlers along the wall. Brézillon and his hatred of the Clermont-Brasseur bastards. The divisionnaire might be attracted by the idea of getting at them via the Comte d'Ordebec. In which case there was a good chance that the Normandy business might be allocated to him. In which case, he'd be facing the Ghost Riders. A prospect that exerted an indefinable attraction for him, welling up from some ancestral depths. He remembered seeing a very young man, one evening, leaning over the parapet of a bridge and staring at the water as it rushed by underneath. He was holding his cap in his hand, and his problem, he confided in Adamsberg, was the overwhelming temptation to throw the cap into the water, although he was fond of it. The young man was trying to understand why he was so strongly drawn to commit an action he didn't actually want to do. In the end he had run off, without letting go of the cap, as if he had had to tear himself away from some magnetic force. Now Adamsberg understood better the odd incident of the cap on the bridge. The cavalcade of black horses was galloping through his thoughts, issuing obscure and pressing invitations, to the point where he felt that the bitter realism surrounding the politico-financial affairs of the Clermont-Brasseur dynasty was but a distraction. Only the memory of Mo's stricken face, a straw being trampled under their feet, gave him the energy to work on it. The Clermont secrets were unsurprising, wearyingly pragmatic, and that only made the horrible death of the aged industrialist more appalling. Whereas the secret of Ordebec was emitting strains of music, unintelligible and dissonant, a composition of fantasy and illusion drawing him towards it like the water under the bridge.

He couldn't allow himself to leave the squad unattended for long on this momentous day, so he took one of the cars to go and see Brézillon. Only at the second traffic lights did he realise he'd taken the one containing the cat and its feeding dishes. He slowed down so as not to spill any water from the bowl. Retancourt would never forgive him if the cat became dehydrated.

Brézillon received him with an impatient smile, and a sympathetic clap on the shoulder. An unusual atmosphere, but that didn't stop him greeting the commissaire with the words he invariably pronounced:

'You know I don't really approve of your methods, Adamsberg. Too much informality, too little clarity either for your superiors or your staff, and not enough factual elements along the way. But your methods might have something to be said for them in present circumstances, since we're navigating in the dark anyway.'

Adamsberg let this opening pass, and embarked instead on the excellent factual element provided by the laces of the trainers, wrongly tied by the arsonist. It wasn't easy to break into the divisionnaire's long monologues.

'I hear you,' said Brézillon, stubbing out his cigarette with one thumb, his usual gesture. 'You'd do well to turn off your mobile before we go any further. Your phones have been tapped since the suspect escaped, i.e. since you showed such pathetic lack of determination to recapture this

Mohamed. That is to say the sacrificial lamb,' he went on, when Adamsberg had turned off the mobile. 'We're in agreement there, are we? I didn't for a moment believe this insignificant young man could have accidentally caused the death of one of the country's top industrialists. They've given you a week, yes, I know, and I can't see you getting very far in that time. For one thing because you're a slow worker, and for another, the road has been blocked. Nevertheless, I'm prepared to support you in any reasonable and *legal* way to try and get under the defence of those brothers. It goes without saying, Adamsberg, that in the meantime I totally subscribe to the official version that this Arab boy is guilty, and whatever happens to the Clermont clan, don't expect any approval from me if you cause a scandal. Up to you to find a way out.'

XVI

AT 5 P.M., ADAMSBERG RETURNED TO HEADQUARTERS, WITH THE cat folded in two over his arm, like a huge floorcloth; he deposited it back on the warm lid of the photocopier. The Inspection team had indeed descended on the offices two hours earlier, scouring the premises ruthlessly and without comment, but had found nothing untoward. Between times, reports had come in from the gendarmeries and police stations, and still Momo was missing. Several officers were out checking the homes of his known contacts. A larger operation was planned for the evening, a complete search of all the flats in the Cité des Buttes, the tower block where Momo lived, and which, unsurprisingly, had a record of torched cars above the national average. They were waiting for reinforcements to arrive from three Paris police stations to surround the block.

Adamsberg motioned to Veyrenc, Morel and Noël, and sat sideways on Retancourt's desk.

'Here's the address of the two Clermont sons. Christian and Christophe: the "two Christs" they call them.'

'Hardly up to the reputation of the Saviour,' remarked Retancourt.

'Their father expected too much of them.'

'*He weeps as he sees them, these men of no worth / His own sons whose virtues he had stifled at birth*,' commented Veyrenc. 'Are you hoping the Clermonts are going to let us in now?'

'No. But I want you to watch them night and day. They both live at the same address, a huge Paris mansion, with two wings on the same site. You'll have to keep changing cars and appearance and, Veyrenc, you'll have to dye your hair.'

'Noël isn't the best choice for a tail,' observed Morel. 'Too easily spotted at a distance.'

'But we need him. Noël may be difficult and grouchy but he doesn't give up. We need his persistence.'

'Thanks a lot,' said Noël, but without irony, because he was well aware of his negative traits.

'Here are photos of them,' said Adamsberg, handing round a few snapshots. 'Their features are fairly alike, but one's on the heavy side and the other's thin. Ages: sixty and fifty-eight. The thin one is the older brother, Christian, to whom we'll give the code name Saviour One. He has thick grey hair and wears it rather long. Elegant, distinguished, a man about town who wears expensive clothes. The tubby one is more reserved, more sober in his habits and he's going bald. Christophe will be Saviour Two. The Mercedes that was burnt belonged to him. So we've got a playboy on the one hand and a workaholic on the other. Not that that means one is better than the other. We still don't know what they were doing the night of the fire, or who was driving the car.'

'So what's going on?' asked Retancourt. 'Are we giving up on Momo?'

Adamsberg glanced at Retancourt and met once more that slightly amused and unreadable expression of disbelief.

'We're looking for Momo, lieutenant, at this very moment, and we're calling on reinforcements to step it up tonight. But we have a problem with the ends of the shoelaces.'

'When did you think of this?' asked Noël, after Adamsberg had explained to them about the shoelaces.

'Last night,' replied Adamsberg nonchalantly.

'So why did you ask him to put one of the shoes on *yesterday*?'

'Just checking his size.'

'Oh, *really*,' said Retancourt, injecting all her scepticism into the word.

'It doesn't mean Mo is innocent,' Adamsberg went on. 'But it's still a bit of a glitch.'

'Quite a big one,' agreed Noël. 'If it was one of the two Christs that torched the car but wanted Mo to carry the can, the case would be holed below the waterline.'

'It is anyway,' said Veyrenc. '*No sooner had the boat pulled away from the shore / Than through cracks in its timbers, the water did pour.*'

Since rejoining the force, Lieutenant Veyrenc had already spouted dozens of bad alexandrines. But nowadays nobody paid him much attention, as if he had become part of the soundtrack, like Mercadet's snores, or the cat's mewing, merging into the everyday background music in the squad.

'If one of the Christs *was* behind it – but we don't know that, and we don't even think it – the suit he was wearing would have had residual traces of petrol vapour.'

'Heavier than air,' Veyrenc agreed.

'And there must also have been a bag or a briefcase he carried to switch the shoes,' said Morel.

'Or why not his front doorknob when he got back home?' said Noël. 'Or his keys?'

'Not if he wiped everything down,' objected Veyrenc.

'We need to check whether one of the brothers had to get rid of a suit. Or sent it to the cleaners.'

'So the long and short of it, commissaire,' said Retancourt, 'is that you want us to check up on the two Christs *as if* they were murderers, while asking us not to believe that.'

'Exactly,' said Adamsberg with a grin. 'Mo is guilty, and we're searching for him. But your job is to stick to the Clermonts like ticks.'

'Just for the beauty of the manoeuvre,' said Retancourt.

'A little beauty never comes amiss. An aesthetic pleasure will make up for our raid on the Cité des Buttes tonight, which will not be a pretty sight. Retancourt and Noël, you can take the older brother, Christian, aka Saviour One, and Morel and Veyrenc, you take Christophe, Saviour Two. Use the code, because my phones are being tapped.'

'We ought to have two night teams.'

'We'll have Froissy taking care of multidirectional mikes, and Lamarre,

Mordent and Justin can relieve you. Their town house has security protection.'

'What if we're spotted?'

Adamsberg thought for a few minutes then shook his head, unable to come up with an answer.

'We won't be spotted,' Veyrenc concluded.

XVII

HIS NEIGHBOUR, LUCIO, STOPPED ADAMSBERG AS HE WAS CROSSING the little garden on the way to his house.

'*Hola, hombre!*' the old man called.

'*Hola*, Lucio.'

'A nice cool beer would do you good. In this heat.'

'Not now, Lucio.'

'And with all the trouble you're in.'

'I'm in trouble?'

'You certainly are, *hombre*.'

Adamsberg never disregarded Lucio's pronouncements and he waited in the garden until the old Spaniard returned with two chilled beers. Lucio was in the habit of pissing against the beech tree and Adamsberg wondered if that was why the grass was dying at the base of the trunk. Or perhaps it was just the heat.

The old man took the tops off the bottles – never any cans for him – and held one out.

'Two men came prowling around,' Lucio said between swigs.

'Here?'

'Yes. Pretending not to. Trying to look like ordinary passers-by. But the more casual you try to look, the more you look like something else. Shit-stirrers, they were. Shit-stirrers never walk with their heads up or looking down like ordinary people. Their eyes are everywhere, as if they were tourists. But our street isn't a tourist attraction, is it, eh, *hombre*?'

'No.'

'Shit-stirrers, they were, and your house was what interested them.'

'Staking it out?'

'Noting when your son came and went, maybe to know when the house was empty.'

'Shit-stirrers, eh,' murmured Adamsberg. 'People who'll end up being choked with a mouthful of bread.'

'Why do you want to choke them with bread?'

Adamsberg simply spread his arms wide.

'Well, I'm telling you,' Lucio carried on, 'if some shit-stirrers are hoping to get into your place, it means you've got problems.'

Adamsberg blew on the mouth of the bottle to make a little whistling noise – something you can't do to a beer can, as Lucio rightly pointed out – and sat down on an old packing case his neighbour had placed under the tree.

'Have you done something stupid, *hombre*?'

'No.'

'Who are you going after?'

'I'm going into unknown territory.'

'Not a good plan, *amigo*. If you need it, and if you've got someone or something you need to put in a safe place, you know where my spare key is.'

'Yes, under the bucket of gravel behind the shed.'

'You'd better put it in your pocket. Up to you, *hombre*,' said Lucio, moving off.

The table had been laid, using the plastic sheet still stained by Hellebaud. Zerk and Momo were waiting for Adamsberg before starting their supper. Zerk had cooked pasta with steamed tuna chunks and tomato sauce, a variant of the rice with tuna and tomato sauce he had served up a day or two earlier. Adamsberg thought of asking him to ring the changes a bit, but immediately rejected the thought, there was no point criticising his previously unknown son over a bit of tuna. Still less in front of an unknown Mo. Zerk put some bits of fish on the side of his plate and Hellebaud attacked them with gusto.

'He looks a lot better,' said Adamsberg.

'Yep,' Zerk confirmed.

Adamsberg was never concerned by silence falling in company and felt no need to try and make conversation come what may. Angels could pass and pass again as far as he was concerned. His son appeared to be of similar disposition, and Mo was at first too intimidated to try and launch a subject for table talk. But he was the kind of person who was bothered by the angels passing.

'Are you a diabolist?' he asked the commissaire in a hesitant voice.

Adamsberg looked at the young man in incomprehension, chewing on his mouthful. Steamed tuna fish is dense and dry and that was what he had been thinking about when Mo put the question.

'I don't understand, Mo.'

'Do you like playing diabolo?'

Adamsberg poured some more tomato sauce over his tuna and thought that perhaps being a diabolist or playing diabolo might mean something like 'playing with the devil' in the youth slang of Mo's milieu.

'Sometimes you have to,' he replied.

'But not professionally?'

Adamsberg stopped chewing and swallowed some water.

'I don't think we can be talking about the same thing. What do you mean by "diabolo"?'

'It's a game,' Mo explained, blushing. 'This double cone made of rubber, you roll it on a string with two handles,' he said, miming the action.

'Oh, I get it, diabolo,' said Adamsberg. 'No, I don't play that. Or yo-yos either.'

Mo plunged his nose back in his food, disappointed with the failure of his initiative, and casting about for something else to say.

'Is he really important to you? The pigeon?'

'Well, Mo, they've tied *your* feet together too.'

'Who's "they"?'

'The powers that be, they've got their eye on you.'

Adamsberg got up, moved aside a corner of the curtain pinned across the door, and looked out on the garden as night fell. Lucio was sitting on the packing case, reading his newspaper.

'We're going to have to think a bit,' he said, starting to pace round the table. 'Two shit-stirrers were seen in the street today. Don't worry, Mo, we've got a bit of time, they weren't actually looking for you.'

'Cops?'

'More likely someone attached to the Ministry. They want to know what I've got in mind for the Clermont-Brasseurs. They're worried about the shoelaces. I'll explain later. It's the weak point in their armour. Your escape has panicked them.'

'What are they looking for here?' asked Zerk.

'They want to see if I have any papers indicating an unofficial investigation into the Clermont-Brasseur family. They want to break in while we're out. So there's no way Mo can go on staying here.'

'Do we have to move him tonight?'

'There are roadblocks everywhere, Zerk. We'll have to think a bit,' he repeated.

Frowning, Zerk drew on his cigarette. 'If they're watching the street, we can't get Mo into a car.'

Adamsberg kept pacing round, simultaneously registering that his son was capable of fast action and even of a pragmatic approach.

'We'll go out through Lucio's place, and then into the street behind these houses.'

Adamsberg stiffened, as he heard the grass outside being trampled. There came an immediate knock on the door. Mo had already jumped to his feet holding his plate and moved towards the stairs.

'It's Retancourt,' came the loud voice of the lieutenant. 'Can I come in, commissaire?'

With his thumb, Adamsberg directed Mo to the cellar, before opening the door. It was an old house, and the lieutenant had to bend down to avoid hitting her head on the lintel as she stepped in. The kitchen suddenly seemed smaller once Retancourt was inside.

'It's important,' she said.

'Have you had your supper, Violette?' asked Zerk, whose face had lit up at her arrival.

'Not so important.'

'I'll warm some up for you,' said Zerk, busying himself at the cooker.

The pigeon jumped up on to the table and walked to within a few centimetres of Retancourt's arm.

'He recognises me a bit, don't you think? He looks better.'

'Yes, but he can't fly.'

'We don't know if it's physical or mental,' explained Zerk very seriously. 'I tried taking him into the garden, but he just stayed pecking about as if he'd forgotten how to take off.'

'OK,' said Retancourt, seating herself on the most solid of Adamsberg's chairs. 'I've got an alteration to your plan for trailing the Clermont brothers.'

'You don't like it?'

'No. Too classic, too long-term, too risky, and precious little hope of getting anywhere.'

'You could be right,' admitted Adamsberg, who was aware that since the previous day he had had to take a whole series of hasty and ill-judged decisions. He was never upset by criticism from Retancourt.

'Have you got a better idea?' he asked.

'Insider intelligence. Can't see any other way.'

'Also classic,' Adamsberg rejoined. 'But impossible. We can't get inside their house.'

Zerk put a plate of reheated pasta and tuna in front of Retancourt. Adamsberg presumed that Violette would get through the fish without even noticing.

'You don't have a spot of wine to go with this, do you?' she asked. 'No, don't bother getting up, I know where it is, I'll fetch it.'

'No, no, let me,' said Zerk quickly.

'Well, virtually impossible, yes, so I've taken a risk.'

Adamsberg shuddered. 'You should have consulted me, lieutenant.'

'You said your phone was tapped,' said Retancourt, plunging her fork into a large piece of fish which gave her no trouble to demolish. 'By the way, I've brought you a clean mobile, with a changeable SIM card. It used to belong to this fence in La Garenne, "the Shark", remember him? But anyway, no matter, he's dead. And I also have a personal message for you; it came to the office this evening. From the divisionnaire.'

'Retancourt, what have you been doing?'

'Nothing special. I went round to the Clermont house and told the concierge that I'd heard there was a job going. I don't know why, but I impressed him and he didn't just tell me to get lost.'

'I'll bet he didn't,' admitted Adamsberg. 'But he must have asked where you got your information from.'

'Of course. I told him it was via Clara de Verdier, who's a friend of Christophe Clermont's daughter.'

'They'll check that kind of thing, Retancourt.'

'Yes, maybe they will,' said the lieutenant, helping herself from the bottle which Zerk had uncorked. 'Delicious, this dinner, Zerk. Well, they can check all they like, because it's true. Also true that there was a job going. In big houses like that they have so many staff there's always a service job going somewhere. Especially since Christian Saviour One has a reputation for being hard on his employees. There's a very quick turnover. The Clara I mentioned used to be my brother Bruno's girlfriend, and I got her out of trouble once over an armed robbery. I called her up, and she'll confirm it if she has to.'

'Uh, yeah, right,' said Adamsberg, feeling somewhat stunned. He was the first to revere Retancourt's abnormal problem-solving powers, all-purpose and adaptable for any kind of work, but he always felt a bit taken aback when he was actually confronted with them.

'So, in that case,' said Retancourt, wiping up the last of the sauce with some bread, 'if you have no objection, I start tomorrow.'

'A bit more detail, lieutenant. The concierge let you in?'

'Naturally. And I got to see Christian Saviour One's PA, a rather disagreeable little Napoleon, who wasn't disposed to give me the job at first.'

'What kind of job is it?'

'Managing the household accounts on a computer. To cut a long story short, I demonstrated my talents rather forcefully, and in the end the guy hired me.'

'He probably didn't have any choice,' said Adamsberg softly.

'Probably not.'

Retancourt finished her glass and put it on the table noisily.

'Your tablecloth isn't very clean,' she remarked.

'It's the pigeon. Zerk cleans it as best he can, but pigeon shit leaves a stain on the plastic. I wonder what chemicals it contains.'

'Acid or something. So. Do I take this job or not?'

In the middle of the night, Adamsberg woke up and went down to the kitchen. He had forgotten the message from the divisionnaire, delivered by Retancourt, which was still sitting on the table. He read it, smiled, and burnt it in the fireplace. Brézillon was handing him the Ordebec investigation.

Now he had to face the Ghost Riders.

At six thirty, he woke Zerk and Mo.

'Lord Hellequin has come to our aid,' he said, and Zerk thought this announcement sounded rather like a sentence heard in church.

'So has Violette,' Zerk said.

'Yes, but she always does. I've been put in charge of the Ordebec affair. Be ready to leave today. Before you go, clean the house thoroughly, disinfect the whole bathroom, wash Mo's sheets, wipe down any surface where he might have left prints. We'll take him in my police car and put him in a safe house up there in Normandy. Zerk, you go and fetch my own car from the garage and buy a birdcage for Hellebaud. Money on the sideboard.'

'Will there be prints on pigeon feathers? Hellebaud doesn't like me rubbing him with a cloth.'

'No, no need to clean him.'

'Why? Are we taking him with us?'

'If you go, he'll have to go. I'll need you up there to look after Mo in his hiding place.'

Zerk nodded agreement.

'I don't know whether it's best if you come with me too, or come separately in my car.'

'You still have to think about it?'

'Yes, and I've got to think fast.'

'Tricky,' said Zerk, fully appreciating the problem.

XVIII

ONCE MORE THE MEMBERS OF THE SQUAD WERE MEETING IN THE chapter room, with the ceiling fans going full blast. It was Sunday, but all leave had been cancelled on the Minister of the Interior's orders, until the Mohamed case was resolved. For once, Danglard had managed to get there in the morning, which made him look as though he had already given up on life. Everyone knew that his face would be inside out until about midday. Adamsberg had had time to pretend to read the reports on the police raid on the Cité des Buttes which had gone on until 2.20 a.m. without result.

'Where's Violette?' asked Estalère as he served the first round of coffees.

'She's on a mission inside the Clermont-Brasseur household, she's got herself taken on to the staff.'

Noël gave a long appreciative whistle.

'None of us must mention that, or try to contact her. Officially she's gone to Toulon, for a crash course on computers.'

'How did she get herself in there?' asked Noël.

'She was determined to do it, and she put her intention into practice.'

'A very stimulating example,' drawled Voisenet. 'If only we could all put our intentions into practice.'

'Forget it, Voisenet,' said Adamsberg. 'Retancourt isn't a role model for anyone, she's a one-off: her faculties are unique.'

'You said it,' said Mordent, seriously.

'Therefore, we call off the previous surveillance plan. We move on to something else.'

'But we keep searching for Mo, surely?' said Morel.

'Yes, of course, that has to be the number-one priority. But I need a few people to be available. We're off to Normandy: we've been assigned to the Ordebec affair.'

Danglard's head shot up and a frown of displeasure crumpled his face. 'You fixed this, commissaire?'

'No, it wasn't me. Capitaine Émeri is on his knees. He had attributed one murder to a suicide and an attempted murder to an accident, and he's been taken off the case.'

'But why has it landed on us?' asked Justin. 'And not the local gendarmes?'

'Because I happened to be there both when the first body was found and when the second victim was attacked. Because Capitaine Émeri pressed for it. And because there is a possibility of finding another route into the Clermont-Brasseur fortress from up there.'

Adamsberg was lying. He didn't believe in the miraculous string-pulling capacities of the Comte d'Ordebec. Émeri had simply dangled the idea under his nose as a pretext. Adamsberg was going to Ordebec because the Ghost Riders were drawing him there almost irresistibly. And because it would make a good place for Mo to go to ground.

'I don't see the link to the Clermonts,' remarked Mordent.

'Well, there's some old nobleman there who might be able to open a few doors for us. He used to do business with Antoine Clermont.'

'Even if that's so,' said Morel, 'what's it all about? What's happened up there?'

'There's been one murder, of a man, and an attempted murder of an old woman. She's not expected to survive. And three more deaths have been foretold.'

'*Foretold*?'

'Yes. Because these crimes are directly linked to a sort of cavalcade of horsemen; it's a very old story.'

'A cavalcade of what?'

'Armed corpses. It's been roaming round the countryside there for centuries and it carries off guilty mortals.'

'Fine,' said Noël. 'It can do our job for us.'

'A bit more than that, it kills them. Danglard, could you explain quickly about the Ghost Riders?'

'I don't agree with us getting mixed up in this,' Danglard grumbled. 'You must have been meddling somehow, for us to be assigned to the case. And I'm not in favour of it, not at all.'

Danglard put up his hands in a gesture of refusal, wondering at the same time where his repugnance for the Ordebec affair was coming from. He had dreamed twice now about Hellequin's Horde since the evening when he had quite enjoyed himself describing it to Zerk and Adamsberg. But he had definitely not enjoyed the dreams, where he was fighting the troubling feeling that he was racing towards his destruction.

'Tell the story all the same,' said Adamsberg, looking affectionately at his deputy, and sensing fear in his reluctance. In Danglard's mind, for all he was an authentic atheist, not inclined to mysticism, superstition could still find a clear way in, by taking the broad pathways of his perpetual anxiety.

The commandant shrugged, assumed a confident air and stood up, as was his habit, to explain the medieval situation to the officers of the squad.

'The short version please, Danglard,' Adamsberg asked. 'No need to quote the documents.'

This was a fruitless request, as Danglard's presentation took forty minutes and distracted the squad from the gloomy reality of the Clermont affair. Only Froissy slipped away for a few moments to go and eat some pâté and crackers. There were a few complicit nods. People knew that she had just renewed her store with some delicious terrines, including hare pâté with truffles, which tempted some of the others. When Froissy sat back down, Danglard's eloquence was holding the entire attention of the squad, as was the story of Hellequin's ghostly band of riders – a formidable sight in the literal sense of the word, the commandant told them, that is such as to inspire terror.

'Could it be this Lina that killed the hunter then?' asked Lamarre. 'Perhaps she's going to kill all the people she saw in her vision?'

'Perhaps she's obeying it, in some way?' suggested Justin.

'Maybe,' said Adamsberg. 'In Ordebec they say the entire Vendermot family is wrong in the head. But in the village, everyone feels the influence of the Riders. The legend's been in the region too long, and these aren't the army's first victims. Nobody feels at ease, and a lot of them are genuinely terrified by it. If another victim dies, the whole place will have a panic attack. Especially when it comes to the fourth victim as yet unnamed.'

'So plenty of people might imagine they're in line to be number four,' remarked Mordent, who was taking notes.

'People with a guilty conscience?'

'No, people who are really guilty,' said Adamsberg. 'Criminals, killers who have gone unsuspected and unpunished, sinners who are more terrified of Hellequin coming to get them than of the arrival of the police. Because in Ordebec, they are convinced that Hellequin knows everything, can see everything.'

'The exact opposite of what they think of the cops then,' said Noël.

'Let's just suppose,' said Justin, who liked precision, 'that some person is afraid of being the fourth victim picked out by Hellequin. The fourth "seized" person, you called him. It's still hard to see why he would kill the other three.'

'Yes, there could be a reason,' said Danglard, 'because there's a subsidiary tradition, though not everyone agrees, that anyone who executes Hellequin's plans might be saved from his own fate.'

'In exchange for services rendered,' commented Mordent, who collected tales and legends and was still taking notes about this one, which he had not encountered.

'A collaborator getting his reward, eh?' said Noël.

'Yes, that's the idea,' Danglard agreed. 'But that only appears from the early nineteenth century. Another dangerous hypothesis is that some other person, who doesn't think they're in line to be "seized", believes Hellequin's accusations and wants to carry out his orders. So as to render "true and faithfulle justice".'

'This Léo person, what would she know about it?'

'We can't tell. She was alone when she found Herbier's body.'

'So what's the plan?' Justin asked. 'Who does what?'

'There is no plan. I haven't had time to make plans for anything for a while.'

You never have, thought Danglard, his revulsion for the whole Ordebec operation aggravating his bad temper.

'I'll go up to Ordebec, with Danglard if he agrees, and call on some of the others as I need you.'

'And we're still under orders to find Mo?'

'Exactly. Find that kid for me. Keep a permanent link open to the national network.'

Adamsberg took Danglard aside after the meeting.

'Come with me to see what sort of state Léo is in,' he said, 'and then you'll really feel like taking on the Riders. Some maniac has been carrying out the desires of Lord Hellequin.'

'It makes no sense,' said Danglard, shaking his head. 'We need someone to be in charge of the squad here.'

'Danglard, what are you scared of?'

'I'm not scared.'

'Yes, you are.'

'All right,' Danglard admitted. 'I have this feeling I'll leave my bones in Ordebec. It'll be my last case.'

'Good Lord above, Danglard! What makes you think that?'

'I've dreamed about it twice. About a horse with only three legs.' Danglard shivered, and almost vomited.

'Come and sit down,' said Adamsberg, pulling him gently by the sleeve.

'It's being ridden by a man in black,' Danglard went on, 'he hits me, I go down, I'm dead, and that's it. I know, I know, commissaire, we don't believe in dreams.'

'Well then.'

'What it is, I feel somehow I set all this in motion by telling you the story of the Furious Army. If I hadn't, you'd have gone on thinking it was "curious" and it would have stopped there. But I opened up the box, for fun, to show off my knowledge. And that was the challenge. Hellequin is after my skin now. He doesn't like people trifling with him.'

'No-o, I should think not. He doesn't sound like a guy with a great sense of humour.'

'No jokes please, commissaire.'

'You can't be serious, Danglard. Not that serious. Surely.'

Danglard shrugged his shoulders with lassitude. 'No, of course not. But I wake up obsessed by this idea and it haunts me when I go to bed.'

'Danglard, this is the first time I've seen you afraid of anything except yourself. That gives you two enemies. Too many to face.'

'So what do you suggest?'

'We'll go there this afternoon. And we'll have dinner in a local restaurant. With a good bottle of wine?'

'And if I die there?'

'That'll just be too bad.'

Danglard smiled and looked at the commissaire with a changed expression. 'That'll just be too bad.' The kind of answer that suited him, ending his complaint, as if Adamsberg had pressed a button, disconnecting him from his fears.

'What time?'

Adamsberg looked at his two watches.

'Meet me at my place in two hours. Ask Froissy to give you two new mobiles, and look up the name of a good restaurant.'

When the commissaire got home, the house had been cleaned from top to bottom, Hellebaud's cage was ready and the rucksacks were almost packed. In Mo's, Zerk was putting cigarettes, books, coloured pencils and crosswords. Mo was watching, as if the rubber gloves he was wearing prevented him moving. Adamsberg knew that being a wanted man, a hunted beast, can paralyse the body's natural movements for the first few days. After a month, one hesitates to make a sound underfoot, and after three months, one hardly dares breathe.

'I bought him a new yo-yo too,' said Zerk. 'Not a champion one like he had before, but I couldn't go out for long. Lucio took over, and sat in the kitchen with his radio. Why does he always carry around this radio that just buzzes? You can't make out anything on it.'

'He likes to hear voices, but not what they're saying.'

'Where'm I going?' asked Mo timidly.

'To this safe house, it's just a wooden cabin with concrete floors, a little way out of town. The man who lived there has been killed. So the gendarmerie has put the seals on it, couldn't be better as a shelter.'

'But what do we do about the seals?' asked Zerk.

'We'll undo them and do them up again. I'll show you. Anyway, the gendarmerie won't have any reason to come back.'

'Why was this guy killed?' asked Mo.

'Some sort of local monster called Hellequin had it in for him. Don't worry, he's no cause to be after you. What are these coloured pencils for, Zerk?'

'In case he wants to do some drawing.'

'OK. Will you want to do any drawing, Mo?'

'Dunno. Don't think so.'

'OK,' repeated Adamsberg. 'Mo will go with me in the squad car, but in the boot. The journey will last about two hours, and it'll be very hot in there. You'll have some water to drink. Think you can do it?'

'Yes.'

'You'll hear the voice of another man in the car, it'll be Commandant Danglard. Don't worry, he knows you're on the run under our protection. At least he's guessed as much and I couldn't stop him. He doesn't actually know that I'm taking you up there with us. But he'll soon work it out, Danglard is brilliant, he foresees and guesses almost everything, even the deadly designs of Lord Hellequin. I'll drop you in the empty house, before we reach Ordebec. Zerk, you'll come on with my car and the rest of the luggage. And while we're there, since you know how to use a camera, we'll say you're on a photographic course, and working on a freelance project which means you have to go here and there. Let's say it's for a Swedish magazine. Because we'll have to explain why you disappear from time to time. Unless you can think of a better plan.'

'No,' replied Zerk simply.

'So what can you take pictures of?'

'The landscape? Churches?'

'Too obvious. Do something that takes you out into the fields and woods. Because you'll have to be our link with Mo.'

'Flowers?' suggested Mo.

'Leaf mould,' proposed Zerk.

Adamsberg put down the rucksacks by the door.

'Why would you want to photograph leaf mould?'

'It was you that asked me to photograph something.'

'Yes, but why leaf mould?'

'Because it's interesting. Do you know what you get in leaf mould? Just in ten square centimetres? Insects, worms, larvae, gases, fungus spores, bird droppings, roots, microorganisms, seeds. So I'm doing a special feature on leaf mould for the *Svenska Dagbladet*.'

'Svenska?'

'It's a Swedish magazine. Didn't you just suggest that yourself?'

'Yes, so I did,' said Adamsberg and looked at his watches. 'Right, take Mo and the bags to Lucio's place. I'm going to park the squad car behind his back door, and when Danglard turns up, I'll let you know I'm ready to leave.'

'I'm glad I'm going, it'll be fun,' said Zerk, with the naive pleasure that often appeared when he spoke.

'Yeah, well, be sure to tell Danglard that. He's not at all happy about it.'

Twenty minutes later, Adamsberg was on the way out of Paris on the western motorway, with the commandant sitting alongside him, fanning himself with a road map. Mo was curled up in the boot with a cushion under his head.

After driving for three-quarters of an hour, the commissaire called Émeri.

'I'm just leaving Paris,' he said. 'Don't expect me to get there before about two.'

'Glad you're coming. That bastard in Lisieux is furious about it.'

'I'm thinking of lodging in Léo's guest house. That's if you have no objection.'

'No.'

'Right, I'll tell her.'

'She won't be able to hear you.'

'I'll tell her all the same.'

Adamsberg put the phone back in his pocket and stepped on the gas.

'Do you have to drive so fast?' asked Danglard. 'There's no hurry.'

'We're going fast because it's hot.'

'And why did you tell Émeri we'd only arrive at two? That's not true.'

'Don't ask so many questions, commandant.'

XIX

FIVE KILOMETRES FROM ORDEBEC, ADAMSBERG SLOWED DOWN AS they went through the little village of Charny-la-Vieille.

'Right, Danglard, I've got a small errand to run before we get to Ordebec proper. I suggest you wait for me here, and I'll be back to pick you up in half an hour.'

Danglard nodded. 'So if I know nothing, my hands will be clean.'

'You could say that.'

'Kind of you to try and protect me. But when you made me write that false report, you got me up to the neck in this business of yours.'

'Nobody asked you to come along and stick your nose into it.'

'My job is to come round after you, putting up the safety barriers.'

'I'm waiting for an answer, Danglard. I'm going to drop you off here, OK?'

'Not OK. I'm coming with you.'

'You won't like it.'

'I already don't like Ordebec.'

'You're wrong, it's very picturesque. When you arrive, you see the big church right away, up on the hill, then the little town at its feet, half-timbered houses, they should appeal to you. There are fields all around in every shade of green and they've installed hundreds of cows, all standing still, against the green. I haven't seen a single cow move yet, I don't know why.'

'You have to keep looking at them for a long time.'

'I suppose so.'

Adamsberg had located the places described by Madame Vendermot: the house of the neighbours, Monsieur and Madame Hébrard, the Bigard wood, the old rubbish dump. He went past the Herbier mailbox without stopping, and continued for a hundred metres before turning the car into a rutted country lane.

'We'll go in the back, through the little wood.'

'Go in where?'

'Into the house where the first murder victim used to live, the hunter. We'll have to go in fast, without making a noise.'

Adamsberg drove on down a track which was hardly fit for vehicles, and parked under the trees. He went quickly round to open the boot.

'OK, Mo, you'll be cooler now. The house is thirty metres away through these trees.'

Danglard shook his head silently as he saw the young man clamber out of the boot. He had been imagining that Mo had been spirited away to the Pyrenees or even abroad, with false papers, given the lengths to which Adamsberg had been going. But it was even worse. To have transported Momo with them in the car appeared the height of folly to him.

Adamsberg undid the seals on the door, put Momo's bags down and looked quickly round the house. One well-lit sitting room, a small bedroom, more or less clean, and a kitchen with a view across some fields, where six or seven cows were standing.

'Hey, that's pretty,' said Mo, who had seen the countryside only once, briefly, in his life, and never the sea. 'Trees, fields, sky. Wow!' he said suddenly. 'Are those cows? Over there?' he added, pointing to the window.

'Get back, Mo! Get away from the window. Yes, they're cows.'

'No shit.'

'Never seen cows before?'

'Not real ones.'

'Well, you'll have plenty of time to look at them, and maybe even see them move. But stay a few feet back from the windows. At night, don't put any lights on, of course. If you want to smoke, sit on the floor because a burning cigarette can be seen from a long way off. You can warm up food, because the cooker isn't visible through the window. And you'll be able to wash, because the water hasn't been cut off. Zerk will be along soon, with some provisions.'

Mo looked around his new domain, without apparently feeling too overcome by the idea of being sequestered there, his eyes returning to the window from time to time.

'I never met anyone like Zerk,' he said. 'Never met someone who buys coloured pencils, except my mother. But if you brought him up, commissaire, that must be why he's like he is.'

Adamsberg judged it was not the moment to explain to Mo that he had only been aware of his son's existence for a few weeks, and that it would be pointless to shatter his illusions by confessing that he had neglected Zerk's mother through his unmitigated insouciance. The girl had written to him, he had not read her letter carefully, and he had ended up not knowing he had a son.

'Yes, he's very well brought up,' commented Danglard, who never joked about fatherhood, an area on which he considered Adamsberg beneath contempt.

'I'm going to put the seals back on, as I go out. Don't use the mobile unless there's an emergency. Even if you get bored to tears, no social calls, don't even think about it, all your pals' phones are being tapped.'

'No sweat, commissaire. Plenty to look at. All those cows, man. About twelve of them. In prison, I'd have ten guys on my back all the time, and no windows. All on my own, cows and bulls to look at, s'brilliant.'

'There aren't any bulls out there, Mo, they don't put them together except for mating. Just cows.'

'Got you.'

Adamsberg checked that there was no one in the wood before saying goodbye to Mo and opening the door. He took out a wax gun and calmly replaced the seals. Danglard was looking around anxiously.

'I don't like this at all,' he muttered.

'Save it for later, Danglard.'

Once on the main road, Adamsberg called Émeri to alert him that he was arriving at Ordebec.

'I'm going to the hospital first,' he said.

'She won't recognise you, Adamsberg. Would you like to join me for dinner here tonight?'

Adamsberg looked across at Danglard, who shook his head. In his black moods, and he was undoubtedly going through one now, all the worse for having no real motive, Danglard tried to keep going by fixing himself modest daily treats, such as choosing a new suit, buying some antique book, or eating out at a fancy restaurant. As a result, every episode of depression dug an alarming hole in his finances. To deprive Danglard of the anticipated meal at the Running Boar, which he had selected with care, would be to blow out the humble candle he had lit that night.

'I've promised to take my son to the Running Boar. You'd be welcome to join us, Émeri.'

'It's a good restaurant, but I'm sorry to hear that,' replied Émeri rather frostily. 'I had been hoping you would do me the honour of dining with me.'

'Another time, Émeri.'

'I think we must have touched a nerve there,' remarked Adamsberg after finishing the call. He looked surprised, since he was quite unaware of the capitaine's obsession with his Empire dining room, to which he was attached as if by an umbilical cord.

Adamsberg met Zerk in front of the hospital as agreed. The young man had already done some shopping and Adamsberg gave him a welcoming hug, taking advantage of it to slip into his rucksack the wax gun, the seal and the plan of how to find Herbier's house.

'What's the house like?' he asked.

'Perfectly clean. The gendarmes have taken away all the game from the freezer.'

'What'll I do with the pigeon?'

'He's there, he's waiting for you.'

'No, I don't mean *Mo*, if that's what you thought, I meant *Hellebaud*. He's been in the car for hours and he doesn't like it.'

'Oh, take him with you,' said Adamsberg after a moment's thought. 'Give him to Mo to look after, it'll keep him company, someone to talk to. He can look at the cows, but round here they don't seem to move.'

'Was the commandant with you when you dropped our big pigeon off?'

'Yes.'

'How did he take it?'

'Not too well. He thinks I'm crazy and that it's against the law.'

'Does he? It seems perfectly OK to me,' said Zerk, picking up the shopping bags.

XX

'SHE LOOKS TINY, DOESN'T SHE?' SAID ADAMSBERG SOFTLY TO
Danglard: he was appalled to see for the first time Léo's changed face,
propped up on pillows. 'In real life she's very tall. Much taller than me,
at least if she wasn't stooped.'

He sat on the edge of the bed and patted her cheeks with his hands.

'Léo, I've come back. I'm the policeman from Paris. We had supper
together. We had soup and veal, and we had a little Calva in front of the
fire, with our Havana cigars.'

'She's not moving,' said the doctor who had just come into the room.

'Has anyone been to see her?'

'The Vendermot daughter, and the capitaine. She didn't react at all.
Clinically, she ought to be showing some sign of life. But nothing's
happening. She's not in a coma now, the internal haematoma has been
fairly well absorbed. The heart's functioning reasonably well, though it's
damaged by her cigar smoking. Technically, she ought to be able to open
her eyes and say something. But no, nothing, and the worst is that her
temperature is too low. It's as if the whole mechanism has closed down.
But I can't find a spanner to fix it.'

'Can she carry on for long like this?'

'No, at her age, without moving or eating, she can't last long, just a
few days.'

The doctor looked disapprovingly at Adamsberg's hands on the aged
Léone's face.

'Don't move her head,' he said.

'Léo,' Adamsberg repeated. 'It's me. I'm here, I've come to stay. I'm going to sleep at your place, with my assistants. I hope that's all right with you. We'll be very careful.'

Adamsberg picked up a comb from the bedside table and started to comb Léo's hair, one hand still stroking her cheek. Danglard sat on the only chair in the room and prepared for a long session. Adamsberg would not give up easily on the old lady. The doctor went out, shrugging his shoulders, and returned an hour and a half later, intrigued by the intensity with which this policeman was trying to get Léo to respond to him. Danglard too was watching Adamsberg, who carried on speaking quietly without interruption, and whose face had taken on that luminosity he knew well, when he was in one of his rare episodes of total concentration: it was as if the commissaire had swallowed a lamp that was diffusing its light from beneath his dark complexion.

Without turning round, Adamsberg put his arm out towards the doctor to forestall any intervention by him. Under his hand, Léone's skin was still as cold as ever, but her lips had moved. He signalled to Danglard to come closer. Another twitch of the lips and then a sound.

'Danglard, did you hear her say "*Ello*"? That's what she said, wasn't it?'

'Could have been "L.O."'

'That's her way of greeting people. *Hello*, Léo, it's me.'

'*Ello*,' Léo said more distinctly.

Adamsberg took her hand in his and shook it a little.

'*Hello*, Léo, I'm listening to you.'

'Fleg.'

'Fleg's fine. Brigadier Blériot is looking after him.'

'Fleg.'

'Yes. He's OK. He's waiting for you.'

'Sugar.'

'Yes, the brigadier is giving him his sugar every day,' said Adamsberg, who didn't really know if this was true. 'He's being well looked after, they're taking good care of him.'

'*Ello*,' she repeated.

And that was all. Her lips closed again, and Adamsberg realised she was exhausted.

'Congratulations,' said the doctor.

'It's nothing,' said Adamsberg, without thinking. 'Can you call me if she shows any more signs of wanting to communicate?'

'Leave me your card. But don't be too hopeful. It might have been a final effort.'

'Doctor, you're very keen to bury her before her time,' said Adamsberg, moving towards the door. 'There's no hurry, is there?'

'I'm a geriatric specialist, I know my job,' said the doctor, clamping his mouth shut.

Adamsberg noted his name from his badge, Jacques Turbot, and left. He walked to the car without speaking and let Danglard take the wheel.

'Where now?' asked Danglard, starting the engine.

'I don't like that doctor.'

'He's got a lot to contend with. Can't be much fun being called Turbot.'

'Name suits him. He's a cold fish all right.'

'You still haven't said where to,' said Danglard, who was driving at random through Ordebec's narrow streets.

'You saw her, Danglard. Like an egg that's been chucked on the floor and cracked.'

'Yes, you said.'

'We'll go to her place first, it used to be a guest house. Turn right here.'

'Funny that she says "Ello" instead of "Bonjour."'

'It's English, though they say it with an H.'

'I know *that*,' said Danglard, but didn't insist.

The Ordebec gendarmes had been expeditious and Léo's house had been set to rights after being inspected. The floor of the dining room had been cleaned and if there was any blood, it didn't show against the ancient dark red tiles. Adamsberg took the room he had slept in before and Danglard chose one at the far end of the building. As he unpacked his few belongings, the commandant watched Adamsberg through the window. He had sat down cross-legged in the middle of the courtyard, under an apple tree, elbows on thighs and head bent, and didn't look as if he intended moving. From time to time, he seemed to try and catch something at the back of his neck.

A little before 8 p.m., as the sun was sinking, Danglard went across to him, his shadow falling across the commissaire's feet.

'Time to go,' he said.

'The Blue Boar,' said Adamsberg, looking up.

'Not blue. The Running Boar.'

'Can boars run?' asked Adamsberg, putting out a hand so that Danglard could haul him to his feet.

'They can do thirty-five kilometres an hour, I believe. Though I don't know a lot about wild boars. Except that they can't sweat.'

'What do they do then?' asked Adamsberg, rubbing his trousers but without greatly caring about the answer.

'They wallow in mud to cool down.'

'That's what our killer is like. A muddy creature, weighing about two hundred kilos, but who can't sweat. He'll go about his work without batting an eyelid.'

XXI

DANGLARD HAD RESERVED A ROUND TABLE AND SAT DOWN WITH a satisfied air. This first meal in Ordebec, in an old inn with low beams, marked a restful interlude in the midst of his fears. Zerk arrived on time and gave them a quick wink to indicate that all was well at the house in the woods. Adamsberg had asked Émeri again if he would join them, and this time the capitaine had agreed.

'The Pigeon likes the idea of the pigeon,' said Zerk to Adamsberg in a low voice. 'I left them chatting to each other. Hellebaud likes it when the Pigeon plays yo-yo. When it hits the ground he goes and pecks it.'

'I get the feeling Hellebaud is getting further from his state of nature. We're waiting for the local capitaine of gendarmes, Émeri, his name is. A big military-looking guy, fair hair, impeccable uniform. You must call him "capitaine".'

'OK.'

'He's a descendant of Marshal Davout, one of Napoleon's right-hand men, who was never defeated, and it matters a lot to him. No joking about it.'

'Course not.'

'Here they come. The fat man with dark hair is Brigadier Blériot.'

'So I call him "brigadier"?'

'Precisely.'

When the entrée was served, Zerk started to eat before the others, just as Adamsberg used to do before Danglard had impressed upon him some of the rules of good table manners. Zerk also made a lot of noise when he ate; he'd have to have a word with him about that. He hadn't noticed back in Paris. But in this rather formal atmosphere as the meal began, he had the impression that all anyone could hear was his son munching.

'How's Fleg doing?' Adamsberg asked Blériot. 'Léo managed to say a few words today. She's worried about her dog.'

'She spoke?' asked Émeri in surprise.

'Yes, I stayed about two hours by her bed and she said a few words. The doctor, Halibut or whatever his name is, didn't look very happy. My methods can't have pleased him.'

'Turbot,' Danglard whispered.

'And you waited till now to tell me?' said Émeri. 'What did she say, for god's sake?'

'Very little. She just tried to say hello. And she said "Fleg" and "sugar". That's all. I told her the brigadier here was giving Fleg his ration of sugar.'

'Yessir, I am,' said Blériot, 'though I don't say as I like it. But that dog, he sits in front of the sugar dish, six o'clock every day. He's got a clock inside him like an addict.'

'Good, I wouldn't want to have misled her. Now that she's talking,' Adamsberg said to Émeri, 'I think it would be wise to put a guard outside her door.'

'God Almighty, Adamsberg, how many men do you think I've got here? Just Blériot, and one man who splits his time between Ordebec and Saint-Vernon. A half-timer in every sense of the word. Half cunning, half stupid, half obedient, half disobedient, half clean and half dirty. How am I supposed to manage that?'

'We could put that CCTV in her room,' suggested Blériot.

'Two cameras,' said Danglard, 'one to film anyone coming in, the other by her bed.'

'All right,' agreed Émeri, 'but the technicians will have to come from Lisieux, don't expect anything to be up and running before tomorrow afternoon.'

'As for protection for the other two named men,' said Adamsberg, 'we could get someone from Paris. For the glazier in the first place.'

'I spoke to Glayeux,' said Émeri, shaking his head. 'He refuses to have any kind of guard. I know this fellow, he'd be humiliated if anyone were to imagine he was impressed by that Vendermot woman's nonsense. He's not the sort of man to do what he's told.'

'Tough guy, then?' asked Danglard.

'No, aggressive more like, violent, well educated, a real artist, and ruthless. He *is* very talented with his stained-glass windows, you can't deny that. But he's a disagreeable man, like I said, and you'll see for yourselves. I'm not saying that because he's homosexual, but he is a homosexual.'

'Is that generally known in Ordebec?'

'He doesn't make any secret of it, the boyfriend lives here too, he works on the local paper. He's quite different, nice chap, people like him.'

'They live together?' asked Danglard.

'No, no, Glayeux lives with Mortembot, the nurseryman.'

'What! The Riders' next two victims live under the same roof?'

'Have done for years, they're cousins, they've been inseparable since they were boys. But Mortembot isn't a homosexual.'

'Was Herbier?' asked Danglard.

'Are you starting to think about a homophobic killer?'

'Could be.'

'No, Herbier wasn't gay, definitely not. More like a heterosexual rapist if you ask me. And don't forget it was Lina who named the "seized" men. I've got no reason to think she's got anything against gays. Lina has a, well, rather an unconventional sex life herself.'

'Fantastic tits,' said the brigadier. 'Good enough to eat.'

'That'll do, Blériot,' said Émeri, 'we can do without that kind of comment.'

'Everything's worth noting,' said Adamsberg, who was, like his son, forgetting to be on his best behaviour and mopping up his sauce with his bread. 'Émeri, since the people chosen by the Riders are supposed to be wicked, how does that square with the glazier and his cousin?'

'Not only does it make perfect sense, but it's well known all over town.'

'What are they supposed to have done?'

'There are two shady episodes that have never properly come to light.

I investigated, and got no results, and I was furious myself. Do you mind if we move somewhere else for coffee? There's a little side room here, where they let me smoke.'

As he got up, the capitaine looked again at Zerk, scruffily dressed in an outsize T-shirt, and appeared to wonder what on earth Adamsberg's son was doing there.

'Your boy's working with you?' he asked, as he led them to the other room. 'He wants to be a cop or what?'

'No, he's doing a photographic feature on leaf mould. For a Swedish magazine.'

'*Leaf* mould? Bit weird, isn't it?'

'He's interested in the micro-environment of decomposing leaves,' Danglard intervened to help Adamsberg out.

'Oh, right,' said Émeri, choosing a very upright chair for himself, while the others sat on couches.

Zerk offered cigarettes all round, and Danglard ordered another bottle of wine. Having to share only two bottles among five people had caused him a nagging pain throughout the meal.

'So, as I was saying, there were two violent deaths of people close to Glayeux and Mortembot,' Émeri explained as he filled the glasses. 'Seven years ago, Glayeux's assistant fell from the scaffolding of the church in Louverain. They were both working there, about twenty metres up, restoring the windows of the nave. And four years ago, Mortembot's mother died in the stockroom of the nursery. She fell off a stool, and she grabbed at a set of metal shelves full of flowerpots and troughs of earth. It all came down with her and killed her. Both deaths were pure accidents, apparently. But with something in common: a fall. Anyway, I opened inquiries into both of them.'

'On what grounds?' asked Danglard, who was gulping down his wine with a sense of relief.

'Well, really because both Glayeux and Mortembot are bad hats, the pair of them. Sewer rats, if you ask me.'

'Some rats can be OK,' said Adamsberg. 'Toni and Marie for instance.'

'Who?'

'Two rats who are sweethearts. Never mind,' said Adamsberg with a shake of his head.

'Well, these two are certainly not OK, Adamsberg. They'd sell their souls for money and success, and I'm pretty sure that's what they did.'

'Sold out to Lord Hellequin?' suggested Danglard.

'Why not, commandant? I'm not the only one round here who thinks that. A farmhouse up the way, Le Buisson, burnt to the ground and neither of them gave a cent to help the family. That's the way they are. They think the people in Ordebec are dumb yokels, unworthy of interest.'

'So what were your grounds for opening the first investigation?'

'Glayeux had a motive for getting rid of his assistant. Tétard, this other craftsman, he was much younger, but getting very good at the job, excellent in fact. The authorities in charge of church repairs round here were tending to give him work, preferring to deal with him rather than with Glayeux. Obviously he was going to take over sooner or later. A month before he fell, the town of Coutances – you know the cathedral there?'

'Yes,' supplied Danglard.

'Well, Coutances had chosen Tétard to restore the stained glass in the transept. Big commission. And if the youngster made a good job of it, his career would be launched. Glayeux would be humiliated, and his business would go downhill. But Tétard had a fatal fall. So the Coutances people called in Glayeux instead.'

'Naturally,' muttered Adamsberg. 'So the scaffolding was checked?'

'It was faulty, the planks weren't well fitted to the metal tubes, there was some play in the connections. Glayeux and Tétard were working on different windows, so they weren't standing on the same section. Glayeux could perfectly well have loosened some joints, or shifted a plank overnight, because he had the church key, so he could have destabilised part of the scaffolding. Easy.'

'But impossible to prove.'

'Exactly,' said Émeri bitterly. 'We couldn't even get Glayeux for incompetent workmanship, because Tétard was officially in charge of erecting the scaffolding, with a cousin. And same thing in Mortembot's case, no proof. He wasn't in the stockroom when his mother had her fall, he was taking some deliveries in the shop. But it isn't that impossible to make a stool fall over from a distance. All you'd have to do is tie a string to one of its feet and pull. When he heard the noise, Mortembot rushed in with one of his assistants. No string anywhere.'

Émeri looked meaningfully at Adamsberg, seeming to challenge him to come up with an answer.

'He didn't knot it,' said Adamsberg. 'He just looped some string round the leg of the stool. And then afterwards all he had to do was pull one end to reel in the rest, a few seconds if it slipped through easily.'

'Precisely. And no traces left.'

'Not everyone can leave a trail of breadcrumbs.'

Émeri helped himself to more coffee, realising that Adamsberg said a number of things to which there was no point responding. He had believed in this Paris cop's reputation at first; but without judging too much in advance, it seemed as if Adamsberg didn't exactly work by normal methods. Or perhaps he wasn't all that normal himself. At any rate he seemed a calm sort of person, who, as Émeri had hoped, wasn't challenging him all the time over the investigation.

'So Mortembot didn't get on with his mother?'

'Well, as far as I know, it wasn't that bad. In fact, he was rather under her thumb. But the thing was, she didn't like him living with his cousin, because Glayeux's gay, like I said, and she was ashamed of that. So she nagged her son about it, she insisted he come and live with her, or she'd disinherit him. He agreed, just to have a bit of peace, but in fact he dragged his feet. The scenes had begun again. Money, the house, his freedom, that's what he wanted. He must have thought she was past it, and I dare say Glayeux encouraged him. She was the kind of woman who'd live to a hundred and still be minding the shop. She was a maniac about the business, but she wasn't wrong. Since her death, people say the quality of the plants has gone down. Mortembot sells fuchsias that die in their first winter. And they're not easy to kill. He makes a mess of his grafting is what they say.'

'Oh, really,' said Adamsberg, who had never grafted a plant in his life.

'In both cases, I was on their backs for a while, had them under twenty-four-hour observation, and all that. Glayeux viewed the whole business with contempt and waited for it to die down. Mortembot didn't even have the decency to appear to mourn for his mother. He got to be the sole owner of the nursery and its branches, it's quite a big business. He's more phlegmatic, a casual guy, doesn't react to provocation or threats. I had to give up, but in my view, both of them are cynical killers, out of pure self-interest. And if Lord Hellequin existed, yes, you bet, they're exactly the kind of man he'd choose to carry off.'

'So how did they react to the threats from the Riders?'

'Same way they react to everything. Couldn't give a damn, and they think Lina's just a hysterical woman. Or a murderess.'

'That could be true, couldn't it?' said Danglard, half closing his eyes.

'You'll see the family. Don't be surprised: the three brothers are equally crazy. Like I told you, Adamsberg. They've plenty of excuse. The father abused them all brutally when they were kids. But if you want to get anything out of them, be careful how you approach Antonin.'

'Why, is he dangerous?'

'No, the opposite. He'll be frightened when he sees you coming, and the whole family will protect him. He thinks his body's partly made of clay.'

'Ah yes, you said.'

'Crumbly clay. Antonin thinks he'll break into pieces if he gets a knock. Totally barmy. Apart from that, he looks normal.'

'He's able to work?'

'He spends all day on his computer, never leaves the house. And don't be surprised if you can't understand Hippolyte, the oldest. Everyone calls him Hippo, like a hippopotamus. Actually that's not far off the mark, he's a big guy, strapping, not fat though. But when he wants to, he speaks backwards.'

'What, he uses back slang?'

'No, he says the *words* backwards, letter by letter.'

Émeri stopped to think, then, giving up, got out a pencil from his bag.

'Suppose he wants to say: "Good morning, commissaire." Well, it would come out like this.' And Émeri applied himself to write out, letter by letter:

Doog gninrom, eriassimmoc.

He passed the sheet of paper across to Adamsberg, who looked at it flabbergasted. Danglard had opened his eyes again, intrigued by the possibility of a new intellectual experience.

'You'd have to be a genius to do that,' said Adamsberg with a frown.

'He *is* a genius. The whole family are, in their own peculiar way. That's why people round here respect them, but they don't go too close. As if they were aliens. Some people think they should be put away, others say it's dangerous to approach them. Hippolyte's talented all right, but he's never tried to hold down a job. He looks after the house, the kitchen garden, the orchard and the poultry. They're self-sufficient up there.'

'And the third brother?'

'Martin is less impressive but don't be fooled by appearances. He's tall and thin, with long legs, like an insect. And he goes out in the woods and fields, picking up all kinds of creatures, and then he eats them: grasshoppers, caterpillars, ants, butterflies, whatever. It's revolting.'

'He eats them raw?'

'No, he cooks them. As a main course or in a sauce. Turns your stomach. But he has people round here who like his little concoctions of insects, for therapeutic reasons.'

'And the family eats them too?'

'Antonin mainly. It was because of him that Martin started collecting the creatures, to help strengthen his clay. Or his "yalc" as Hippolyte calls it.'

'And the sister? Apart from having visions of the Ghost Riders?'

'Nothing much else to say about her, except that she understands Hippo's backwards words. It's not as hard as making them up, but it still takes a lot of brain work.'

'Do they open the door to visitors?'

'They can be very hospitable if you're prepared to go and see them. Open, friendly, even Antonin. But people who are afraid of them say that's all just an act to tempt you over there, and once in, you've had it. They don't like me, for the reasons I told you about, and also because *I* think they're all damaged, but if you don't mention me, you'll get on all right with them.'

'So where does the super-intelligence come from? The mother or the father?'

'Neither. You saw the mother in Paris, I think, didn't you? Very ordinary. Quiet as a mouse, looks after the everyday chores. If you want to make her happy, take her some flowers. She likes that, because the torturer, the old brute, her husband, never gave her any. Then she'll dry them, hanging them upside down.'

'Why do you call him the torturer?'

Émeri stood up and pulled a face.

'Go and see them. But first,' he said with a smile, 'go along the Chemin de Bonneval and pick up a bit of earth to put in your pocket. They say hereabouts that'll protect you from Lina's magic powers. Don't forget that girl is the door between the living and the dead. With a handful of earth, you'll be all right. But it's complicated too, don't get closer than a metre away, because they say she can smell it if you have earth from that path about you. And she doesn't like it.'

As he walked back to the car with Danglard, Adamsberg put his hand over his trouser pocket, and wondered what spirit had inspired him, long before all this, to pick up a bit of earth from Bonneval. And why he had brought it with him.

XXII

ADAMSBERG WAS WAITING OUTSIDE THE OFFICE OF THE LOCAL
solicitors – Deschamps and Poulain – in one of Ordebec's steep streets.
It seemed to him that wherever you stood on the upper levels of the little
town, you could see cattle standing like statues under the apple trees. Lina
would be out to meet him any minute, so he wouldn't have time to see
any of them move. Perhaps it would be a better strategy to fix his eyes
on just one, instead of sweeping the whole field.

He hadn't wanted to rush things by summoning Lina Vendermot to
the gendarmerie, so he had invited her 'to the Blue Boar', where you could
have a quiet conversation under the low beams. On the phone, her voice
had sounded warm, with no sign of either fear or embarrassment. By
fixing his eyes on a single cow, Adamsberg was trying to eliminate his
desire to view Lina's magnificent bosom, inspired by Blériot's spontaneous
praise. He was also trying to put out of his mind the idea that if her sex
life was as free as Émeri had said, it might be easy to go to bed with her.
The Ordebec team, entirely composed of men, was a bit bleak, as far as
he was concerned. But nobody would appreciate it if he slept with a
woman at the top of the suspect list.

His second mobile indicated a text and he went into the shade to look
at it. Retancourt, at last. The idea of Retancourt plunging alone into the
deep chasm of the Clermont-Brasseur household had caused him some
anguish the previous night, before he fell asleep in the hollow of his soft
mattress. There were so many sharks in the ocean depths. Retancourt had

done some deep-sea diving at one time and she had been willing to touch the scaly skin of some of them. But human sharks were more vicious than the fishy kind. The text ran as follows: *Night of fire Saviours 1 + 2 + father gala Steel Fed. Drink taken. Sv 2 drove Merc + called cops. SV 1 left early own car. Told later. Checked both suits: OK, no smell petrol + not sent cleaners. Sv 1 had 1 suit cleaned but not worn same night. Photos attached note suits + ID photos bros. Nasty to staff.*

Adamsberg looked at the photos she attached: Christian, Saviour 1, was wearing a navy suit with a fine stripe, while Christophe, Saviour 2, was wearing a navy blazer, as if he owned a yacht. Which he probably did anyway. Sharks might well own yachts so that they could rest after roaming the seas and gobbling up a few squid. Another shot showed a three-quarter view of Christian looking elegant, this time with shorter hair, and one of his brother looking podgy and graceless.

Maître Deschamps came out of his office before his assistant, and looked carefully right and left before crossing the narrow street and heading straight for Adamsberg: he walked hurriedly and mincingly, which fitted the way his voice had sounded on the phone that morning.

'Commissaire Adamsberg,' said the lawyer, shaking hands, 'you've come to give us a hand, I see. That reassures me, yes, indeed. I've been very worried about Caroline.'

'Caroline?'

'Lina, if you prefer. In the office she's Caroline.'

'And is Lina worried?' asked Adamsberg.

'If she is, she's trying not to show it. Naturally the whole story must have upset her a bit, but I don't think she's entirely grasped the consequences it might have for herself and her family. They could be ostracised by the townspeople, or some vengeance could be planned, or god knows what. It's very worrying. It seems you can work miracles, since you got Léone to speak yesterday.'

'Yes.'

'Would it be breaking confidence to tell me what she said?'

'Not at all. She said "Ello", "Fleg" and "Sugar".'

'Does that help you?'

'Not a bit.'

It seemed to Adamsberg that the little solicitor was relieved, perhaps because Léo hadn't mentioned Lina.

'Do you think she will say any more?'

'The doctor doesn't think she'll survive. Is this Lina?' asked Adamsberg, as he saw the office door open again.

'Yes. Treat her gently, please. She's had a hard life, one and a half wage packets isn't much for a family of five, with the mother's little pension. It's the devil's own job to keep going – sorry, not what I meant to say, don't misinterpret it please!' said the solicitor, before moving off quickly, as if he were running away.

Adamsberg shook hands with Lina.

'Thank you for agreeing to see me,' he said formally.

Lina wasn't a classical beauty, far from it. Round-shouldered and slightly buck-toothed, she was running a little to fat, and her heavy bust was out of proportion to her slim legs. But the brigadier was right, her breasts were indeed good enough to eat, like the rest of her: lovely smooth skin, round arms, a radiant face, a little broad perhaps, high cheekbones with a rosy glow, very Norman, and a dusting of freckles like specks of gold.

'I've never heard of the Blue Boar,' Lina was now saying.

'Opposite the flower market, just round the corner. Delicious food and not dear.'

'Opposite the flower market, that's the *Running* Boar.'

'Oh, yes, you're right. Running.'

'Not Blue.'

'No, not Blue.'

As he accompanied her through the narrow streets, Adamsberg realised that his desire to eat her was stronger than the wish to go to bed with her. This woman literally excited his appetite, suddenly reminding him of a kind of cake filled with honey, known as a *kouglof*, which he had once eaten as a child, when staying with his aunt in Alsace. He chose a table near the window, wondering how he was going to conduct a proper interrogation with a warm slice of honey-coloured *kouglof*, the exact shade of Lina's hair which curled over her shoulders. Shoulders that the commissaire couldn't see, because Lina was wearing a long blue silk shawl, oddly for a warm summer day. Adamsberg hadn't prepared his opening question, preferring to wait till he saw her and then improvise. And now that he was sitting opposite Lina, with her blonde radiance shining at him, he found it impossible to associate her with the black spectres of the ghostly Riders, or to imagine that she was the one who saw horrors and transmitted them. But that's what she had done. They ordered their food, then both waited in silence, nibbling at pieces of bread. Adamsberg glanced across at her. Her face was still open and attentive, but she made no attempt to help him. He was a cop, she had unleashed a storm on Ordebec, he suspected her, she knew people thought she was mad, and those were the simple facts of the situation. He swung round in his seat and looked over at the bar.

'Looks a bit like rain,' he said finally.

'Yes, threatening from the west. Might rain tonight.'

'Or this evening. So. Mademoiselle Vendermot, it all started with you.'

'Call me Lina.'

'It all started with you, Lina. Not the rain, but the storm raging in Ordebec. And nobody knows where this storm will end, how many victims it will cause, or if it will turn against you.'

'*Nothing* started with me,' said Lina, gathering her shawl round her shoulders. 'It all started with Lord Hellequin and his horde. The Riders went past and I saw them. What am I supposed to do about it? There were four people in the procession, there'll be four deaths.'

'But you told people about it.'

'Anyone who sees the Riders has to tell, you've got to. You don't understand. Where are you from?'

'From the south-west, Béarn.'

'There you are, you really can't understand. This is an army that gallops over the northern plains. The people who've been sighted with it might try to protect themselves.'

'The ones who are "seized", you mean?'

159

'That's right. That's why you've got to tell. Not that they often manage to get away, but it does happen. Glayeux and Mortembot, now, they don't deserve to live, but they still have a chance to escape and survive. They've got a right to that chance.'

'Do you have any personal reason for disliking them?'

Lina waited for their meal to arrive before replying. She was clearly hungry or at least wanted to eat, and eyed her food with an eager expression. Logical enough, Adamsberg thought, that such an edible woman should have a healthy appetite.

'A personal reason, no,' she said, attacking her food. 'But everyone knows they both have blood on their hands. People try to avoid them, and it didn't surprise me to see them among the Riders.'

'Like Herbier?'

'Herbier was a disgusting human being. He was always shooting things. But he had a screw loose as well. Glayeux and Mortembot aren't like that. They killed because it suited them. Worse than Herbier, probably.'

Adamsberg forced himself to eat more quickly than usual to keep up with the young woman. He didn't want to find himself facing her with his plate half full.

'But in order to see the Riders, people say you have to have a screw loose too. Or else to be lying.'

'It's up to you, if you think that. I see them, and I can't help it. I see them on the path, I'm on the path, and my bedroom is three kilometres away.'

Lina was using her fork to plunge slices of potato into a creamy sauce, devoting surprising energy and concentration to the task. Her eagerness was almost upsetting.

'Or else it could be a vision,' Adamsberg went on. 'A vision, personal to you, into which you put people you don't like. Herbier, Glayeux, Mortembot.'

'I've seen doctors, you know,' said Lina, savouring her mouthful. 'They put me through a battery of tests at the hospital in Lisieux, physiological and psychiatric tests, two years' worth. I was an interesting case, because of St Teresa of Lisieux, of course. You're looking for some kind of reassuring explanation, but I've been there too. There isn't one. They couldn't find any lithium deficiency or anything else that makes you see the Virgin Mary here and there, or hear voices. They said I was perfectly well balanced, stable, and even that I seem to be a very reasonable person. And they let me go home without giving me any diagnosis.'

'So what *is* the diagnosis, Lina? That these ghostly horsemen really exist, that they really come galloping along the Chemin de Bonneval, and that you really see them?'

'I can't tell you if they exist, commissaire. But I can tell you I've seen them. As far back as people can remember there's always been someone here who sees the Riders of Ordebec go past. Perhaps there's an ancient cloud round here, some mist, a disturbance, a memory still hanging in the air. And I just walked into it like walking into a fog bank.'

'So what does he look like, this Lord Hellequin?'

'Oh, very striking,' Lina replied at once. 'A grand majestic head, and he has long blond hair, kind of bedraggled, flowing to his shoulders, over his armour. But terrifying. Well,' she added hesitantly and in a much lower voice, 'it's because his skin isn't normal.'

Lina interrupted herself, in order to clear her plate, well ahead of Adamsberg. Then she leaned back in her chair looking even more glowing and relaxed after eating her fill.

'Enjoy the food?' asked Adamsberg.

'Fantastic,' she replied sincerely. 'I've never been here before. Can't afford it.'

'We'll order some cheese and dessert,' said Adamsberg, hoping that the young woman would reach a state of complete relaxation.

'Finish your dish first,' she said kindly. 'You don't eat fast, do you? And people say policemen do everything in a rush.'

'I'm incapable of doing anything in a rush. Even when I run, I run slowly.'

'Anyway,' Lina was saying, 'to prove I'm telling the truth, the first time I saw the Riders, nobody'd ever told me about them.'

'But I hear that in Ordebec everyone knows about them, even without being told. Apparently people drink it in with their mothers' milk.'

'Not in our house. My parents always lived a bit away from everyone. I bet you've been told that people didn't want to know my father.'

'Yes.'

'It's quite true. When I told my mother what I'd seen – I was crying and screaming back then – she thought I was ill, nervous exhaustion, as they used to say in those days. She'd never heard of Hellequin and his Riders, nor had my father. And he used to come back late from hunting, by the Chemin de Bonneval. But everyone who *knew* about this legend, they took good care not to go down that path after nightfall. Even people who don't believe it avoid going there.'

'So when was the first time you saw the Riders?'

'I was eleven. It was just two days after my father had been killed – his skull was split open with an axe. I'll have some floating islands, with a lot of flaked almonds please,' she said to the waitress.

'An axe?' said Adamsberg, somewhat stunned. 'Was that how your father died?'

'Yep, felled like a pig,' said Lina and calmly mimed the action, bringing down the edge of her hand on the tabletop. 'He was struck on the head and chest.'

Adamsberg observed this lack of emotion and reflected that his honey *kouglof* was perhaps without a soft centre.

'After that I had nightmares for ages, and the doctor gave me sedatives. Not because of my father being chopped in two, but because I was terrified of seeing those horsemen again. You have to realise they're all rotten, decayed, like Lord Hellequin's face. Decomposed,' she added with a shudder. 'They don't have all their limbs, the men or the horses, they make this horrible noise, but the cries of the living creatures they take away with them, they're even worse. Well. Luckily nothing happened after that for about eight years, and I thought I was out of it and it had just been, you know, some nervous thing when I was little. But then when I was nineteen, I saw them again. You do understand, don't you, commissaire, this isn't a nice story, it's not one I'm making up to show off. It's ghastly, it's a burden, it's my fate, and I even tried to kill myself twice. Then this psychiatrist from Caen, he managed to make me accept I've got to live with the Riders. They scare me and I don't want to see them, but at least now they don't stop me living my life more or less normally. Could I have a few more almonds please?'

'Of course,' said Adamsberg, raising his hand to call the waitress over.

'It's not going to cost too much?'

'The police will pay.'

Lina laughed, as she waved her spoon. 'For once the police will pay to make amends.'

Adamsberg looked blank.

'Amends, almonds, just a joke.'

'Sorry, I'm a bit slow on the uptake. Would you mind telling me a bit more about your father? Did they find out who killed him?'

'No, never.'

'Was anyone suspected?'

'Yes, of course.'

'Who?'

'Me,' said Lina, smiling again. 'I heard this yelling and I ran upstairs, and I found him in his bedroom, covered in blood. My brother Hippo, who was only eight, saw me holding the axe. And he told the gendarmes. He didn't mean any harm, he was just answering their questions.'

'What do you mean, you were holding the axe?'

'I picked it up. The gendarmes thought I'd wiped the handle, because they didn't find any fingerprints on it except mine. In the end, after Léo and the count came along and helped us, they left me in peace. The window was open, it would have been easy for the killer to get away. Nobody liked my father, just like nobody liked Herbier. Whenever he had one of his violent turns, people said it was the bullet shifting inside his head. I didn't understand what they meant when I was little.'

'Neither do I. What was shifting?'

'The bullet. My mother says before the Algerian war, when she married him, he was more or less OK. But when he was over there, he got this bullet lodged in his brain and they couldn't get it out. He was taken off active service and they put him on to interrogations. Torturing people. I'm going to leave you for a few minutes, I'm going outside for a smoke.'

Adamsberg joined her, taking out a half-crushed cigarette from his pocket. He had a close-up view of the honey-coloured hair, unusually thick for a woman from Normandy, and the freckles on her gleaming shoulders when the shawl slipped, though she quickly twitched it back.

'Did he beat you?'

'Did yours?'

'No. He was a shoemaker.'

'That's nothing to do with it.'

'No.'

'Well, he never touched *me*. But he beat my brothers to pulp. When Antonin was a baby, he picked him up by his heels and threw him downstairs. Just like that. Fourteen fractures. He was in plaster from head to foot for a year. And Martin wouldn't eat his food. He used to secretly put stuff from his plate into the hollow leg of the table. One day my father saw him, and he made him get it back out of the table leg with a hook and eat it all. It was rotten of course. Stuff like that, that's how he was.'

'What about Hippo?'

'Even worse.'

Lina ground out her cigarette underfoot and pushed the stub neatly into the gutter. Adamsberg got out his mobile – the second secret one – feeling it vibrate in his pocket.

Arriving tonite, address svp. LVB

Veyrenc. Veyrenc would snatch his lovely *kouglof* from under his nose, with his tender face and his girlish mouth.

No! all OK here, he texted back.

All not OK. Address svp.

Phone me.

Fckng address fast.

Adamsberg came back to the table and typed in Léo's address unwillingly, his mood darkened. Clouds gathering in the west, rain tonight.

'Problems?'

'A colleague is coming out here,' said Adamsberg, pocketing the mobile.

'Well, we were always round at Léo's,' Lina continued regardless. 'She educated us, her and the count. They say she isn't going to survive, that her mechanism can't function any more. You found her, they say. And she said something to you.'

'Just a minute,' said Adamsberg, holding up his hand to make her stop. He took out a pen and wrote 'mechanism' on his paper napkin. A word which the doctor with the name of a fish had used. A word that made his eyes mist over, and awakened an idea in there somewhere, but he couldn't identify it. He put the napkin in his pocket and looked at Lina with the eyes of a man waking from sleep.

'So did you see your *father* among the Riders, when you were eleven?'

'There was one man with them, yes, but there was all this flame and smoke, he had his hands up to his face, screaming. So I couldn't be sure it was him. But I suppose it was. I recognised his shoes.'

'And was anyone seized the second time?'

'That time, there was an old woman. We knew her, she used to go round throwing stones at people's shutters, and shouting curses, she was the kind of woman who scared the local kids.'

'Was she supposed to have murdered anyone?'

'No, I don't think so. Unless perhaps her husband. He'd died long before.'

'And did she die?'

'Yes, nine days after the army appeared. But peacefully, in her bed. After that I never saw the Riders until this last time, a month ago.'

'And the fourth living person, did you not recognise them? Man, woman?'

'A man, but I'm not sure. Because a horse had fallen on him, and his hair was on fire, you see. I couldn't make out his face.'

Lina put her hand on the curve of her stomach, as if to appreciate with her fingers the meal she had eaten so voraciously.

It was four thirty by the time Adamsberg arrived back at Léo's house on foot. His body was feeling the strain from having struggled against its desires. From time to time, he took out the paper napkin, looked again at the word 'mechanism' and put it back in his pocket. No, the word meant absolutely nothing to him. If there was an idea in there somewhere, it must be lying in the deepest recesses, wedged under a rock in the ocean and masked by fronds of seaweed. Sooner or later, it would release itself and float zigzagging up to the surface. It was the only way Adamsberg knew how to think. Wait, cast his net across the surface of the water, and see what it caught.

In the guest house, Danglard, his sleeves rolled up, was in charge of preparations for supper, while holding forth under the attentive gaze of Zerk.

'It's very rare for anyone's little toe to look good,' he was saying. 'It's usually twisted, deformed and turned under, not to mention the nail, which is very reduced in size. Now, when they've browned on one side, you can turn them over.'

Adamsberg leaned against the jamb of the door and watched as his son obeyed the commandant's instructions.

'And it's our shoes that do that to it?' Zerk was asking.

'Evolution. We walk less than we did, so the little toe has atrophied, it's gradually disappearing. One day, thousands of years from now, it will just be a fragment of toenail on the side of the foot, like on a horse. But shoes don't help of course.'

'Like wisdom teeth. They don't have room to come through.'

'Correct. The little toe is the wisdom tooth of the foot, so to speak.'

'Or the wisdom tooth is the little toe of the mouth.'

'Yes, but if you put it that way, it's less easy to understand.'

Adamsberg came inside, and poured himself a cup of coffee.

'How did it go?' Danglard asked.

'She irradiated me.'

'Bad vibes?'

'No, golden. She's a bit plump, her teeth stick out a bit, but she irradiated me.'

'Dangerous,' commented Danglard disapprovingly.

'I don't know if I ever told you about this kind of honey cake I once had at my aunt's when I was little, called a *kouglof*. She's like that, only life-size.'

166

'Remember that this Vendermot woman is a morbid fantasist.'

'Possibly. But that's not the way she seems. She's both confident and childlike, chatty and prudent.'

'Perhaps her toes are not so pretty.'

'Shrinking with evolution,' put in Zerk.

'Doesn't bother me.'

'If it's reached that stage,' Danglard said, 'you're no longer fit to pursue this inquiry. You can cook the dinner and I'll take over from you.'

'No, I'm going to visit her brothers at seven. Veyrenc is coming down this evening, commandant.'

Danglard took the time to pour half a glass of water on to the pieces of chicken, covered the pan and turned down the gas.

'Now you let it simmer for an hour like that,' he said to Zerk, before turning to face Adamsberg again. 'We don't need Veyrenc. Why did you ask him to come?'

'He invited himself, for no reason. Danglard, in your view, why would a woman put a shawl round her shoulders if it's a hot day?'

'It might rain,' said Zerk. 'There are clouds in the west.'

'To hide something she's ashamed of,' Danglard contradicted him. 'A blemish perhaps or the mark of the devil.'

'Well, it still doesn't bother me,' Adamsberg repeated.

'Those who see the Furious Army, commissaire, are not sunny, benevolent individuals. They must be dark and sinister souls. Irradiated or not, you'd do well to bear that in mind.'

Adamsberg didn't answer, but brought out his napkin once more.

'What's that?' Danglard asked.

'It's a word that doesn't mean anything to me, "mechanism".'

'So who wrote it?'

'I did of course.'

Zerk nodded, as if he understood perfectly.

XXIII

LINA SHOWED HIM INTO THE MAIN ROOM, WHERE THREE MEN WERE waiting, lined up behind the large table and looking wary. Adamsberg had asked Danglard to come along, so that he could verify the irradiation for himself. The commissaire easily identified the middle brother, Martin: tall, skinny and brown, like a branch of dried wood, the one who had had to eat the food scraped out of the table leg. Hippolyte, the oldest brother, aged about forty, had an impressive head, and blond hair rather like his sister's, but without the same radiance. Tall and solidly built, he was extending a large, slightly deformed hand. At the end of the table, Antonin watched apprehensively as the two men approached. Thin and dark like Martin, but better proportioned, he was holding his arms folded tightly across his waist in a posture of protection: the youngest one, the one made of clay. About thirty-five, looking a bit older perhaps, because of his drawn face, in which his anxious eyes seemed very large. From her armchair in an inconspicuous corner of the room, the mother made only a slight movement of her head. She was wearing a shabby grey blouse instead of the flowered overall.

'We wouldn't have let Émeri across the threshold,' Martin explained, waving his arms about jerkily like a huge grasshopper. 'But you're different. We were waiting for you before having an aperitif.'

'Very nice of you,' said Danglard.

'We're nice people,' said Hippolyte, agreeing calmly, and putting glasses on the table. 'Which one is Adamsberg?'

'I am,' said Adamsberg, sitting down on an old chair, the legs of which were tied together with string. 'This is my deputy, Commandant Danglard.'

He noticed then that all the chairs were reinforced with string, no doubt to stop them breaking and causing Antonin to fall. Perhaps that was also the explanation for the rubber cladding nailed to the surrounds of the doors. It was a big house, but sparsely equipped and in poor repair, with holes in the plaster, cheap plywood furniture, draughts under the doors, and walls which were almost bare. There was a buzzing sound in the room, so loud that Adamsberg instinctively put his hand to his ear, as if his tinnitus of the previous months had returned. But Martin moved quickly towards a closed wicker basket.

'I'll take this out,' he said. 'If you're not used to it, the noise they make's annoying.'

'Crickets,' Lina explained in a whisper. 'He's got about thirty in the basket.'

'Is Martin really going to eat them tonight?'

'The Chinese eat them,' Hippolyte assured him, 'and the Chinese have always been years ahead of us. Martin cooks them in pastry with sausage meat, eggs and parsley. I prefer them in a quiche.'

'The flesh of crickets helps strengthen the clay,' Antonin put in. 'The sun does too, but you have to be careful or it dries out.'

'Émeri told me about it. How long have you had this clay problem?'

'Since I was six.'

'What does it affect, your muscles, or is it ligaments, nerves?'

'No, it affects parts of my bones. But the muscles are attached to the bones so they find it harder to work the clay bits. So I'm not very strong.'

'I see.'

Hippolyte opened a bottle of port and poured it into the glasses – which were old mustard pots, either opaque or badly wiped. He took one across to his mother who hadn't budged from her corner.

'*Eno yad eh si gniog ot eb deruc,*' he said with a broad grin.

'One day he is going to be cured,' Lina translated, in some embarrassment.

'How do you do that?' asked Danglard. 'Saying the letters backwards.'

'You just have to read the word backwards in your head. What's your name, your full name?'

'Adrien Danglard.'

'*Neirda Dralgnad*. Sounds quite nice, Dralgnad. You see, it's not so hard.'

And for once, Danglard felt he had been bested by an intelligence absolutely superior to his, or at least one which had developed extraordinarily in a certain direction. He was outclassed and for a moment distressed. Hippolyte's natural talent seemed to sweep away all his classic culture, which seemed stale and second-hand. He knocked back his port in one mouthful. It took the roof off your mouth, no doubt the cheapest in the shop.

'So what do you want from us, commissaire?' asked Hippolyte with his big grin – producing an effect that was vaguely attractive, jolly even, but at the same time rather sinister. Perhaps because he seemed to have kept some of his baby teeth, which made his mouth look irregular. 'Do you want us to tell you what we were doing the night Herbier died? Which was when anyway?'

'July the twenty-seventh.'

'What time?'

'We don't know that, because the body was only found much later. The neighbours saw him going off at 6 p.m., and from his house to the chapel would take about a quarter of an hour. He must have had to push the moped the last thirty metres or so. The murderer was waiting there, at about 6.15, let's say. And yes, I do need to know where you were.'

The four siblings looked at each other as if they had been asked a ridiculous question.

'But what would that prove?' asked Martin. 'If people don't tell you the truth, what would you do?'

'If you lie to me, I'll be suspicious of course.'

'But how would you know?'

'I'm a cop. I hear thousands of lies. Over time, you get to recognise when people are lying.'

'How?'

'It's something about the way they look or blink, or move parts of their body, or in the tremors in their voice, or how quickly they speak. It's as if the person suddenly developed a limp, instead of walking normally.'

'For instance,' said Hippolyte, 'if I don't look you in the eye, that means I'm lying?'

'It could be the opposite,' said Adamsberg with a smile. 'The twenty-seventh was a Tuesday. I'd like to hear from Antonin first.'

'All right,' said the youngest brother, hugging his arms to his body. 'I practically never go out. What I mean is, it's dangerous for me to be out of doors. I work from home, on websites, buying and selling antiques and second-hand furniture. It's not much, but it's a sort of job. On Tuesdays I don't go out at all, because it's market day in town, and there's always a lot of pushing and shoving until late in the afternoon.'

'No, he didn't go out,' put in Hippolyte, refilling the only empty glass on the table – Danglard's. 'Nor did I. *Ew erew lla ereh rof erus.*'

'He said we were all here for sure,' Lina translated. 'But no, Hippo, that's not true. I stayed late at the office to finish a file. We had to put in a big report by the thirtieth. I came home to make the supper. Martin came to the office sometime in the afternoon, to bring us some honey. He had his baskets.'

'Yes, that's right,' said Martin, who was pulling on his long fingers and making the joints crack. 'I went to collect stuff from the forest, and was probably out until about seven. After that it's too late, the creatures are back in their holes.'

'*Sey, ouy era thgir,*' admitted Hippo.

'After supper, if there's nothing on the telly, we often play dominoes, or dice games,' said Antonin. 'That's fun,' he said naively. 'But that night, Lina didn't play with us, she was reading over her file.'

'*Ton os doog nehw ehs si ton gniyalp.*'

'Oh, stop it, Hippo,' said Lina, 'the commissaire isn't here to play games with you.'

Adamsberg looked at all five of them, the mother shrinking into her chair, the luminous sister who provided their income and keep, and the three brothers who were all some kind of crazy genius.

'The commissaire knows,' said Hippolyte, 'that Herbier was killed because he was evil, and also our father's best mate. He died because the Riders decided to seize him. If we'd wanted to kill him, we could have done it ages ago. What I don't understand is why Lord Hellequin seized our father thirty-one years ago, and only came for Herbier so long after. But we're not supposed to question Hellequin's plans.'

'Lina tells me that no one has ever been charged with the murder of your father. And you don't suspect anyone, Hippo? You came in and found Lina holding the axe?'

'The murderer,' said Hippo, tracing a circle in the air with his deformed hand, 'comes from who knows where, like black smoke. We'll never know, any more than we will for Herbier and the three others.'

'Are they going to die?'

'Certainly,' said Martin, getting up. 'Excuse me, it's time for Antonin's massage. Half past seven just struck. If we go past the time, it's not good. But carry on, we can still listen.'

Martin went to fetch a bowl of yellowish mixture from the fridge while Antonin shyly took off his shirt.

'It's mainly celandine extract and formic acid,' Martin explained. 'It stings a bit, but it's very good for absorbing the clay.'

Martin started spreading the ointment over his brother's bony torso, and by the glances exchanged in the room, Adamsberg gathered that none of the others really believed that Antonin was half made of clay. But they played the game, looking after their brother and reassuring him. Because he had been smashed to bits when the father threw him downstairs as a baby.

'Yes, we're nice people,' Hippolyte repeated, rubbing his long blond, rather grubby curls. 'But we won't shed any tears over our father or the other arseholes she saw being carried along by the horsemen. Have you noticed my hands, commissaire?'

'Yes.'

'I was born with six fingers on each hand. An extra little finger.'

'Hippo is very special,' said Antonin with a smile.

'It's not common, but it happens sometimes,' remarked Martin, who was now attacking his brother's left arm, applying the ointment very precisely.

'Six fingers on your hand is a sign of the devil,' said Hippolyte with an even bigger grin. 'That's what people have always said round here. As if anyone could believe such foolishness.'

'You believe in the Riders, don't you?' said Danglard, asking with a glance if he could help himself to another finger of port, rotgut though it was.

'We know Lina sees the Riders, that's different. If she sees them, she sees them. But we don't believe in signs of the devil and rubbish like that.'

'But you *do* believe in dead men riding on horseback along the Chemin de Bonneval.'

'Commandant Dralgnad,' said Hippolyte, 'the dead can return without being sent by god or the devil. Anyway, their leader is Hellequin, not the devil.'

'That's right,' said Adamsberg, who didn't want Danglard to start an argument about Lina and her vision of the Riders. For a few minutes, he had not been following the conversation closely, but trying to work out what his own name was spelled backwards.

'My father was ashamed of my hands with their six fingers. He made me wear mittens, he made me eat my food off my knees so as not to have my hands on the table. He was disgusted at the sight of them, and humiliated that a son of his looked like that.'

Smiles once more spread over the faces of the siblings, as if this sorry affair of the sixth finger amused them all greatly.

'Tell them, tell them,' said Antonin, looking delighted at the prospect of hearing the story again.

'One night when I was eight years old, I put my hands on the table without mittens. Our father got into a terrible rage, worse than Hellequin. He fetched his axe. The same one he was chopped in two with later.'

'It was the bullet twisting in his head,' put in their mother suddenly, in a plaintive voice.

'Yes, *maman*, it must have been the bullet,' said Hippo impatiently. 'He got hold of my right hand and he chopped off the finger. Lina says I fainted. Mother screamed, the table was covered in blood and Mother rushed at him. But he just picked up my left hand and cut off the other finger too.'

'The bullet moved in his brain.'

'It must have moved a lot, *maman*,' said Martin.

'My mother picked me up and ran to the hospital. I'd have bled to death on the way if the count hadn't seen her on the road. He was coming back from this grand reception, wasn't he?'

'Very grand,' said Antonin, putting his shirt back on, 'and he rushed our mother and Hippo to hospital, getting blood all over his fancy car. What I mean is, the count is a good man, he'll never get picked up by the Riders. And he took our mother in every day to visit Hippo.'

'The doctors didn't sew him up very well,' said Martin bitterly. 'These days, when someone is born with six fingers, they can fix it so you hardly notice. But Turbot's cack-handed, he was there in those days too. He massacred Hippo's hands.'

'It doesn't matter, Martin,' said Hippolyte.

'Well, we go to Lisieux if we want a doctor now, we don't go to Turbot.'

'There are people,' Martin went on, 'who have their sixth finger removed and then they regret it all their lives. They say they've lost their identity when they lost their extra finger. Hippo says it doesn't bother him. There was this girl in Marseille, she went to get her fingers back out of the bin in the hospital and kept them in a jar. Imagine! We think Mother may have done that too, but she won't say.'

'Don't be silly,' said his mother.

Martin wiped his hands on a cloth and turned towards Hippolyte with the same engaging smile.

'Tell them the rest,' he said.

'Yes, please do,' insisted Antonin.

'Perhaps that's not necessary,' said Lina prudently.

'*Grebsmada yam ton ekil siht.* He's a cop after all.'

'He says you may not like it,' translated Lina.

'Grebsmada, that's my name, is it?'

'Yes.'

'Could be Serbian. It sounded a bit like that.'

'Hippo had this dog,' Antonin said. 'It was his own special dog, they were inseparable; actually I was jealous. He was called Sooty.'

'He'd trained him perfectly.'

'Tell them, Hippo.'

'Two months after he cut off my fingers, my father made me sit on the floor in the corner as a punishment. It was the night when he forced Martin to swallow all the stuff from the table leg, and I'd tried to defend him. Yes, I know, *maman*, the bullet must have twisted again.'

'Yes, my love, it must have.'

'Twisted several times, *maman*.'

'Hippo was in the corner,' Lina said, taking up the story. 'He was cuddling Sooty. Then he whispered something in the dog's ear and Sooty leapt up like a mad thing. He went for our father's throat.'

'I wanted the dog to kill him,' Hippo explained calmly. 'But Lina made me call him off, and I told Sooty to get down. Then I got him to eat the stuff from the table leg.'

'It didn't bother the dog,' Antonin said, 'but Martin was ill with colic for four days.'

'Anyway, after that,' Hippo went on in sadder tones, 'when our father came back from hospital with stitches in his throat, he got his gun and he shot Sooty while we were at school. He put my dog's corpse outside the front door so we'd see it before we even reached the house. That's when the count came to fetch me. He decided I wasn't safe here. He kept me in the chateau for a few weeks. He bought me a puppy. But I didn't get on with his son.'

'His son's an idiot,' said Martin.

'A *ytrid elttil dratsab*,' Hippolyte confirmed.

Adamsberg looked to Lina to interpret.

'A dirty little bastard,' she said reluctantly.

'A *dratsab* – that sounds quite suitable,' remarked Danglard, looking intellectually satisfied.

'Well, because of that little dratsab, I came back home, and Mother hid

175

me under Lina's bed. I was living here in secret and Mother didn't know how to manage. But Hellequin found the solution. He split my father's head in two. And it was just after that when Lina saw them for the first time.'

'The Riders?' asked Danglard. 'How do you say that backwards?'

'Oh no, we don't have the right to say their name backwards,' Hippolyte said, shaking his head decisively.

'I see,' said Adamsberg. 'So your father was killed how long after you got back from the chateau?'

'Thirteen days.'

'His head split open with an axe.'

'And his chest,' said Hippolyte cheerfully.

'The monster was dead,' said Martin.

'It was the bullet's fault,' whispered their mother.

'So in the end,' Hippolyte summed up, 'Lina should never have made me call Sooty off. It would have been settled that night once and for all.'

'You can't blame her,' said Antonin, shrugging his shoulders cautiously. 'Lina's just too soft-hearted, she's too nice.'

'We're all nice people,' said Hippolyte, nodding.

As she got up to wish them goodbye, Lina's shawl slipped to the ground and she gave a little cry. With an elegant gesture, Danglard swept it up and placed it round her shoulders again.

'So what do you make of that, commandant?' asked Adamsberg as they walked slowly back up the track to Léo's house.

'Could be a whole *family* of killers,' said Danglard coolly, 'self-contained, sheltered from the outside world. All of them with a screw loose, they've been badly abused, they're wild, incredibly talented and very engaging.'

'I meant the radiation. Did you notice it? Although when she's with her brothers she holds back a bit.'

'Yes, I did notice,' admitted Danglard reluctantly, 'the honeyed bosom and so on. But not a good kind of radiation. Infrared or ultraviolet, dark light.'

'You're saying that because of Camille. But, Danglard, these days, Camille only wants to kiss me on the cheek, like a friend. A very precise and determined kiss that means we'll never sleep together again. No relenting.'

'Mild punishment, considering the crime.'

'But what do you want me to do about it? Go and sit under an apple tree and wait for Camille for years?'

'Doesn't have to be an apple tree.'

'And I'm not allowed to notice this woman with her fantastic breasts?'

'You're right, they are,' conceded Danglard.

'Just a sec,' said Adamsberg, stopping on the path. 'Message from Retancourt. Our battleship diving into the shark-infested abysm.'

'Abyss, you mean,' corrected Danglard, peering across at the phone. 'And battleships don't dive.'

Sv 1 home v late night of fire. Didnt know but reaction normal so not involved? But acted edgy.

How edgy? Adamsberg texted.

Sacked chmbermaid.

Why?

Complicated not important.

Tell anyway.

Sv gave labrador sugar when home.

'Danglard, what is it with all these people, they're forever feeding sugar to their dogs?'

'They want to be loved. Go on.'

Lab refused. Chmbrmd tried. Refused again. Chmbrmd criticised sugar. Sv 1 sacked her same night. Jumpy.

Coz dog not eat sugar?

I sed. Drop it. Cheers.

Zerk came bounding towards them, with his cameras slung from his neck.

'The count came by. He wants to see you after supper, at ten.'

'Is it urgent?'

'He didn't ask, he more or less ordered.'

'What's he like?'

'Every inch a count. Old, elegant, bald-headed, and wearing a scruffy gardening jacket. Commandant, I've finished cooking the chicken.'

'You added the cream and herbs, like I told you?'

'Yes, right at the end. I took some to the Pigeon. He loved it. He's spent the day drawing cows with the pencils.'

'So is he any good at drawing after all that?'

'Not really, but cows are hard. Harder than horses.'

'OK, let's eat our chicken, Danglard, and then we'll go up there.'

XXIV

NIGHT WAS FALLING AS ADAMSBERG STOPPED THE CAR IN FRONT of the chateau's iron gates, up on the hill overlooking the citadel of Ordebec. Danglard extracted his long body from the front seat with unaccustomed agility, and went at once to stand at the gate, gripping it with both hands and looking at the building. Adamsberg read on his face unadulterated delight, a state of mind free of melancholy, which Danglard achieved only rarely. He glanced up at the great chateau built of pale stone, which no doubt represented for his deputy a kind of honey *kouglof*.

'I told you you'd like it here. Is it very old, this chateau?'

'The first lords of Ordebec are recorded in the eleventh century. But it was above all at the Battle of Orléans in 1428 that the Comte de Valleray distinguished himself when he joined the French troops commanded by the Comte de Dunois, known as Jean, the bastard son of Louis, the Duc d'Orléans.'

'OK, Danglard, but what about the chateau?'

'That's what I'm explaining to you. Valleray's son, Henri, built it after the Hundred Years War, at the end of the fifteenth century. The west wing that you can still see and the west tower date from then. But the main body of the chateau was rebuilt in the seventeenth century, and the big arches are eighteenth-century additions.'

'Shall we ring the bell?'

'There are at least three or four dogs barking. We can ring and then wait for an escort. I don't know what it is with these people and their dogs.'

'And sugar,' added Adamsberg, tugging the bell pull.

Rémy François de Valleray, Comte d'Ordebec, was waiting for them in the library, and received them informally, still wearing the shabby blue canvas jacket that made him look like a farm labourer. But Danglard noted that each of the cut-glass goblets on the table would have cost easily a month of his salary. And that judging simply by its colour, the alcohol which they were being served made the journey from Paris entirely worthwhile. Not like the grocer's port he had drunk out of mustard pots at the Vendermots' house, which had made his stomach protest. The library must have contained about a thousand volumes, and the walls were lined with about forty paintings, at which Commandant Danglard's jaw dropped. In short, the kind of surroundings to be found in an aristocratic mansion where money had not yet run short, except that any solemnity the room might have had was dispelled by the incredible disorder. Boots, sacks of seed, medicines, plastic bags, screws, melted candles, boxes of nails, papers were strewn everywhere on the floor, tables and shelves.

'Gentlemen,' said the count, putting aside his walking stick, and holding out his hand. 'Thank you for answering my appeal.'

He was indeed every inch a count. The tone of voice, the rather imperious gestures, the direct gaze and the confidence in his perfect right to meet them wearing a peasant's jacket. At the same time, one could also easily glimpse in him the old Norman countryman, with his ruddy cheeks, dirty fingernails and a secret amusement directed at himself. He filled the glasses with one hand, leaning on his stick with the other, and gestured to them to be seated.

'I hope you like this Calva, it's the one I give Léo. Ah, come in, Denis. May I introduce my son. Denis, these gentlemen are from the Criminal Division of the Paris Police.'

'I didn't realise you had company,' said the man who had entered, shaking hands coolly, without smiling.

White hands and well-kept nails, a solid if plump body, grey hair combed back.

So this was the filthy little *dratsab*, as the Vendermots had called him, the one who had cut short Hippolyte's refuge at the castle. Well, Adamsberg observed, the man did have a rather *dratsab*-like face, jowly with thin lips and a furtive or remote gaze, at any rate one that indicated he was keeping his distance. He poured himself a glass of Calvados, from politeness rather than any desire to stay. Everything about his body language indicated that the guests didn't interest him, nor, for all intents and purposes, did his father.

'I just came to say that Maryse's car will be ready tomorrow. We'll have to ask Georges to be here to receive it, because I'll be in the salerooms all day.'

'You couldn't find Georges, then?'

'No, the brute must have got drunk and he's probably in the stables. Damned if I'm going to go and crawl under some horse's belly to wake him.'

'All right, I'll see to it.'

'Thank you,' said Denis, putting down his glass.

'Don't let us chase you away.'

'No, I'm going anyway. I'll leave you to your guests.'

The count pulled a slight face as the door clicked shut.

'Apologies, gentlemen. My relations with my stepson are not the best, especially since he knows what I want to talk to you about, and he doesn't like it. I want to talk about Léo.'

'I'm very fond of Léo,' said Adamsberg without having prepared his reply.

'I believe you. And you'd only known her a few hours. You were the one who found her when she'd been injured. And you've succeeded in getting her to speak. Which probably prevented Dr Turbot declaring her brain-dead.'

'I had a few words with the doctor.'

'That doesn't surprise me. He can be a *dratsab* sometimes. Not all the time though.'

'You like using Hippolyte's words, monsieur le comte?' asked Danglard.

'Just call me Valleray, that's simpler. I've known Hippo since he was a baby. I like the word, it fits.'

'When did he start reversing letters?'

'When he was thirteen. He's an exceptional chap and the brothers and sister are too. Lina has this extraordinary luminosity.'

'Something that didn't escape the commissaire,' remarked Danglard, who was feeling profoundly relaxed, what with the succulence of the Calvados and the sight of the chateau.

'But you didn't notice it?' asked the count, surprised.

'All right, yes, I did,' Danglard admitted.

'Good. And the Calva?'

'It's perfect.'

The count dipped a lump of sugar in his drink and sucked it unconcernedly. Adamsberg felt himself momentarily besieged by lumps of sugar coming at him from all directions.

'This is what I always used to drink with Léo. I have to tell you that I loved that woman with all my heart. I married her, and my family, which contains a good number of *dratsabs*, believe me, beat me down. I was young and weak. I gave in, and we were divorced two years later. This may seem strange to you,' he went on, 'but never mind. If Léo survives her injuries from this vicious attacker, I intend to marry her again. I had decided and she had accepted. And that's where you come in, commissaire.'

'To catch the killer.'

'No, to bring Léo back to life. Don't go thinking this wedding is just an old man's fancy. I've been thinking about it for over a year. I was hoping to bring my stepson round to it, but nothing doing. So I'll just have to go ahead without his blessing.'

The count stood up with some difficulty, walked with the stick to the huge fireplace and threw on a couple of large logs. The old man was still strong, and determined enough to decide on this marriage of two near-nonagenarians, over sixty years after their first marriage.

'You don't find this idea shocking?' he said, rejoining them.

'On the contrary,' said Adamsberg, 'I'll willingly come to the wedding if you invite me.'

'You certainly will, commissaire, if you can bring her back from where she is. And you will do it. Léo telephoned me an hour before the attack, she was delighted with the evening you spent at her place and her opinion's good enough for me. There must be some fate operating, if you'll forgive this rather simple-minded idea. We who live near the Chemin de Bonneval are all a bit inclined to believe in fate. You and you alone managed to rescue her from speechlessness, got her to speak.'

'Only three words.'

'Yes, I heard. How long had you been at her bedside?'

'Getting on for two hours, I think.'

'Two hours, talking to her, combing her hair, stroking her cheek. I know all about it. What I'm asking you to do is be there ten hours a day, fifteen if necessary. Until you can bring her back up to you. I'm sure you can do it, Commissaire Adamsberg.'

The count paused and his gaze wandered round the walls of the room.

'If you can, I'll give you this,' he said, pointing carelessly with his cane towards a little picture near the door. 'It's made for you.'

Danglard gave a start and looked at the canvas. It showed an elegant knight posed in front of a mountain landscape.

'Take a closer look, Commandant Danglard,' said Valleray. 'Do you recognise where it is, Adamsberg?'

'I think that's the summit of the Gourgs Blancs.'

'Precisely. Not far from your own stamping ground, if I'm not much mistaken.'

'You're well informed about me.'

'Obviously. When I need to find something out, I usually manage it. The remains of ancient privileges, but still quite effective. I also know that you're going after the Clermont-Brasseur family.'

'No, monsieur le comte. Nobody is "going after" the Clermont-Brasseurs, not me nor anyone else.'

'Late sixteenth century?' Danglard asked, as he peered at the painting.

'School of François Clouet?' he added, lowering his voice, and sounding less confident.

'Yes, or if we indulge in a little wishful thinking, by the master himself, a break from his usual work as a portraitist. Of course, we don't know for certain that he ever travelled to the Pyrenees. But he did do a portrait of Jeanne d'Albret, Queen of Navarre in 1570, possibly in her own city of Pau.'

Danglard came back to sit down, awed, his glass empty. The picture was a real rarity and worth a fortune, though Adamsberg seemed unaware of that.

'Help yourself, commandant. It's an effort for me to get up. And you can refill my glass too, if you will. It isn't often that such hopes enter my house.'

Adamsberg wasn't looking at the picture, nor at Danglard or Valleray. He was thinking of that word *mechanism*, which had suddenly swum up out of the seabed and had bumped up against Dr Turbot and the young man made of clay and the remembrance of Martin's fingers applying the mixture to his brother's skin.

'I can't do it,' he said. 'I don't have the gift.'

'Yes, you do,' the count insisted, banging his stick on the polished parquet floor, and realising that Adamsberg's expression, which he had already thought absent-minded, seemed to have drifted off into the distance.

'No, I can't,' Adamsberg repeated in an absent voice. 'I've got an investigation to conduct.'

'I'll talk to your superiors. You can't let Léo go now.'

'No, I can't.'

'Then what can we do?'

'*I* can't, but there is someone who can. Léo's alive, she's conscious, but the whole mechanism has seized up. I do know someone who can fix this kind of breakdown, the kind that has no name.'

'Some sort of quack?' said Valleray, raising his hoary eyebrows.

'A scientist. But he practises his science with inhuman talent. He can get people's circuits moving again, reoxygenate the brain, he can fix kittens who won't feed, and he can unblock lungs that have solidified. He's a genius. I think he's our only hope, monsieur le comte.'

'Valleray.'

'Our only hope, Valleray. He might be able to pull her out of this. But I can't make any promises.'

'How does he operate? With drugs?'

'With his hands.'

'Sort of magnetism?'

'No, he presses on the levers, he gets the organs to slip back into place, he works the handles, unblocks filters, he gets the mechanism working again.'

'Well, get him here,' said the count.

Adamsberg was pacing round the room, making the old parquet creak and shaking his head.

'That's the problem,' he said. 'I can't.'

'He's abroad?'

'No, he's in prison.'

'Good Lord!'

'We'd have to get special permission for him to be let out.'

'And who would grant that?'

'The judge in charge of prisoners serving sentences. In the case of our doctor, it's a judge called Varnier, a stubborn old goat who wouldn't even hear of it. Getting a prisoner out of Fleury jail just so that he can treat an elderly lady in Ordebec isn't the kind of emergency the judge would recognise.'

'Raymond de Varnier?'

'Yes,' said Adamsberg, still pacing the library and without glancing at the School of Clouet painting.

'No problem, he's a friend of mine.'

Adamsberg turned towards Valleray, who was now smiling with raised eyebrows.

'Raymond de Varnier can't refuse me anything. We'll get your expert out.'

'You'll have to have a cast-iron, genuine and verifiable reason.'

'Since when have judges needed that kind of thing? Not since St Louis.

185

Just give me the name of this doctor, and the place he's being kept. I'll call Varnier first thing in the morning and we'll have your man here by tomorrow night.'

Adamsberg looked at Danglard, who nodded approvingly. Adamsberg was kicking himself for not having thought of this earlier. As soon as he had heard Dr Turbot speak irreverently about Léo as a mechanism that had broken down, he ought to have thought of the doctor, currently in prison, who had used the same expression. Perhaps he had thought of him, but without realising it. Not even when Lina had repeated the word 'mechanism'. But it had stirred him enough to make him write it on his paper napkin. The count held out a notebook and he wrote down the details.

'There's another obstacle,' Adamsberg said as he handed it back. 'If I get into any trouble, they won't let our protégé out again. But for the doctor to bring her back to consciousness, he'll no doubt need several sessions. And I could be pulled off the job four days from now.'

'I know about that.'

'Do you know everything?'

'I know a lot about you. I'm afraid for Léo and I'm afraid for the Vendermots. You arrived, I made enquiries. I know that you're going to be in big trouble if you don't catch Antoine Clermont-Brasseur's killer, who got away from your headquarters, and worse still from your very office when you were supposed to be in charge of him.'

'Exactly.'

'You're under suspicion yourself, commissaire, did you know that?'

'No.'

'Well, best to be on your guard. There are some gentlemen in the Ministry who are keen to launch an inquiry into your own actions. They're not far off thinking you actually let the young man go.'

'That wouldn't make sense.'

'Of course not,' said Valleray with a smile. 'But for now, this man is missing. And you're nosing into the affairs of the Clermont-Brasseur family.'

'There's no access there, Valleray. I can't go nosing about.'

'But you did want to question the two sons, Christian and Christophe?'

'I was refused permission. And that was that.'

'But you don't like that.'

The count put the rest of his sugar lump on a saucer, licked his fingers and wiped them on his blue jacket.

'So what was it exactly that you wanted to find out? About the Clermonts.'

'How the evening had proceeded before the fire. And what sort of mood the sons were in.'

'Normal, quite jolly, if you can ever call Christophe jolly. Plenty of champagne, the best.'

'How do you know?'

'I was there.'

Valleray took another sugar lump and dipped it carefully in his glass.

'In this world there exists a small atomic nucleus in which industrialists are always on the lookout for aristocrats and vice versa. The exchanges between them, which can be marital, increase the potential energy of the whole. I belong to both circles, industry and nobility.'

'I know you sold your steelworks to Antoine Clermont.'

'Our friend Émeri told you that, did he?'

'Yes.'

'Antoine was a thoroughgoing predator. He operated in the stratosphere, but you had to admire him in a way. You can't say the same for his sons. But if you've got it into your head that one of them set fire to their father, you're barking up the wrong tree.'

'Antoine was intending to marry his housekeeper.'

'Rose, yes,' the count agreed, sucking on his sugar lump. 'I think it was more that he wanted to provoke the family, and I'd warned him about it. It was just that it got on his nerves, seeing in his sons' eyes that they were eagerly waiting for him to die. For some time he'd been feeling wounded, depressed, and given to erratic behaviour.'

'Which of them wanted to get power of attorney?'

'Christian mostly. But he would never have managed it. Antoine was of perfectly sound mind, as could easily be established.'

'And then, providentially, along comes some youth, who sets fire to the Mercedes, just when Antoine was sitting in it alone.'

'I can see that bothers you. Do you want to know why Antoine was alone?'

'Yes, I would indeed. And why the chauffeur wasn't driving them.'

'The chauffeur had been invited into the kitchens during the reception and Christophe decided he was too drunk to drive. So he left with his father, and they walked to the car, which was parked in the rue Henri-Barbusse. Then just as he had taken the wheel, he realised he'd lost his mobile phone. So he asked his father to wait while he retraced their steps. He found the phone on the pavement in the rue du Val-de-Grâce. When he came back round the corner, he saw the car was on fire. Believe me, Adamsberg, Christophe was a couple of hundred metres away from the Mercedes and two witnesses saw him. He shouted and started to run, and the witnesses ran with him. It was Christophe who called the police.'

'Did he tell you that?'

'No, his wife did. We know each other very well – I introduced her to her husband. Christophe was devastated. Horrified. However bad your relationship, it's no joke to see your father burnt to death.'

'No, I understand,' said Adamsberg. 'What about Christian?'

'Christian had left the party earlier, he'd had a lot to drink and wanted to go to bed.'

'But apparently he only *reached* home very late.'

The count scratched his bald head for a moment.

'It's not giving away any secrets to say that Christian is seeing another woman, well, more than one, actually, and that he takes advantage of official functions to come home late. And I have to tell you again, both the brothers were in a good mood that evening. Christian was dancing, he gave an excellent imitation of the Baron de Salvin, and Christophe, who doesn't easily relax, was frankly enjoying himself for a few moments.'

'So everything was fine, a perfectly normal party.'

'Perfectly. Look, on the mantelpiece over there, you'll find an envelope with a dozen photos of the evening, which Christophe's wife sent me. She doesn't understand that at my age one has no interest in seeing photographs of oneself. Take a look, it'll give you an idea of the atmosphere.'

Adamsberg examined the ten or so photos, and indeed neither Christian nor Christophe had the tense expression of someone who was about to burn his father to death.

'OK. I see,' said Adamsberg, offering back the photos.

'Keep them, if they'd help convince you. And hurry up and find this young man. What *I* can quite easily do is plead with the Clermont brothers to get an extension of the deadline.'

'I think that's essential,' said Danglard suddenly: he had been walking from one picture to another, like a wasp torn between several drops of jam. 'That young Mohamed has got clean away.'

'He'll need money sooner or later,' said Adamsberg with a shrug. 'He didn't have anything in his pockets. His friends will only be able to help him for so long.'

'Yes. Help always lasts only so long,' murmured Danglard, 'while cowardice lasts for ever. That's the general principle we apply – you'll always catch runaways in the end. On condition you don't have the Ministry dangling a sword of Damocles over your head. It tends to hamper progress.'

'I understand,' said Valleray with a laugh. 'So we'll try and get the sword removed.'

As if, thought Danglard wryly, being himself the son of a miner from northern France, as if it were a mere matter of pushing a chair out of the way, the better to move about. He had no doubt the count would manage it.

XXV

VEYRENC WAS WAITING FOR THEM WITH ZERK, IN FRONT OF THE door to Léo's house. It was a warm evening, and the clouds had finally moved away to shed their rain somewhere else. The two men had taken chairs outside and were smoking in the darkness. Veyrenc looked calm enough but Adamsberg didn't feel reassured. The lieutenant's Roman face, round, solid and comfortable-looking, softly contoured without any sharp outlines, was a compact mass of resolution and obstinacy. Danglard shook hands briefly and vanished inside the house. It was past 1 a.m.

'Let's go for a stroll in the fields,' suggested Veyrenc. 'Leave your phones behind.'

'Want to see some cows move?' asked Adamsberg, taking a cigarette from him. 'You know, here, unlike back home, the cows hardly budge at all.'

Veyrenc signed to Zerk to accompany them and waited until they were some distance from the house, before stopping at the gate to a field.

'There's been a new summons from the Ministry that I didn't like the sound of.'

'What didn't you like?'

'The tone. Very aggressive, because Mo hasn't been traced. He's got no money, his photo is up all over the place, so where could he have gone? That's what they're saying.'

'Aggressive, well, they've been that all along. So what else about the tone?'

'A certain sarcasm. The guy who called didn't seem very subtle. In his voice you could hear that he was so proud of knowing something that he couldn't hide it.'

'For instance?'

'For instance, something they've got on you. I don't have much to go on, to explain the sarcasm, the secret gloating I was hearing, but I got the distinct impression that they've been dreaming up a scenario.'

Adamsberg held out his hand to ask for a light.

'Something you've been dreaming up too?'

'That's not what matters. All I know is that your son came down here, in a second car. And they know that too, you can be sure.'

'Zerk is doing a photo feature about leaf mould for a Swedish magazine.'

'Yes. That's unusual.'

'That's the way he is, impulsive, he seizes opportunities.'

'No, Jean-Baptiste, that isn't how Armel is. I didn't see the pigeon in your house. Where is it?'

'Flown away.'

'Good. But why did Zerk come in a separate car? Wasn't there room in your boot for three suitcases?'

'So what are you trying to do, Louis?'

'I'm trying to convince you that they have come up with some kind of scenario.'

'And you think they *have*.'

'For example, that Mo disappeared like magic. That too many pigeons have flown the coop. I think Danglard knows. He's not that good at hiding things. Since Mo escaped, he's been like a worried hen sitting on an ostrich egg.'

'You've got too much imagination. You think I'm capable of doing something as daft as that?'

'Absolutely. I didn't say it was daft, by the way.'

'Come on, Louis, get it off your chest.'

'I don't think it'll be long before they're descending on you here. I've no idea where you've put Mo, but I think he should probably leave tonight. As soon and as far away as possible.'

'But how? If you or I or Danglard were to leave, it would be obvious, we'd be spotted in an hour.'

'Your son,' said Veyrenc, looking at Zerk.

'You don't think I'm going to get him mixed up in this, do you, Louis?'

'He already is.'

'No, there's no evidence of that. But if they find him driving a car with Mo inside, he'll go straight to jail. If you're right, we're just going to have to sacrifice Mo. We'll send him off about a hundred kilometres from here, and he'll allow himself to be caught.'

'You said yourself – once the examining magistrate gets his claws into him, he'll never get out. He's being framed.'

'So what's the solution?'

'Zerk must leave tonight. There are fewer roadblocks at night. And most of them aren't serious. The guys are tired.'

'I'm up for it,' said Zerk. 'No, don't stop me,' he insisted, pulling Adamsberg's arm, 'I'll take him. But where, Louis?'

'You know the Pyrenees as well as we do, you know the crossing points into Spain. Head for Granada.'

'Then what?'

'Hole up there and wait for instructions. I've got the names of a few hotels. I've also brought two number plates for the car, insurance, some money, two ID cards and a credit card. When you've got some distance from here, go off the road somewhere and get Mo to cut his hair so he looks more respectable.'

'That's proof enough he didn't torch the Merc,' said Zerk. 'His hair's quite long at the moment.'

'So what?' asked Adamsberg.

'Well, he told me, when he's torched a car, his hair always gets singed, so he shaves his head afterwards for it not to show. His mates call him Skinhead Mo.'

'All right, Armel,' said Veyrenc, 'but we've got to get a move on. Where've you put him? Is it far?'

'Three kilometres,' said Adamsberg, who was feeling dazed. 'Two through the woods.'

'We should get moving right away. While the boys pack up, you and I can change the plates and wipe off any prints.'

'Just when he was taking to drawing,' said Zerk.

'And just when it looks as though the Clermont brothers are off the hook,' added Adamsberg, treading out his cigarette.

'What about the pigeon?' asked Zerk suddenly in alarm.

'What do you mean, what about him? You're taking him to Granada.'

'No, the actual pigeon, Hellebaud.'

'Leave him here with us. It'll make you look suspicious.'

'He still needs antiseptic on his feet every couple of days. Promise me you'll do it, promise me you'll remember.'

It was almost four in the morning as Adamsberg and Veyrenc watched the rear lights of the car fade away. The pigeon was cooing gently in its cage at their feet. Adamsberg had filled a Thermos of coffee for his son.

'I hope you haven't sent him off for no good reason,' he said quietly. 'And I hope you haven't sent him straight into a trap. They're going to have to drive all night and all tomorrow. They're going to be exhausted.'

'You're worrying about Armel?'

'Yes.'

'He'll manage. *The project's audacious, of his courage a test / But your brave-hearted son with good luck will be blessed.*'

'Why did they get suspicious about Mo?'

'You went at it too fast. Well played, yes, but too quick off the mark.'

'Not enough time, no choice.'

'I know. But you played it too much as a lone star as well. *All alone without help, how could you see it through? / Call first on your comrades, they were all there for you.* You should have called me.'

XXVI

LATE THAT NIGHT AND EARLY NEXT MORNING, THE COUNT WENT into action to impressive effect, indicating how strongly he cared for his dear Léone: the doctor arrived discreetly at Ordebec hospital at eleven thirty. Valleray had woken the elderly judge at 6 a.m., issued his orders, and the gates of Fleury prison had opened at nine to let out a convoy escorting the prisoner to Normandy.

The two unmarked cars drove into the staff car park, out of sight of passers-by. Surrounded by four men, the doctor got out, wearing hand-cuffs, but with a satisfied and even jovial air, which reassured Adamsberg. He had still heard nothing from Zerk, and not a word from Retancourt. For once, he thought his Retancourt torpedo must have been disarmed and was inoperable. And that might confirm the count's theory. If Retancourt didn't find anything, that meant there was nothing to find. Apart from the fact that Christian had come home late – the only thing he could now hang on to – there was no reason to suspect either of the Clermont brothers.

The doctor came towards him with his usual mincing gait, looking spruce and well dressed. He hadn't lost an ounce of weight in prison, indeed it seemed that he had even put some on.

'Thank you for arranging this little excursion, Adamsberg,' he said, as they shook hands. 'Very refreshing to see the countryside. But please don't use my real name in front of these people. I want to preserve my reputation.'

'What are we to call you then? Dr Hellebaud perhaps?'

'Very well. And how is your tinnitus? Come back, no doubt. As I recall, you only had two sessions.'

'Gone, doctor. Just a bit of a whistle in the left ear.'

'Capital. I'll fix it before I go away again with these gentlemen. And the kitten?'

'She'll be weaned soon. And how is prison life, doctor? I haven't had time to visit you since your sentence.'

'What can I say, *mon ami*? I'm up to my ears in work. I have to treat the governor – very long-standing back trouble; the prisoners – who suffer from depression and childhood traumas of every kind, quite fascinating cases, I confess. And the warders – a lot of them are addicts or suffer from repressed instincts of violence. I only see five patients a day, I've been very firm about that. I don't accept payment of course, I'm not allowed to. But you know how it is, I get plenty of compensation. Nice cell, special treatment, good food, all the books I want, I can't complain. So with all my cases, I'm writing a book that's going to be a rather remarkable study of prison trauma. Now tell me about our patient here. What happened to her? What have they diagnosed?'

Adamsberg spent about a quarter of an hour briefing the doctor in the basement, then they went to the first floor where a reception committee was waiting outside Léone's room: Capitaine Émeri, Dr Turbot, the Comte de Valleray and Lina Vendermot. Adamsberg introduced them to 'Dr Paul Hellebaud' and one of the guards removed the handcuffs with respectful care.

'This guard,' the doctor whispered to Adamsberg, 'thinks I saved his life. He'd become impotent. Poor lad was devastated. He brings me my coffee in bed every morning now. Who's that scrumptious woman, good enough to eat?'

'Lina Vendermot. She's the one who started it all, causing the first murder.'

'A killer?' the doctor asked with a surprised and disapproving air.

'We don't know that. She had this deadly vision, she told people about it, and everything started after that.'

'What kind of vision?'

'It's an old local legend, about a cavalcade of ghostly riders that have been coming through here for centuries. They're dead, but they carry with them living people who have sinned.'

'Ah, do you mean Hellequin's Horde?' the doctor asked, looking alert.

'Yes indeed. Do you know about them?'

'Who doesn't, *mon ami*? So Lord Hellequin comes galloping in these parts, does he?'

'Three kilometres from here.'

'What a fantastic place to find myself,' said the doctor appreciatively, rubbing his hands, a gesture that reminded Adamsberg of the time the doctor had once served him some excellent wine.

'And the old lady was caught up in the cavalcade?'

'No, no, but we think that she knew something.'

When the doctor went across to the bed and looked down at Léone, still lying there cold and white, his smile abruptly vanished and Adamsberg brushed away the bubble of electricity that had returned.

'Something bitten you?' the doctor whispered, without taking his eyes off Léone, as if he were inspecting a programme of works.

'Nothing, a little bubble of electricity that comes now and then.'

'No such thing,' said the doctor dismissively. 'We'll look into that later. The old lady's case is more touch and go.'

He asked the four guards to stand back against the wall and not to speak. Dr Turbot was enhancing his reputation as a *dratsab* by his super-cilious and suspicious smile. Émeri was virtually standing to attention as if under review by the Emperor, and the count, for whom a chair had been brought, was clasping his hands together to stop them trembling. Lina stood behind him. Adamsberg felt his mobile vibrate, clandestine phone number two, and glanced at the text message. *They are here. Searching Léo's. LVB*. He showed the message discreetly to Danglard. Let them search, he thought, sending a grateful thanks to Lieutenant Veyrenc.

The doctor had put his large hands on Léo's cranium, and seemed to be listening for a long time, then he moved to the neck and chest. He went round the bed, without speaking and felt her thin feet, massaging and manipulating them, stopping and starting for a few minutes. Then he came towards Adamsberg.

'The whole mechanism's stalled, Adamsberg. The fuses have blown, the circuits are disconnected, the mediastinal and encephalic fascias are blocked, the brain's under-oxygenated, the breathing is decompressed, and the digestive system is in stasis. How old is she?'

Adamsberg heard the count's breathing come more quickly.

'Eighty-eight.'

'Right. I'll have to do a first session of forty-five minutes or so. And another, shorter one at about 5 p.m. Is that all right, René?' he asked, turning to the senior guard. The formerly impotent guard nodded immediately, with total veneration in his eyes.

'If she responds to the treatment, I'll need to return in a fortnight to stabilise her.'

'That won't be a problem,' said the count, in a strained voice.

'Now if you will all be good enough to leave the room, I should like to be alone with the patient. Dr Turbot can stay if he wishes, provided he can control his sarcastic expression. Or I might ask him to leave too.'

The four guards consulted each other, checked the imperious look from Valleray and the doubt on Émeri's face, and in the end, René, the senior one, gave his agreement.

'But we'll be outside the door, doctor.'

'Naturally, René, that goes without saying. Besides, if I'm not mistaken, there are two CCTV cameras in the room.'

'That's correct,' said Émeri. 'For her protection.'

'So I'm not going to fly away. I have no intention of doing so anyway, because it's a fascinating case. Everything is functioning, but nothing is working. Unquestionably the effect of terror, which through an unconscious survival reflex has paralysed all her functions. She doesn't want to relive the attack, she doesn't want to have to come back and face it. You may deduce from that, commissaire, that she may know her assailant and that the knowledge is intolerable. She's taken flight, very far away, too far away.'

Two of the guards took up position outside the door, the other two went into the courtyard to stand under the window. The count, limping on his stick into the corridor, took Adamsberg by the elbow.

'He's going to treat her just with his fingers?'

'Yes, Valleray, I told you.'

'My god.'

The count looked at his watch.

'Only seven minutes so far, Valleray.'

'Can't you go in and see how it's going?'

'When Dr Hellebaud is on a difficult case, he works so intensely that he comes out dripping with sweat. We can't disturb him.'

'I understand. You haven't asked how I moved the sword.'

'The sword?'

'The sword of Damocles the Ministry was dangling over your head.'

'Tell me.'

'It wasn't easy to convince Antoine's sons. But it came through in the end. You've got one more week to catch your Mohamed.'

'Thank you, Valleray.'

'But the minister's private secretary sounded a bit strange. When he agreed, he added, "That is, if they don't find him today." About Mohamed. As if he was laughing. Do they have some information about him?'

Adamsberg felt the bubble of electricity sting his neck more intensely than ever. No such thing, the doctor had told him, it doesn't exist.

'I haven't been informed,' he said.

'Are they running a parallel search behind your back or something?'

'No idea, Valleray.'

By now the special team of undercover agents from the Ministry would have finished searching everywhere he had been since he arrived in Ordebec. Léo's guest house, the Vendermot house – Adamsberg hoped that Hippolyte would have addressed them entirely in backwards-speak – and the gendarmerie – and here he hoped with all his might that Fleg had gone for them. It was very unlikely that they would have visited Herbier's house, but an abandoned building would always interest police doing a search. He ran through the precautions he and Veyrenc had taken: wiping off all fingerprints, washing the dishes in boiling water, sheets off the bed and the two young ones told to dispose of them once they were well away from Ordebec – and the wax seals replaced. The only thing left was the pigeon's droppings, which they had cleaned off as best they could, but some stains remained. He had asked Veyrenc if he knew the secret of this phenomenal lasting power of bird droppings, but Veyrenc knew as little as he did about it.

XXVII

THE TWO YOUNG MEN HAD TAKEN TURNS, THROUGH THE NIGHT, one driving while the other slept. Mo now had much shorter hair and was sporting glasses and an improvised moustache, a hasty but reassuring change, in order to look more like the photo Veyrenc had glued on the false papers. Fascinated by his new ID, Mo kept turning it over, admiring it and saying that the cops were way better at getting round the law than his gang of amateurs in the Cité des Buttes. Zerk had plotted their route to avoid motorway tolls, and they met their first roadblock on the Saumur bypass.

'Pretend to be asleep, Mo,' Zerk hissed through his teeth. 'When we stop, I'll wake you, you faff about in your pocket, pull out the ID. Try to look like you're dozy and not very bright. Think of something simple, like Hellebaud, just concentrate on him.'

'Or the cows?' whispered Mo anxiously.

'Yeah, and don't say anything, just shake your head as if you're still sleepy.'

Two gendarmes approached the car slowly, looking bored rigid and pleased to have something to break the monotony. One of them went round the car with his torch, the other flashed his rapidly across the youngsters' faces, as he looked at their papers.

'New plates, eh?' he said.

'Yes, sir,' said Zerk. 'I put 'em on a fortnight ago.'

'Seven-year-old car, new plates?'

'That was in Paris, officer,' Zerk explained. 'Plates were knocked in, front and back, had to change 'em.'

'Why, weren't they readable any more?'

'Yeah, but you know what it's like, Paris, if your plates are fucked up, they just think they can, like, bash your car any time they park.'

'You're not from Paris then?'

'O-oh no. Pyrenees, us.'

'Ha, better than Paris, anyway,' said the gendarme with a hint of a smile as he handed back their papers.

They drove in silence for a few minutes, letting their heartbeats settle down.

'Hey, you were ace,' said Mo. 'I could never have done that.'

'We'd better stop and rearrange the plates a bit. Kick 'em a few times.'

'Put on some soot from the exhaust.'

'We'll grab a bite same time. Put your ID in your back pocket, so it gets a bit distressed. Looks too new.'

At 11 a.m. they met a second roadblock at Angoulême. At four in the afternoon, Zerk stopped the car on a mountain road near Laruns.

'Let's take an hour to rest here, Mo. But no more. Got to get across now.'

'This is the frontier?'

'Practically. We'll get into Spain at this crossing point, Les Socques. And then, know what we'll do? We'll eat like kings at the cafe in Hoz de Jaca. We'll stay at Berdún and tomorrow Granada, another twelve hours on the road.'

'Get a shower, too? We both stink.'

'Yeah, we do, and two guys who stink get noticed.'

'Your dad's going to be in big trouble. All because of me. What'll he do?'

'Dunno,' said Zerk, between gulps of water from a bottle. 'I don't really know him.'

'What?' said Mo, grabbing the bottle.

'He only found me couple of months ago.'

'He found you? Adopted you? But you look like him.'

'No, I said he *found* me, when I was twenty-eight. Before that he didn't know I existed.'

'Shit, man,' said Mo, rubbing his cheeks. 'My dad's the opposite. He knew fine I existed but he didn't want to know.'

'Nor did mine. I found him first. Fathers. Complicated.'

'We better get some sleep.'

Mo had the impression that Zerk's voice had cracked. Maybe talking about his dad. Maybe just from exhaustion. The two young men bumped up against each other trying to find a comfortable position to sleep.

'Zerk.'

'Yeah?'

'There's one little thing I could do for your dad, make it up to him.'

'Find whoever killed Clermont?'

'No, find whoever tied the pigeon's feet.'

'Some little toerag.'

'Yeah.'

'It'd really be something. But you can't do that.'

'In your house, the basket you brought Hellebaud in?'

'Yeah?' said Zerk, sitting up.

'There was this string in it, been round his legs.'

'Yeah, my dad kept it, to get it analysed. What about it?'

'Well, it's string from off a diabolo.'

Zerk sat up properly, lit a cigarette, gave one to Mo and opened the car window.

'How d'you know?'

'You use special string. If you don't, it gets worn out, it frays, and the diabolo won't work properly.'

'Like a yo-yo or what?'

'No, no, no. Because the diabolo wears out the string in the middle, it can even break, so you need this special strong nylon string.'

'So?'

'You can't get it in just any shop, you have to go to a diabolo store. And there's not that many in Paris.'

'Well,' said Zerk, after a moment's thought, 'I don't see you finding whoever tortured our pigeon by watching people going in and out the shops.'

'No, there's a way,' Mo insisted. 'It wasn't professional string. I don't think it was heart-woven.'

'*What?*' said Zerk.

'Reinforced centre – real pros have this very pricey string. You get it in rolls of ten metres, twenty metres, whatever. But this wasn't like that. It was just the kind you get in a kit, with a diabolo and sticks.'

'I'm still not with you, Mo.'

'It didn't look to me like it was worn at all. But maybe the guys that work with your dad, they could look at it with a magnifier?'

'Microscope probably,' said Zerk. 'But anyway, what if it *was* new?'

'Well, why would a kid use the string from his new diabolo set? Why doesn't he just take some string from round the house?'

'Because he's got plenty of it?'

'*Yeah,* see? His dad runs the shop. So he takes some string off of a big roll, and of course he doesn't take the expensive stuff. So his dad's maybe a dealer, sells string to people who make the kits? So there, you're talking, can't be many of them in Paris. Most likely near your dad's office, because Hellebaud couldn't walk after that, could he?'

Zerk was smoking with his eyes half closed, looking at Mo.

'You must've been thinking a lot to come up with that,' he observed.

'Nothing else to do when I was in that house. But you think it's rubbish?'

'No, I think if we could get on the Internet, we'd soon get a name and address for the little bastard.'

'But we can't, it's too big a risk.'

'Yeah, we could be on the run for ages. Unless you can find whoever tied *your* legs.'

'It's not a fair fight, is it? These Clermonts, it's like we're taking on the whole country.'

'Quite a few countries, probably.'

XXVIII

IN THE HOSPITAL CORRIDOR, ANXIETY HAD REPLACED INSTINCTIVE politeness, and nobody spoke a word. Lina shivered, her shawl slipped off again and fell to the floor. Danglard was quicker than Adamsberg. With two of his clumsy steps, he was behind her, replacing the shawl with old-fashioned fussiness.

Irradiated, thought Adamsberg, while Émeri, blond eyebrows locked in a frown, looked disapproving. All of us irradiated, Adamsberg concluded. All putty in her hands, she can say what she likes, catch whoever she wants. Then everyone's eyes once more turned to keep watch on the closed door of Léo's room, hoping for the handle to turn, as if waiting for the curtain to rise on an exceptional show. They all stood as still as cows in the fields.

'There we are, engine's turning over again,' said the doctor simply, as he emerged from the room.

He pulled a large white handkerchief from his pocket and mopped his brow methodically, still holding the door back.

'*You* can go in,' he said to the count, 'but don't say a word. And don't try to get her to talk either. Not for another two weeks. She needs all that time to come to terms with things, she absolutely mustn't be rushed, or she'll go back into the dark again. If I have your solemn word, all of you can look at her.'

The heads nodded together.

'But who will see that you all do what I ask?' the doctor insisted.

'I will,' said Dr Turbot, whom nobody had noticed as he followed Hellebaud out, looking somewhat dazed and overcome.

'Very well, my dear colleague, I'll take your word for it. You'll have to accompany any visitor or see that they are accompanied. Or I'll hold you responsible for any relapse.'

'Trust me, I'm a doctor. I won't let anyone interfere with this cure.'

Hellebaud nodded and let the count approach the bed. Danglard was supporting his trembling arm. Valleray stopped still, open-mouthed as he saw Léo with colour in her cheeks, breathing regularly and able to greet him with a smile and a meaningful look. He stroked the old woman's hands, which were now warm again. Turning to the doctor to thank him, or to express his veneration, he suddenly collapsed on to Danglard's arm.

'Look out,' said Hellebaud, pulling a face. 'He's had a shock, it's given him a bit of a turn. Sit him down, take off his shirt and check his feet – are they going blue?'

Valleray allowed himself to be moved on to a chair, but Danglard had trouble getting his shirt off. In his confusion, the count was resisting as forcefully as he could, apparently refusing absolutely to be stripped and humiliated in a hospital room.

'He always hates being undressed,' Dr Turbot commented laconically. 'I've seen him act like that once before, up at the chateau.'

'Does he often get attacks like this?' asked Adamsberg.

'No, the last time was a year ago. Just stress, it's not too serious. He's more alarmed than ill. Why do you ask, commissaire?'

'For Léo's sake.'

'Don't worry, he's as tough as old boots, she'll have him for a few years yet.'

XXIX

JUST THEN, CAPITAINE ÉMERI, LOOKING DEEPLY ALARMED, CAME into the room and shook Adamsberg's elbow.

'Mortembot has just found his cousin Glayeux dead. Murdered!'

'What? When?'

'Last night apparently. The police doctor's on the way. And you haven't heard the worst – his skull was split open. With an axe. The murderer is returning to his original method.'

'Are you thinking of the Vendermots' father?'

'Obviously, it must have started everything. A brute creates brutality all round him.'

'But you weren't even living here when that happened.'

'Doesn't matter. Ask yourself why nobody was ever arrested for that at the time. Or why perhaps somebody didn't *want* anyone arrested.'

'Who do you mean by "somebody"?'

'Round here, Adamsberg,' Émeri said in a strained whisper, while Danglard escorted the count out of the room, his shirt having been removed, 'the only real law is what the Comte de Valleray d'Ordebec wants. He has the right of life and death on his estate and far beyond, if only you knew.'

Adamsberg hesitated, remembering the orders he had received the previous night at the chateau.

'Look at the facts,' Émeri said. 'He needs your prisoner to treat Léo? He gets him. You need an extension for the investigation? He gets that too.'

'How did you know I've got an extension?'

'He told me himself. He likes you to know how far his writ runs.'

'But who would he have been protecting?'

'It was always thought one of the kids had killed the father. They found Lina wiping the axe.'

'She hasn't denied that.'

'She couldn't, it was all stated at the inquest. But she might have been wiping it to protect Hippo. You know what his father had done to him?'

'Yes, the fingers.'

'Hacked off with an axe. But Valleray could have decided to kill the monster himself, to protect the kids. What if Herbier knew that? And what if he decided to blackmail Valleray?'

'What, thirty years later?'

'He could have been doing it for years.'

'But what's that got to do with Glayeux?'

'Just a bit of local colour to cover his tracks.'

'But you're suggesting that Lina and Valleray are in league. She announces that the Riders have come through, so that Valleray can get rid of Herbier. And all the others, Mortembot, Glayeux, whoever, are red herrings to get you chasing after some local maniac who believes in the Hellequin cavalcade and is carrying out His Lordship's wishes.'

'Well, it fits, doesn't it?'

'Possibly, Émeri. But I'm inclined to think that there *is* a maniac out there, someone who takes the Riders seriously. Either one of those seen with them who's trying to save his skin, or someone who thinks they might be a victim in future and is trying to win favour from Hellequin by serving him.'

'What makes you think that?'

'I don't know,' Adamsberg admitted.

'It's because you just don't know the people round here. What did the count offer you if you could cure Léo? A work of art perhaps? Don't hold your breath. He does it all the time. And why is he moving heaven and earth to get her treated?'

'Because he's fond of her, Émeri, you know that.'

'Or to find out what she knows?'

'Christ, Émeri, he almost fainted just now. He wants to *marry* her if she survives.'

'That would be convenient, wouldn't it? A wife's testimony couldn't be taken in a court of law.'

'Make up your mind, Émeri, whether you suspect Valleray or the Vendermots.'

'Vendermot, Valleray, Léo – they're all part of the same gang. The Vendermot father and Herbier were the diabolical side of it. The count and the children are the seemingly innocent side. But if you mix the two you get a damned unpredictable mixture, with some clay thrown in.'

XXX

'HE MUST HAVE BEEN ATTACKED LAST NIGHT AT ABOUT MIDNIGHT,'
reported Dr Chazy, the pathologist. 'Two blows from the axe. But the first
was the one that did the damage.'

Glayeux's body, fully clothed, was stretched out in his office. His head
had been split open with two blows, and blood had drenched the carpet,
the table and some preliminary sketches he had spread out on the floor.
Through the bloodstains, it was still possible to see the head of a madonna.

'Horrible,' said Émeri, pointing to it. 'The Virgin Mary covered in blood,'
he added with disgust, as if this revolted him even more than the scene
of butchery before them.

'Lord Hellequin certainly doesn't do things by halves,' Adamsberg
murmured. 'And he wasn't even impressed by the Virgin Mary.'

'Obviously,' said Émeri gloomily. 'Glayeux had a commission in hand
for the church in Saint-Aubin. He always worked late. The killer must
have come in, whoever it was, man or woman, they knew each other.
Glayeux asked them inside. If the killer attacked him with an axe, they
must have been wearing a waterproof of some kind. That would look a
bit out of the ordinary with this heat.'

'Remember there was a threat of rain. Clouds to the west.'

From outside the door came the sound of Michel Mortembot's sobbing,
or rather his stifled cries, the kind produced by men who find it hard to
shed tears.

'He didn't cry like that when his mother died,' said Émeri maliciously.

209

'Do you know where he was yesterday?'

'He'd been in Caen for two days, with a big order of pear trees. Plenty of people will confirm that. He only got back late this morning.'

'And at midnight last night?'

'He was in this nightclub in Caen, called Shake It Up. A night out with whores and faggots, so now he's feeling guilty. When he's stopped snivelling, the brigadier will take him off to get a statement from him.'

'Émeri, calm down, getting tetchy won't solve anything. When will the SOC people get here?'

'They've got to get here from Lisieux, work it out. If only that wretched Glayeux had listened to me and at least let us keep a watch on the house.'

'OK, OK, cool it, Émeri. Is it because you feel sorry for him?'

'No, not at all, he can go to Hellequin for all I care! But what I'm seeing now is that two of the people "seized" by the Riders have been killed. Know what effect that will have in Ordebec?'

'Panic.'

'Most people wouldn't give a toss if they saw Mortembot go the same way. But we don't know the name of the fourth victim. We can protect Mortembot, but not the whole town. If I wanted to find out who's got something on their conscience, someone who's afraid they've been picked out by Hellequin, this would be the moment to keep a close watch. By seeing who seems agitated and who seems calm. Then I could make a list.'

'Wait for me,' said Adamsberg, closing his phone. 'Commandant Danglard's outside, I'm going to fetch him.'

'Can't he come in on his own?'

'I don't want him to see Glayeux.'

'Why ever not?'

'He can't stand the sight of blood.'

'And he's a *cop*?'

'Cool it, Émeri.'

'He'd have run away on a battlefield then.'

'It's not a big deal. He's not descended from a marshal. All his fore-fathers were down the pit. Just as tough, but no glory attached.'

A small crowd had gathered in front of Glayeux's house. People knew he had been one of those seen in the ghostly cavalcade, they had seen the gendarmes' car arrive, and that had been enough to spread the word. Danglard was standing at the back of the crowd, making no attempt to move forward.

'I've got Antonin with me,' he explained to Adamsberg. 'He wants to talk to you and Émeri. But he doesn't dare try to push through the crowd on his own, we need to clear a passage for him.'

'Let's go round the back,' said Adamsberg, gently taking hold of Antonin's hand. He had understood, during the home massage, that the hand was solid but the wrist was made of clay. It had to be handled with care.

'How's the count now?' Adamsberg went on.

'Back on his feet. And dressed again, furious that they removed his shirt. Dr Turbot has completely changed sides, by the way. He humbly arranged a room, and his colleague Hellebaud is this minute holding forth and having lunch with the warders. Turbot's sticking to him like a leech, he looks as if his preconceptions have been blown away by a cyclone. So what's happened to Glayeux?'

'You'd better not see him.'

Adamsberg and Danglard went round the house, protecting Antonin from each side. They met Mortembot, trudging out like a harassed ox, and being shown, quite kindly, by Brigadier Blériot towards the car. Blériot stopped the commissaire with a discreet gesture.

'The capitaine's blaming you for Glayeux's death. He's saying – pardon my language, sir – that you've done fuck all to solve the case. I'm just saying that to warn you, he can be very, erm, tetchy.'

'Yes, I saw.'

'Don't take too much notice, it'll pass.'

Antonin sat down carefully on one of the chairs in Glayeux's kitchen and placed his arms under the table.

'Lina's at work, Hippo went to buy some wood and Martin is in the forest,' he explained. 'So I came.'

'Right, we're listening,' said Adamsberg patiently.

Émeri was standing somewhat to the side, making it quite plain that he wasn't in charge of inquiries, and that Adamsberg, famous as he was, had made no more headway in the case than he had.

'People are saying that Glayeux has been killed.'

'That's right.'

'You know that Lina saw him crying for mercy in among the Riders?'

'Yes, and Mortembot, and another one we don't know.'

'Well, what I came to say is that when the Riders kill someone, they do it their own way. Not with modern weapons, I mean. Not guns. Because Hellequin didn't have those, he's too ancient.'

'That wasn't the case for Herbier.'

'All right, but perhaps it wasn't Hellequin who killed Herbier.'

'It's true for Glayeux,' admitted Adamsberg. 'He wasn't killed with a gun.'

'But was it with an axe?'

'How do you know?'

'Because our axe has disappeared. That's what I came to say.'

'Fancy that,' said Émeri with a short laugh, 'you've come all this way, fragile as you are, to tell us about the murder weapon! Very kind of you, Antonin.'

'My mother said it might help.'

'Aren't you afraid it might get you into trouble? That is, unless you think we'll find it anyway, and you prefer to get in first.'

'Cool it, Émeri,' said Adamsberg. 'Antonin, when did you notice the axe had gone?'

'This morning, but before I heard about Glayeux. I never use it, it's too dangerous for me. But I noticed it wasn't where it usually is, by the woodpile.'

'So anyone could have taken it?'

'Yes, but people don't.'

'Does it have any distinguishing marks, this axe, so we could recognise it?'

'Hippo had carved a V on the handle.'

'And you think someone else has used it so that you'll be accused?'

'That's possible, but what I mean is, that wouldn't be very clever, would it? If we had wanted to kill Glayeux, we wouldn't have used our own axe, would we?'

212

'Of course you might. Very clever,' interjected Émeri. 'It would look so stupid that nobody would believe you'd done it. Especially not you, the Vendermots, the smartest family in Ordebec.'

Antonin shrugged his shoulders cautiously.

'You don't like us, Émeri, so I'm not going to listen to you. Even if your ancestor *was* a good soldier, outnumbered or not.'

'Leave my family out of it, Antonin.'

'Well, you've got it in for *my* family, haven't you? But do you take after your ancestor? You go charging off after the first hare you see, you never look around, you never ask what other people think. Anyway, you're not in charge of the case now, so I'm talking to the commissaire from Paris.'

'Bravo,' said Émeri with his warlike grin. 'As you can see, he's been super-efficient ever since he arrived.'

'His way's not yours. It takes time, to work out what people are thinking.'

The SOC team from Lisieux was arriving, and Antonin looked up, his delicate features expressing alarm.

'Danglard will take you home, Antonin,' said Adamsberg. 'Thank you for coming to see us. Émeri, I'll see you tonight, and take up your dinner invitation, if it's still on offer. I don't like quarrelling. Not out of the good-ness of my heart, but because I find it tiring, whether justified or not.'

'All right,' said Émeri after a moment. 'My table?'

'Your table. I'll leave you with the technical team. Keep Mortembot in the cells as long as you can, say you're holding him to help with inquiries. At least in the gendarmerie he'll be safe.'

'What are you going to do? Have lunch? See someone?'

'I'm going for a walk, I need to walk.'

'You mean you're going searching for something?'

'No, just for a walk. You know that Dr Hellebaud says these bubbles of electricity don't exist.'

'Then what is it?'

'Let's have a word about it later.'

All his ill humour had vanished from the capitaine's face. Brigadier Blériot was right, it went over quite quickly, which was a rare advantage.

XXXI

ANXIETY WOULD REACH A HIGHER PITCH IN ORDEBEC NOW, FEAR would spread, people would be seeking answers and, thought Adamsberg, they were more likely to be wondering about the haunting of the area by the ghostly riders than about the failures of the Parisian commissaire. For who around here would seriously believe that a man, a mere mortal, could thwart the darts of Lord Hellequin? Nevertheless, Adamsberg chose to take a little-frequented route, to avoid meeting anyone and answering questions – although he knew Normans were not the kind to ask directly. But they made up for that with long stares or heavy insinuations that stabbed you in the back, and forced you in the end to tackle the question head-on.

Under a scorching sun, he went round the edge of Ordebec, past the pond with its dragonflies, cut through the wood of the Petites Alindes, and headed for the Chemin de Bonneval. There was no risk of meeting anyone on this cursed path in present circumstances. He ought to have come here before and walked the length of it. Because it was here and here alone that Léo must have discovered or realised something. But he had had to deal with Mo, with the Clermont-Brasseurs, with Retancourt going under cover, with Léo's coma, the count's commands, and he hadn't acted fast enough. It was also possible that a certain fatalism had got to work on him, causing him to blame everything on Lord Hellequin instead of looking for the real-life man, the mortal, who went round killing people with an axe. There was no news from

Zerk. In that respect, his son was following instructions – he had been forbidden to contact him. Because by now, after the arrival of the men from the Ministry, his second mobile had surely been detected and tapped. He would have to warn Retancourt not to contact him either. God knows what fate awaited a mole uncovered in the great rabbit warren of the Clermonts.

At a crossroads on the way was an isolated farm, guarded by a dog that was tired of barking. There was no chance this phone would be tapped. Adamsberg tugged several times on the old bell pull and called out. Receiving no answer, he pushed open the door and found a telephone on a table in an entry porch full of letters, umbrellas and muddy boots. He picked it up to ring Retancourt.

Then he replaced it. He had suddenly become aware that in the back pocket of his trousers was a bulky packet, containing the photos Valleray had given him the day before. Going back outside, he took shelter behind a hay barn to take a longer look at them, without understanding why they had suddenly seemed to call insistently for his attention. There was Christian doing his imitation of somebody or other, in front of a crowd of laughing admirers, Christophe looking clumsy but smiling, with a gold tiepin in the shape of a horseshoe. All the guests were holding champagne glasses, the dishes were decorated with flower arrangements, the women's dresses were low-cut, there were jewels everywhere, rings embedded in the flesh of aged fingers, waiters in tuxedos. Plenty for a zoologist who specialised in the parades and habits of the super-rich, but nothing for a cop trying to find a parricide. He was distracted by a flight of wild ducks in an impeccable V-shape, and looked up at the pale blue sky – still with some clouds to the west – then he put the photos back again, patted the nose of a nearby mare who was shaking her mane over her eyes, and consulted his watches. If anything had happened to Zerk, he would surely have been informed. By now they should be getting near Granada, safe from the most diligent searchers. He hadn't foreseen that he would start worrying about Zerk, and couldn't work out whether it was because of guilt, or a growing affection he was as yet unaware of. He imagined the two youngsters approaching the city, looking rather dishevelled; he saw

Zerk's small bony face bearing a grin, and Mo with a nice short haircut like a good boy. *Skinhead Mo.*

Replacing the photos quickly in his pocket, he hurried back to the still-deserted farm, checked the surroundings and dialled Retancourt's mobile.

'Violette,' he said, 'you know the photo you took of Saviour 1?'

'Yes.'

'His hair is very short. But in the photos from the evening reception, his hair was longer. So when did you take it?'

'The day after I got here.'

'So three days after the father's death. Try to find out when he got his hair cut. To the hour. Before or after he returned from the reception. You've got to find this out.'

'I've made friends with the grouchiest butler in the house. He won't speak to anyone else but he makes an exception for me.'

'That doesn't surprise me. Send me the answer somehow but don't use the mobiles any more and then get out of there fast.'

'A problem?' Retancourt asked placidly.

'Yeah, big time.'

'OK.'

'If he actually cut his hair that night before getting back, there could be some on the headrest. Has he driven himself anywhere since the murder?'

'No, he's always had the chauffeur drive him.'

'Well, look and see if there are any tiny bits of hair on the driver's seat.'

'But without a search warrant.'

'Correct, lieutenant, we'd never get one.'

He walked on for twenty minutes before reaching the Chemin de Bonneval, his mind occupied but confused by Christian Clermont-Brasseur's unexpected haircut. But he hadn't been driving his father in the Mercedes. He'd left earlier, having drunk a lot, and if he had visited a woman later, her name would never be discovered. And it was quite possible that after the news he'd cut his hair in order to look more respectable in mourning.

Well, maybe. But what about Mo, whose hair sometimes got singed by the flames from his fires? If Christian really had set the car alight, and if his hair had been slightly singed, he would have made haste to cover that up with a quick haircut. But Christian hadn't been at the scene, and that was what he always returned to. Nothing exhausted Adamsberg so much as going round in circles, contrary to Danglard, who could doggedly pursue a problem to the point of vertigo, going round and round in his own footsteps.

Adamsberg forced himself to ignore the blackberries, so that he could concentrate on the path, and any traces left by Léo. He passed the big tree trunk where he had sat down with her, and paused to send heartfelt wishes for her recovery, then he spent some time by the Chapel of St Antony, who helps people find things they have lost. His mother had always annoyed him by sending up prayers to the saint whenever she had lost the slightest thing: St Antony of Padua, finder of everything.

As a child, Adamsberg had been a bit shocked that his mother was not embarrassed to call on St Antony just to find a thimble. But now the saint wasn't being any help, and there was nothing to be seen on the path. He decided conscientiously to retrace his steps back to the beginning and, at the halfway point, sat down on the felled tree trunk, this time having collected a few blackberries which he laid down beside him. He looked again, on his mobile, at the photos Retancourt had sent him, and compared them with those Valleray had given him. Suddenly there was a rustling sound behind him, and Fleg bounded out of the woods with the happy expression of a lad who had just made a successful visit to the girl at the farm. Fleg put his drooling head on Adamsberg's knee and looked up at him with that pleading expression that no human being can reproduce as obstinately. Adamsberg patted his head.

'I suppose you want some sugar now? But I haven't got any, old fellow. I'm not Léo.'

Fleg insisted, putting his muddy paws up on Adamsberg's trousers, begging more insistently.

'No. Sugar. Fleg,' said Adamsberg slowly. 'The brigadier will give you some this evening at six. What about a blackberry?'

Adamsberg offered him one, but the dog refused. Seeming to realise that his request would not be granted, or that this man was stupid, he started digging around Adamsberg's feet, sending the leaves flying.

'Fleg, you are destroying the vital microcosm of leaf mould.'

The dog stopped and looked up meaningfully at Adamsberg and then down at the ground. One of his paws had unearthed a little piece of white paper.

'Yes, I see, it's the wrapping from the sugar. But it's old. It's empty.'

Adamsberg swallowed a handful of blackberries, and Fleg insisted, moving his paw and guiding this human who was so slow on the uptake. Within a minute, Adamsberg had found six old sugar-lump wrappings in the leaves.

'They're all empty, old boy. I know what you're trying to tell me: there's a sugar mine here. I know this is where Léo used to give you sugar lumps after you came back from the farm. Yes, I know you're disappointed, but I haven't got any sugar.'

Adamsberg stood up and walked on a few paces, with the idea of distracting Fleg from this pointless obsession. The dog followed him, whining slightly, then Adamsberg turned suddenly back and went to sit in the exact position where he had sat with Léo, revisiting the scene in his memory, their first words, the dog's arrival. If Adamsberg's mind was useless at remembering long words, he had a near-photographic memory for images. He could see again Léo's gestures, as clearly as if they were drawn with a pen. She hadn't unwrapped the sugar lump, because it didn't have paper round it. She had given it directly to the dog. She wasn't the kind of woman to have pre-wrapped sugar, she'd have taken some straight from the packet at home, and couldn't care less about dirt in her pockets, on her fingers or on the sugar.

Carefully, he picked up the six papers Fleg had found. Someone else had been eating sugar here. These papers must have been there a couple of weeks, all together as if they had been thrown down at the same time. But so what? Well, they were on the Chemin de Bonneval, that's what. Some teenager could have been sitting there one night, waiting to see the Riders – since this was a famous rite of passage – and might have been eating sugar to keep his strength up. Or he might even have been there the night of the murder, and seen the murderer go past.

'Fleg,' he said to the dog, 'did you show the papers to Léo perhaps? Hoping for an extra reward?'

Adamsberg thought back to the hospital bed and considered differently the only three words that the old woman had whispered. 'Ello, Fleg, sugar.'

'Fleg,' he said again, 'Léo must have seen the papers, is that it? She saw them here? And I'll tell you when she saw them. The day she found Herbier's body. Otherwise she wouldn't have mentioned them in hospital, since she had so little strength left. But why didn't she say anything that night? Do you think she only understood later? Like me? Much later? Next day? But what did she understand, Fleg?'

Adamsberg slipped the papers carefully into the packet of photographs.

'But what, Fleg?' he said as he went down the short cut that Léo had used. 'What did she suddenly understand? That someone had witnessed a murder? But how could she know that the papers had been thrown *that* night? Because she came the same way the day before the murder with you and they weren't there then?'

The dog bounded down the path, taking care to lift its leg against the same trees as before, as they approached Léo's house.

That must be it. A witness who was eating sugar. Who didn't understand the significance of what he had seen until he later heard about the murder, and when it took place. But a witness who didn't dare come forward because he was frightened. Léo might have known which teenager had been sent to brave out his initiation rite on the path that night.

Fifty paces from the house, Fleg started running towards a car parked on the side. Brigadier Blériot came to meet the commissaire, and Adamsberg walked faster, hoping he had been to the hospital and might have some news.

'No, nothing to be done, we can't find out what's wrong with her,' he told Adamsberg without any more formal greeting, spreading his short arms in a gesture like a sigh.

'Hell, Blériot, what's happened?'

'This rattling sound, when she moves.'

'*Rattling?*'

'Yes, she gets out of puff soon as you push her. But downhill or on the flat, no problem.'

'Blériot, who on earth are you talking about?'

'This car, sir. Will the prefecture replace it for us? When the cows come home.'

'Right, brigadier. But what did you find out when you questioned Mortembot?'

'He can't tell us nothing about nothing. Like a wet rag, he is, sir,' said Blériot with a touch of pity, as he stooped to pat the dog, which was rubbing against his legs. 'Without Glayeux, he's completely lost.'

'He wants his sugar,' Adamsberg said.

'He wants to stay in the cell. Stupid pillock, he shouted at me, he even tried to have a go at me, wanted me to put him in jail for a long stretch. Can't put anything over me.'

'Blériot, we're at cross purposes again,' said Adamsberg, wiping his face with his T-shirt sleeve. 'I was just saying the *dog* wants his sugar.'

'Ah, well, it's not time yet.'

'I know that. But we've been in the woods, he's been to see his girlfriend at the farm and he wants some sugar.'

'Well, you'll have to give it to him yourself, commissaire. Because I've been fiddling with the engine, and when my hands smell of petrol, he won't take it from me.'

'But I haven't got any sugar,' explained Adamsberg patiently.

Without replying, Blériot pointed to his shirt pocket, stuffed with sugar lumps wrapped in paper.

'Help yourself,' he said.

Adamsberg took a lump out, unwrapped it and gave it to the dog. At least that was one minor victory.

'Do you always cart around a pocketful of sugar?'

'So what if I do?' muttered Blériot.

Adamsberg sensed that the question had been far too direct and had touched a nerve with Blériot. Perhaps he suffered from diabetes, causing those sudden drops in blood sugar level which made you sweat and stumble and collapse – like a wet rag indeed. Perhaps Blériot was a horse lover. Perhaps he put sugar lumps in his enemies' petrol tanks. Or dipped sugar in his morning Calvados.

'Can you give me a lift to the hospital, brigadier? I need to see the doctor before he leaves.'

'They say he's brung Madame Léo up from the depths, like a fish off of a riverbed,' said Blériot, getting back into the car as Fleg jumped in the back. 'It's like one day, I got this old brown trout from out the Touques. I just picked her up in my hand. Must have knocked herself out on a rock or something. What it was though, I couldn't bring myself to eat her. Dunno why, I just put her back.'

'What are we doing about Mortembot?'

'Oh, that one, wimp like he is, he'll be in the gendarmerie overnight. He can stay till two tomorrow afternoon, that's his rights. After that, I dunno what's going to happen. Bet he wishes he hadn't killed his mother now. He'd have been all right with her around, tough old bird she was, wouldn't take no nonsense. If he'd just have kept his hands off her, Hellequin wouldn't've got the army after him.'

'Do you believe in the army, brigadier?'

'No, no, course not,' muttered Blériot, 'just saying what people say, that's all.'

'These teenagers who go on to the path at night, does that happen much?'

'Yes. Stupid little perishers, they don't dare run away neither.'

'Who tells them what to do?'

'These other daft kids, only older ones. Round here, it's like the thing to do. You got to spend a night in Bonneval, or you got no balls. Simple as that. Did it myself when I was a lad of fifteen. Tell you what though, at that age, you don't feel very brave. And you can't light a fire neither, that's another of their daft rules.'

'The ones who've been there this year, would you know their names?'

'Not this year or any other year. Nobody boasts about it after. Because the gang's waiting for you at the end of it, and they want to see if you've

221

pissed your pants. Or worse. So none of them is going to blab. It's like a sect, commissaire. It's secret.'

'Do girls have to do it?'

'Between ourselves, sir, girls are a lot less stupid than lads for that kind of thing. They're not going to scare themselves to death for no point. No, course not, they don't do it.'

Dr Hellebaud was finishing a light snack in the room placed at his disposal. He was chatting away to two nurses and Dr Turbot, now completely won over and looking relaxed and affable.

'Now, *mon ami*,' Hellebaud said, greeting Adamsberg, 'you find me having a little afternoon tea before I leave.'

'How is she?'

'I did a second treatment, just to check, and I'm quite satisfied everything seems to be in the right place. Unless I'm mistaken, the vital functions will now gradually return, day after day. You should see a real difference in four days, then she'll go into a consolidation phase. But look here, Adamsberg, none of your police-type questioning, what did you see, who was it, what happened? – all that. She isn't capable of facing this memory yet. If you try to force her back there, it would destroy all our progress.'

'I'll see to that personally, Dr Hellebaud,' said Turbot obsequiously. 'Her room will be locked and no one will go in without my permission. No one will speak to her either without my being there.'

'I'll count on you, my dear colleague. Adamsberg, if you can arrange another outing for me, I ought to see her again in two weeks. It's been delightful.'

'Well, I have to thank you, Hellebaud, really.'

'Come, come, *mon ami*, I'm just doing my job. By the way, what about your so-called bubble of electricity? Shall we deal with that now? René,' he said, turning to the chief warder, 'can we have five minutes? That's all I need with the commissaire. He's abnormally asymptomatic.'

'All right,' said René, checking the clock. 'But we've got to be away by six, doctor, no later.'

'I won't need that long.'

The doctor smiled, patted his lips with his paper napkin and took Adamsberg into the corridor, followed by two warders.

'You don't need to lie down, just sit on this chair, that'll do. Take off your shoes. Now where is this famous bubble? On the back of your neck?'

The doctor worked for a few minutes on the commissaire's skull, neck and feet, and spent some time on his eyes and cheekbones.

'As odd as ever, *mon ami*,' he said at last, gesturing to him to put his shoes back on. 'We'd only have to sever a few ties linking you to the earth for you to drift up to the clouds, without even having an ideal. Like a balloon. Watch out, Adamsberg, I've already warned you about that. Yes, real life is despicable and mediocre, a pile of shit in fact, we can agree about that. But we're obliged to wade through it, *mon ami*. Obliged. Luckily, you're also a fairly simple soul and part of you is held to earth, like a bull with its hoof in the mud. That's your good fortune and I've consolidated it on the occipital condyle and the cheekbone.'

'What about the bubble?'

'The bubble came physiologically from a zone compressed between your vertebra C1, which was locked, and C2. Somatically, it was created by a major guilt episode.'

'I don't think I've ever felt guilt.'

'If not, you're a lucky exception. But *I* would say – and you know very well how closely I was involved with this resurrection – that the impact on your life of a previously unknown son, unbalanced by your absence, indeed debilitated by your negligence, could generate a whole truckload of guilt. Hence this reaction between your vertebrae. I have to go now, *mon ami*. We may meet again in a fortnight, if the judge will sign another laissez-passer. Did you know that Varnier was totally corrupt, rotten to the core?'

'Yes, it's because of that we could get you here.'

'Good luck, *mon ami*,' said the doctor, shaking hands. 'It would give me pleasure if you were to visit me at Fleury.'

He referred to 'Fleury' as if to his country residence, as if he were simply inviting a friend to spend an afternoon at his rural manor, rather than a prison. Adamsberg watched him leave, with a feeling of esteem, very rare for him and no doubt the instant effect of the treatment he had just received.

Before Dr Turbot locked the door, the commissaire was able to slip into Léo's room, touch her now warm cheeks and stroke her hair. He thought about, but immediately rejected, mentioning the sugar wrappers.

'*Hello*, Léo, it's me. Fleg has been to see his girlfriend at the farm. He's happy now.'

XXXII

IN THE VESTIBULE OF A RATHER GLOOMY HOTEL ON THE OUTSKIRTS of Granada, Zerk and Mo logged off the ancient computer they had consulted, and strolled with a deliberately casual air towards the stairs. You never think about the way you're walking unless you think you're being watched, whether by the police or by a lover. And then nothing is more difficult than to imitate the natural walk one has suddenly lost. They had agreed not to use the lift, a place where hotel guests might, for want of anything else to do, observe them more closely.

'Maybe going on the Internet wasn't so bright,' said Mo, closing the door of their room.

'Cool it, Mo. Nothing's more suspicious than someone looking tense. At least we found what we were after.'

'It wouldn't be a good idea either to phone the cafe in Ordebec, what's it called?'

'The Running Boar. No, I agree. We've got the number just for emergencies. But now we know the name of the games shop with the diabolos, Strung Out. We'll easily get the name of the guy who runs it and if he has kids. I'm guessing a boy, twelve to sixteen.'

'Yeah, gotta be a boy,' agreed Mo. 'I don't think a girl would go tying a pigeon's legs together.'

'Or torch cars either.'

Mo sat on his bed, stretched his legs and tried to take deep slow breaths. He had the feeling he had a second heart beating constantly in his stomach.

Adamsberg had explained to him in the house with the cows that it was probably little bubbles of electricity here and there. He put a hand on his stomach to try and make them go away, then started leafing through a French newspaper from the previous day.

'Still,' Zerk went on, 'a girl might *watch* the kid tying up the pigeon, and think it was funny, or watch the guy torching the car, come to that. Anything there about Ordebec?'

'No. But I bet your dad's got better things to do than worry about the kid from the diabolo shop.'

'No, not really. My guess is the boy who likes torturing pigeons, and the Ordebec murderer, and whoever burnt Clermont-Brasseur, all of them are going round in his head, without him really seeing much difference between them.'

'I thought you said you didn't know him.'

'Yeah, but I'm starting to feel like I'm like him. Mo, I think we better have a regular time to leave in the mornings, starting tomorrow, say 8.50. Every day the same. Give the impression we've got some regular job to go to. If we're still here, that is.'

'Ah. Did you notice him too?' said Mo, still rubbing his stomach.

'The guy looking across at us downstairs?'

'Yeah.'

'He did kind of stare, didn't he?'

'Yeah. Make you think of anything?'

'A cop, right?'

Zerk opened the window, to smoke near the fresh air. From their room, all you could see was a little courtyard, a lot of waterpipes, clothes lines and zinc roofs. He threw his fag end out of the window, and watched it fall into the shadows.

'I think we'd better get out of here right now,' he said.

XXXIII

ÉMERI HAD PROUDLY OPENED THE DOUBLE DOORS INTO HIS DINING room, eagerly awaiting the expressions on his guests' faces. Adamsberg looked surprised but indifferent (uneducated, Émeri thought) but Veyrenc's open-mouthed astonishment and the admiring comments made by Danglard pleased him enough to wipe away the last traces of the argument earlier that day. In reality, although Danglard appreciated the quality of the furniture, he found this recreation of an Empire salon over-meticulous and rather excessive.

'What a marvellous room, capitaine,' he concluded, however, accepting an aperitif, since he had far better manners than either of his two Pyrenean colleagues. For that reason, it was Danglard who did most of the talking over dinner, with that sincere show of interest that he was so good at faking, and for which Adamsberg was always grateful to him. Especially since the quantity of wine dispensed, from period carafes engraved with the arms of the Prince of Eckmülh, was sufficiently generous to prevent the commandant having any fear that it would run out. Encouraged by Danglard, who was on equally brilliant form whether talking about the county of Ordebec or the battles fought by Marshal Davout, Émeri drank a good deal and let himself go, sounding familiar and even sentimental. It seemed to Adamsberg that the marshal's cloak, and the posture it forced upon his descendant, was gradually slipping from his shoulders and falling to the ground.

At the same time, however, Danglard's expression was somehow altered.

Adamsberg knew him well enough to realise that the hint of amusement in his eyes was not just the effect of the alcohol. It was a slightly mischievous look, as if the commandant had something up his sleeve but wasn't going to reveal it. And, Adamsberg thought, that something might be aimed at Lieutenant Veyrenc, towards whom Danglard was being almost friendly, for once, which was a potential danger sign. The little something up his sleeve was making him smile at a man he was going to pull a trick on later.

The events of Ordebec, which had been temporarily put aside during the chat about imperial times, finally surfaced when they reached the after-dinner Calvados.

'What are you going to do about Mortembot, Émeri?' asked Adamsberg.

'If your men can back us up, we could have a team of six or seven on watch during the week. Could you get them here?'

'I've got one lieutenant who's worth ten men, but she's gone scuba-diving. I'd rather call on a couple of normal men.'

'Could your son give us a hand?'

'No, I'm not exposing my son to danger, Émeri. He's not got the training and he can't handle a gun. Anyway, he's gone off on his travels.'

'I thought he was doing a photo shoot about rotten leaves.'

'Yes, he was, but this girl phoned him from Italy and he went like a shot. You know what they're like.'

'Yes,' said Émeri, leaning back in his chair, as far as its upright Empire form allowed. 'I used to play the field myself, then I met my wife, she's from these parts. When she followed me to Lyon, she was already getting bored, but I still loved her. I thought getting a posting back to Ordebec would please her. Go back home, meet up with old friends. So I moved heaven and earth to get the job here. And then what did she do, but stay in Lyon? I did everything wrong my first two years here. I did the rounds of the red-light district in Lisieux, but that was no fun. I'm not like my illustrious ancestor, my friends, if I can so call you. I lost every fight I took on, apart from a few arrests any fool could have made.'

'I don't know if winning and losing are the right words for judging one's life,' said Veyrenc. 'That is, I don't really think you should judge your life at all. We're all forced to do it, but it's a crime.'

'Worse than a crime, a blunder,' said Danglard, automatically quoting the famous reply Fouché is supposed to have made to the Emperor about the murder of the Duc d'Enghien.

'Ah yes, well said,' said Émeri, looking reinvigorated. He got up rather unsteadily to pour out a second round of Calvados. 'We found the axe,' he announced without transition. 'Chucked over the wall of Glayeux's garden, and lying in the field behind.'

'If one of the Vendermots killed him,' said Adamsberg, 'do you really think they'd have used their own axe? And anyway, if they did, the easiest thing to do would be to take it back home, wouldn't it?'

'You could read it either way, Adamsberg, like I said. It could make them look innocent, clever way of doing so.'

'Not as clever as they are, though.'

'You like them, don't you?'

'I've got nothing serious against them, so far anyway.'

'But you do like them.'

Émeri left the room for a few moments and returned with an old school photograph which he put on Adamsberg's knee.

'Take a look at this,' he said. 'We're all between eight and ten years old. Hippo was already very big, he's third from the left in the back row. He's still got his six fingers on each hand. You know the ghastly story?'

'Yes.'

'I'm in the row in front of him, the only one not smiling. So, you see, I've known him a long time. Well, I can tell you, Hippo was a terror. Not the nice guy he likes to show to you. We were very wary of him, even me, and I was two years older.'

'Did he beat people up?'

'Didn't need to. He had a more powerful weapon. With his six fingers, he said he was an arm of the devil, and he could make all kinds of curses fall on us if we were nasty to him.'

'And the kids *were* nasty to him?'

'Yes, at first. You can imagine how a school playground reacts to a boy with six fingers. When he was five or six, he was teased and persecuted mercilessly. It's true. There was one gang that really went for him; the leader was a boy called Régis Vernet. One time, he put tacks on Hippo's chair and Hippo sat on them. When he stood up he was bleeding, six holes in his backside, and everyone was laughing. Another time he was tied to a tree and everyone pissed on him. But one day Hippo got his revenge.'

'He turned his six fingers on the lot of you.'

'Exactly. His first victim was the nastiest one, Régis. Hippo threatened him, then he held out his two hands, with this weird expression. And you can believe me or not, but five days later, Régis was knocked down by a Parisian's car and lost both legs. Horrible. In school, we knew it wasn't the driver's fault, it was the curse of Hippo. And he didn't deny it. On the contrary, he said the next person who crossed him they'd lose their arms *and* their legs, and their balls, come to that. So then everything went into reverse and we were all scared stiff. Later on, Hippo stopped all that nonsense. But I can assure you that even today, believe it or not, nobody likes to cross him in any way. Not him, not his family.'

'Is this Régis still around. Can we see him?'

'He's dead. I'm not making this up, Adamsberg, he had terrible luck all his life: illness, couldn't hold down a job, family all died, he had no money. He drowned himself in the Touques three years ago. He was only thirty-six. All of us who were at school with him knew that it was Hippo's revenge all the time. Hippo had said so. He said if he decided to point his fingers at you, well, you were going to have bad luck all your life.'

'So what do you think about that today?'

'Luckily for me, I left the region when I was eleven, and I could forget all about it. If you ask Émeri the cop, he'll tell you this kind of story is a load of rubbish. But if you were to ask Émeri the schoolkid, I find myself thinking that Régis did have a curse on him. Let's say that Hippo, as a boy, defended himself the only way he could. He was treated as if he was a limb of Satan, a misbegotten monster from hell, so he started living up to it. But he went on playing up spectacularly, even after his fingers were chopped off. So, whatever you think of the story, I can tell you he may not be a servant of the devil, but he's very tough, and possibly dangerous. He suffered with that father worse than anyone can imagine. When he set his dog on his father, he really meant to kill him. And I wouldn't be sure he's over it yet. How could the Vendermots become good little angels, after all they've been through?'

'Do you lump Antonin in with the others?'

'Yes. I don't think a baby who's had every bone in his body broken can ever develop a normal nature, do you? People think Antonin would be too scared of shattering again to actually do anything. But he might be able to pull a trigger. Or even lift up an axe, I don't know.'

'He says not.'

'But he'd blindly back up everything that Hippo does. It's plausible that his visit today, about the axe, was on his brother's orders. Same goes for Martin, the one who eats like a wild animal and always shadows his big brother.'

'That leaves Lina.'

'Who sees Hellequin's ghostly cavalcade, and isn't any saner than her brothers. Or who pretends to see it, Adamsberg. The main thing is to point the finger at future victims, and get everyone in a panic, like Hippo with his hands. And then Hippo might kill these victims, while the rest of the family provides him with all the alibis he needs. That way they'd be able to spread terror through Ordebec and they'd look like avengers, because the victims so far were real bastards, however you look at it. But I'm more inclined to think Lina's simply seeing things. That started it all off. And her brothers have taken the vision literally and decided to follow it through. They believe it. Because Lina's first vision happened about the same time as the father's death. Before or after, I'm not sure which.'

'Two days later. She told me.'

'She'll tell anyone who'll listen. You saw how she didn't turn a hair?'

'Yes,' said Adamsberg, seeing again Lina bringing down the side of her hand on the table. 'But why would Lina keep quiet about the fourth victim?'

'Either she really didn't see him, or else they're keeping that secret to get the locals scared stiff. They're smart in that family. A terrifying threat like this would bring all the rats out of their holes. And that amuses them, it makes them feel good, and they'd think it was justice being done. Like the death of their father.'

'You're probably right, Émeri. Unless, that is, someone is exploiting the apparent guilt of the Vendermots to commit murders. That someone can kill with impunity because he can be sure the townspeople will accuse the so-called family from hell.'

'But what motive could he have?'

'Terror of the Ghost Riders. You said yourself that plenty of people in Ordebec believe in them, didn't you, and some people are so scared they won't even pronounce their name. Think about it, Émeri. We could make a list of them all.'

'Too many for that!' said Émeri, shaking his head.

Adamsberg walked home in silence, Veyrenc and Danglard strolling calmly along in front of him. The clouds in the west had still not come to anything and the night was overpoweringly hot. From time to time, Danglard passed some remark to Veyrenc, which was another surprising thing, to put alongside that cunning little air of concealing a secret.

Émeri's accusations against the Vendermots troubled Adamsberg. With the details about Hippo's childhood he had heard, they were credible. It would be hard to see how any wisdom or grace could have blessed the Vendermot children allowing them to escape from their anger and desire for vengeance. But a piece of grit was also whirling round inside his random thoughts. Old Léo. He couldn't see any of the four Vendermots being capable of hitting her or pushing her to the ground. Even if one of them had approached her, Adamsberg supposed that Hippo – for the sake of argument – would have found a less brutal way of silencing the old woman who had been good to him throughout his childhood.

He went to the cellar before going to bed and hid the sugar wrappings and the photos in an empty cider keg. Then he sent a message to the squad to ask for two more men by 2 p.m. Estalère and Justin would be best, since both of them were immune to the boredom of keeping a watch over someone, the former because of his 'cheerful nature' as some called it (what they meant was 'not very bright'), and the other because patience was a feature of his perfectionism. Mortembot's house, he'd gathered, shouldn't be too difficult to protect. It had two windows in front and two at the back, all with shutters. The only weak spot was the little window of the lavatory on the side, without shutters but barred. The murderer would have to come very close and break the glass before aiming through a narrow space, and that would be impossible with two men patrolling the house. Anyway, if it was supposed to be in the tradition of killings by Lord Hellequin, bullets wouldn't be used. Axe, sword, club, stone, strangling, any medieval method of killing could only be carried out inside the house. Except that Herbier had been killed with a sawn-off shotgun and that sounded a false note.

Adamsberg closed the cellar door and walked across the large courtyard. The lights in the house were out. Veyrenc and Danglard were already asleep. With his fists, Adamsberg made an even bigger hollow in his woollen mattress and curled up in it.

XXXIV

ZERK AND MO LEFT BY AN EMERGENCY EXIT ON TO THE HOTEL FIRE escape, and reached the street without meeting anyone.

'Now where?' asked Mo, getting into the car.

'We'll find some little village in the south, where it's easy to cross to North Africa. Lots of boats with captains ready to do a deal to take us over.'

'You think we'll have to cross?'

'We'll have to see.'

'Zerk, I saw what you put in your bag.'

'The gun?'

'Yeah,' said Mo, looking unhappy.

'When we stopped in the Pyrenees, when you were asleep, I was only a kilometre from my home village. It just took me twenty minutes to go and get my grandad's gun.'

'You're crazy, man, what the fuck you want a revolver for?'

'It's an old pistol, 1935A, 7.7mm. From 1940, but it works.'

'And bullets, you got bullets too?'

'Yeah, boxful.'

'Shit, Zerk, what for?'

'Cos I know how to use it.'

'But fuck, man, you're not going to shoot at a cop?'

'No, but we could *really* need to get across, right?'

'I thought you were the quiet type. Not a nutter.'

'I am the quiet type. My dad got us out of the trap but we've got to use our wits not to get back in it.'

'So we go to Africa right away?'

'We'll ask around the boats. Mo, if they find you, my dad's in deep, deep shit. I may not know him that well, but I don't like that idea.'

XXXV

VEYRENC WASN'T ASLEEP. HE WAS STANDING UP, KEEPING WATCH from his window. Danglard had been behaving oddly all evening: anticipating some amusement, a victory over someone: he was planning some kind of coup. A professional coup, Veyrenc guessed, since the commandant wasn't the kind of man to go round the red-light district of Lisieux, as suggested by Émeri. Or, if so, he would have said as much, without making any secret of it. The bonhomie he had shown towards Veyrenc, suppressing his usual childish jealousy, had put the latter on high alert. He imagined that Danglard was on the point of making some breakthrough in the inquiry without telling anyone, thus overtaking his colleague and scoring extra brownie points with Adamsberg. Tomorrow, he'd proudly present the commissaire with whatever he had found. Well, Veyrenc wasn't too bothered about that. Nor was he irritated at whatever plan was disturbing the commandant's usually calm judgement. But in an inquiry where the bodies were piling up, one shouldn't go venturing out alone.

By 1.30 a.m., Danglard hadn't appeared. Disappointed, Veyrenc lay down on his bed, fully dressed.

Danglard had set his alarm for 5.50 and had gone to sleep quickly, which was rare for him, except when the prospect of a job to do demanded that he sleep quickly and well. At 6.25, he was in the driver's seat, releasing the handbrake and letting the car roll silently down the slope, so as not to wake anyone. He started the engine once he was on the road and drove slowly for twenty-two kilometres, with the sunblind down. His correspondent, man or woman, had asked him not to make himself conspicuous. The fact that this correspondent had apparently mistaken him for the commissaire had been a stroke of luck. He had found the message in his jacket the previous day, a clumsily pencilled note, apparently by someone without much education. *Comisaire I got something about Glayeux but on condision I stay hidden. Too dangearous. Meet me at Cérenay Station Platform A, 06.50 sharp tomorrow. THANKS. Please be discrete* ('discreet' and 'discrete' had been written and crossed out a couple of times) *and don't be late.*

By thinking back over the events of the previous day, Danglard was convinced that the writer of the message could only have slipped it into his jacket pocket when he was standing in the small crowd outside Glayeux's house. It hadn't been there earlier, when he was at the hospital.

The commandant parked under a line of trees and went on to Platform A, tiptoeing discreetly round the little station building. It stood outside the village, and was locked and deserted. There was no one on the platforms either. Danglard looked at the timetable and noted that no train would be stopping at Cérenay before 11.12 a.m. So there was no likelihood that anyone would be there for another four hours. The correspondent had chosen one of the few places where isolation was assured.

At 6.48 by the station clock, Danglard sat down on a bench, hunched over as usual, feeling impatient and somewhat shattered. He had had only a few hours' sleep and without his usual nine hours his energy was at a low ebb. But the idea of beating Veyrenc to the winning post was a stimulus, making him smile and feel cheerful. He had been working with Adamsberg now for over twenty years, and the spontaneous complicity between the commissaire and Veyrenc made him literally bristle with jealousy. Danglard was too insightful to fool himself: he knew perfectly well that his aversion to Veyrenc was a shameful form of envy. He wasn't even certain that Veyrenc was trying to take his place, but the temptation was irresistible. Get one over on Veyrenc. Danglard lifted his head, swallowed some saliva and expelled a vague sense of unworthiness. Adamsberg was neither his point of reference nor his model. On the contrary, the behaviour and ideas of his boss often annoyed him. But Adamsberg's esteem, and indeed affection, were necessary to him, as if that vague individual could somehow protect him or justify his existence. At 6.51 he felt a sharp blow on the side of his neck, put his hand up to feel it, then fell headlong on to the platform. A minute later, the commandant's body was lying across the rails.

Visibility along the platform was so clear that Veyrenc had had to hide a couple of hundred metres away, behind the signal box, in order to observe Danglard. His angle of vision was not good, and when he saw him, the unknown assailant was only a couple of metres from the commandant. The blow to Danglard's neck and Danglard's collapse took only a couple of seconds. As the man started rolling the body over towards the edge of the platform, Veyrenc had immediately set off at a run. He was still about forty metres away when Danglard fell on to the rails. The assailant was already making his escape, at an athletic pace.

Veyrenc jumped down on to the tracks and grabbed Danglard's head: his face was livid in the early-morning light, the mouth was open and slack, the eyes closed. Veyrenc found a pulse, then raised the eyelids on unseeing eyes. Danglard was out for the count, drugged or dying. On the side of his neck around a puncture mark, a large bruise was already forming. Grabbing him under the armpits, the lieutenant started to hoist his colleague up on to the platform, but the ninety-five inert kilos of this unconscious body were too much for him to lift. He needed help. He stood up, sweating, and was about to phone Adamsberg, when he heard the unmistakable whistle of a distant train approaching at high speed. Panic-stricken, he could already see the engine coming straight down the line from the left. Veyrenc flung himself on Danglard's body, and with a supreme effort, managed to lie him between the rails, arms by his sides. The train gave a loud hoot like a cry of despair, Veyrenc hauled himself on to the platform in the nick of time, and rolled away from the edge.

The carriages roared through the station with an ear-splitting noise, quickly fading into the distance, leaving him unable to move, either because his muscles were paralysed by his efforts, or because he couldn't face looking down at Danglard. Head encircled by his arms, he felt tears pouring down his cheeks. One piece of information was going round inside his head. 'The space between the surface of the body and the undercarriage of a train is only twenty centimetres.'

It must have been a quarter of an hour later that the lieutenant was finally able to raise himself on his elbows and crawl to the edge of the platform. Holding his head with his hands, he opened his eyes. Danglard looked like a corpse, neatly lined up in the track between the shining rails as if lying on a luxurious stretcher. But he was untouched. Veyrenc let his head fall on his arms, felt for his mobile and called Adamsberg. *Come quickly, Cérenay station.* Then he pulled out his gun, slipped off the safety catch and held it in his right hand, finger on trigger. He shut his eyes again. 'The space between the surface of the body and the undercarriage of the train is only twenty centimetres.' Now he remembered where he had heard that: last year, on the track between Paris and Granville, a man had fallen on the rails, in such a state of intoxication that the express train had passed clean over him; his absence of reflexes had saved his life. Veyrenc felt pins and needles in his legs and tried to move them slowly. They seemed simultaneously to have turned into cotton wool and to feel like lumps of granite. Twenty centimetres. It was good luck that Danglard's conspicuous lack of a muscular frame had allowed him to lie flat between the rails like an inert package.

When he heard running steps behind him, he was still sitting cross-legged on the platform, his gaze fixed on Danglard as if by keeping his attention concentrated on him he could prevent another train from coming along, or Danglard sliding towards death. He had addressed a few words to him – 'hold on', 'don't move', 'take deep breaths' – but without getting a flicker of response. Now, though, he could see Danglard's slack lips moving slightly with each breath and he was watching the small movements intently. His mind had started working again. Whoever had arranged to meet Danglard here had planned it carefully, pushing him under the

Caen–Paris express at a time when there was no risk of anyone else witnessing it. He would have been found hours later, when any trace of the anaesthetic, whatever it was, had disappeared from his body. And nobody would even have thought of looking for it. What would the inquest have said? That Danglard's habitual melancholy had got worse lately, that he had been afraid Ordebec would be the death of him. That he had got completely drunk and lain down on the railway line to die. It would certainly have been an extraordinary choice, but the madness of a suicidal man who was dead drunk couldn't be measured by ordinary standards, and that is what would have been concluded in the end. He turned to look at the hand pressing his shoulder – it belonged to Adamsberg.

'Down there,' said Veyrenc. 'Quick. I can't move.'

Émeri and Blériot had already taken hold of Danglard's body under the arms, and Adamsberg jumped down on the track to take his legs. Afterwards, Blériot couldn't manage to hoist himself on to the platform, and had to be hauled up by grabbing his hands.

'Dr Turbot is on his way,' said Émeri, bending over Danglard's chest. 'In my view, he's drugged but not in danger. There's a pulse, slow but regular. What happened, lieutenant?'

'This guy,' said Veyrenc, still struggling to speak.

'You can't get up?' asked Adamsberg.

'Can't seem to. You wouldn't have a drop of something?'

'Yessir, I have,' said Blériot, bringing out a cheap hip flask. 'But it's not even eight yet, it'll slam into your guts, it will.'

'Just what I need,' Veyrenc assured him.

'Eaten anything this morning?'

'No, up all night.'

Veyrenc took a gulp, and pulled a face showing that, yes indeed, it was slamming into his guts. He took another and passed the flask back to Blériot.

'Can you talk properly now?' asked Adamsberg, sitting cross-legged beside him and noting the traces of tears on Veyrenc's cheeks.

'Yeah, it's just the shock, that's all. I've used up all my strength.'

'Why were you up all night?'

'Because Danglard was plotting some damfool scheme on his own.'

'Ah, you noticed too?'

'Yeah. He wanted to steal a march on me, I thought it might be risky. I thought he'd go out late last night, but he only went off at six thirty this morning. I took the other car, and followed him at a distance. We got here,' Veyrenc said, waving his hand around. 'Then this guy hit him on the neck, and must have injected him with something, I think, and pushed him down on the track. I started running, the other man got away, and when I tried to haul Danglard up, I just couldn't. And this train appeared.'

'The Caen–Paris fast train,' said Émeri, looking serious. 'Goes through here at 6.56 every day.'

'Right,' said Veyrenc, his head sinking on to his chest, 'well, it certainly *is* fast.'

'Oh shit,' said Adamsberg through clenched teeth.

Why was it Veyrenc who had been shadowing Danglard? Why not him? Why had he allowed his lieutenant to get into this diabolical situation? Because Danglard's scheme had been directed at Veyrenc, and Adamsberg had regarded it as of no consequence. Just a bit of macho posturing.

'I just had time to move Danglard, and lie him down between the rails, don't know how, and then pull myself up, don't know how either. Heck, he was really heavy, and the platform's really high. I felt the air from the train going past. Twenty centimetres. That's the space between the undercarriage of the train and a body between the rails – if it's someone drunk or relaxed – just twenty centimetres.'

'I dunno as I'd have thought of that,' said Blériot, looking at Veyrenc with a stupefied expression. He was also fascinated by this officer's hair, dark brown but speckled with a dozen or so abnormal red locks, like poppies on a ploughed field.

'So this man?' asked Émeri. 'Was he big? Like Hippolyte?'

'Yeah, he looked a big fellow. But I was a long way off and he was wearing a hoodie and gloves.'

'What else was he wearing?'

'Trainers, maybe a sweatshirt and jogging pants. Dark green, navy, I don't know. Help me, Jean-Baptiste, I think I can stand up now.'

'Louis, why didn't you call me before you started following him? Why did you go off on your own?'

'It was between him and me. Some hare-brained plot of Danglard's, no point getting you involved. I had no idea this would get so heavy. *He went off all alone, with a heart full of bile . . .*'

Veyrenc broke off the verse he had started, and shrugged his shoulders.

'No,' he said to himself, 'no stomach for it.'

Dr Turbot had arrived and was attending to Danglard. He kept shaking his head and muttering 'went under the train, under the train!' as if convincing himself of the exceptional nature of the event he was being called to.

'It was probably a strong dose of anaesthetic,' he said, looking up and motioning to the two paramedics accompanying him, 'but I think it's almost worn off now. We'll take him back and I'll go on reviving him, but carefully. He won't be capable of speaking for a couple of hours, so don't come before that, commissaire. He's got some bruising, with the blow to the side of the neck and falling on to the track, but I don't think anything's broken. Survived going under the train, can't get over that!'

Adamsberg watched Danglard being stretchered to the ambulance with a wave of retrospective distress. But the bubble of electricity hadn't reappeared on his neck. Down to Dr Hellebaud, presumably.

'And how is Léo?' he asked the doctor.

'Last night she sat up and had something to eat. We've taken the catheter out. But she can't speak, she just gives us a smile from time to time. Looking as if she's got something to say, but she can't get there. Almost makes me think your Dr Hellebaud has blocked her powers of speech, like turning down a dimmer switch. And he'll turn it back up again when he sees fit.'

'That's pretty much how he operates, yes.'

'I wrote to him at his Fleury place, to report on her progress. I addressed it to the governor as you suggested.'

'Fleury *jail*,' said Adamsberg meaningfully.

'I know that, commissaire, but I don't like saying it or thinking it. Like I know that it was you that arrested him, and I don't want to hear what he'd done. Not medical malpractice at least?'

'No.'

'Under the train, can't get over that. Only suicides throw themselves under trains.'

'Quite, doctor. Not a normal MO for murder. But since it is indeed a normal method of killing oneself, Danglard's death might easily have been thought a suicide. For your hospital staff, the suicide version will be best, and make sure no wind of anything gets outside. I don't want the murderer to be alerted. Right now, he must be imagining that his victim has been cut to bits by the wheels of an express train. Let's let him think that for a few hours.'

'I see,' said Turbot, taking on a would-be knowing expression by screwing up his eyes. 'You want to take him by surprise, watch and wait.'

In fact, Adamsberg did nothing of the kind. As the ambulance moved off, he walked up and down Platform A, on a short stretch of twenty metres, not wanting to go too far from Veyrenc, to whom Blériot – he noticed – had given three or four lumps of sugar. Blériot the sugar carrier. Without intending to, he noticed too that the brigadier didn't drop the wrappings on the ground, but screwed them up in tiny balls which he put into his trouser pocket. Émeri, whose uniform was less impeccable than usual, since he had had to dress in a hurry when called, came towards him shaking his head.

'I can't see any sign of anything on the bench. Nothing, Adamsberg. Nothing to go on.'

Veyrenc gestured to Émeri, asking for a cigarette.

'I'd be surprised if Danglard can help us,' Veyrenc said. 'The attacker came from behind, he didn't even have time to turn his head.'

'How come the train driver didn't see him?' Blériot asked.

'This time of day, he'd be driving into the sun, facing due east,' Adamsberg replied.

'Well, even if he had seen him,' Émeri said, 'he wouldn't be able stop the train for several hundred metres. Lieutenant, why did you decide to follow him?'

'Obeying rules, I suppose,' said Veyrenc with a smile. 'Saw him go out and decided to tail him. Because you shouldn't go off alone in a case like this.'

'But why did *he* go off alone? He looked the careful type to me.'

'Yes, but inclined to do things by himself,' said Adamsberg, trying to excuse Danglard.

'And whoever arranged this rendezvous probably insisted he come alone,' sighed Émeri. 'Always the way. Let's meet up again back at the gendarmerie to organise surveillance at Mortembot's place. Adamsberg, can you get the backup from Paris?'

'Couple of men should be here by two o'clock.'

Veyrenc had recovered enough to drive, and Adamsberg followed him to Léo's place, where the lieutenant ate some tinned soup and then went straight to bed. As he returned to his room, Adamsberg remembered that he had forgotten to feed the pigeon any birdseed the night before. And the window had been open.

But Hellebaud had nestled into one of Adamsberg's shoes, the way some of his fellow pigeons might settle on a chimney pot, and was patiently waiting for him.

'Now come on, Hellebaud,' said Adamsberg, lifting up the shoe, pigeon and all, and putting it on the windowsill. 'We need a serious talk. You're getting away from the state of nature, you're sliding down the slope towards civilisation. Your feet are better, you can fly. Look out there! Sunshine! Trees! Female pigeons! And all the grubs and insects you want.'

Hellebaud cooed, which seemed a good sign, and Adamsberg placed him more firmly on the windowsill.

'Take off when you want,' he said. 'No need to leave a note, I'll understand.'

XXXVI

ADAMSBERG HAD REMEMBERED THAT ONE OUGHT TO OFFER FLOWERS to Madame Vendermot, and at 10 a.m. he was knocking gently at the door. It was Wednesday, so there was a chance Lina would be there, since she had the morning off to make up for coming in on Saturdays. It was the two of them that he wanted to see, Lina and Hippo, separately, for more serious questioning. He found the whole family sitting round the breakfast table, the younger members not yet dressed. He greeted them all in turn, examining their sleepy faces. Hippo's crumpled look was convincing, but with the already oppressive heat of the day, it would perhaps be easy to give the impression of someone who had just woken up. The puffy eyes of one roused from a night's sleep are hard to fake, but Hippo's eyelids were naturally heavy and as a result he did not always look either wide awake or friendly.

The mother, the only one who was properly dressed, accepted the flowers with real satisfaction and immediately offered the commissaire a cup of coffee.

'I hear something bad's happened at Cérenay station,' she said, and it was the first time he had heard her speak more than a few words since Paris, in a voice that was as humble as it was clear and calm. 'Is it this horrible case going on? Has something happened to Mortembot?'

'Who told you?' asked Adamsberg.

'Was it Mortembot?' she insisted.

'No, it wasn't him.'

'Holy Mother of god,' she went on with a sigh. 'Because if this goes on, we'll all have to move away, me and my children.'

'No, no, *maman*,' said Martin automatically.

'I know what I'm talking about, son. You none of you want to see anything, the way you are. But one of these days, someone's going to come along and kill us all.'

'No, forget it, *maman*,' said Martin. 'They're all too scared of us.'

'They don't understand,' the mother went on, addressing Adamsberg this time. 'They *won't* understand that people think we're all guilty. My poor girl, if only you'd held your tongue.'

'I didn't have the right to,' said Lina rather severely, without seeming to be troubled by her mother's anxiety. 'You know that perfectly well. You have to let the people who are seized take their chances.'

'Well, that may be,' said her mother, sitting back down at the table. 'We've got nowhere to go, but I've got to protect them,' she said, turning to Adamsberg again.

'*Maman*, nobody's going to touch us,' said Hippolyte, lifting his two deformed hands up towards the ceiling, and everyone burst out laughing.

'See, they don't understand a thing,' the mother repeated quietly, looking distressed. 'Don't play games with your fingers, Hippo, when someone's been killed at Cérenay.'

'What happened?' Lina asked. Adamsberg tried not to look her way, since her breasts were strikingly visible through her white pyjamas.

'*Maman* told you,' said Antonin. 'Someone threw himself under the Caen train. Suicide, that's what she meant.'

'How did you hear about it?' Adamsberg asked Madame Vendermot.

'I was down at the shops. The stationmaster was up there at a quarter to eight and he saw the police cars and the ambulance. He asked one of the paramedics.'

'Quarter to eight? But no train stops there before eleven.'

'The train driver had phoned through. He thought he'd seen someone or something on the track, so the stationmaster went in to check. Do you know who was killed?'

'Did they tell you?'

'No,' said Hippo. 'Perhaps it was Marguerite Vanout.'

'Why would it be her?' asked Martin.

'You know what they say in Cérenay. *Yttun sa a ekactiurf.*'

'Nutty as a fruitcake,' Lina translated.

'Oh really?' said Antonin, looking frankly interested, as if unaware that he inclined slightly towards the fruitcake end of the spectrum himself.

'Since her husband left her. She goes round shouting, she tears her clothes, she writes on the walls of the houses. On the walls.'

'What does she write?'

'Pigs. She writes it all over the village and in Cérenay they're starting to get really fed up with her. Every day, the mayor has to get someone to clean off the graffiti she wrote in the night. And she's got plenty of money, so she hides banknotes here and there, under stones, up trees, and next morning the village people can't help going looking for them, like a game of hide-and-seek. Makes 'em late for work. So just this one woman, she's got everyone running in circles. Still, it's not a *crime* to hide banknotes.'

'No, it's funny,' said Martin.

'Yeah, 'tis rather,' Hippo agreed.

'It's not funny at all,' answered their mother sharply. 'She's just a poor woman who's lost her wits and is suffering.'

'Yeah, but it's still funny,' said Hippo, bending down to kiss her cheek.

His mother was instantly transformed, as if she suddenly realised that any reprimand was either pointless or unfair. She patted her son's big hand and went to sit in her armchair in the corner, from where she was unlikely to take any further part in the conversation. It was as if a character had quietly left the stage, while still remaining in sight.

'We should send flowers to her funeral though,' said Lina. 'After all, we do know her aunt.'

'I'll go and pick some in the forest,' suggested Martin.

'No, you don't send wild flowers to a funeral.'

'No, that's right,' put in Antonin, 'you got to buy florist's flowers. We could get some lilies.'

'No, lilies are for weddings.'

'Anyway, we can't afford lilies,' said Lina.

'What about anemones?' said Hippo. '*Ton raed, senomena.*'

Adamsberg had let them go on arguing about the kind of flowers they should send for Marguerite. And their conversation, unless it was being invented for his benefit by a set of geniuses, proved to him, better than anything else could, that none of the Vendermots had been involved in the Cérenay incident. Still, they were all strangely gifted, there was no getting away from that.

'No,' he said in the end. 'It's not Marguerite that's dead.'

'No flowers then,' said Hippolyte emphatically.

'But who is?' asked Martin.

'Nobody's dead. The man involved lay down between the rails and the train went over him without touching him.'

'Wow,' said Antonin. 'That's what I call an artistic experience.'

As he spoke, the young man passed a large sugar lump across to his sister, and Lina understood at once and broke it in two for him. It needed strong pressure from her fingers, something Antonin didn't want to risk. Adamsberg looked away. This constant presence of sugar lumps here, there and everywhere was giving him a strange feeling, as if he were surrounded by a multiple adversary throwing sugar bricks at him from sugar walls.

'If someone wanted to kill himself,' said Lina, looking at Adamsberg, 'he'd have lain *across* the rails.'

'Quite right, Lina. He didn't want to kill himself, someone pushed him on to the line. He was my deputy, Danglard, you've met him. Someone tried to kill him.'

Hippolyte frowned. 'Using a train as a weapon's a rather risky way to do it,' he said.

'Yes, but if you wanted to make it look like suicide,' said Martin, 'it's quite clever. People will think of suicide if someone's killed on a railway line.'

'I suppose so,' said Hippolyte, pulling a face. 'But planning that kind of thing must come from a very twisted brain. Someone ambitious but weird. *Yllatot driew.*'

'Hippo,' said Adamsberg, pushing away his cup, 'I need to talk to you on your own. And then Lina, if possible.'

'*Driew*, really *driew*,' Hippo went on.

248

'I do need to have a word with you,' Adamsberg insisted.

'I don't know who tried to kill your deputy.'

'No, it's not about that. It's about your father's death,' Adamsberg went on in a low voice.

'All right then,' said Hippo, glancing across at his mother. 'We'd better go outside. Let me just get dressed.'

Adamsberg was presently walking along the stony little lane, alongside Hippolyte, who was a head taller than him.

'I don't know anything about his death,' said Hippo. 'He was hit on the head and in the chest with an axe, while he was asleep, that's all.'

'But you knew that Lina had wiped the handle.'

'That's what I said at the time, but I was only little.'

'Hippo, why would Lina wipe the handle?'

'*I* don't know,' said Hippo sulkily. 'But not because she killed him. Come on, I know my sister. Not that she *couldn't* have wished him dead, we all did. But she went the other way. Stopped my dog Sooty going for his throat.'

'She could have wiped the handle because she thought someone else in the family killed him, Martin or Antonin.'

'But they were only six and four years old!'

'Or you.'

'No! We were all far too scared of him to try and do something like that. We weren't big enough.'

'But you did set your dog on him.'

'Then it would have been the dog's fault, not mine. See the difference?'

'Yes.'

'So then the bastard, he killed my dog. We all thought, any of us lift a finger against him, he'd be capable of killing us too, like the dog. My mother and all. Perhaps he would have too, if the count hadn't taken me away to his place.'

'Émeri says you weren't scared of anything. He says you caused chaos in school when you were a kid.'

249

'Yeah, I created mayhem all right,' said Hippo, giving one of his big grins. 'What does he say, Émeri? That I was a little shit going round terrorising everyone?'

'Yes, that's more or less what he said.'

'That's *exactly* what he said. But Émeri was no angel either. And he didn't have any excuse. He was properly looked after, his family was well off. Before Régis's gang of villains got going, there was this other boy, Hervé, who persecuted me. And let me tell you, Émeri wasn't backward when they were all dancing round me and hitting me. No, commissaire, I don't regret anything, I had to defend myself. All I had to do was wave my hands in the air at them, and they'd run away squealing. It was fun for me. But it was their fault, they started it. They said I had devil's hands, and I was a cripple from hell. I wouldn't have thought of that kind of thing if it wasn't for them. So I made use of it. No, if there's one thing in my life I'm sorry about, it's that I'm the son of the biggest fucking bastard in the region.'

By now Lina had got dressed, in a tight-fitting T-shirt, giving Adamsberg a fresh thrill. Patting her arm, Hippolyte left her to walk back with the commissaire.

'It's all right, little sis, he won't eat you. But you have to watch out for him. He likes to know where people have hidden their dirty linen, it's not a nice job.'

'He saved Léo,' said Lina, frowning at her brother.

'But he's wondering whether I killed Herbier and Glayeux. He's poking about in my dirty linen. Aren't you, commissaire?'

'It's normal if he's asking questions,' Lina retorted. 'I hope you were polite at least.'

'Very,' said Adamsberg with a smile.

'But since Lina has no dirty linen to hide, I can safely leave her with you,' said Hippo, walking away. 'But mind, *tnod hcout a riah fo reh daeh.*'

'What?'

'Don't touch a hair of her head,' said Lina. 'I'm sorry, commissaire, it's the way he is. He feels responsible for all of us. But we're *nice* people, you know.'

'We're nice people.' The simple-minded motto of the Vendermots. So naive and simple-minded that Adamsberg was half inclined to believe it. Their idea of themselves, their watchword to the world: 'We're nice people.' And what were they hiding behind that? Émeri would have said. A man as intelligent as Hippolyte, and that was an understatement, a guy who could talk backwards as if he were playing marbles, couldn't just be 'nice'.

'Lina, I'm going to ask you the same thing as Hippolyte. When you found your father had been killed, why did you wipe the handle of the axe?'

'Just a reflex, I suppose, for something to do.'

'Lina, you're not eleven years old any more. You can't think an answer like that is good enough. Did you wipe it to remove the fingerprints of one of your brothers?'

'No.'

'You didn't think Hippo could have hit him on the head? Or Martin?'

'No.'

'Why not?'

'We were all too scared to go into his bedroom. We didn't even dare go up there. It was forbidden.'

Adamsberg stopped in the middle of the lane, faced Lina and drew his finger down her pink cheek, in all innocence, like Zerk stroking the pigeon.

'Well then, who *were* you protecting, Lina?'

'The killer,' she said suddenly, looking up. 'And I didn't know who it was. I wasn't shocked when I found him lying there, covered in blood. I just thought that someone, at last, had put a *stop* to him, and he would never come back, and it was a big relief. I wiped the prints off the axe so whoever did it would never be punished. Whoever it was.'

'Thank you, Lina. Tell me, Hippo, when he was in school, was he a holy terror?'

'He was protecting us. Because my brothers, the little ones, in the infants' playground, they were being bullied too. When Hippo was brave enough to face them out with his poor deformed hands, we had a bit of peace at last. We are nice people, but Hippo had to protect us.'

'He told them he was the devil's disciple and he could curse them.'

'Yes and it worked!' she said with a laugh, showing no regret. 'They would run away when we came. And then we were in heaven. We were like kings. Only Léo warned us. Revenge is a dish best eaten cold, she used to say, but I didn't understand that at the time. And now,' she said, looking more serious, 'we're paying for it. With people remembering Hippo the devil, and Hellequin's Horde, I understand why my mother is anxious for us. In 1777, you know, they killed this man, François-Benjamin, he was a pig farmer, with pitchforks.'

'Yes, I was told that. Because he saw the Riders.'

'And he could name three victims, but couldn't recognise the fourth, just like me. The crowd attacked him after the second victim died, and they were two hours at it, spilling his guts And François-Benjamin passed the gift on to his nephew Guillaume, who passed it to his cousin Élodine, then it went on to Sigismond the tanner, then to Hébrard, then to Arnaud the cloth merchant, then to Louis-Pierre who played the harpsichord, and then to Aveline, and then to Gilbert. And apparently Gilbert passed it on to me, when I was baptised. Did your deputy know something, is that why someone tried to kill him?'

'No idea.' *He went off all alone, with a heart full of bile*, Adamsberg said to himself, surprised to find this little line of Veyrenc's verse resurfacing.

'Don't worry looking in that direction,' she said, suddenly sounding determined. 'It wasn't *him* they wanted to kill, it was you.'

'No.'

'Yes. Because you may not know anything today, but you'll end up knowing everything tomorrow. You're much more dangerous than Émeri. Your time's running out.'

'Mine?'

'Yours, commissaire. You'd better get going and run. Nothing stops the Lord and his troops. Don't stand in his way. You can believe me or not, I'm trying to help you.'

This pronouncement was so harsh and weird that Émeri would probably have arrested her on the spot for less. Adamsberg didn't move.

'I've got to protect Mortembot,' he said.

'Mortembot killed his own mother. He's not worth bothering about.'

'That's not my problem, Lina, you know that.'

'You don't understand. He'll die whatever you do. You'd better get away before that.'

'When?'

'Now.'

'I mean, when will he die?'

'Hellequin will decide. Just go away. You and your men.'

XXXVII

ADAMSBERG WALKED SLOWLY INTO THE COURTYARD OF THE hospital, which was becoming as familiar to him as the bar opposite his Paris office. Danglard had refused to wear the regulation blue hospital gown, made of disposable tissue, and was sitting on his bed wearing his suit, crumpled and dirty as it was. The nurse had strongly disapproved, saying it was unhygienic. But since this was a case of attempted suicide and since he had been under a train and survived – something which commanded respect – she hadn't dared insist.

'I need some proper clothes,' was the first thing Danglard said. At the same time, his eyes were directed at the cream-coloured walls, not wanting to meet Adamsberg's expression where he would see reflected his own shame, disgrace and depression. Dr Turbot had filled him in briefly on the sequence of events, without making any comment, and Danglard now didn't know how to live with himself. He had been unprofessional, he'd been grotesque and, worse than everything, stupid. Him, Danglard, the mighty brain. Basic jealousy, his burning desire to best Veyrenc, hadn't left a corner in his mind for dignity and intelligence. Well, maybe, in some remote recess a tiny voice had indeed tried to tell him something, but he hadn't listened, hadn't wanted to know. Like the worst of idiots, the kind that leads to destruction. And it was the very man he had wanted to humiliate who had protected him, and had almost been killed himself under the wheels of the train. It was Louis Veyrenc de Bilhc who had had the reflexes, the courage and the strength, to lie him down between the rails. Whereas he, himself, he reflected, would certainly not have had those three qualities. He wouldn't have thought of moving the body; in any case, he wouldn't have had the physical strength; and perhaps, worst of all, he would have tried to save his own skin first, by scrambling back on to the platform.

The commandant's face was grey with distress. He looked like a cornered rat, not one cheerfully sitting inside a loaf of bread in the kitchen of Tuilot, Julien.

'Does it hurt?' asked Adamsberg.

'Only if I turn my head.'

'Apparently you weren't conscious of the train going over you,' said Adamsberg, without letting any note of consolation enter his voice.

'No. Pretty annoying to have that happen and not remember it, isn't it?' said Danglard, trying to introduce a little irony to his tone.

'That's not what's annoying.'

'And I wasn't even as sloshed as usual.'

'No, indeed not, Danglard. On the contrary, you took care not to drink too much at Émeri's so as to have a clear head for your one-man expedition.'

Danglard looked up at the cream-painted ceiling and decided to keep looking. He had glimpsed Adamsberg's expression and seen the gleam in his eyes. A gleam that carried far, and one that he wanted to avoid. It was a rare kind of gleam, one that only appeared when the commissaire was very angry, deeply interested, or had suddenly had an idea.

'Veyrenc *did* feel the train go past,' Adamsberg said meaningfully.

Furious with Danglard's lamentable behaviour, yes, disappointed, distressed, he was all of those. He felt the need to force his deputy to look him in the eye and be aware of that. *He went off all alone, with a heart full of bile.*

'How is he now?' asked Danglard, articulating scarcely audibly between his teeth.

'He's sleeping, he's getting over it. But we'll be lucky if he hasn't got a few more red hairs afterwards. Or white ones.'

'How did he know?'

'Same way I did. You're not much good as a plotter, commandant. Your excitement about some secret project, your pride and joy, could be read all over your face and in your body language right through dinner.'

'Why did Veyrenc stay up all night?'

'Because he put two and two together. He thought that if you were so worked up about something, some stunt you were going to keep for yourself, it was probably because you hoped to put one across him. Picking up some new information for instance. Whereas you, commandant, forgot that if an informer really wants to stay anonymous, he doesn't usually want to meet you. He writes a note but doesn't give a rendezvous. Even Estalère might have smelt a rat. You didn't. But Veyrenc did. And finally and most importantly, he thought that, given the body count, it was best not to act alone. Unless, that is, a certain person was keen to win some kind of medal, so much so that he couldn't see the bleeding obvious. Because you *did* receive a message didn't you, Danglard? Giving you a rendezvous at the station?'

'Yes.'

'When? Where?'

'I found this note in my pocket. Someone must have got in among the little crowd outside Glayeux's house.'

'And you kept it?'

'No.'

'Brilliant. Why not?'

Danglard bit the inside of his cheek several times before replying.

'I didn't want anyone to know I'd kept the message for myself. That I was acting with premeditation. What I meant to do, after collecting the information, was invent a plausible version.'

'Such as?'

'That I saw someone in the crowd. Asked around about him. And went to Cérenay to find out a bit more. Something banal.'

'And more dignified, you mean.'

'Yes,' sighed Danglard, 'more dignified.'

'Didn't work out, did it?' said Adamsberg, getting up and pacing the small room, going round the commandant's bed.

'OK,' said Danglard. 'I fell in the shit. And I'm in it up to my neck.'

'It happened to me before you, remember that?'

'Yes.'

'So you're not the only one. The difficult bit isn't falling in, it's cleaning oneself up afterwards. What did the message say?'

'It looked as if it was written by someone illiterate, several spelling mistakes. Either real or fake, could be either. But if it was faked, it was quite convincing: crossings-out and so on.'

'And it said?'

'That I should be at Cérenay station at 6.50 exactly. I presumed the writer lived there.'

'I don't think so. The advantage of Cérenay is that trains go through. At 6.56. The Ordebec branch line is disused now. What did Turbot say about the drug?'

Adamsberg's eyes had returned more or less to normal. To their underwater, 'seaweedy' state as some people called it, inventing a word to describe the melting, vague, almost opaque aspect.

'According to the first tests, it's gone from my bloodstream. He thinks it was an anaesthetic vets use: it knocks someone out for about fifteen minutes, then disappears. Probably a weak dose of ketamine chlorohydrate, because I didn't suffer from hallucinations. Commissaire, can I ask you to do something? I mean, can this whole sorry escapade be kept from the rest of the squad?'

'I've got no objection. But there are three of us who know about it. It's not me you should ask, but Veyrenc. After all, he might be tempted to take his revenge. Understandably.'

'Yes.'

'Shall I tell him to come and see you?'

'Not yet.'

'In the end,' Adamsberg said, as he headed for the door, 'you weren't wrong when you imagined your life would be at risk in Ordebec. But as for finding out why someone wanted to kill you, commandant, you'll have to start thinking, and dredge up all the little clues. Discover what it was about you that scared the killer.'

'No!' Danglard almost shouted, as Adamsberg was opening the door. 'No, not me! The killer mistook me for you. The letter was addressed to the commissaire – even if it was spelt wrong. It was *you* they wanted to kill. You don't look like a cop down from Paris, but I do. When I turned up at Glayeux's house in a dark suit, the killer must have thought I was the commissaire.'

'Lina thinks the same as you. But I don't know why she thinks that. I'll leave you now, Danglard, we need to sort out the shifts round Mortembot's house.'

'Will you be seeing Veyrenc?'

'If he's awake.'

'Can you say something to him for me?'

'Absolutely not, Danglard. That's something you'll have to do yourself.'

XXXVIII

THE CHARACTERISTICS OF THE INTERVENTION SITE (AS ÉMERI CALLED it), otherwise known as Mortembot's house, had been explained at length to the combined team of cops from Ordebec and Paris, and shifts had been drawn up. Émeri's part-timer, the one he described as half-this and half-that, had been detached full-time by the Saint-Venon gendarmerie, because of the emergency situation. So there were four two-man teams, allowing round-the-clock shifts. One officer would take the back of the house, which gave on to the fields, covering that side and the east wall. The other would take the front of the house overlooking the street, and the west side with its gable. It wasn't a long house, so every angle would be within a line of sight. At 14.35, Mortembot, having settled his large body on a small plastic chair, was sweating as he listened to his instructions. He was confined to the house until further notice, and was to keep the shutters closed. He had no objection. If he could, he would have begged them to put him inside a concrete drum. They worked out a code so that Mortembot would know when it was a policeman knocking at the door, bringing him food or information. The code would be changed every day. He was of course forbidden to open the door to anyone, the postman, employees from his nurseries, or friends anxious to hear any news. Brigadiers Blériot and Faucheur would handle the first shift until 9 p.m. Justin and Estalère would take over until 3 a.m., Adamsberg and Veyrenc until 9 a.m., and finally Danglard and Émeri would relieve them, staying until 3 p.m. Adamsberg had had to negotiate, using made-up excuses, so that Danglard and Veyrenc would not share a shift:

he considered shotgun reconciliations futile and in poor taste. The programme was to last three days.

'And then what, when three days are up?' asked Mortembot, running his fingers again and again through his sweat-soaked hair.

'We'll just see,' said Émeri coldly. 'We won't need to be watching over you for weeks if we catch the killer.'

'But you'll never catch him,' said Mortembot, almost whining. 'You can't catch Lord Hellequin.'

'So you believe in him? I thought you and your cousin didn't believe in the supernatural.'

'Jeannot didn't. But I've always thought there was some power lurking in the Forest of Alance.'

'Did you say so to Jeannot?'

'No, no. He thought it was all a lot of nonsense, only idiots believed it.'

'Well, if you believe it, you must know why Hellequin chose you. You know why you're frightened of him?'

'No, no, I've no idea.'

'Oh yeah!'

'Perhaps because I was close to Jeannot.'

'*And Jeannot killed young Tétard?*'

'Yes,' said Mortembot, wiping his eyes.

'And you helped him?'

'No, honest to god.'

'Doesn't bother you, does it, telling on your cousin now that he's dead?'

'Hellequin asks for contrition.'

'Oh, that's it, is it? So he'll spare you. In that case, you'd do well to explain to him what happened with your mother.'

'No! I never touched her! She was my mother!'

'You touched something though, you pulled the stool away with a string. You're a piece of shit, Mortembot. Get up, we're going to lock you in now. And since you'll have plenty of time to think, settle your accounts with Hellequin, draw up your confession.'

* * *

Adamsberg went back to the guest house where he found Hellebaud the pigeon nestled into the hollow on his own bed, and Veyrenc up, showered, changed and sitting eating some warmed-up pasta straight from the saucepan.

'We have to take the shift from 3 a.m. to 9 a.m. Is that OK?'

'Fine. I think I'm back to normal now. But seeing a train bearing down on you is indescribable. I nearly chickened out, I nearly left Danglard on the rails and got back on the platform.'

'You'll get an award,' said Adamsberg with a brief grin. 'Police gallantry medal. Solid silver.'

'No. That would mean reporting the whole thing and stabbing Danglard in the back. I don't think our poor old colleague would get over it. Albatross fallen to earth, intelligence failed.'

'He's already crawling on the ground, Louis. He doesn't know how to get himself out of this mess.'

'Yeah, right, normal enough.'

'Yes.'

'Want some pasta? I can't eat all this,' said Veyrenc, passing over the saucepan.

Adamsberg was still eating the lukewarm spaghetti, when his mobile pinged. He opened it with one hand and read Retancourt's message. At last.

Sv 1 told butler hair cut 3am Friday cos shock + grief. Sacked chmbrmaid sez hair already cut post-party. But chmbrmd unreliable wtness hates Sv guts. Will check car.

Adamsberg showed the text to Veyrenc, his heart beating fast.

'Don't understand,' said Veyrenc.

'I'll tell you.'

'I've got something to explain too,' said Veyrenc, lowering his girlish eyelashes. 'They're off.'

He stopped and drew a map of Africa on a piece of paper they had used for a shopping list.

When did you find out? Adamsberg wrote, under the words *cheese, bread, lighter, birdseed.*

Text an hour ago, Veyrenc wrote.

From?

Pal of your son.

What happened?

They spotted a cop in Granada.

Where now?

Casares. 15 km from Estepona.

?

Facing the African coast.

'Let's go for a walk,' said Adamsberg. 'I've lost my appetite.'

XXXIX

'NOTHING TO REPORT,' SAID JUSTIN, WHEN VEYRENC AND ADAMSBERG arrived to take over at 3 a.m.

Adamsberg walked round to the back and found Estalère, conscientiously pacing up and down, looking in turn out at the fields and at the house.

'Nothing,' Estalère confirmed. 'But he's still not asleep,' he added, pointing to the lights shining through the shutters.

'He's got plenty to think about, and it'll keep him awake.'

'I guess.'

'What are you eating?

'Lump of sugar, good for energy. Want some?'

'No thanks, Estalère. Just now, when I see a sugar lump, I feel sick.'

'Allergy?' asked the young brigadier, opening wide his big green eyes.

Adamsberg hadn't been able to sleep either, despite having tried to nap before going on duty. Zerk and Mo were in danger, on the verge of disappearing to North Africa, and why was his Zerk going all the way with Mo, sharing his fate? As for the Ordebec killer, he was slipping through his fingers like the ghastly ghost that he was: it was enough to make you think the locals were right and that no one could take hold of Lord Hellequin with his flowing locks. The Clermont family still seemed untouchable, although there was this business of the haircut. Such a fragile clue that it would melt away the moment it was examined. Unless, that is, the sacked chambermaid was telling the truth and Saviour 1, Christian, really had come home that night with his hair already cut. Going out at 8 p.m. with long hair, back at 2 a.m. with short hair. Like Mo, who shaved his head after getting scorched. So that no one could see his singed locks. So that the cops wouldn't suspect him. But it was Christophe, not Christian, who had been driving their father. And both of them had completely undamaged suits, neither of which had been sent for dry-cleaning.

Adamsberg concentrated on the guard duty. The fields and the edge of the woods were visible by moonlight, although Émeri had announced that clouds were piling up in the west. It seemed that after two weeks of heatwave and no rain, the people of Normandy were at last starting to feel concern at the unusual weather. Those clouds in the west were becoming an obsession.

At 4 a.m., the lights in the house were still on, in both ground-floor rooms, and the kitchen and bathroom. Mortembot might be awake and that wouldn't be surprising, but most insomniacs known to Adamsberg turned out the lights except in the room they were in. Perhaps Mortembot was so paralysed with fear that he didn't want the house to be in darkness. At 5 a.m., Adamsberg went over to meet Veyrenc.

'Does that look normal to you?' he asked.

'No, it doesn't.'

'Shall we take a look?'

'Yes.'

Adamsberg knocked at the front door, using the prearranged code: four long, two short, three long. He tried several times, without getting any response.

'Open up,' he said to Veyrenc, 'and have your gun ready. Stay outside, while I check what he's up to.'

Adamsberg, holding his own gun cocked for action, went through the empty rooms, hugging the walls. No books lying around, no TV on, no sign of Mortembot. In the kitchen were the remains of a cold meal, which he had not had the stomach to finish. In the bathroom, he found the clothes Mortembot had been wearing earlier in the day at the police station. The only way Mortembot could have escaped was through the skylight on the roof, by waiting for one of the cops to go round the corner, and then jumping down to the ground. Perhaps he didn't trust them, and thought it best to disappear. Then Adamsberg pushed open the door of the lavatory, and Mortembot's large body collapsed on to the floor, face up, his trousers round his thighs. The tiles were covered with blood: Mortembot's throat had been pierced by a long steel object. The bolt from a crossbow, if Adamsberg was not mistaken. He had been dead a few hours. The narrow little window was broken, the glass lying on the floor.

The commissaire called Veyrenc.

'Shot in the neck while he was taking a leak. Look at the angle,' said Adamsberg, standing outside the lavatory door, looking at the window. 'The bolt got him in the throat.'

'Good god, Jean-Baptiste, that window's barred, the gap's not more than twenty centimetres either side. What kind of arrow is it? An archer firing through the window – surely Estalère would have seen him?'

'It's a bolt, a very powerful crossbow bolt.'

Veyrenc whistled, in either anger or surprise. 'Well, that's certainly something from the Middle Ages.'

'No, not really, Louis. I think, from looking at the way it's lodged in the wound, it must have been a hunting bolt. Very contemporary. They're light, solid and accurate, and they have razor-sharp wings that cause a haemorrhage. Deadly, for sure.'

'Provided you're a good shot,' said Veyrenc, moving round the body and peering at the bars on the window. 'Look how narrow the gap is – I can hardly get my arm through. Even with a bit of luck, whoever shot it would have to be within five metres to get his target and not hit the bar. Estalère would *surely* have seen him. There's light here from the street lamp.'

'Not if the killer was lucky and had a pulley-driven crossbow, a compound for instance. It can be aimed from forty metres, and with telescopic sights and night vision, he couldn't miss. Fifty metres even, if he's good. And if he's got a weapon like that, he must be good. But either way, it means the killer was in the woods, hiding just at the edge. The shot would be quite silent, he'd have plenty of time to get away before any cop noticed what had happened.'

'You know a lot about crossbows.'

'On my military service, I had to train as a marksman. They had me learning every kind of weapon in the arsenal.'

'That's odd,' said Veyrenc, turning round. 'He's changed.'

Adamsberg was calling Émeri on his phone. 'Changed what?'

'His clothes. Mortembot changed his clothes. He's wearing a grey track-suit now. But why do that when he was at home?'

'To feel cleaner after his time in the police cells, probably? Normal enough, surely? Émeri? Did I wake you? Look, get here fast, Mortembot's dead.'

'But why didn't he wait till the morning?' Veyrenc was asking.

'What?'

'To change.'

'Hell's bells, Louis, what's it matter? He went to take a leak, the killer was just waiting for that moment. Mortembot could be seen head-on, through that window, standing still with the light on. Ideal target. He collapsed, didn't make a sound. Lord Hellequin got him, and in his old-fashioned way, what's more.'

'Well, old-fashioned, but updated for commando purposes, you said so yourself.'

'It's the only explanation I can see for a shot like that. But still a cross-bow's a heavy thing, weighs more than three kilos and it's about a metre long. Even if he's got one that folds up, you can't hide it under a jacket. The killer must have known how to get rid of it afterwards.'

'But who'd own a thing like that these days?'

'Hunters, plenty of them. It's typically used by big-time poachers, because it's noiseless. It's still officially classed as a sixth-category weapon, allowed without a permit because it's considered suitable for "sport and recreation". Some sport.'

'Why didn't you think of it before?'

Adamsberg looked hard at the window, the broken glass and the iron bar.

'I thought that with the glass as a barrier, any attempt to shoot would have been deflected, bullet or arrow. The result wouldn't be certain enough for anyone to try and shoot through it. But look at this glass, Louis. That's what we didn't check.'

Émeri came into the house, only two of the buttons on his tunic done up this time.

'Émeri, I'm sorry,' said Adamsberg. 'It was a crossbow bolt through the lavatory window. When he was taking a leak.'

'That window? But it's barred.'

'But that's what happened. And it got him in the throat.'

'A crossbow? Not a serious weapon. You could just about wing a deer with one, at ten metres.'

'Not this kind, Émeri. Did you call Lisieux?'

'They're on their way. It's your responsibility, Adamsberg. You're in charge of the case, and your men were on the watch.'

'My men can't be expected to see forty metres into the woods. And you might have foreseen the gap at this window. You checked out the place for access.'

'Why would I think of a crossbow being used to get through a mousehole?'

'A rathole, I'd call it.'

'The rathole was blocked with thick glass, impossible to get a clear shot through it. The killer wouldn't choose that angle.'

'Take a look at the window, Émeri. There's not a single shard of glass attached to the frame. It must have been cut out carefully beforehand, so that a slight pressure, even a finger, would make it fall out.'

'So that it wouldn't deflect the shot?'

'No. And we didn't notice the trace left by the glass-cutter close to the window frame.'

'That still doesn't explain why he chose a crossbow.'

'Because it's silent. And the killer must have been familiar with Mortembot's mother's house. There are fitted carpets everywhere, even in the toilet. So the glass didn't make a clatter when it fell out either.'

Émeri adjusted his tunic collar, muttering crossly. 'Round here, they mostly have shotguns. If he wanted not to be heard, he could have used a silencer and a subsonic bullet.'

'Even that would make a noise. Something like a .22 airgun and a lot more than a crossbow.'

'But the cord vibrates and makes a noise.'

'Yes, but not the kind of sound people would be listening out for. And from that distance it wouldn't sound much louder than a bird flapping its wings. Anyway, it fits the idea of Hellequin's weapon, doesn't it?'

'Yeah, right,' said Émeri bitterly.

'Think about it, Émeri. It's not only the perfect choice of weapon but an artistic one. Historic and poetic.'

'He didn't kill Herbier poetically.'

'Let's say he's refining his methods. More subtle.'

'You reckon the killer thinks he's Hellequin himself?'

'I don't know about that,' said Adamsberg. 'All we know is he's a crack shot with a crossbow. At least that's a clue to start with. We could try checking the local shooting clubs, and get hold of their membership lists.'

'Why did he change his clothes?' Émeri asked, looking down at Mortembot's body.

'To get rid of the smell of the police cell,' said Veyrenc.

'The cells are perfectly clean at my station. And the blankets. What do you think, Adamsberg?'

'I'm wondering why you and Veyrenc are getting so steamed up about his changing his clothes. Although it all counts,' the commissaire added, looking wearily at the window. 'Even a hole big enough for a rat. Especially that.'

XL

ADAMSBERG HELPED SEARCH THE WOODS UNTIL 7 A.M., BEING JOINED
by the five other men who had all been called from their beds. Danglard
looked worn out. He wouldn't have been able to sleep much either,
Adamsberg reflected: he would have been searching for a safe haven
for his thoughts, as one tries to shelter from the wind. But for the
moment, Danglard had no place of shelter. His brilliant mind, normally
incapable of anything stupid or shameful, was lying in pieces at his
feet.

At first light, they quite quickly ascertained where the killer had lain
in wait. Faucheur called the others. Unusually, it was apparent that the
assassin, protected by a many-branched oak tree, had sat on a small
camping stool, and the marks of its metal base could be seen imprinted
on the carpet of leaves.

'I've never seen anything like it!' said Émeri, who seemed almost scan-
dalised. 'A murderer who takes trouble over his comfort. He's preparing
to kill a man, but he doesn't want to tire his legs.'

'Perhaps he's old,' ventured Veyrenc. 'Or someone who has trouble
standing for a long time. He could have had hours to wait before
Mortembot went into the lav.'

'Not as old as all that,' said Adamsberg. 'To draw a crossbow and take
the recoil, you have to be pretty strong. Sitting down would enable him
to aim with more precision. And you make less noise than trampling the
undergrowth. How far are we from the target?'

'Forty-two or forty-three metres,' said Estalère, who had, as Adamsberg had always remarked, very good eyesight.

'In Rouen Cathedral,' said Danglard, in a very quiet voice, as if his lost eminence now disqualified him from speaking normally, 'the heart of King Richard is preserved. He was killed in battle by a crossbow.'

'Oh really?' said Émeri, who always perked up at any mention of glorious battlefields.

'Yes. He was wounded at the siege of Châlus-Chabrol in March 1199 and died eleven days later of gangrene. And in his case at least, we know the name of the murderer.'

'Who was it?' asked Émeri.

'Pierre Basile, a minor noble from the Limousin.'

'For crying out loud, what's that got to do with anything?' said Adamsberg, irritated by the fact that even in a state of collapse, Danglard persisted in showing off his knowledge.

'It's just,' said Danglard still in his muted voice, 'that he was one of the most famous victims of a crossbow.'

'And after Richard the Lionheart, the despicable Michel Mortembot,' said Émeri. 'What a comedown,' he concluded, shaking his head.

The men continued to search the forest, beating down undergrowth, looking without much hope for any trace of the murderer's tracks. The leaves underfoot were dry with the summer heat and retained no footprints. Émeri called the searchers together with a whistle after a further three-quarters of an hour. He was standing to attention, his tunic by now buttoned, a few metres from the far edge of the wood, in front of a patch of newly dug earth, imperfectly covered with scattered leaves.

'The crossbow!' said Veyrenc.

'I think so,' said Émeri.

The hole wasn't deep, only about thirty centimetres, and the men quickly unearthed a plastic sheath.

'That's it all right,' said Blériot. 'Didn't want to destroy his precious weapon, did he? He buried it here, quickly like. Must have dug the hole before.'

'Like he cut the glass in the window earlier.'

'How could he have guessed that Mortembot would barricade himself in like that?'

'Not so difficult to work out that after Glayeux's death Mortembot would be in his mother's house,' said Émeri. 'It's very carelessly buried,' he added, looking scornful. 'Just like he didn't bother hiding the axe properly.'

'Perhaps he's not much of a thinker,' suggested Veyrenc. 'Someone good at immediate action but who doesn't work out the long term. With gaps in the thinking.'

'Or perhaps this weapon belongs to someone else, like the axe did,' said Adamsberg, who was starting to feel dizzy with fatigue. 'For example one of the Vendermots. And the killer wanted us to find it.'

'You know what I think of them,' said Émeri. 'Still, I don't know that Hippo has a crossbow.'

'What about Martin? He's always in the forest, collecting things.'

'I can't see him capturing insects with a modern weapon. But someone who certainly *did* have one of these was Herbier.'

'Two years ago,' Faucheur confirmed, 'we found a wild sow with a crossbow bolt in its side.'

'The killer could well have taken the crossbow from his house, after his death and before the seals were placed on it.'

'Although,' Adamsberg remarked gently, 'there are ways and means of replacing the seals.'

'Got to be a professional, though, to do that.'

'That's true.'

Émeri's team collected up the material to be taken to Lisieux, fenced off the area round the hole, and the place where the stool had been, and left Blériot and Faucheur waiting for the SOC team.

They returned to Mortembot's house, arriving at the same time as Dr Turbot, who had been called in to make a preliminary report. The regular pathologist, Dr Chazy, was in Livarot, where a slater had fallen from a roof. No suspicious circumstances at first sight but the gendarmes had preferred to call her in, because the slater's wife had said, shrugging her shoulders, that her husband had had a bellyful of cider.

Turbot looked down at Mortembot and shook his head. 'If a man can't even take a piss in safety,' he said simply.

Rather a bleak funeral oration, Adamsberg thought, but to the point. Turbot confirmed that the shot must have hit him between about 1 and 2 a.m., certainly no later than three. He extracted the bolt without moving the body, so as to leave the scene unchanged for his colleague.

'Bloody savage weapon,' he said, waving it in front of Adamsberg. 'My colleague will do the autopsy but it looks as if the bolt went through the larynx to the oesophagus. I think he choked to death before the haemorrhage set in. Shall we adjust his pants?'

'We can't, doctor. Crime scene team has to check him.'

'All the same,' said Turbot with a grimace.

'Yes, doctor, I know.'

'And as for you,' said the doctor, looking at Adamsberg intently, 'you'd better get some sleep as soon as possible. And he should too,' he said, gesturing towards Danglard. 'Some people round here aren't getting enough sleep. You'll keel over like skittles if you don't watch it.'

'Go on,' said Émeri, tapping Adamsberg on the shoulder. 'I'll wait for the others. Blériot and I have had some sleep.'

Hellebaud had left signs in the bedroom of his morning walk, leaving birdseed scattered everywhere. But he had returned to occupy the commissaire's left shoe, and he cooed when he saw Adamsberg arrive. There was one big advantage to this choice of shoe, unnatural though it might be. The pigeon no longer left droppings as it flew round the room, but strictly inside the shoe. When he had slept, Adamsberg thought, he'd clean it out. With what? A knife? A spoon? A shoehorn?

The violence of the hunting crossbow had made him feel sick, the sharp wings of the bolt piercing holes in the victim's neck as he stood taking a piss. Much worse than the bread in the old woman's throat. Tuilot, Lucette:

that method of killing, in its rather homespun way, was even strangely touching. And then Danglard had got on his nerves, spouting about Richard the Lionheart, as if that had any relevance. Veyrenc was no better, fussing about Mortembot having changed his clothes. Adamsberg's irritability had come over him quickly, and was unfair, only proving how exhausted he was. Mortembot had taken off his blue jacket – which probably smelt of the cell, whatever anyone said, if only because of the disinfectant – and had put on a grey tracksuit, jogging pants with dark grey piping. Well, so what? What if Mortembot had felt like being more comfortable? Or looking smarter? Émeri had also annoyed him once more, with his habit of announcing that he was letting Adamsberg carry full responsibility for this new disaster. Émeri, not the bravest of soldiers. This third murder would finally rouse Ordebec to a state of panic, and it would spread to the entire region. The local papers were already going to town about Lord Hellequin and his sinister fury, and some readers had already written in, pointing the finger at the Vendermot family, without naming them directly. It had seemed to him the day before that the streets emptied much more quickly than usual in the evening. Moreover, if the murderer could attack from a distance with a crossbow, nobody was safe in their little ratholes. Himself least of all, since somebody had intended him to be sliced in three by a train. If the murderer could have known how much at a loss he was, and how little he knew, he wouldn't have gone to all that trouble of arranging for a train to kill him. But perhaps Lina Vendermot's splendid breasts were blinding him to the possibility of finding fault with the Vendermot family.

XLI

ADAMSBERG OPENED HIS EYES THREE HOURS LATER, CONSCIOUS OF the buzzing of a fly that was crashing furiously around the room without noticing – nor did Hellebaud – that the window was wide open.

On waking, his first thought was not for Mo and Zerk on the verge of danger, nor of the victims of Lord Hellequin, nor even old Léo. He was asking himself why he had thought that Mortembot was wearing a blue jacket in his police cell, since it had actually been brown.

He opened the door, and scattered some birdseed on the step, to encourage Hellebaud to venture at least a metre away from the shoe, then went into the kitchen to fix some coffee. Danglard was already there, not speaking, his eyes fixed on a newspaper without reading it, and Adamsberg began to feel some pity for his old comrade, still unable to heave himself out of the cesspit he was in.

'They say in the *Ordebec Reporter* that the Paris cops haven't caught anyone. To put it briefly.'

'They're not wrong,' commented Adamsberg, pouring hot water on to the ground coffee in the filter.

'They say that back in 1777 it was the same; Lord Hellequin dodged the constables of the day easily.'

'That's not untrue either.'

'There is something though. Nothing to do with the case, but I'm thinking about it all the same.'

'If it's King Richard's heart, please don't bother, Danglard.'

Adamsberg went out into the large courtyard, leaving the water boiling on the gas. Danglard shook his head, heaved up his body which seemed ten times more ponderous than normal, and finished pouring hot water on to the coffee grounds. He went over to the window to look at Adamsberg strolling under the apple trees, hands in the pockets of his shapeless trousers, and his gaze, it seemed, empty and vacant. Danglard busied himself with the coffee – should he take it outside, or drink it on his own without calling Adamsberg? – while watching the courtyard out of the corner of his eye. Adamsberg disappeared from his field of vision, then re-emerged from the cellar and walked rather quickly back to the house. He sat down more heavily than usual on a bench in the kitchen, put both hands on the table and looked hard at Danglard without speaking. Danglard didn't feel at this moment any right to question or criticise, but put two cups on the table and poured out the coffee like a kindly house-wife, for want of anything else to do.

'Danglard,' said Adamsberg, 'what colour jacket was Mortembot wearing when he was up at the gendarmerie?'

'Brown.'

'Exactly. But I saw it as blue. Or rather, when I thought about it later, I remembered it as blue.'

'Yes?' said Danglard prudently, more alarmed at Adamsberg's moments of concentration than when the gleam flashed in his seaweedy eyes.

'But why, Danglard?'

The commandant raised his cup to his lips but said nothing. He was tempted by the idea of adding a drop of Calvados to it as people round here did, 'as a heart-starter', but he had the feeling that at this time of day such an action would reawaken Adamsberg's anger, which had barely subsided. Especially since the *Ordebec Reporter* was saying that the Paris cops were a waste of space and (he had spared the commissaire this) that they didn't give a damn about the case anyway. On the other hand, Adamsberg would be so far away he might not notice. He was just about to get up and fetch his little drop, when Adamsberg took a packet of photographs out of his pocket and spread them in front of him.

'The Clermont-Brasseur brothers,' he said.

'Right,' said Danglard. 'The photos the count gave you.'

'Quite. Dressed as for this famous evening party. Christian here in a blue jacket with a pinstripe and there's Christophe wearing a yachting blazer.'

'Bit vulgar,' said Danglard, sotto voce.

Adamsberg got out his mobile, flipped across a few images and held it out to Danglard.

'Here's the photo Retancourt sent, showing the suit Christian was wearing when he got back that evening. The one that was *not* sent to the cleaners. Neither were his brother's clothes. She checked.'

'So we have to believe her,' said Danglard, looking at the small image.

'Navy pinstripe for Christian, see? Not brown.'

'No.'

'So why did I think Mortembot's jacket was navy?'

'By mistake?'

'Because he *changed*, Danglard. See the connection?'

'Frankly, no.'

'Because I knew, somewhere in my mind, that Christian must have changed. Like Mortembot.'

'But why did Mortembot change?'

'Mortembot doesn't matter, dammit,' said Adamsberg. 'Anyone would think you were trying on purpose not to understand.'

'Well, don't forget I've been under a train.'

'OK, granted,' Adamsberg acknowledged. 'Well, Christian Clermont *changed his clothes*, it's been staring me in the face for days. So much so that when I thought about Mortembot's jacket I saw it as navy too. Like Christian's. Look at them carefully, Danglard: the suit he was wearing during the reception, and the one photographed by Retancourt, that is, the one he wore to come home.'

Adamsberg placed in front of Danglard the photo he had received from the count, and the one on the mobile. He seemed only then to notice the coffee in front of him and swallowed half a cup.

'Well, Danglard?'

'I only see it because you pointed it out. Christian's two suits are very alike, both navy, but not quite the same.'

'See.'

'The pinstripe is a bit thicker on the second one, the lapels are a bit wider, the sleeves a bit narrower.'

'There you are,' said Adamsberg with a smile, getting up and taking long strides between the fireplace and the door. 'There you are. Between the time Christian left the reception, at about midnight, and the time he got home, at about two, he'd changed his clothes. Very close match, hardly noticeable, but there it is. The suit he sent to the cleaners next day *wasn't* the one he was wearing when he got back, Retancourt wasn't wrong. But it *was* the one he wore to the party. And why, Danglard?'

'Because it smelt of petrol,' said the commandant, managing a weak smile once more.

'And it stank of petrol because Christian had bloody well torched the Mercedes with his father strapped inside. And another thing,' he said, striking the table with his fist. 'He cut his hair before he went home. Look at the photos again. At the party, his hair is fairly long and he has a bit of a fringe. But when he returned, according to the sacked chambermaid, his hair was very short. Because, as has happened before to Mo, the fierce flames singed his hair and it was obvious. So he cut it, made it look the same all over, and he put on a different suit. And what does he tell his valet next morning? That in the night he cut his hair short as a grief reflex, an act of despair. Christian the Skinhead.'

'There's no direct evidence,' Danglard said. 'Retancourt's photo wasn't taken the same night and nothing proves either she or the chambermaid who told her didn't make a mistake. The suits are very similar.'

'We might find some hairs in the car.'

'It'll have been cleaned since then.'

'Not necessarily. It's very hard to remove all the tiny hairs after a haircut, especially if we're lucky and the headrests are made of cloth. We can suppose Christian would have done it in haste, not thinking he was taking a risk. He probably didn't think he'd even be questioned. Retancourt will have to examine the car.'

'But how will she get permission to get inside it?'

'She won't. And a third thing, Danglard, the dog and the sugar.'

'That's your business with Léo.'

'No, I'm talking about another dog, another lump of sugar. We're going through a period infested with sugar lumps, commandant. Some years there are plagues of ladybirds, other times sugar lumps.'

Adamsberg looked up the messages from Retancourt about the sacked chambermaid and got the commandant to read them.

'I don't get it,' said Danglard.

'That's because you've been under a train. Yesterday on the road, Blériot asked me to give some sugar to Léo's dog, Fleg. He'd just been fixing the engine in the police car and explained that Fleg wouldn't touch the sugar if his hands smelt of petrol.'

'Ah, very good,' said Danglard, more alert now, getting up to fetch some Calvados from the cupboard.

'What are you doing, Danglard?'

'I'm just getting a wee drop, to cheer up my coffee and the cesspit as well.'

'Dammit, commandant, that's Léo's Calva, the one Valleray gives her. What will it look like when she gets back? Like some soldiers from an occupying army have been billeted here.'

'OK, you're right,' said Danglard, quickly putting a drop in his coffee, as Adamsberg turned away to start pacing towards the fireplace.

'That's why the chambermaid was fired. Christian had changed his clothes, and cleaned himself up, but his hands still smelt of petrol. It can cling to your skin for hours. And a dog would sniff it out, no trouble. Which is what Christian realised when his pet refused the sugar. A lump of sugar that the chambermaid had picked up. And which she criticised. He had to get rid of the contaminated sugar lump. *And* the chambermaid, so he sacked her on the spot.'

'She'll need to be called as a witness.'

'About that and the haircut. She's not the only person to have seen Christian that evening. There were the two cops who came to inform him of the news. And then he went and shut himself in his room. We need to know more about what Retancourt says here: *Chmbrmaid criticsed sugar* – what was she criticising? Get Retancourt to work on it tonight.'

'Tonight?'

'In Paris. You're going back, Danglard, to brief Retancourt, and then you're going to vanish like a shadow.'

'To Ordebec?'

'No.'

Danglard drank his coffee-Calva and thought for a moment.

Adamsberg was fiddling with the two mobiles, taking out the batteries.

'You want me to go after the two kids? That it?'

'Yes. You should find them quite quickly in Casares. Once they get to North Africa, though, it would be another matter. If the cops spotted them in Granada, they might well be looking in all the towns on the coast, as we speak. You've got to get there before them, Danglard. Get down there fast and bring them back.'

'It seems a bit premature to me.'

'No, I think our case will stand up. But we need to organise their return carefully. Zerk has to look as if he's back from Italy, after some girlfriend trouble, and Mo will have to be picked up hiding out in the home of one of his friends. The friend's father cracks and reports him. It has to look plausible.'

'How will I contact you?'

'Call the Blue Boar, but use coded messages. I'll say that from tomorrow either Veyrenc or I will eat there every night.'

'Running Boar,' Danglard corrected automatically, then he slumped dramatically, his long arms at his sides. 'But for god's sake, Adamsberg, it was *Christophe* who was driving the Mercedes, Christian had already left the party.'

'They must both be in it together. Christian took his own car earlier, and parked it near the Mercedes, then he waited for his brother to come along. He'd be all ready, wearing the new trainers. But he laced them like an oldster. When Christophe walked away from the Mercedes, leaving their father belted into the front seat, supposedly to look for his lost mobile – which he had indeed deliberately dropped on the pavement – Christian

279

poured the petrol over the car, lit it and then ran back to his own car. Christophe was a safe distance away when it caught fire, he called the police, and he even ran to help, as the witnesses said. Christian then finished off the operation. He dumped the trainers at Mo's place, having lured him away. The door of Mo's flat is easy to force. Then he changed his suit, putting the one he was wearing into the car boot. He realised some of his hair was singed. So he cut it himself. Next day he retrieves his suit and sends it to the cleaners. All that remains to do then is to get Mo arrested.'

'And why would Christian have scissors or a razor with him?'

'These guys always have a travelling bag with them in the boot of the car. They have to be ready to catch a plane at the drop of a hat. So he'd have had them.'

'No examining magistrate will listen to this,' said Danglard, shaking his head. 'They've put up a big wall round it, the system's impregnable.'

'Well, we'll get in through the system. I don't think the Comte de Valleray would appreciate the fact that the brothers killed his old friend Antoine. So he can pull some strings.'

'When should I go?'

'Right now, I think, Danglard.'

'I don't like leaving you alone to face Lord Hellequin.'

'I don't think it's Lord Hellequin who tries to kill people with the Paris express. Or with a commando-style crossbow.'

'A bit tasteless. Not his style.'

'Exactly.'

XLII

DANGLARD WAS PUTTING HIS BAGS IN THE BOOT OF ONE OF THE cars when he saw Veyrenc in the courtyard. He had not yet found either the strength or the words, still less the humility, to speak to the lieutenant. Mortembot's death had made it possible to put off the reckoning. The idea of simply holding out his hand and saying 'Thank you' seemed to him to be ridiculously pompous.

'I'm going to pick up the kids,' he said, rather shamefacedly, as he came up beside him.

'Risky,' said Veyrenc.

'Adamsberg has found a way through, a rat run to get into the Clermonts. We may be able to build the case against the two brothers.'

Veyrenc's expression lightened, his lip lifted in that dangerously girlish smile. Danglard remembered that Veyrenc loved his nephew, Armel, aka Zerk, like a son.

'When you get there,' said Veyrenc, 'check something. That Armel hasn't nicked his grandfather's pistol.'

'Adamsberg said he didn't know how to use a gun.'

'He doesn't know the boy at all. He can handle a gun all right.'

'Oh my god, Veyrenc,' said Danglard, forgetting for a moment the embarrassment which was inhibiting his powers of conversation. 'I meant to tell Adamsberg something, nothing to do with the case, but all the same. Can you give him a message?'

'What is it?'

'In the hospital, I picked up the shawl that Lina let fall from her shoulders. However hot it is, she always wears it. And later I helped the doctor to carry Valleray out, when he had a fainting fit. He had his shirt taken off and he was trying to resist as hard as he could. And here,' Danglard said, putting his finger on his shoulder blade, 'he has a rather disfiguring birthmark, a port wine stain, looks a bit like a woodlouse, about two centimetres long. And the thing is, Lina has one just the same.'

The two men looked at each other, almost directly.

'Lina Vendermot is Valleray's daughter,' said Danglard. 'I'm as sure of that as of the shit I've been going through. And since she and her brother Hippo look as alike as two peas, with their fair hair, they make a pair. But the two darker ones, Martin and Antonin, must be Vendermot's children.'

'My god. Do they know?'

'Well, the count must know. That's why he was struggling not to have his shoulder exposed. I wouldn't know about the children. Doesn't look like it.'

'But why would Lina hide her birthmark?'

'She's a woman. The birthmark's rather ugly.'

'I'm trying to think of any way this might change the Hellequin manoeuvres.'

'Haven't had time to think about that, Veyrenc. I leave it all to you,' Danglard said, holding out his hand. 'Thank you,' he said.

He'd done it. He'd said it.

Like the most ordinary of people. Like any common mortal for a mediocre resolution of a drama, he thought, wiping his damp palm before getting into the car. To shake hands and say thank you was easy perhaps, and banal, possibly taking some courage, but now it was done, and deserved. He would say more at some later stage, if he could manage it. A sudden feeling of angry pleasure came over him and made him sit up straighter as he drove off, at the thought that Adamsberg had nailed the murderers of Clermont *père*. Thanks to Mortembot's jacket, and never mind what the reasoning was, since Danglard hadn't really been able to follow the logic. But the means were in place now and for the moment that consoled him for all the moral failings of the world, and even to some extent for his own.

At nine in the evening he had joined Retancourt on the terrace of the cafe outside her flat in Seine-Saint-Denis. Every time he saw Violette again, even after three days, he found her taller and more solid than in his memory and was impressed. She was sitting on a plastic chair, the legs of which splayed under her weight.

'Three things,' said Retancourt, who had spent only a short time enquiring after the feelings of her colleagues dealing with the Ordebec quagmire, since empathy wasn't her thing. 'The car belonging to Saviour 1, Christian. I found out that it's parked in their private garage with the cars of his brother and their wives. If I'm to examine it, I'll have to get it out of there. So I'll have to immobilise the alarm and jump-start it. No bother, Noël can do that. But I won't take the risk of getting it back, they'll have to work it out themselves, it's not our problem.'

'We won't be able to use the samples if we don't go through official channels.'

'Yeah, but we'd never get permission. So we go with plan B. Illegal collection of clues, put together the file and then charge head-on.'

'If you say so,' said Danglard, who rarely challenged Retancourt's somewhat strong-arm tactics.

'Second point,' she said, putting her powerful index finger on the table, 'the suit. The one he sent to the cleaners discreetly. Petrol vapour, like hair, is very hard to eliminate completely. With a bit of luck, there should be some left in the cloth. Of course, that means stealing the suit.'

'Difficult.'

'Not really. I know the daily routine. I know when Vincent, the butler, is on the door. I turn up with a bag, saying I've left behind a jacket or some other clothes on the first floor, and I follow my nose.'

Improvisation, cheek and confidence, all means that Danglard never employed.

'What excuse did you give for leaving?'

'My husband was trying to find me, he'd caught up with me and I had to get away, in my own interests. Vincent expressed sympathy, though he seemed surprised that I was married and even more that a husband was chasing me with such determination. But I don't think Christian even noticed I'd gone. Third point, the sugar. The chambermaid, Leila. She's really pissed off, she'll certainly talk if she can remember anything. Whether the sugar or the haircut. How did Adamsberg get the idea of the changed suit?'

'I can't tell you exactly, Violette. It was all held together by some kind of spider's web, incomplete and rather mixed up.'

'I can imagine,' said Retancourt, who had often argued against the commissaire's nebulous mental system.

'Here's to the arrest of the Clermont-Brasseur brothers,' said Danglard, filling up Retancourt's glass, simply for an excuse to replenish his own. 'It will be great to see, ethically correct, hygienic and satisfying, but it won't last long. The empire will be passed on to some nephew and it'll all start again. Don't try to call me on my mobile. Report to Adamsberg at this restaurant called the Running Boar in the evenings. It's in Ordebec. If he tells you to call him at the Blue Boar, don't worry, it's the same place, but he never gets the name right. I don't know why he keeps thinking the boar is blue. I'll write down the number for you.'

'You're off somewhere, commandant?'

'Yes, tonight.'

'Somewhere we can't reach you. I mean, we won't know where you are?'

'Right.'

Retancourt nodded without showing surprise, which made Danglard fear that she had understood the whole business with Mo.

'And you want to get away without anyone knowing?'

'Yes.'

'And how do you think you're going to do that?'

'Well, I'll sneak away. On foot, taxi, not sure yet.'

'Bad idea,' said Retancourt, shaking her head disapprovingly.

'Well, I can't think of anything better.'

'I can. We'll go upstairs to my place for a last drink, looks quite natural.

And my brother will drive you. You know Bruno's got a police record? Well known to all the cops round here.'

'Yes.'

'He's so harmless and dumb that if ever they stop him when he's in a car, they just give him a little sign of recognition and wave him on. He's no good at anything much except driving. He can take you tonight wherever you want to go. Strasbourg, Lille, Toulouse, Lyon, wherever. What direction are you going in?'

'Let's say Toulouse?'

'Right. You can get a train on from there to your mystery destination.'

'Sounds perfect, Violette.'

'Except for your clothes. Wherever you're going, I presume you don't want everyone to know you're from Paris, not a good idea. Take a couple of Bruno's outfits, they might be a bit long in the leg and tight in the waist but they'll do. They'll be a bit showy. You won't like them. You'll look a bit flash, that's good.'

'Vulgar, you mean?'

'Yep, pretty much.'

'That'll be fine.'

'One last thing. When you get to Toulouse, let Bruno get away fast. Don't get him mixed up in whatever mess you're sorting out, he's got enough on his plate.'

'I wouldn't dream of getting anyone into trouble,' said Danglard, but he couldn't help thinking at the same time that he had almost got Veyrenc killed.

'And how's the pigeon doing?' Retancourt asked simply as she stood up.

Thirty-five minutes later, Danglard was leaving Paris lying on the back seat of her brother's car, wearing a cheap suit that was too tight in the sleeves and carrying a new mobile. Bruno had said he could sleep if he wanted. Danglard closed his eyes and felt that at least until he reached Toulouse he would be protected by the powerful sovereign arm of Violette Retancourt.

XLIII

'LIKE A *WOODLOUSE*?' ADAMSBERG REPEATED A SECOND TIME.

He had returned from the gendarmerie and the hospital only at 7 p.m. Veyrenc was waiting for him at the end of the path to the guest house and summed up the essentials of the inquiry so far. The analysis by the technicians from Lisieux had yielded little. The killer had had a very common type of camping stool, the sort used by all fishermen, and the crossbow was indeed Herbier's and carried only his fingerprints. Estalère and Justin had returned to the squad in Paris, and Léone had recovered a little more strength but had still said nothing.

'A woodlouse two centimetres long. On Valleray's left shoulder, and on Lina's.'

'Like a sort of big insect painted on their backs?'

'I don't want to sound as pedantic as Danglard, but a woodlouse isn't actually an insect, it's a crustacean.'

'A crustacean? Like a shrimp, you mean, a shrimp out of water?'

'Yes, a little land shrimp. It has fourteen legs. Insects have six legs. That's how you know that spiders, which have eight legs, aren't insects either.'

'Are you kidding me? Are you saying spiders are land shrimps too?'

As Veyrenc explained the paths of science to Adamsberg, he wondered why the commissaire hadn't reacted more strongly to the news that Hippolyte and Lina might be the natural children of Valleray.

'No, they're arachnids.'

'Well, it alters something,' said Adamsberg, starting to walk slowly along the path, 'but what?'

'It doesn't really alter one's view of a woodlouse. It's a non-edible crustacean, that's all. One wonders what Martin might do with them.'

'I'm talking about Valleray. If a man has a birthmark like that, and someone else does too, does that necessarily mean they're related?'

'Yes, absolutely. And Danglard's description was precise. Two centimetres, port wine colour, long oval, with something like two antennae at the top.'

'A crustacean then.'

'Yes. And if you add that to the fact that Valleray was very resistant to anyone seeing him without his shirt, you might deduce that he knew very well the birthmark would give him away. So he knows that two of the Vendermot children must be his.'

'But they *don't* know, Louis. Hippo said to me, and he was bitterly sincere, that the only regret he had in life was being the son of the biggest bastard in the district, i.e. his godawful father, Vendermot.'

'So that means the count had taken care that they shouldn't know. He looked after them when they were small, he got Léo to educate them, he rescued young Hippo when he was under threat, but he refuses to recognise his children. Letting them live in poverty with their mother,' said Veyrenc drily.

'Fear of scandal, need for stable succession. That doesn't make Valleray look good at all.'

'But you liked him?'

'Like isn't strong enough. I found him sincere, determined. Generous, indeed.'

'Whereas he's really cunning and cowardly.'

'Or perhaps glued to the rock of his ancestors without daring to budge. Like an anemone. No, please don't tell me what anemones are. Molluscs, I suppose.'

'No, cnidarians.'

'OK,' Adamsberg conceded, 'a cnidarian. Just reassure me Hellebaud's a bird, and things will be fine.'

'Yes, he's a bird. Or at least he was. Since he's mistaken your shoe for his natural habitat, things have changed.'

Adamsberg took one of Veyrenc's cigarettes and pursued his slow pacing.

'After Valleray married Léo, when they were very young,' he said, 'they gave in to pressure from the Valleray clan, and he divorced her to marry a woman of higher status, who was already widowed with a child.'

'So Denis de Valleray isn't his son?'

'No, Louis, and everyone knows that, he's his mother's son, and the count adopted him when he was three.'

'No other children?'

'Not officially. The gossip is that the count is sterile, but now we know that isn't true. Imagine when Ordebec finds out that he had two children with a maidservant.'

'Was the Vendermots' mother employed at the chateau?'

'No, but she worked for about fifteen years in a sort of chateau hotel not far from Ordebec. She must have been an irresistible girl if she had breasts like Lina's. Have I already mentioned them to you?'

'Yes, you did, and I've even seen them. I met her coming out of her office.'

'And?' said Adamsberg, glancing quickly at his lieutenant.

'Like you, I looked.'

'And?'

'Well, you're right. Mouth-watering.'

'The count must have met the young Madame Vendermot at this chateau place. Result: two children. But he had nothing to fear from the mother. She wasn't going to tell everyone that Hippo and Lina were his children. Because from what we know of her husband, he could have killed her, and the kids as well.'

'She could have spoken up after his death.'

'Question of dishonour,' said Adamsberg, shaking his head. 'She had her reputation to protect.'

'So Valleray could feel safe. Except for the birthmark that could give him away. But what has this got to do with Lord Hellequin?'

'Well, in the end, nothing. The count has two illegitimate children, OK. Nothing to do with the three murders. I'm tired of thinking, Louis, I'm going to sit under the apple tree.'

'It might rain on you.'

'Yes, I saw, clouds coming up in the west.'

Without knowing why, Adamsberg decided to spend part of the night on the Chemin de Bonneval. He walked right to the end, failing to glimpse a single blackberry in the darkness, then came back to sit on the tree trunk where Fleg had begged for sugar. He sat there for over an hour, in a passive and even receptive mood, ready for any impromptu visit by the Lord of the Riders, who did not however deign to turn up. Perhaps because he felt nothing in these lonely woods, neither unease nor apprehension, not even when a stag dashed noisily past and made him look round. Not even when a ghostly barn owl brushed past not far from him with a human-sounding screech. Hoping that the owl was indeed a bird, as he assumed. But on the other hand he had reached the conclusion that Valleray was rather contemptible, something which troubled him. Autocratic, selfish, without affection for his adoptive son. Bowing to the code of honour of the family. But why had he decided to marry Léo again when they were eighty-eight years old? Why take this provocative step? Why, on the last stretch of his journey, was he reviving the scandal, after a lifetime of submission? Possibly to try and shake off that very submission. Some worms turn at the last moment. In which case it changed everything of course.

A greater noise gave him a brief moment of hope, what sounded like a cavalcade of snorting beasts. He stood up, watchfully, ready to get out of the way of the Lord with the long hair. But it was only a herd of wild boar pressing on towards its wallow. No, Adamsberg thought as he set off back, Hellequin has no interest in me. The ancient ancestor preferred women like Lina, and who was to say he was wrong?

XLIV

'IN WHICH CASE IT WOULD CHANGE EVERYTHING,' ADAMSBERG announced to Veyrenc over breakfast.

The commissaire had carried their coffee and bread out under the apple trees in the yard. While Adamsberg filled their bowls, Veyrenc was throwing little cider apples in front of him.

'Think about it, Louis. My photo appeared in the *Ordebec Reporter* the day after I arrived. The killer couldn't have mistaken Danglard for me. So it *was* him someone tried to kill on the railway, not me. But why? Because Danglard had seen these woodlice. There's no other explanation.'

'And who would know that he'd seen them?'

'You know Danglard's no good at keeping a secret. He's been around in Ordebec, asking questions and talking to people. He might have let something drop, without meaning to. So we have a link between the murders and the woodlice. The killer doesn't want anyone to know about the origins of the Vendermot children.'

'*Hide all your descendants, the fruit of ancient sin / They'll return one fine day, to call the reckoning in,*' muttered Veyrenc, tossing another apple.

'Unless the count doesn't want them to be hidden any more. The worm began to turn a year ago, when old Valleray decided to remarry Léo. To repair what he had broken through his own feeble-mindedness. He's obeyed other people all his life, he knows it, and he's redeeming himself. So we might think he would do the same towards his children.'

'How?' asked Veyrenc, throwing his seventh apple.

'By writing them into his will. Dividing the inheritance into three. As surely as a sea anemone isn't a mollusc, I'm prepared to bet Valleray has willed them something, and that Hippolyte and Lina will be recognised after his death.'

'And he won't have the courage before that?'

'Apparently not. What are you doing with those apples?'

'Aiming at vole holes. Why are you so sure about the will?'

'Last night in the forest, it came to me.'

As if the forest could dictate truths in some way. Veyrenc preferred to disregard the typical lack of coherence in Adamsberg's reply.

'What on earth were you doing in the forest?'

'I spent some of the evening on the Chemin de Bonneval. There were some wild boar, I heard a stag bellowing and I saw a barn owl. Which is a bird, isn't it? Not a crustacean or a spider.'

'A bird. The owl that screeches like a human.'

'Exactly. And why are you aiming at vole holes?'

'I'm playing golf.'

'You've missed all the holes.'

'Yes. So you mean that Valleray will have divided his will among the three children and that will have changed everything. But only if someone knows that.'

'Someone does know that. Denis de Valleray doesn't like his stepfather. He must have been watching him for a long time. We might imagine that his mother warned him, so that he wouldn't be done out of two-thirds of his fortune by some grubby little bastards from the village. I'd be very surprised if he doesn't know about his father's will.'

Veyrenc put down his handful of apples and helped himself to a second coffee, holding out his hand to Adamsberg to ask for the sugar.

'I'm fed up with all these stories about sugar,' said the commissaire, passing him a lump.

'It's over now. Fleg's sugar lump led you to Christian Clermont's sugar lump; you can pack up the box.'

'I certainly hope so,' said Adamsberg, leaning hard on the lid of the sugar box, which was tricky to close. 'We'd better put a rubber band round it, that's what Léo does and we should respect her little ways. She must find everything in its place when she gets back. Danglard's already helped himself to her Calvados, and that's quite enough. So I think it's certain that Denis is no mollusc and that he knows about his father's will. Perhaps he's known for a year, ever since the count started his rebellion. If his father dies now, he'll be in trouble financially and socially. Vicomte Denis de Valleray, high-class auctioneer in Rouen, finds he's the brother of two peasants, brother of the madman with six fingers and the madwoman who sees visions, and the stepson of a count who has strayed from the path.'

'Unless he eliminates the Vendermot children. That would be a big step to take.'

'Not necessarily. Denis probably sees the Vendermots as negligible people. I should think he despises them in a spontaneous instinctive manner. Their disappearance would even seem legitimate to him. From where he sits, not a serious loss. Comparable to you trying to stop up the vole holes.'

'I'll unblock them again though.'

'But anyway, infinitely less important than losing two-thirds of his inheritance and all his social status. He could be playing for very high stakes.'

'You've got a wasp on your shoulder.'

'An insect,' said Adamsberg, sweeping it away with a gesture.

'Yes. And if Denis knows about the will – if it exists – he wouldn't just despise the Vendermots, he'd detest them.'

'And will have done for a year or more. We don't know when the count might have done it.'

'But it's not Hippo and Lina who've been killed.'

'I know,' said Adamsberg, putting the sugar box behind him, as if the sight of it troubled him. 'So this isn't an impulsive killer. He thinks, he prowls. To get rid of Hippo and Lina would be risky. Suppose someone else knows about their birth. If Danglard worked it out in a day or two, one might think other people are in on it. So Denis might hesitate. Because if the two Vendermots were to die, he'd automatically be suspected.'

'By Léo for instance. She looked after them when they were little and she's known Valleray for seventy years.'

'It must have been Denis who hit her on the head. And in that case, the attack wouldn't have anything to do with Léo's discovery in the woods. The wasp's on you now.'

Veyrenc blew on his shoulder and turned his bowl over so that the remains of the sweet coffee wouldn't attract the insect.

'Turn your bowl over too,' he instructed Adamsberg.

'I didn't take sugar.'

'I thought you did.'

'I told you, right now the very thought of sugar annoys me. As if sugar were an insect. At any rate, it seems to be surrounding me like a swarm of wasps.'

'In the end,' Veyrenc said, 'Denis was waiting for a suitable occasion for him to kill without being suspected. And the perfect opportunity presented itself when Lina had her vision.'

Adamsberg leaned against the tree trunk, almost turning his back on Veyrenc, who was occupying the other half of the tree. At nine thirty the sun's warmth was getting through. The lieutenant lit a cigarette and passed another over his shoulder to the commissaire.

'Yes, the perfect opportunity,' Adamsberg agreed. 'Because if the three "seized" men were to die, the terror of the local people would be directed at the Vendermots. Against Lina, who's responsible for the vision, as an intermediary between the living and the dead. But also against Hippo, because everyone knows he had six fingers on each hand, the mark of the devil. So in an atmosphere like that, the murder of those two wouldn't surprise anyone, and half the inhabitants of Ordebec could be suspects. Exactly like the villagers in seventeen-something who took their pitchforks to some chap called Benjamin who had also described the people seized by the Riders. So to put an end to the deaths, the mob killed him.'

'But this isn't the eighteenth century, the method will change. Nobody's going to massacre Lina and Hippo on the market square, it will be much more discreet.'

'So Denis kills Herbier, Glayeux and Mortembot. Apart from Herbier, he does it in an ancient manner, more or less observing the ritual, to make people scared. He's the kind of guy who'd belong to a snobbish crossbow club, wouldn't he?'

'That's the first thing we'd better check,' said Veyrenc, throwing his twentieth apple.

'You won't aim very well while you're sitting down. And since the three victims were notorious bastards and probably guilty of murder themselves, Denis has all the fewer scruples in killing them.'

'So that, as we speak, Lina and Hippo are in mortal danger.'

'Not before nightfall.'

'You do realise that for now the whole story depends on the purple woodlouse.'

'We can take a look at Denis's alibis.'

'You won't be able to get close to him, any more than you did the Clermonts.'

The two men remained silent for a long moment, after which Veyrenc threw all the remaining apples away and started to collect up the dishes on a tray.

'Look,' whispered Adamsberg, catching him by the arm. 'Hellebaud's coming out.'

And indeed the pigeon had ventured about two metres from the door of Adamsberg's bedroom.

'Did you put some birdseed out there?' asked Veyrenc.

'No.'

'Well, in that case, he's looking for insects on his own.'

'Insects, crustaceans, arthropods.'

'Yes.'

XLV

CAPITAINE ÉMERI LISTENED TO ADAMSBERG AND VEYRENC, LOOKING stunned. No, he had never seen the birthmarks, he had never heard it said that the Vendermot children had been fathered by Valleray.

'He certainly slept around, yes, everyone knew that. And also that his second wife hated him: she turned young Denis against him.'

'And we heard later, didn't we, sir, that his wife wasn't too particular either,' said Blériot.

'It's not appropriate to wash more dirty linen, Blériot. The situation is difficult enough as it is.'

'Yes. Émeri,' insisted Adamsberg, 'we *do* need to wash the dirty linen. There's this crustacean and that can't be dodged.'

'What crustacean?' asked Émeri.

'The woodlouse,' Veyrenc explained, 'it's a crustacean.'

'What the fuck's that got to do with anything?' exploded Émeri, getting up abruptly. 'Don't just stand there, Blériot, go and get us some coffee. I warn you, Adamsberg, and please listen carefully, I refuse to entertain the slightest suspicion of Denis de Valleray. You hear me? I refuse.'

'Because he's a nobleman?'

'Don't insult me. You're forgetting that Empire nobility has no truck with *ancien régime* aristocracy.'

'Well, why then?'

'Because your story doesn't make sense. You think someone would kill three people, just to be able to get rid of the Vendermots?'

'It makes perfect sense.'

'No, it doesn't, unless Denis is either wicked or bloodthirsty. I know him, he's neither. He's sly, he's opportunistic and he's ambitious.'

'He's also status-conscious, pompous and arrogant.'

'All of that, all right. But he's lazy, careful and timid, he's just not a decisive character. You're barking up the wrong tree. Denis would never have the nerve to shoot Herbier in the face, to chop Glayeux up with an axe or fire a crossbow at Mortembot. We're looking for someone who's audacious and crazy, Adamsberg. And you know perfectly well where crazy and audacious people are to be found in Ordebec. What's to say it isn't the other way round? What's to say it isn't Hippo who killed these three men, before planning to attack Denis de Valleray?'

Blériot put the tray down and gave out the cups clumsily, very differently from Estalère's precise service. Émeri took his without sitting down and passed round the sugar.

'Go on,' he said, 'what's to prove it isn't that way round?'

'I hadn't thought of that,' Adamsberg admitted. 'Yes, it's not impossible.'

'It's extremely possible. Imagine that Hippo and Lina have found out who their father is, and about the will. They could have, couldn't they?'

'Yes,' said Adamsberg, firmly refusing the sugar which Émeri was offering him.

'Your reasoning could then apply perfectly well, but the other way round. It's entirely in their interests to get rid of Denis. But as soon as the will becomes known, they'd be the first to be suspected. So Lina invents this vision, leaving the fourth victim unidentified.'

'Yes, OK,' admitted Adamsberg.

'Victim number four would be Denis de Valleray.'

'No, that doesn't work, Émeri. That wouldn't put the Vendermots above suspicion, on the contrary.'

'Why?'

'Because it would seem as if it was Hellequin's Riders who had carried off the four men, and that still leaves the finger pointing at the Vendermots.'

'Hell's teeth,' said Émeri, putting down his cup. 'Think of something else then.'

'OK, first of all let's check whether Denis de Valleray can use a crossbow,' said Veyrenc, who had kept one little green apple and was rolling it between his palms.

'What about local gun clubs?'

'There are lots of them,' said Émeri, looking discouraged. 'Eleven in the region and five just in our *département*.'

'Is there one club that's more exclusive than the others, among the eleven?'

'The Compagnie de la Marche, in Quitteuil-sur-Touques. You have to be proposed for it by two members.'

'Perfect. Ask them if Denis is a member.'

'How'm I going to do that? They'd never tell me. These circles protect their members. And I don't want to reveal to them that the gendarmerie has opened an investigation of the count's stepson.'

'No, it's too early, that's true.'

Émeri paced round the room, squaring his shoulders, hands behind him, face looking stern.

'All right,' he said after a moment, faced with Adamsberg's insistent gaze. 'I'll bluff it out. But please leave me alone to do it. I hate telling lies in public.'

Ten minutes later, the capitaine opened the door and signalled to them to come back in, with an angry gesture.

'I called myself François de Rocheterre. I explained that the Vicomte de Valleray had agreed to sponsor me. I asked if that was enough or if I needed two sponsors.'

'Very good, sir,' said Blériot appreciatively.

'Forget it, brigadier. I like being straightforward, I don't like this kind of subterfuge.'

'Result?' asked Adamsberg.

'Yes,' sighed Émeri. 'Valleray does belong to the club. And he's a good shot. But he's never agreed to take part in the Normandy championships.'

'Too common, probably,' commented Veyrenc.

'Yes, sure. But there's a problem. The club secretary was chatting on too much. Not for the pleasure of giving me information, but because he seemed to be testing me. I'm sure he smelt a rat. And that means the Compagnie de la Marche may well phone Denis de Valleray to check if he knows a certain François de Rocheterre. Then Denis will understand that someone with a false name has been asking questions about him.'

'And about how good he is with a crossbow.'

'Precisely. Denis is no genius, but he'll soon realise he's being suspected of killing Mortembot. Either by the cops or some unknown person. He's going to be on his guard.'

'Or he'll want to get the job finished quickly. To get Hippo and Lina out of the way.'

'That's ridiculous,' said Émeri.

'Denis has everything to lose,' Adamsberg insisted. 'Think about it seriously. It would be best to have the chateau watched.'

'Out of the question. I'd have Valleray and Denis on my back – in other words, my superiors would come down on me like a ton of bricks. Non-motivated surveillance, damaging suspicions, professional misconduct.'

'He's right,' said Veyrenc.

'Well, in that case, we watch the Vendermot house. But it's much less safe. Can you get hold of Faucheur again?'

'Yes.'

'We won't need him before it gets dark. We can start at 10 p.m. and stop at 6 a.m. Eight hours, we can manage that.'

'Very well,' admitted Émeri, looking suddenly tired. 'But where's Danglard gone now?'

'He's had a delayed reaction, gone home to recover.'

'So there are just the two of you.'

'It'll be enough. If you take 10 p.m. to 2 p.m., I'll relieve you with Veyrenc. We'll have time to have a meal at the Boar first.'

'No, let's do it the other way round. I'll take the second watch with Faucheur from two to six. I'm exhausted, I'll sleep first.'

XLVI

FOR THE PAST THREE DAYS, ADAMSBERG HAD BEEN TAKING ONE OF Léo's books into the hospital. He would comb her hair, then sit beside her, leaning on one arm, and read her about twenty pages. It was an old book, the story of a passionate love affair ending in catastrophe. It didn't seem to awake any passion in the old woman, but she had been smiling a lot while he read, moving her head and fingers as if she were listening to a song rather than a story. Today, Adamsberg had decided to pick another book. He read out a technical chapter on how to help mares foal, and Léo seemed to dance in just the same way. And indeed the nurse, who never missed the half-hour's reading, didn't seem to react any differently. Adamsberg was beginning to be alarmed by this bland and peaceful state, since when he had first met Léo she was quite different: talkative, brusque and rather sharp-tongued. Dr Turbot, who maintained total confidence in his colleague Hellebaud – which Adamsberg was now starting to lose – assured him that the case was following the exact course predicted by the osteopath, whom he had had permission to telephone the previous day in his 'place at Fleury'. Léone was quite capable of thinking and speaking, but her unconscious had put these functions on pause, with the doctor's help. The old woman was being shielded in this way in a kind of health-giving refuge, and it would be several more days before the protective mechanism would be lifted.

'It's only a week so far,' said Turbot. 'Give it time.'

'You haven't told her about Mortembot?'

'Not a word. We're following instructions. Did you see the paper yesterday?'

'The one that said the Paris cops are a waste of space?'

'More or less.'

'Well, they're right. Two deaths since I got here.'

'But two were avoided: Léone's and the commandant's.'

'Avoiding isn't the same as fighting, doctor.'

Dr Turbot spread his hands in sympathy. 'Doctors can't give a diagnosis without symptoms, and policemen can't work without clues. Your killer shows no symptoms. He leaves no traces, he passes like a ghost. It's not normal, commissaire, not normal at all. Valleray agrees with me.'

'Father or son?'

'Father of course. Denis couldn't give a toss about what's going on here.'

'Do you know him well?'

'So-so. We don't see much of him in Ordebec. But twice a year the count organises a dinner for the local professionals and I get an invitation. Not much fun, but you have to go. The food's excellent though. Why, is Denis a suspect?'

'No.'

'You're right. He'd never be tempted to kill anyone and you know why? It would need decisiveness and he's quite incapable of it. He didn't even choose his own wife, so you can imagine. At least that's what they say.'

'We'll have a word about that again, doctor, when you have a moment.'

Hippolyte was hanging clothes on the line, a blue string attached to two apple trees. Adamsberg watched him: he shook out the creases in one of his sister's dresses before hanging it up carefully. It was out of the question of course to come out with some direct statement about his birth. It would only precipitate an unpredictable, perhaps violent reaction and the killer was too elusive and mobile for any more unforeseen events to be added to a situation which was already out of control. Hippolyte stopped what he was doing as he saw Adamsberg approach, and automatically wiped the edge of his right hand.

'*Ruojnob*, commissaire.'

'Bonjour,' said Adamsberg. 'Have you hurt your hand?'

'It's nothing, just the missing finger. When there's rain in the air it itches. It looks a bit threatening in the west.'

'It's been doing that for days now.'

'But this time it's for sure,' said Hippo, carrying on with his task. 'It's going to rain a lot. It's really itching.'

Adamsberg wiped his brow hesitantly. Émeri would have suspected that it wasn't the missing finger that was troubling Hippo, but the edge of his hand, after having used it to hit Danglard on the neck.

'It doesn't do the same on the left?'

'Sometimes it's the one, and sometimes the other, and sometimes both. It's not mathematical.'

Abnormal intelligence, sharp wit, not particularly friendly manner. If Adamsberg hadn't been running the investigation, Émeri would surely have had Hippo under lock and key by now. Hippo, putting his sister's vision into practice, killing the 'seized' men, and then eliminating the heir to the Valleray fortune among them. Hippo seemed perfectly calm. Just now he was shaking out one of Lina's flowery tops, which immediately brought the image of her breasts before Adamsberg's eyes.

'She changes her clothes every day, makes a massive amount of work.'

'Hippo, tonight your house is going to be under surveillance. That's what I came to say. If you see two men outside, don't get out your gun. Veyrenc and I will be here from ten to two and Émeri and Faucheur will take over until daylight.'

'Why?' asked Hippo, with a shrug of his shoulders.

'Three people have died. Your mother is right to be worried about you. I saw a new graffiti on the walls of the grain store on my way here: "Death to the Vs."'

'Doesn't mean anything,' said Hippo.

'It could mean "Death to the Vendermots": the family who've brought the troubles on the town.'

'But what would be the point of anyone killing us?'

'To break the curse.'

'Rubbish. I told you nobody would dare come near us. And keeping watch won't do any good if you ask me. After all, Mortembot was killed. Not wishing to be rude, commissaire, but you haven't got anything done here. You were all round his house, circling like buzzards, and they killed him right under your noses. Can you help me with this?'

Hippolyte offered one side of a sheet to Adamsberg in all simplicity and the two men shook it out in the warm air.

'The murderer,' Hippo went on, giving the commissaire two clothes pegs, 'was sitting comfortably on a stool, he must have had a good laugh afterwards. The cops have never stopped anybody killing if he's a mind to. Once he wants to, it's like a bolting horse. He just gets over the obstacles and that's it. And this one, he really has a mind to. You've got to be a cold-blooded bastard to push a man on to the railway track. Do you know why your deputy was attacked?'

'No, we still don't know,' said Adamsberg, on alert. 'Apparently he may have been mistaken for me.'

'Rubbish,' Hippo said once more. 'Someone like this, he doesn't make mistakes. I'd be careful if I were you, while you're on watch tonight.'

'There's no point killing cops, they're like thistles, there'll always be more coming up.'

'Maybe so, but this guy, he's got some kind of bloodlust. Axe, crossbow, train, horrible. A shot from a gun's cleaner, isn't it?'

'Well, not always. Herbier's head was practically blown off. And it makes a lot of noise.'

'True,' said Hippo, scratching his neck. 'And this one's like a ghost. Just flits about and nobody sees him.'

'That's what Turbot said.'

'Well, for once he's not wrong. Watch all you like if you think it'll help, commissaire. At least it'll reassure my mother. She's all over the place just now. And she's got Lina to look after.'

'Lina's ill?'

'Here,' said Hippo, pointing to his forehead. 'When Lina's seen the army, she's on edge for weeks. She gets these panic attacks.'

Danglard's call came through to the Running Boar shortly before nine. Adamsberg got up feeling apprehensive. He moved slowly towards the telephone, wondering how he was going to code the conversation. Word games weren't his strong suit.

'You can reassure your dispatcher,' said Danglard. 'I picked up the two packets from left luggage, the key was the correct one.'

Right, Adamsberg thought with relief, Danglard has found Zerk and Mo, they must still be in Casares.

'Not too much damage?'

'The paper was a bit torn and the string coming off, but in reasonable overall condition.'

Right, thought Adamsberg, the two youngsters are a bit tired but OK.

'So what should I do about them now?' Danglard asked. 'Return to sender?'

'If it's not too inconvenient, can you hang on to them for a bit? I need to contact the sorting office.'

'Well, it is a bit inconvenient. Where am I going to put them?'

'Not my problem. Have you eaten?'

'Not yet.'

'Perhaps it's aperitif time over there, so raise a glass of port and drink my health.'

'Never touch the stuff.'

'Well, I do, so have some for me, just this once.'

All right, Danglard said to himself. Rather heavy-handed but not stupid. Adamsberg wanted him to take the boys to Porto, that is, in the opposite direction from the one they had so far taken. And there was still no news from Retancourt. So it was too soon to bring them back across the frontier.

'How's Ordebec?'

'Nothing much happening. Tonight maybe.'

Adamsberg rejoined Veyrenc at the table and finished his meat, which was getting cold. A clap of thunder suddenly made the windows rattle.

'Clouds gathering in the west,' murmured Adamsberg, raising his fork.

The two men began their night-time vigil under pouring rain and resounding claps of thunder. Adamsberg lifted his face up to the deluge. During a storm, and at such moments only, he felt himself to be somehow linked to the mass of energy exploding up there, without any objective or motive, simply the deployment of fantastic and futile power. Power was what he had singularly lacked over the last few days; the power had been entirely in the hands of the enemy. And that night, it was finally consenting to flow over him.

XLVII

THE GROUND WAS STILL DAMP IN THE MORNING, AND ADAMSBERG was sitting under the apple tree for breakfast, having put Léo's sugar container out of sight behind him. He could feel his trousers soaking up the moisture. He was pulling at blades of grass with his bare toes. The temperature had fallen about ten degrees, and the sky was misty, but the dauntless morning wasp wasn't discouraged and had returned to find him. Hellebaud was pecking about, four metres from the doorway, and that was significant progress. But none had been made regarding the ghostly killer: the night had passed without incident.

And now, Blériot was coming towards him, moving his large body as fast as he could.

'Voicemail full up!' he puffed as he reached Adamsberg.

'What?'

'Your voicemail. Must be full. Couldn't reach you.'

He had rings under his eyes and hadn't shaved.

'What is it, brigadier?'

'It's Denis de Valleray. No chance *he'd* try to kill the Vendermots in the night. He's dead, commissaire! Hurry up, you're wanted at the chateau.'

'Dead! But how?' cried Adamsberg, hastening barefoot to his room.

'Threw himself out of the window,' Blériot shouted back, which troubled him, because it isn't the sort of thing you want to yell out loud.

Adamsberg didn't bother to find dry trousers, but picked up his phone, thrust on the nearest pair of shoes and ran to shake Veyrenc awake. Four minutes later, he was getting into the brigadier's ancient car.

'Go ahead, Blériot, I'm listening. What do we know?'

'The count found Denis's body at 8.05 this morning. He called Émeri. The capitaine went up there without you, because we couldn't reach you. He sent me to fetch you.'

Adamsberg clenched his teeth. Coming back from their late-night watch, he and Veyrenc had disabled their phones, so as to talk about the young people on the run. And he had forgotten to switch it back on again before going to sleep. He had for so long considered his mobile as a personal enemy, which it was, that he had not paid it enough attention.

'What does he say?'

'That Denis de Valleray killed himself, no question. The body stinks of whisky, can't miss it, sir. Émeri says Denis must have drunk a lot to give himself courage. I wouldn't know about that. Anyway, seems he was ill, he'd leaned over and puked out the window. His room's on the second floor and the yard underneath is cobbled.'

'Could he have fallen by accident?'

'Yessir, could have, right enough. The windowsills up the chateau, they're pretty low. But there are all these bottles of tranquillisers, and they're empty and his bottle of sleeping pills was open, so the capitaine thinks he must have wanted to kill himself.'

'Do we know when?'

'Midnight to one this morning. For once the police doctor got there fast, and the technical team. They get a move on when it's for the toffs.'

'Did he usually take a lot of pills?'

'You'll see, his bedside table's covered with 'em.'

'Did he drink a lot too?'

'So they say. Though you never saw him drunk or the worse for wear. Trouble is, sir,' Blériot said, pulling a face, 'Émeri says he'd never have done it at all if you hadn't started asking questions about the crossbow club.'

'So it's *my* fault?'

'Sort of. See, yesterday the secretary of this club turned up at the chateau for drinks.'

306

'They didn't waste any time then.'

'Still, after that, or so the count says, Denis didn't seem too bothered at dinner. But then in that family, they don't really notice each other. They eat at different ends of their great big table and don't hardly talk. Nobody else was there; Denis's wife is off in Germany with her children.'

'Émeri *ought* to be thinking that if Denis did kill himself, it was because he was guilty.'

'Yeah, he says that too. But you know the capitaine, he gets on his high horse – well, he is the great-great-grand-something of the marshal – then he comes down again. He just says you should have gone about it another way. More cautious like, collect the evidence in secret, and have Denis watched. Then he wouldn't be dead.'

'But sentenced to life and his murders revealed for everyone to see. Exactly what he didn't want. How is the count taking it?'

'He's in shock, he's shut himself in the library. I wouldn't say he's that grieved though. They couldn't stand each other no more.'

Adamsberg called Émeri on the mobile when they were two kilometres from the chateau.

'I've found the paper,' said the capitaine in a hostile voice.

'What paper?'

'The bleeding will, what do you think? And yes, the two Vendermot brats inherit, a third each. The only bonus for Denis was that he would have kept the chateau.'

'Have you spoken to Valleray about that?'

'Can't get a word out of him about that, he clammed up. I don't think he knows how to deal with it.'

'And what about the murders Denis committed?'

'He refuses to believe any of that. He'll admit he didn't like his stepson and it was mutual. But he says no way Denis could have killed three men or hit Léo on the head or pushed your man on to the railway track.'

'Any reason for that?'

'Because he's known him since he was three years old. He'll cling to his version. Afraid of scandal, you'll understand.'

'So what's his version?'

'That Denis had too much to drink, made himself ill over some personal problem we don't know about. Then he felt sick, and ran to the window to vomit. The window was open, to let in fresh air, because of the storm. And because he was feeling dizzy, he fell.'

'And what do you think?'

'I think it's partly *your* fault,' muttered Émeri. 'That visit from the secretary of the Compagnie de la Marche sounded the alarm. Denis took a mixture of pills and alcohol and he died of it. Not the way he would have chosen. He meant to die in his bed, just losing consciousness. But when he staggered to the window and leaned out to be sick, he must have lost his balance.'

'All right,' said Adamsberg, without picking up on the capitaine's reproach. 'So how did you get the will out of the count?'

'Put pressure on him. Said I knew what was in it. He was cornered. Nasty business, Adamsberg. Despicable. No poetry, no grandeur.'

Adamsberg looked down at Denis's shattered head, examined the height of the window and the low sill, the position of the corpse and the signs of vomit on the ground. He had certainly fallen from the bedroom. Inside the large room, a bottle of whisky had rolled on the carpet and three bottles of pills were open on the bedside table.

'Tranquillisers, antidepressants and sleeping pills,' said Émeri, pointing to each in turn. 'And he was in bed when he took them.'

'Yes, I see,' said Adamsberg as he viewed the traces of vomit, some on the sheet, some on the carpet about twenty centimetres from the window, and some on the sill. 'So when he felt sick, his reflex sent him towards the window. A matter of dignity.'

Adamsberg sat on a chair to one side, as two technicians took over in the bedroom. Yes, the questions to the shooting club must have precipitated Valleray's suicide. And yes, Denis, after three murders and two attempted murders, had chosen his own way out. Adamsberg thought about the bald head he had seen in the courtyard below. No, Denis de Valleray had neither the stature nor the attitude of a brazen killer. There was nothing savage or intimidating about him, he'd been a man who was distant, aloof, sarcastic at most. But he had done it. Gun, axe, crossbow. It was only at this point that the commissaire realised that the Ordebec case was closed. That the separate events, each steeped in its own context, had suddenly all come together, in a single mass, like the clouds in the west releasing their rain. That he would go and see Léo one last time, and read her another instalment of the romance, or something about mares in foal. He'd see for one last time the Vendermots, Dr Turbot, the count, Fleg, he'd see Lina, the hollow in the mattress, and his place under the apple tree. At the thought of leaving, and having to forget all these people and things, he was overtaken by a nagging feeling of incompleteness. As light as Zerk's fingers on the pigeon's feathers. Tomorrow he'd take Hellebaud back to town, tomorrow he'd be driving to Paris. The Ghost Riders would fade away, Lord Hellequin would retreat back into the shadows. Having, Adamsberg told himself with irritation, accomplished his mission. Nobody conquers Lord Hellequin. Everyone had said that, and it was true. This year would go down in the lugubrious annals of Ordebec. Four men seized and four men dead. He had only been able to prevent some human interventions. Well, he had at least saved Hippo and Lina being savaged with pitchforks.

The pathologist grabbed his elbow unceremoniously to get his attention.

'I'm sorry,' Adamsberg said, 'I didn't see you come in.'

'It wasn't an accident,' she said. 'Tests will confirm it, but a preliminary examination suggests he'd absorbed a lethal dose of benzodiazepines and especially neuroleptics. If he hadn't fallen out of the window, he'd probably be dead anyway. Suicide.'

'Confirming that,' said one of the technicians coming up. 'Just the one set of prints here, looks like they're all his.'

'So what happened?' asked the doctor. 'I know his wife's gone off to live in Germany with her sons, but they hadn't really been a couple for years.'

'He'd just learned that he'd been found out,' said Adamsberg wearily.

'What? Money troubles, ruin?'

'No, the police investigation. He'd killed three people, almost killed another and the old lady, Léone. And he was preparing to kill two more, or four or five.'

'Him?' said the doctor, glancing at the window.

'Surprise you?'

'I'll say. This was a man who never chanced his arm.'

'What do you mean?'

'Well, once a month I try my luck at the casino in Deauville. I used to see him there. I never really talked to him, but you can learn a lot watching someone gambling. He hesitated over his decisions, he'd ask people for advice, he'd hold the whole table up in an exasperating way, all that for a small stake. He wasn't a bold player, not someone who'd go for it, he was a timid gambler. I'd find it hard to imagine him having ideas of his own, let alone the determination to do something savage like that. He was only keeping going because of his rank, his prestige and his relatives' help. They were his safety net. Like for a trapeze artist.'

'And if the net looked as if it might be about to break?'

'Well, I suppose in that case anything would be possible,' said the pathologist, moving away. 'When an alarm signal goes off, human responses are unpredictable and can be devastating.'

Adamsberg registered her sentence; he could never have formulated it himself. This might help him to calm the count down. Brutal murder, an unexpected suicide, one should never corner an animal, however sophisticated and well brought up. Everyone knew that. But there were various ways of putting it. He went down the polished oak staircase, murmuring the words to himself, and felt the mobile vibrate in his back pocket. Which reminded him, as his hand encountered some dried mud, that he hadn't troubled to put on clean trousers to come out. He stopped at the door of the library, reading Retancourt's text: *6 cut hairs on left headrest 2 on party suit. Chmbrmd sez yes haircut + sugar smlt like garage.* Adamsberg clutched the phone, feeling that puerile sensation of power that had gone through him the night before, during the storm. It was a primal joy, brutal and barbaric; he'd triumphed against overwhelming odds. He took two deep breaths, smoothed his face to remove the smile and knocked at the door. By the time he had heard the count's answer, angry and accompanied by the sound of his stick on the floor, the doctor's sentence had completely disappeared, lost in the opaque waters of his brain.

XLVIII

HE HAD BEEN TO VISIT LÉO, HAD READ HER A CHAPTER ABOUT TWIN births in horses, kissed the old woman on the cheek and told her: 'I'll be back.' He had said goodbye to Dr Turbot. He had gone to the Vendermot house, where he'd interrupted the brothers who were installing a hammock in the courtyard: he had explained the situation briefly to them, without mentioning the crucial element of the Comte de Valleray's paternity. He was going to leave that to Léo or the count himself, if he ever had the courage. Valleray's anger had subsided, but with the shock that had shaken the chateau, Adamsberg doubted he would have enough bravado to carry out his plan to marry Léo. The following day the national press would be full of the crimes committed by his stepson and would be sniffing at the trail of blood leading to the chateau.

The press conference was due to take place at 9 a.m. and Adamsberg was leaving Émeri to take all the credit, as fair return for his collaboration, which had been pretty friendly, all in all. Émeri had thanked him warmly, without suspecting, since he himself loved announcements and formal parades, that Adamsberg was heartily glad to escape. Émeri had insisted they should celebrate the end of the case, by inviting him to take an aperitif in his Empire room, with Veyrenc, Blériot and Faucheur. Blériot had cut up the salami, Faucheur had prepared some sickly-sweet kirs and Émeri had raised his glass to the defeat of the enemy, taking the chance to refer in the same breath to the great victories of his ancestor, Ulm, Austerlitz, Auerstadt, Eckmühl and, his favourite one, Eylau. On that occasion, Davout, being attacked on the right flank, had received reinforcements from Marshal Ney's army. It was the one when the Emperor, spurring on his men, had shouted to Murat: 'Are you going to let yourself be devoured by those people?'

Looking jovial and satisfied, the capitaine had stroked his stomach repeatedly as if he were now completely rid of the bubbles of electricity.

He had been to see Lina at her office, casting a final glance at the object of his desire. With Veyrenc, he had tidied up Léo's house, hesitating over whether to put a little water in the Calvados bottle to restore the level. That was the sort of sacrilegious thing ignorant teenagers do, Veyrenc had decreed. You should *never* water a Calva as good as that. He had scraped the pigeon droppings from his left shoe, swept up the birdseed from the floor, and pummelled the mattress back into shape. He had filled up the petrol tank, packed his rucksack and climbed to the highest point in Ordebec. Sitting on a warm wall in the last ray of sunshine, he looked carefully at all the meadows and hills around, watching to see if any of the impassive cows should move. He would have to wait to have supper at the Blue Boar before leaving, that is, to wait for Danglard's phone call, so as to tell him he could bring the young men back. The commandant was to send Zerk to Italy, and he was to drop Mo off at the home of one of his friends, whose father had agreed to 'report' him to the police. He had no need to refer to these instructions in code, having agreed them with Danglard before his departure. It would be enough simply to give him the green light. Not one cow decided to move, and faced with this setback, Adamsberg felt the same sensation of incompleteness as in the morning. Just as light, just as clear.

In the end, it was as his old neighbour Lucio was always telling him: Lucio, who had lost his arm as a child, during the Spanish Civil War. The problem, Lucio would explain, wasn't so much the missing arm as that when it happened he had had a spider bite on it which he hadn't finished scratching. And seventy years later, Lucio was still scratching away at empty space. Something that isn't finished with properly will irritate you for ever. But what hadn't he completed at Ordebec? The movement of the cows? Léo's final restoration to health? The flight of the pigeon? For sure the conquest of Lina, whom he had not so much as touched. At all events, something was still itching, and since he couldn't work out what was causing it, he concentrated on the motionless cattle in the fields.

He and Veyrenc left at nightfall. Adamsberg gave himself the task of shutting up the house, and took his time. He put the birdcage in the boot, picked Hellebaud up in the shoe and installed him on the front seat. The pigeon now seemed sufficiently tame, that is to say de-natured, not to flutter about during the drive. The rain from the storm had leaked inside the car and no doubt into the engine as well, and he had trouble starting it, evidence that his own squad cars were no better than Blériot's, and a far cry from the top-of-the-range Mercedes belonging to the Clermont-Brasseurs. He glanced down at Hellebaud, peacefully perched on the seat, and spared a thought for the old man Clermont, sitting like that in the front seat of the car, waiting trustingly while his two sons prepared to set fire to him.

Two and a half hours later, he was crossing the dark little garden of his house and waiting for old Lucio to appear. His neighbour would surely have heard him arrive, and would inevitably turn up with some beer, pretending to take a leak by the tree before starting a conversation. Adamsberg had just time to go inside with his bag and Hellebaud, whom he put on the kitchen table, still in the shoe, when Lucio appeared in the dark, holding two bottles of beer.

'Things going better now, *hombre*,' Lucio diagnosed.

'I think so.'

'The shit-stirrers came back twice. But now they've disappeared. Have you sorted out your affairs?'

'Almost.'

'In the country too, sorted that one out?'

'It's over. But it ended badly. Three deaths and a suicide.'

'The killer?'

'Yes.'

Lucio nodded, seeming to appreciate the macabre balance sheet, and uncapped the beer bottles, levering them against a branch.

'When you piss against it, you're damaging its roots,' Adamsberg protested, 'and now you're tearing off its bark.'

'Not at all,' Lucio retorted indignantly. 'Urine's full of nitrates, best thing there is for compost. Why d'you think I piss against the tree? Nitrates, that's why, did you know that?'

'I don't know much, Lucio.'

'Sit down, *hombre*,' said the old Spaniard, pointing to a packing case. 'It's been hot here,' he said, drinking straight from the bottle, 'we really suffered.'

'It was hot there too. Clouds kept building up in the west but never amounted to anything. Then finally it all came to a head yesterday, end of the hot spell and the case, both. There was a woman up there, with breasts good enough to eat. You can't imagine. I really thought I ought to, I felt I'd left things unfinished.'

'Still itching, is it?'

'Yes, that's what I wanted to talk to you about. It's not my arm that's itching, it's inside my head. Like a door banging somewhere, a door I didn't close properly.'

'You'll have to go back then, *hombre*. Or it'll go on banging all your life. You know the principle.'

'The case is closed, Lucio. I don't have anything more to do there. Or perhaps it was because I didn't see any cows move. In the Pyrenees, yes. But up there, no, nothing doing.'

'You can't get off with the woman? Rather than watch cows?'

'I don't want to, Lucio.'

'Ah.'

Lucio drank off half his bottle of beer, swilling it down noisily, then belched, reflecting on the difficult case Adamsberg had presented to him. He was extremely sensitive to things that hadn't stopped itching. This was his home ground, his speciality.

'When you think about her, do you think of any food in particular?'

'Yes, a *kouglof* with almonds and honey.'

'What's that?'

'A sort of special cake.'

'Well, that's very definite,' said Lucio, with the air of a connoisseur. 'But insect bites always are well defined. You should try and get hold of one of these *kouglofs*. That should do it.'

'You can't find real ones in Paris. It's a speciality of eastern France.'

'I could always ask Maria to make one for you. There must be some recipes, surely?'

XLIX

THE DEBRIEFING SESSION STARTED IN THE SQUAD HEADQUARTERS
on the Sunday morning, 15 August, at nine thirty, with fourteen members
present. Adamsberg had been waiting impatiently for Retancourt, and
as a sign of gratitude and admiration, had squeezed her shoulder in a
bluff, rather military show of emotion, a gesture Émeri might have
approved of. An accolade for the most brilliant of his troops. Retancourt,
who lost any subtlety when on emotional ground, had tossed her head
like a sulky and evasive child, keeping her satisfaction for later, that is
for herself alone.

The officers were seated round the large table. Mercadet and Mordent
were taking notes, for the minutes. Adamsberg wasn't keen on these big
meetings when he had to sum up, explain, give orders and conclude. His
attention would wander at the slightest pretext, neglecting his immediate
duty, and Danglard was always at his side to bring him back to reality
when necessary. But just now, Danglard was in Porto with Momo, having
dispatched Zerk to Rome, and was no doubt preparing to return to Paris.
Adamsberg was hoping that would be by the end of the day. Then they
would wait a few days to make it look less unlikely, and the pseudo-
informer would alert the squad. Mo would be brought back as a trophy
in Adamsberg's hands. Adamsberg was revising his part in this charade,
while Lieutenant Froissy was reporting on the tasks carried out in the
previous few days, among other things a bloody confrontation between

two employees of an insurance company, when one had called the other a 'lunary perv' and had ended up with a ruptured spleen, having been stabbed with a paperknife, and only just escaping with his life.

'Apparently,' said Justin with his usual attention to detail, 'it wasn't the perv that was the problem but the lunary.'

'But what is a lunary perv?' asked Adamsberg.

'Nobody knows, not even the man who said it. We asked.'

'OK,' said Adamsberg, already starting to doodle on the notepad he was resting on his knees. 'And what about the little girl with the gerbil?'

'The tribunal agreed that she can be taken in by a half-sister who lives in the Vendée. The judge ordered psychiatric counselling for the little girl. The half-sister has agreed to take the gerbil. Which is also a girl, according to the vet.'

'Brave woman,' pronounced Mordent, twisting his long thin neck as he did every time he passed a comment, as if to mark it. Since Mordent always looked to Adamsberg like an old heron with bedraggled plumage, this gesture reminded him of the bird swallowing a fish. If, that is, the heron was a bird and the fish a fish.

'And the great-uncle?'

'In detention. The charges are kidnapping, holding against her will, violence and ill-treatment. But no sexual offences, at least. The thing is, the great-uncle didn't want anyone else to have her.'

'Right,' said Adamsberg, who was sketching the apple tree under which he used to eat his breakfast. Although he could barely remember the doctor's report for more than a few seconds, every branch and twig of the apple tree remained precise and intact in his memory.

'Now, Monsieur Tuilot, first name Julien,' announced Noël.

'The breadcrumb murderer.'

'Exactly.'

'A unique weapon,' remarked Adamsberg, turning over another leaf in his notebook. 'As silent and effective as a crossbow, but requiring close proximity.'

'What's a crossbow got to do with it?' asked Retancourt. Adamsberg signalled to her that he'd explain later, and began to sketch a portrait of Dr Turbot.

'He's under arrest,' Noël said. 'A cousin is prepared to pay a defence lawyer, on the grounds that his wife's tyranny made his life a misery.'

'Madame Tuilot, Lucette.'

'Yes. The cousin has brought him crosswords in prison. He's only been there twelve days, and has already organised a tournament for some of the promising remand prisoners, beginner level.'

'So he's on good form, if I understand you.'

'Never so blooming, according to the cousin.'

A silence fell next, as everyone looked towards Retancourt, knowing as they did, though without the details, her key role in the Clermont-Brasseur case. Adamsberg signalled to Estalère to bring them all some coffee.

'We're still searching for Momo,' Adamsberg began, 'but it wasn't him that burnt the Mercedes.'

During Retancourt's lengthy account – covering the first pinstripe suit of clothes, the second suit, the haircut, the chambermaid, the Labrador, the smell of petrol – Estalère served everyone coffee, and offered his colleagues milk and sugar, going round the table carefully and attentively. Lieutenant Mercadet raised his hand without speaking to refuse sugar, which mortified Estalère, who prided himself on knowing which colleagues, in this case the lieutenant, usually took sugar.

'Given it up,' Mercadet explained in an undertone. 'Dieting,' he said, patting his stomach.

Reassured, Estalère was finishing his round, while Adamsberg suddenly froze, for no reason. A question from Morel surprised him and he realised that Retancourt was finishing her recital and that he'd missed some of it.

'Where's Danglard?' Morel repeated.

'He's taking a rest,' Adamsberg said quickly. 'He went under a train. He wasn't hurt, but it's a shock, takes some getting over.'

'He went under a *train*?' asked Froissy, with the same admiring and stupefied expression as Dr Turbot.

'Yes, Veyrenc acted quickly and pushed him between the rails.'

'There are twenty centimetres between the surface of a body and the underside of a train,' Veyrenc explained. 'He wasn't conscious.'

Adamsberg rose clumsily to his feet, leaving his notebook on the table.

'Veyrenc will take over and do the Ordebec report,' he said. 'I'll be back.'

'I'll be back,' he always said, as if it was highly possible that one day he would go away and never come back. He went out of the room with a lighter step than usual and escaped into the street. He knew that he had been struck stock-still all of a sudden, like one of the Ordebec cows, and had lost about five or six minutes of the meeting. Why, he couldn't say, and that was what he set out to discover by walking the pavements. He wasn't troubled by these sudden gaps in his consciousness, he was used to them. He didn't know the reason for this one, but he knew the cause. Something had passed through his mind, like the bolt from a crossbow, so fast that he hadn't had time to get hold of it. But it had been enough to turn him to stone. It was an experience like that time he had seen the sparkle on the waters in the port of Marseille, or the poster on a bus shelter in Paris, or when he had been unable to sleep on the Paris–Venice express. And the invisible image which had flashed across had drained the watery morass of his brain, bringing along with it other imperceptible images attached to each other as if in a magnetic chain. He couldn't see either the beginning or the end of it, but he could see Ordebec, and more precisely a car door, the one on Blériot's old banger, a door hanging open to which he hadn't paid any particular attention. It was as he had said to Lucio the day before, as if there was a door somewhere that hadn't been closed properly, a door that was banging, an insect bite that he hadn't finished scratching.

He walked slowly through the streets, going carefully, towards the Seine, where his footsteps always took him when he was troubled. It was at such moments that Adamsberg, normally almost impervious to anxiety or any strong emotion, became as tense as a guyrope, clenched his fists and tried to recapture what he had seen without seeing it, or thought without thinking it. There was no method by which he would succeed in extracting this pearl from the shapeless heap of thoughts inside him. He simply knew that he had to do it quickly, because his mind was so made that everything disappeared in the end. Sometimes he had managed it by standing absolutely still, waiting for the faint image to come trembling back to the surface, and sometimes it was by walking, stirring up his random memories, and sometimes going to sleep and allowing the laws of gravity to operate. And he feared, if he chose a theoretical strategy in advance, that he would miss his target.

After walking for over an hour he sat on a bench in the shade, and cupped his chin in his hands. He had completely lost the thread of the discussion during Retancourt's report. What had happened? Nothing. They had all been sitting still, listening attentively to what she was telling them. Mercadet was fighting sleep and taking notes with difficulty. Everyone had been sitting down, except one. Estalère had moved. Of course, he had been handing round coffees with his habitual punctiliousness. The young man had been a bit miffed because Mercadet had refused sugar even though he always took it, and the lieutenant had patted his stomach. Adamsberg dropped his hands from his chin on to his knees. Mercadet had made another gesture. He had lifted one hand, signifying his refusal. And it was at that moment that the shot had flashed through his brain. Sugar. Damn sugar, there'd been something about it from the very start. The commissaire lifted his hand, imitating Mercadet's gesture. He repeated the gesture several times and saw once more the car door swinging open. Blériot, standing in front of the car when it had broken down. Blériot. Blériot had also refused sugar when Émeri offered him some. He had raised his hand silently, just like Mercadet. In the gendarmerie, the day they had been talking about Denis de Valleray. Blériot, the man whose pockets were always bulging with lumps of sugar, but who didn't take it in his coffee. Blériot.

Adamsberg stopped moving his hand. The pearl was lying there, in the hollow of a rock. The door he hadn't closed. Fifteen minutes later, he stood up, gently, so as not to disturb the still unformed and as yet incompletely understood sensations in his head, and went back to his house, on foot. He hadn't unpacked his rucksack from the day before. He picked it up, put Hellebaud inside the shoe and loaded everything as quietly as he could back into his car. He didn't want to make any noise, fearing that speaking out loud would perturb the particles of his thoughts which were clumsily trying to assemble themselves. So he sent a simple message to Danglard on the mobile Retancourt had given him.

Going back to O: if necesary cntct same place same time. He wasn't sure how to spell 'necesary' and changed it to 'needed': *if needed cntct same place same time.* Then he sent a text to Veyrenc. *Come Léo house 20.30. Essential bring Retancourt + avoid being seen forest entrance bring rope + food.*

L

ADAMSBERG ENTERED ORDEBEC DISCREETLY, ONCE MORE AT TWO IN the afternoon, a good time on a Sunday when the streets were empty. He took the path through the woods to Léo's house, and opened up the room he considered his. Lying down in the hollow in the woollen mattress seemed to be a first priority. He placed the now tame Hellebaud on the windowsill, and curled up on the bed without sleeping, listening to the cooing of the pigeon, which seemed well satisfied to be back in its place. He let his thoughts wander as they would without trying to organise them. He had recently seen a photograph that had struck him as a clear illustration of his own idea of his brain. It showed the contents of a fishing net unloaded on the deck of a large vessel, a pile taller than the fishermen themselves, a heap of all kinds of things defying identification, in which the silvery colours of the fish mingled with the dark brown of seaweed, the grey of the crustaceans – marine ones, not that damned woodlouse – the blue of lobsters, the white of seashells, making it hard to distinguish the different elements. That was what he was always fighting, the confused, multiform and shifting mass, always ready to change or vanish, and float off again into the sea. The sailors were sorting out the pile, throwing back creatures that were too small, lumps of seaweed or detritus, and saving the familiar useful species. Adamsberg, it seemed to him, did the opposite, throwing out all the sensible items and then looking at the irrelevant fragments of his personal collection.

* * *

He went back to the beginning, to Blériot raising his hand to refuse sugar in his coffee, and allowed himself to associate freely the sights and sounds of Ordebec, the decomposed yet handsome face of Lord Hellequin, Léo waiting for him in the forest, the bonbonnière on Émeri's Empire table, Hippo shaking out his sister's wet dress, the mare whose nose he had patted, Mo and his coloured pencils, the ointment being rubbed into Antonin's bony ribs, the blood on the sketch of the madonna by Glayeux, Veyrenc in a state of collapse on the station platform, the cows and the woodlouse, the bubbles of electricity, the Battle of Eylau which Émeri had managed to tell him about three times, the count's cane tapping the old parquet floor, the sound of the crickets in the Vendermot house, the herd of wild boar on the Chemin de Bonneval. He turned over, put his hands behind his head and looked up at the beams in the roof. Sugar. Sugar, that had been irritating him all day and every day, giving him a feeling of intense annoyance, so much so that he had stopped taking it in his coffee.

Adamsberg got up after two hours, his cheeks ablaze. Now he had just one person to see: Hippolyte. He'd wait till seven in the evening, when all the inhabitants of Ordebec would be in their kitchens or taking an aperitif in the cafe. Going round the edge of the village, he could reach the Vendermot house with no risk of meeting anyone. The Vendermots would also be taking their aperitif, and perhaps they'd be finishing up the dreadful port they had bought specially to entertain him. He would gently make Hippo come round to his view, get him to go straight to the particular place he had in mind. 'We're nice people.' A rather peremptory definition for a child with amputated fingers who had terrorised his classmates for years. *We're nice people*. He consulted his watches. He had three calls to make to confirm things. One to the Comte de Valleray, one to Danglard and finally one to Dr Turbot. Then he'd set out in two and a half hours.

He slipped out of the bedroom and went to the cellar. There, by climbing on a cask, he could reach a dusty little window, the only one in the house that looked out on to a meadow with cows in it. He had plenty of time, he'd wait.

As he made his way cautiously towards the Vendermot house, hearing the angelus ringing, he felt satisfied. No fewer than three cows had moved. And they'd moved several metres as well. Without lifting their muzzles from the grass. Which seemed an excellent sign for Ordebec's future.

LI

'COULDN'T SHOP FOR FOOD, EVERYTHING WAS SHUT,' SAID VEYRENC, emptying a bag of provisions on to the table. 'Had to raid Froissy's cupboard, we'll have to replace this double quick.'

Retancourt was leaning against the fireplace, now containing cold ashes, her blonde head reaching far above the stone mantelshelf. Adamsberg wondered where he would be able to lodge her in this house, with its ancient beds that were too short for her outsize dimensions. She was watching Adamsberg and Veyrenc prepare sandwiches of hare pâté and truffles, with a cheerful expression. Nobody knew why some days Retancourt was amiable, other days disgruntled, and they didn't try to find out. Even when she was smiling, this large woman's bearing had something tough and pretty impressive about it, which dissuaded people from opening up to her or asking silly questions. Any more than you would give a friendly slap – a basic lack of respect – to an age-old giant redwood tree. Whatever her mood, Retancourt inspired deference and sometimes devotion.

After their hasty meal – but Froissy's pâté was undeniably very succulent – Adamsberg drew the layout of the site for them. From Léo's house, they would take a path south-east, then cut across some fields, find a path called the Chemin de la Bessonnière and follow it to the old well.

'It's a bit of a hike, six kilometres. The old well was the best place I could find. The Oison Well. I noticed it when I took a walk along the Touques.'

'The Touques?' asked Retancourt, always needing exact information.

'The river here. The well's on the land of the next parish, it's been abandoned for forty years, and it's about twelve metres deep. It would be easy, and tempting, to tip a man in.'

'If the man was leaning over the edge,' said Veyrenc.

'That's what I'm counting on. Because the killer's already done a manoeuvre like that by tipping Denis's body out of the window. He knows how to do it.'

'You mean Denis didn't kill himself?' said Veyrenc.

'No, he was killed, he was the fourth victim.'

'And not the last?'

'No.'

Adamsberg put down his pencil and explained his final arguments – if that was the word for them. Retancourt wrinkled her nose several times, disconcerted as always by the commissaire's methods of reaching his objective. But he had reached it, she had to admit that.

'That explains how he never left a single clue,' commented Veyrenc, looking thoughtful on hearing the new elements.

Retancourt by contrast was more concerned with the practical side of the action.

'Is it wide? The coping round the well?'

'No, thirty centimetres or so. And it's low, that's crucial.'

'Could work,' agreed Retancourt.

'And the diameter of the well?'

'Enough.'

'How will we operate?'

'Twenty-five metres away there's an old farm building, a barn, and it has two big wooden doors, very dilapidated. We can hide in there, no way of getting any nearer. Be careful. Hippo's a big lad. It's very risky.'

'It's dangerous,' said Veyrenc. 'We're putting a life at stake.'

'We've got no choice, there's no evidence except for a few old sugar wrappers, and no context for them.'

'You kept them?'

'Yes; they're in a barrel in the cellar.'

'They might have fingerprints. It hasn't rained for weeks.'

'But that wouldn't prove anything either – sitting on a tree trunk eating sugar isn't against the law.'

'There are Léo's words.'

'The words of a very old woman in a state of shock. And I was the only person who heard them.'

'Danglard did too.'

'He wasn't paying attention.'

'No, there's no case there,' agreed Retancourt. 'The only way is to catch him in the act.'

'Dangerous,' Veyrenc repeated.

'That's why we've got Retancourt here, Louis. She's quicker and more accurate. She'll catch him if he starts to fall. And she'll have the rope if we need it.'

Veyrenc lit a cigarette, shaking his head without protesting. Placing Retancourt's abilities higher than his own was something so obvious you didn't argue about it. She would probably have been able to hoist Danglard on to the station platform.

'If we screw up,' he said, 'a man could die, and us with him.'

'We won't screw up,' said Retancourt calmly. 'If this plan happens at all.'

'Yes. It'll happen,' Adamsberg assured them. 'He has no choice. And to kill this particular man would give him a lot of satisfaction.'

'I suppose so,' said Retancourt, holding out her glass for a refill.

'Violette,' said Adamsberg gently, while obeying her request, 'that's your third glass. We need all our strength.'

Retancourt shrugged, as if the commissaire had made a remark so stupid as to be unworthy of comment.

LII

RETANCOURT HAD TAKEN UP POSITION BEHIND THE LEFT-HAND door of the barn, the two men on the right. Nothing must impede her passage towards the well. In the dim light, Adamsberg held up both hands to his colleagues, all ten fingers splayed: ten minutes to go. Veyrenc crushed out his cigarette and put his eye to a large slit in the wooden wall. Solidly built, the lieutenant was flexing his muscles ready to move, while Retancourt, leaning on the door jamb and in spite of the fifteen metres of mountaineering cord coiled round her torso, gave an impression of total relaxation. Adamsberg was rather concerned at this, given the three glasses of wine.

Hippolyte arrived first and sat on the edge of the well, hands in pockets.

'Tough and self-confident, eh?' Veyrenc murmured.

'Watch out by the dovecote, that's the way Émeri will arrive.'

Three minutes later, the capitaine turned up, walking in his usual very upright way, his uniform buttoned up, but his footsteps a little hesitant.

'That's the problem,' whispered Adamsberg. 'He's more worried.'

'Could give him the advantage.'

The two men started to talk to each other, but their words were inaudible from the barn. They were standing less than a metre apart, looking suspicious and aggressive. Hippolyte was talking more than Émeri. And more rapidly, with aggressive intonations. Adamsberg looked anxiously at Retancourt, who was still leaning on the jamb, not having modified her stance one iota. That wasn't entirely reassuring, since Retancourt was capable of going to sleep standing up, like a horse.

Hippolyte's laugh rang out in the night, a harsh and unkind laugh. He tapped Émeri on the back, but it was not a friendly gesture. Then he leaned over the coping of the well, stretching out an arm, as if to point to something. Émeri raised his voice, shouting something like 'Stupid bugger'. And also leaned over.

'Watch out,' whispered Adamsberg.

The move was more expert and faster than he had anticipated – one man passing his arm under his opponent's legs and sweeping him off his feet – and his own reaction slower than he had hoped. He took off a good second behind Veyrenc, who had hurled himself into motion. Retancourt had already reached the well, while he was still three metres away. With a technique peculiar to herself, Retancourt had thrown Émeri to the ground, and was sitting astride him, keeping his arms pinned to the ground, and implacably blocking his ribcage as he groaned under her weight. Hippolyte was getting up, breathing heavily, his knuckles grazed by the stones he had been flung against.

'Close thing,' he said.

'You weren't in danger,' said Adamsberg, pointing to Retancourt.

He caught the capitaine's wrists, and handcuffed them behind his back, while Veyrenc attached his legs.

'Don't try to move, Émeri. Violette could crush you like a woodlouse, believe me. Like a land shrimp.'

Adamsberg, sweating, and his heart beating fast, called Blériot on his mobile, as Retancourt got up, sat on the coping and lit a cigarette as calmly as if she had just got back from the shops. Veyrenc was pacing up and down swinging his arms, getting rid of the tension. From a distance, his outline faded from view, and only the gleam of his auburn locks shone out.

'Come and join us at the old Oison Well, Blériot,' said Adamsberg. 'We've got him.'

'Got who?' said Blériot, who had only answered after about ten rings and then sounded only half awake.

'The Ordebec murderer.'

'But Valleray . . . ?'

'It wasn't Valleray. Hurry up, brigadier.'

'Where to? Are you in Paris?'

'The Oison Well isn't in Paris, Blériot. Wake up!'

'But who is it?' asked Blériot, after clearing his throat.

'It's Émeri. I'm really sorry, brigadier.'

And he really was. He had worked with this man, they'd walked, drunk and eaten together, they'd toasted victory round his table. That day – only yesterday in fact, as Adamsberg recalled – Émeri had been convivial, chatty, charming. He had killed four men, pushed Danglard on to the rails and knocked Léo's head on the floor. Old Léo who had saved him from the frozen pond. Yesterday, Émeri had raised his glass to the memory of his ancestor, he'd been confident: they'd identified a culprit, even if he wasn't the one expected. His work wasn't over yet: there were two more deaths to be arranged, three if Léo should regain her powers of speech. But things were going well. Four deaths had been accomplished. Two attempts had been thwarted, true, but three others remained to be seen to: well, he had his plan. Seven deaths, a big total for a proud soldier. Adamsberg would soon be on his way back to Paris, convinced that the culprit was Denis de Valleray: case closed, field of battle wide open.

Adamsberg sat down cross-legged on the ground beside him. Émeri, eyes directed up at the sky, was composing his features into those of a combatant who does not flinch before the enemy.

'Eylau,' said Adamsberg. 'One of your ancestor's most famous victories and one of your favourites. You know the strategy by heart, you'll talk about it to anyone, whether they want to listen or not. That's what Léo said: "Eylau". Not "Hello". "Eylau, Fleg, sugar." You were the one she was pointing to.'

'You're making the biggest mistake of your life, Adamsberg,' said Émeri in a hoarse voice.

'Three of us were witnesses. You tried to tip Hippo into the well.'

'Because he's a murderer, a devil! I always told you he was. He threatened me, and I defended myself.'

'He didn't threaten you, he said he knew you were guilty.'

'No, he didn't.'

'Yes, he did, Émeri. I told him what to say to you. He had to say he'd seen a body in the well, and call you to come and see for yourself. You were anxious. Why was he calling you to meet him at night? What was this story about a body in the well? So you came.'

'Of course I bloody came. If there was a corpse somewhere, it was my duty to turn up. Whatever the time.'

'But there was no corpse. Just Hippo, who accused you of murder.'

'On the basis of no evidence whatsoever,' said Émeri.

'Exactly. Since the beginning of the whole thing, there's been no evidence, no clues. Not for Herbier, not for Léo, Glayeux, Mortembot, Danglard, Valleray. Six victims, four deaths and not a single clue. That's rare, a murderer who comes and goes like a ghost. Or like a cop. Because who better than a cop to get rid of any traces? You handled the technical side of things, you passed me the results. Sum total: not a thing, not a fingerprint, not a single clue.'

'There aren't any clues, Adamsberg.'

'I can well believe you've destroyed them all. But there's still the sugar.'

Blériot parked his car near the dovecote, and came running up, flashlight in hand, his great belly before him. He looked down at his capitaine lying handcuffed on the ground, glanced in alarm and anger at Adamsberg, but held himself back from speaking. He didn't know whether he should say anything, he didn't know now who was a friend and who an enemy.

'Brigadier, get me away from these idiots,' Émeri commanded. 'Hippo called me out here, pretending there was a body in the well, he threatened me and I had to defend myself.'

'By trying to push me into the well,' said Hippo.

'I didn't have a gun on me,' said Émeri. 'I'd have raised the alarm at once to get you out. Even if devils like you absolutely deserve to die like that, down in the bowels of the earth.'

Blériot looked from Émeri to Adamsberg, still unable to choose his camp.

'Brigadier,' said Adamsberg, getting to his feet, 'you don't take sugar in your coffee, do you? So all that sugar you keep in your pockets is for your capitaine, isn't it? Not for you.'

'I always have some sugar on me,' said Blériot in a tight, neutral voice.

'To give him some when he has an attack. When his legs fail him and he starts shaking and sweating?'

'We're not supposed to mention it.'

'Why is it you that has to cart all these lumps of sugar around? Is it so that his uniform pockets won't bulge? Or because he's ashamed of it?'

'Well, both, commissaire. But we're not supposed to mention it.'

'And the lumps of sugar, they always have to be wrapped in paper?'

'Yes, sir, it's more hygienic. They can stay in my pockets weeks without him needing any.'

'Your sugar papers, Blériot, are the same ones that I found on the Chemin de Bonneval, by the fallen tree trunk. Émeri had a crisis right there. He sat down and ate six lumps and left the wrappers on the ground. And then Léo found them. *After* Herbier's murder. Because ten days earlier, they weren't there. Léo knows everything. She puts two and two together, details like butterfly wings. Léo knows that there are times when Émeri needs to eat several sugar lumps to recover his normal state. But what was Émeri doing on the Chemin de Bonneval? Well, he came to tell her why, that is, he came to kill her.'

'But that's impossible, sir, the capitaine never carries sugar around himself, he asks me for it.'

'Yes, but *that* night, Blériot, he went alone to the chapel, and he took some with him. Because he knows he's got this problem. Strong emotion and a sudden discharge of energy might set off a diabetic crisis. He didn't want to risk fainting after killing Herbier. How does he tear the paper? From the side? From the middle? What does he do next? He crumples them into a ball? Or leaves them as they are? Or folds them? We all have our little ways of dealing with the wrappers. But you screw them up into a tiny little ball and put them in your pocket.'

'So as not to leave litter.'

'And the capitaine?'

'He opens them from the middle and undoes three sides.'

'And afterwards?'

'He just leaves them like that.'

'Precisely, Blériot. And Léo surely knew that. I'm not going to ask you to arrest your capitaine. Veyrenc and I will put him in the back of the car. You get in the front. And all I'll ask you to do is drive us to the gendarmerie.'

LIII

ADAMSBERG HAD REMOVED THE HANDCUFFS AND FREED ÉMERI'S LEGS ONCE they were inside the interview room. He had alerted Commandant Bourlant at Lisieux. Blériot had been sent to Léo's cellar to fetch the sugar wrappers.

'Unwise to leave his hands free,' said Retancourt, in as neutral a tone as possible. 'Remember how Mo got away. Suspects try to escape at the drop of a hat, you know.'

Adamsberg met Retancourt's eyes and found there without any doubt a glint of provocative irony. Like Danglard, Retancourt had understood how Mo escaped, but had kept her counsel. And yet nothing should have displeased her more than that unorthodox manoeuvre of uncertain result.

'But this time, you're here, Retancourt,' said Adamsberg with a smile. 'So there's no danger. We're waiting for Bourlant,' he said, turning to Émeri. 'I'm not authorised to question you in this gendarmerie where you're still an officer. The station doesn't have a chief, so Bourlant will transfer you to Lisieux.'

'That's fine by me, Adamsberg. At least Bourlant respects principles based on the facts. Everyone knows that you just shovel clouds, and your opinion carries no weight in any police force, whether gendarmes or regular cops. I hope you realise that?'

'Was that why you were so insistent that I come to Ordebec? Or because you thought I'd be easier to deal with than your colleague, who wouldn't have let you get near the inquiry?'

'Because you're nothing, Adamsberg. Wind, clouds, an illiterate mass of ectoplasm, incapable of the slightest reasoning.'

'You're well informed.'

'Obviously. It was *my* investigation, and I had no intention of letting some super-efficient cop take over. As soon as I set eyes on you, I realised that what they say about you is true. That I'd be able to have my hands free, while you were wandering around in the mist. You got precisely nowhere, Adamsberg, you did fuck all, and everyone can testify to that. Including the press. All you achieved was to stop me arresting that bastard Hippo Vendermot. And why are you protecting him? Do you even know that? So that nobody lays a hand on his sister. You're useless and obsessed. All you've done while you were in Ordebec is stare at her tits and fuss over your fucking pigeon. Not to mention that the police disciplinary team came down here to do a search. Think I didn't know about that? So what *were* you doing here, Adamsberg?'

'Picking up sugar wrappers.'

Émeri opened his mouth, then breathed in and said nothing. Adamsberg sensed that what he was about to say was: 'Poor fool, the sugar wrappers won't do you any good.'

Right, that meant he wouldn't find any fingerprints on them. Just some pieces of paper, unidentified.

'You think you can convince a jury with your scraps of paper?'

'You're forgetting something, Émeri. Whoever tried to kill Danglard had also killed those other people.'

'Obviously.'

'A tough man, a good runner. You said, like I did, that Denis de Valleray had committed the murders and that therefore it must have been him who gave Danglard the rendezvous at Cérenay. It's in your first report.'

'Naturally.'

'And that he killed himself when the secretary of that club came and informed him about some kind of inquiry.'

'Not a *club*. The Compagnie de la Marche.'

'Whatever, it doesn't impress me. My own ancestor was a conscript in your famous Napoleonic Wars, and he died aged twenty, in case you're interested. At Eylau, if you want to know why that name stuck in my memory. His legs caught fast in the mud of the battlefield, while your forefather was holding a victory parade.'

'The family curse, eh?' said Émeri with a smile, holding his back straighter than ever, and resting a confident arm on the back of the chair. 'You'll have no better luck than your forefather, Adamsberg. You're already over your knees in mud.'

'Denis killed himself, you wrote, because he knew he was about to be accused. Of the murders of Herbier, Glayeux and Mortembot, and the attempted murder of Danglard and Léo.'

'Of course. You didn't see the final report from the lab. He'd taken enough anxiolytics and neuroleptics to kill a horse and he had almost five grams of alcohol in his blood.'

'Could be, perfectly well. It's quite easy to push all that down the throat of a man who's been knocked half conscious. You pull up his head and the swallowing reflex follows. But you have to ask this question, Émeri: why on earth would Denis have wanted to kill Danglard?'

'Come on, shoveller, you told me yourself. Because Danglard had found out the truth about the Vendermot children. Because of the birthmark like an insect.'

'A crustacean.'

'What the hell does *that* matter?' said Émeri exasperatedly.

'Yes, I did say that to you myself, and I was wrong. Because you tell me, how did Denis de Valleray find out so soon that Danglard had seen the crustacean? And realised what that meant? I only heard it myself the night Danglard left.'

'Rumour, gossip.'

'That's what I thought too. But I called Danglard and he hadn't told anyone else except Veyrenc. The man who slipped the note in his pocket did so very soon after the count had his attack in the hospital. The only people who could have seen Danglard putting Lina's shawl back on her shoulders, and *also* known that Danglard had seen the count with his shirt off, the *only* people who could have seen Danglard stare in surprise at the purple birthmark, were: the count, Dr Turbot, the nurse, the prison warders, Dr Hellebaud, Lina and you. Rule out the warders and Hellebaud, they were far away. Rule out the nurse, who hadn't seen Lina's birthmark, and rule out Lina, who hadn't seen the count's own birthmark.'

'She saw it that day.'

'No, she was at the far end of the corridor, as Danglard confirmed. So Denis de Valleray couldn't possibly know that the commandant had worked out the origins of his half-brother and -sister. So he had no motive to try and push him under the Caen–Paris express. *You* did. Who else would?'

'Turbot. He operated on Hippo's fingers when he was a boy.'

'Turbot wasn't in the little crowd in front of Glayeux's house. And in any case, Valleray's descendants were of no interest to him.'

'Lina could have seen, never mind what your commandant says.'

'But she wasn't at Glayeux's house, either.'

'Yeah, but her clay brother was, yes, Antonin. Who's to say she didn't tell him?'

'Turbot would. Lina didn't leave the hospital until after everyone else. She was chatting to a friend at reception. You can rule her out.'

'That leaves the count,' Émeri declared firmly. 'He didn't want anyone to know they were his children. Not in his lifetime anyway.'

'But he wasn't at Glayeux's house, he was still under observation at the hospital. You're the only one who could have both seen and understood, and you were the only one who could have put the note in his pocket. Probably when he went into Glayeux's house.'

'What the fuck do I care if the count is the father of those devil children? I'm not in the Valleray family. You want to look at my back? Just find one thing that links me to the death of all those lowlifes.'

'Easy, Émeri. Terror. And the need to eliminate the cause of the terror. You've always been lacking in courage and mortified not to be as brave as your ancestor. It was your bad luck that they gave you his name.'

'Terror,' said Émeri, spreading his hands wide. 'For the love of god, what am I supposed to be terrified of? That drip Mortembot, who died with his pants down?'

'No, Hippolyte Vendermot. In your eyes he is the cause of all your failures. For thirty-two years. The thought of ending up like Régis haunts you, you wanted to destroy the man who cursed you when you were both kids. Because you really did believe in the curse. You fell off your bike, and nearly died after he cursed you. You didn't tell me about that. Am I wrong?'

'Why should I tell you everything about my childhood? Every kid in the world falls off a bike and gets hurt. Didn't you?'

'Of course. But not just after being cursed by the satanic little Hippo. Not just after Regis's tragic accident. Everything went downhill for you after that. You failed at school, you had no success in Valence or Lyon, you couldn't have children, your wife left you. Your fear, your caution and your diabetic attacks. You aren't a marshal like your father wanted you to be, you're not even a soldier. And all this catalogue of failure, it's a drama for you, and it gets worse. But it wasn't *your* fault, Émeri, was it? It was Hippo's fault for cursing you. He said you'd have no children, he prevented you from having a glorious career or a happy one, because they're the same thing as far as you're concerned. Hippo's the source of all your pain, your bad luck, and he still terrifies you.'

'Come off it, Adamsberg. Who on earth would be scared of a degenerate who talks backwards?'

'Do you really think you have to be degenerate to know how to invert letters? Of course not. You have to be gifted with a special kind of genius. A diabolical one. You know that, just as you knew that Hippo had to be destroyed if you were to be able to live. You're only forty-two, you've still got time to make a new life. Since your wife left you and since Régis's suicide three years ago, which really panicked you, it's been your obsession. Because you're a man who gets obsessions. Like your Empire dining room.'

'That's a simple mark of respect, you wouldn't understand.'

'No, it's megalomania. Like your impeccable uniform – no sugar lumps in your pockets to make them bulge. Your way of parading like a soldier. There's just one person responsible for what you consider your unjust, unbearable, shameful and above all threatening downward path, and it's Hippolyte Vendermot. But the curse can only be removed by his death. You could argue that what happened at the well was simply a neurotic case of self-defence, if it wasn't that you'd already killed four other people.'

'Well, in that case,' said Émeri, leaning back in his chair, 'why wouldn't I just have killed Hippo?'

'Because you were afraid of being accused of his death. Understandably. Everyone here knows about your childhood, the bike accident when you were ten, after being cursed, the hate you have for the Vendermot family. You needed an alibi, to be above suspicion. An alibi or another culprit. You needed a vast and ingenious strategy, like the Battle of Eylau. A well-thought-out strategy, the only way to victory over a much bigger army, like the Emperor had to have. And Hippolyte Vendermot is ten times stronger than you. But then you're the descendant of a marshal, for heaven's sake, so you'll be able to crush him. "Are you going to let yourself be devoured by those people?" as the Emperor would say. Certainly not. But it means reconnoitring every bump and dip in the terrain. You needed a Marshal Ney to back you up, like when Davout was threatened on the right flank. That's why you went to see Denis.'

'I'm supposed to have gone to see him, am I?'

'A year ago, you were at a dinner at the chateau, with the local dignitaries, like Dr Turbot, Denis of course, the head of the salesroom at Evreux and others. The count had one of his attacks, you took him to his room with Turbot's help. Turbot told me about it. I think it must have been that evening that you learned about Hippo and Lina and the will.'

Émeri laughed out loud, quite naturally. 'You were there, Adamsberg, were you?'

'In a way. I asked Valleray to confirm it. He thought he might die, he asked you to fetch his will, he gave you the key of the deed box. Before dying, he wanted to write his two Vendermot children into the will. So with difficulty, he added a few lines on the paper and asked you to sign as a witness. He trusted to your discretion, as capitaine of gendarmes and a man of honour. But you read those few lines, of course. And you weren't surprised to learn that the count had fathered two limbs of the devil like Hippo and Lina. You had seen the birthmark on his back when Turbot was examining him. You knew about Lina's, because her shawl is always slipping. For you, the mark wasn't a woodlouse with antennae, it was the crimson face of a devil with horns. And it only confirmed in you the idea that this was a bastard and cursed line of descent. And that night, after all the time you'd been looking for the chance to wipe the Vendermot family from the face of the earth – because Lina's just as bad in your eyes – it finally offered itself. Or almost. You had to think about it, you don't rush boldly into action, you weigh everything up, and after a while, you decide to have a chat with Valleray's stepson.'

'I've never had any dealings with Denis, anyone will tell you that.'

'But you can go and visit him any time, Émeri, you're the capitaine of gendarmes. You tell him the truth, about the extra clause written into his father's will. You show him the dark chasm that awaits him. He's a weak man and you know it. But a man like him doesn't decide quickly. You let him think about it. You come back, you press him, convince him and make him an offer. You can get rid of these bastard heirs, on condition he provides you with an alibi. Denis doesn't know what to think, he probably takes more time. But as you suspected, he ends up saying yes. If you do the killing, he doesn't have to do anything except swear you were with him. Cheap at the price. So you've got a deal. You wait for the opportunity.'

'You still haven't answered my question. Why the fuck would I care if the count fathered those creatures? Or that Danglard knew about it?'

'Nothing. It's the creatures themselves that concern you. But if the secret of their birth got around, you'd lose the support of your accomplice, Denis, because it wouldn't be in his interests any more to cover you. And you'd lose the alibi. That's why you pushed Danglard on to the tracks.'

Just then, Commandant Bourlant came in. Having no esteem for Adamsberg, he saluted him without warmth.

'What are the presumed charges here?' he asked.

'Four murders, two attempted murders.'

'Intentions don't count. You've got *evidence*?'

'You'll get my report at ten o'clock tomorrow morning. Then it's up to you whether you refer the case to the examining magistrate.'

'I suppose that's in order. Follow me please, Capitaine Émeri, and don't blame me, because I know nothing about all this. But Adamsberg's in charge of the case and I'm obliged to obey him.'

'We won't spend long in each other's company, Commandant Bourlant,' said Émeri, getting up stiffly. 'He's got no evidence whatever, he's rambling.'

'Did you come alone, commandant?' asked Adamsberg.

'Affirmative, commissaire. It's a bank holiday today, 15 August.'

'Veyrenc and Retancourt, please accompany the commandant. I'll start writing the report while I wait for you.'

'Everyone knows you're incapable of writing three lines,' Émeri threw out derisively.

'Don't worry about that. One last thing, Émeri. The perfect opportunity. Lina gave it you without meaning to. When she saw the Ghost Riders, and all of Ordebec heard about it. She was showing you the way, it was a sign from fate. All you had to do was fulfil her prediction, kill the three named men who had been "seized", and get the townspeople incensed against the Vendermots. *Death to the Vs.* Then you would kill Lina and her accursed brother. People would have thought it was some madman in Ordebec who was scared of the army and determined to get rid of its "go-betweens". Like in 1775 when dozens of them lynched François-Benjamin. There would have been no shortage of suspects.'

'Seventeen seventy-seven,' Veyrenc corrected him in Danglard's absence.

'Not that many, but a couple of hundred.'

'I didn't mean the number of suspects, I meant the date he was lynched, 1777.'

'Oh, OK,' said Adamsberg, unperturbed.

'Hark at him, what an imbecile!' said Émeri between clenched teeth.

'Denis was almost as guilty as you,' said Adamsberg calmly, 'by giving you his cowardly word, his lousy blessing. But when you realised that the Compagnie de la Hache –'

'De la Marche,' Émeri interrupted.

'As you like . . . that the Compagnie was going to tip off Denis, you realised he wouldn't hold out more than a few hours. He'd talk. He'd accuse you. He well knew that you'd killed the "seized" men, to prepare for the death of the Vendermots. You went to see him, you talked to him to calm down his fears, then you knocked him half conscious – with one of your professional blows to the carotid – and forced the pills and alcohol down him. Unpredictably, Denis got up to be sick and made a dash for the window. It was the night of the storm, you remember. The time when power is there for the taking. You just had to tip him up by the legs and out he went. Denis would be accused of the murders, which would be the cause of his suicide. Perfect. It wasn't quite what you'd planned, but in the end it would do. After these four deaths, even if there was now a rational explanation, half of Ordebec would go on believing that the army was behind them. And that basically Hellequin had come to take the four villains. That the count's stepson was his chosen arm to do the killing, just his instrument. But that Hippo and Lina were essentially responsible for the Lord's arrival, again, and always would be. So nothing would prevent everyone saying some madman had decided to kill them both, as limbs of Hellequin. A madman who would never be found thanks to the population closing ranks.'

'Mass slaughter, to try and get one man?' said Émeri drily, smoothing down his tunic.

'Yes, it was, Émeri. But these killings gave you the greatest satisfaction as well. Both Glayeux and Mortembot had teased and humiliated you, they'd both escaped the prosecutions you attempted. And Herbier too, because you were never able to pin anything on him. They were all double-dyed villains, and you were about to eliminate these evil men, Hippo being the last one. But above all, Émeri, you really believe in the Ghost Riders, Lord Hellequin, his servants Hippo and Lina, his victim Régis – it all makes perfect sense to you. By destroying the "seized" men, you would be getting into Lord Hellequin's good graces. That's not negligible. Because you were afraid you might be the fourth man. You never liked the fourth man to be mentioned, the unnamed one. So I suppose that sometime, long ago, you must have already killed someone. Like Glayeux, like Mortembot. But that's a secret you'll probably take with you.'

'That will do, commissaire,' said Bourlant. 'Nothing said here has any official standing.'

'No, I know, commandant,' said Adamsberg with a brief smile, as he propelled Veyrenc and Retancourt to follow the dour chief of the Lisieux gendarmes out of the office.

342

'*The proud son of the eagle comes tumbling to earth / When in the heavens he'd dreamed of his worth,*' murmured Veyrenc.

Adamsberg gave him a look that told him this was not the moment, just as he had done to Danglard when he had blethered on about Richard the Lionheart.

LIV

LINA HADN'T GONE TO WORK: THE ROUTINE OF THE VENDERMOT household had been turned upside down by the news of the arrest of Capitaine Émeri, representative of the forces of order. A little as if Ordebec Church had been tipped up on to its steeple. After reading Adamsberg's report – largely drafted by Veyrenc – Commandant Bourlant had decided that he ought to inform the examining magistrate, and he in turn had recommended holding Émeri on remand. Nobody in Ordebec was now unaware that Louis Nicolas was in a police cell in Lisieux.

But even more momentously, the Comte d'Ordebec had written a formal letter to the Vendermot family, informing them of the true parentage of Hippolyte and Lina. It would be less shameful, he had told Adamsberg, that the children should learn it directly from him before rather than after it became the stuff of local gossip, which would spread quickly and inaccurately, as it always does.

On his return from the chateau at almost midday, Adamsberg found them pacing round their dining room, moving at random like billiard balls hitting each other on a bumpy surface, talking while standing up, and circling their large table, from which the breakfast dishes hadn't been cleared.

Adamsberg's arrival passed almost unobserved. Martin was pounding a few herbs with a pestle and mortar, while Hippo, usually the master of the house, was walking round the room, trailing his index finger along the walls as if drawing an invisible line. A child's game, Adamsberg said to himself. Hippo was reconstructing his life, and there'd be plenty for him to think about. Antonin was anxiously watching the rapid steps of his older brother, moving out of his way every now and then to avoid being knocked. Lina was concentrating on one of the chairs, scraping off little flakes of paint with her fingernail, with such intensity that one would have thought a life depended on her work. Only the mother was not moving. She was huddled in her armchair. Her entire posture, head down, thin legs pressed together, arms hugging her body, cried out the shame that had come upon her and from which she saw no means of escape. Everybody would now know that she had slept with the count, that she had been unfaithful to her husband, and all of Ordebec would go on talking about it for ever.

Without greeting anyone, since he thought they were incapable of hearing him, Adamsberg went over to their mother and put his bunch of flowers on her knees. It seemed, if anything, to make her embarrassment worse. She was unworthy of being presented with flowers. Adamsberg insisted, taking her hands one at a time and placing them round the stems. Then he turned to Martin.

'Martin, could you make us some coffee, please?'

His request, in an affectionate tone, seemed to attract the family's attention. Martin put down his pestle and went over to the cooker, scratching his head. Adamsberg himself got the bowls out of the sideboard and put them on the uncleared table, pushing the dirty dishes to the end. One by one, he asked them to sit down. Lina was the last to accept, and once seated, she started picking at the paint of her chair's leg. Adamsberg, feeling he had no talent as a psychologist, had a sudden desire to run away. He took the coffee pot from Martin's hands, and filled all the bowls. He took one to the mother, who refused, her hands still clasped round the bunch of flowers. He had the feeling he'd never drunk so much coffee as here. Hippo also pushed away the bowl, and opened a can of beer.

'Your mother was afraid *for* you,' Adamsberg began, 'and she was absolutely right.'

He saw them all look down. All four looked at the ground as if they were at Mass.

'Well, if not one of you can be bothered to defend her, dammit, who will?!'

Martin put his hand out towards the mortar then took it back.

'The count saved her from going mad,' Adamsberg hazarded. 'None of you can imagine what hell her life had become. Valleray protected you all, and you owe him that. He stopped Hippo being shot like the dog. You owe him that too. By getting his protection, she got you all protected. She couldn't do it herself. She did her job as a mother. That's all.'

Adamsberg was by no means certain of what he was saying, whether the mother would have gone mad, whether the father would have shot Hippolyte, but this wasn't the time for trifling over details.

'Was it the count who killed our father?' asked Hippo.

The head of the family had broken the silence, a good sign. Adamsberg took a breath, regretting he didn't have a cigarette handy from Zerk or Veyrenc.

'No. Who killed your father, we'll never know. Could have been Herbier.'

'Yes,' said Lina, 'that could be it. They'd quarrelled not long before. Herbier wanted money from our father. They were shouting.'

'Yes, of course,' said Antonin, at last opening his eyes wide. 'Herbier must have found out about Hippo and Lina and he was blackmailing our father. He'd never have stood for the whole town to know.'

'In that case,' Hippo objected, 'surely our father would have killed Herbier.'

'Yes!' said Lina. 'And that's why it was his own axe. Our father tried to kill Herbier but he got the worst of it.'

'Well, anyway,' said Martin, 'if Lina saw Herbier in with the Riders, must mean he'd committed a crime. We knew what Mortembot and Glayeux had done, but not Herbier.'

'That must be it,' said Hippo. 'Herbier attacked our father with the axe.'

'Yes, I'm sure you're right,' said Adamsberg approvingly. 'That ties up the loose ends, and above all, it means it's all over.'

'Why did you say our mother was right to be frightened?' asked Antonin. 'Émeri didn't kill *us*.'

'No, but he was going to. It was his final objective: he wanted to kill

Hippo and Lina and let the blame fall on some local person who was really scared of the dead men in the Furious Army.'

'Like in 1777.'

'Exactly. But the death of Denis de Valleray held him up. It was Émeri who tipped him out of the window. But it's all over now,' he said, turning to the mother, whose expression seemed to have cleared, as if now that her actions had been spoken aloud and even defended, she could emerge a little from her daze. 'The time for fear is over,' he insisted. 'And the curse of the Vendermots is over too. At least these murders will have that result. Everyone will know that none of you had anything to do with them – in fact, you were the victims.'

'So now nobody will be scared of us,' said Hippo with a rueful smile.

'Perhaps that's a pity,' said Adamsberg. 'You'll become just an ordinary five-fingered man.'

'Good thing Mother kept the bits,' sighed Antonin.

Adamsberg stayed another hour before taking his leave and sending a final glance towards Lina. Before he left, he put an arm round the mother's shoulders and asked her to walk to the road with him. The little woman, intimidated, put down the flowers and picked up a basket, explaining that she would fetch in the clothes from the line at the same time.

Adamsberg helped her to unpeg the linen from the line strung between the two apple trees, and they folded it into the basket. He could see no tactful way to broach the question.

'So Herbier might have killed your husband,' he said quietly. 'What do you think about that idea?'

'Sounds right,' whispered the little woman.

'But untrue. It was you that killed him.'

The mother dropped the clothes peg she was holding and gripped the line with both hands.

'We two are the only ones who know, Madame Vendermot. The crime is subject to the statutes of limitation. No one will mention it again. You had no choice. It was him or them. I mean Valleray's two children. He was going to kill them. You saved them the only way you could.'

'How did you know?'

'Because in fact there are three of us who know. You, me and the count. If the matter was hushed up at the time it was his doing. He confirmed that to me this morning.'

'Vendermot wanted to kill the two children. He found out.'

'How?'

'Nobody told him. He delivered some planks to the chateau and Valleray helped him unload. The count got his shirt caught on one of the claws of the digger, and it tore in half. Vendermot saw the birthmark on his back.'

'But there's someone else who knows, or half knows.'

The woman lifted her frightened face towards Adamsberg.

'Lina. She saw you kill him when she was a little girl. That's why she wiped the handle. Then she tried to wipe out the memory as well, to bury it deep in oblivion. That's why she had her first crisis soon afterwards.'

'What crisis?'

'The first vision of the Ghost Riders. She saw Vendermot being seized. So that way, Lord Hellequin could become responsible for the crime, instead of you. And she kept on nourishing this idea, crazy as it was.'

'On purpose?'

'No, as a form of self-protection. But it's important now to help her get rid of the nightmare.'

'We can't. These things are stronger than us.'

'You can, perhaps, if you tell her the truth.'

'Never,' said the little woman, turning back to the line.

'In a corner of her mind, Lina already suspects it. And if she does, then her brothers do too. It would help them to know that you did it and why.'

'Never.'

'It's your choice, Madame Vendermot. To imagine: Antonin will stop thinking he's made of clay, Martin will stop eating insects. Lina will be delivered from her visions. Think about it, you're their mother.'

'The clay, that's certainly troubling,' she said weakly.

So weakly Adamsberg felt sure that at that moment a puff of wind would have been enough to scatter her like dandelion down. A fragile little woman, so at a loss, yet who had split her husband's head open with an axe. The dandelion is a humble but very persistent plant.

'But two things won't change,' Adamsberg continued. 'Hippo will go on speaking backwards. And Hellequin's ghostly army will go on riding through Ordebec.'

'Oh yes, of course it will,' said the mother in a firmer voice, 'that's nothing to do with us.'

LV

VEYRENC AND DANGLARD MANHANDLED MO UNGENTLY INTO Adamsberg's office and sat him down forcibly on a chair. He was hand-cuffed. Adamsberg felt real pleasure on seeing him again, in fact a rather proud feeling of satisfaction that he had saved him from the stake.

Standing either side of Mo, Veyrenc and Danglard played their parts to perfection, their expressions stern and vigilant.

Adamsberg winked surreptitiously at Mo.

'Now you see how it ends if you go on the run, Mo.'

'How did you find me?' the young man asked, in an insufficiently truculent tone.

'We'd have nabbed you sooner or later. We had a list of addresses.'

'So what?' said Mo. 'I had the right to run away, I had to run away. I didn't torch that fucking motor.'

'No, I know that,' said Adamsberg.

Mo took on a moderately astonished expression.

'The two sons of Clermont-Brasseur did it,' Adamsberg went on. 'Right now, they're being charged with premeditated murder.'

Before leaving Ordebec three days earlier, Adamsberg had got Valleray to agree to put some pressure on the examining magistrate. The promise had been extracted without difficulty, since the cruelty of the brothers had deeply shocked the old man. He had had his share of atrocities on his doorstep in Ordebec, and was not disposed to indulgence, including towards himself.

'His sons?' Mo was asking with false surprise. 'His own *sons* torched his car with him inside?'

'And they planned to get you charged with it. Your trainers, your methods. Except that Christian Clermont didn't know how you do up your laces. And the heat of the fire burnt his hair.'

'Yeah, it'll do that every time.'

Mo looked right and left, as if he had suddenly realised that the situation had quite changed.

'Oh, so I'm free to go now?'

'Ha! In your dreams,' said Adamsberg sternly. 'You forgotten how you left here? Armed threats to a police officer, violence and escaping from custody.'

'But I *had* to,' Mo repeated.

'You may think so, son, but that's the law. You're going into preventive custody now, and your case will come up in a month.'

'But I didn't really hurt you,' Mo protested. 'I only knocked you about a bit.'

'Knocking me about a bit gets you up in front of a judge. You're used to it. He'll take the decision.'

'How long could it be?'

'Two years,' Adamsberg guessed, 'because of the exceptional circumstances and degree of damages. You might be out in eight months for good conduct.'

'Eight months, *shit*,' said Mo, this time with near-sincerity.

'You ought to be thanking me for finding who really did set the fire. And I had no reason to help you either. A commissaire who lets a suspect escape, do you realise what trouble he can get into?'

'See if I fucking care.'

'No, I don't suppose you do,' said Adamsberg. 'OK, take him away.'

Adamsberg made a sign with his hand to Mo, signifying 'I did tell you. Eight months. No choice.'

'That's true, commissaire,' said Mo suddenly, holding out his handcuffed wrists. 'I should thank you.'

As he shook hands with Adamsberg, Mo slipped him a ball of paper.

Larger than the wrapping of a sugar lump. Adamsberg shut the door when they had left, leaned against it to stop anyone interrupting him, and read the message. Mo had written out, in very tiny letters, his reasoning about the string they had found attached to Hellebaud's feet. At the end of the note, he gave the presumed name and address of the nasty little so-and-so who had done it. Adamsberg smiled and carefully put the paper in his pocket.

LVI

USING HIS USUAL CHANNELS, THE COMTE DE VALLERAY HAD ARRANGED
for the osteopath to return to Léo's bedside on the appointed day. The doctor
spent twenty minutes with her, accompanied only by Dr Turbot, who didn't
want to miss a minute of the demonstration, and the warder René. In the
corridor, the same scene as before repeated itself, with those waiting pacing
up and down: Adamsberg, Lina, the nurse, the count sitting on a chair and
tapping the lino with his cane, the warders from Fleury guarding the door.
The same silence and tension. But this time, for Adamsberg, the anxiety was
of a different kind. It was no longer a matter of saving Léo's life, but of
finding out whether the doctor could restore her powers of speech. Her
words would reveal – or not – the name of the Ordebec murderer. Without
her testimony, Adamsberg doubted whether the examining magistrate would
uphold the charges against Capitaine Émeri. He wasn't going to take such a
momentous decision on the basis of half a dozen sugar wrappers – which
had indeed turned out to have no fingerprints on them. Nor on the basis
of the assault on Hippo at the well, which proved nothing about the other
murders.

In Valleray's case, it was a matter of finding out whether his old Léo
would regain her former vivacity, or would remain forever locked into
her calm silence. As for the wedding, he hadn't mentioned it again. After
the shocks, scares and scandals that had rocked Ordebec, it was as if the
little town was exhausted, its apple trees more weighed down, the cows
turned to statues.

A wave of cool weather with rain had returned Normandy to its normal aspect. So Lina, instead of one of her low-cut blouses, was wearing a high-necked sweater. Adamsberg was concentrating on this problem when Dr Hellebaud at last came out of the room, looking sleek and satisfied. His lunch had been laid for him at a table in the nurse's office as before. They all accompanied him there in silence and the doctor rubbed his hands together energetically, before assuring them that next day, Léo would be able to speak normally. She had recovered enough psychological strength to face up to the situation, so he had been able to lift the protective fences. Turbot watched him eating, leaning his cheek on his hand, rather in the pose of an old man in love.

'There is something,' the osteopath said between mouthfuls, 'that I would like to know. If a man pounces on you and tries to kill you, it would throw anyone into shock. And if a friend did it, that would seriously increase the trauma. But something much more powerful than that has affected Léo, so she was resolutely refusing to face up to it. It was as if, for example, her own son had attacked her. Absolutely. So I don't understand that. But I'd say it wasn't just an acquaintance who hurt her. It must have been someone more important to her.'

'Yes indeed,' said Adamsberg pensively. 'A man she didn't often see any more. But she had known him long ago in special circumstances.'

'Which were?' asked the doctor, gazing at him with a very concentrated glint in his eyes.

'When this man was three years old, Léo plunged into a frozen pond to rescue him from drowning. She saved his life.'

The doctor nodded his head several times. 'Yes, that'll do,' he said.

'When can I see her?'

'Right away. But don't ask her any questions until tomorrow. Who brought her those ridiculous books? A bizarre love story and a book on horse management. What an idea.'

'I liked the love story,' said the nurse.

* * *

Adamsberg retraced his steps along the Chemin de Bonneval, strolled past St Antony's Chapel, walked as far as the old Oison Well, and arrived, feeling somewhat shattered, to dine at the Boar – Blue or Running, whatever it was. Zerk, now back from his sentimental journey to Italy, phoned during the meal to say that Hellebaud had flown away for good. It was excellent news, though Adamsberg could hear the distress in his son's voice.

At seven next morning, he had taken his breakfast under the apple tree. He didn't want to be late for the beginning of visiting time, and above all for Commandant Bourlant to forestall him at Léo's side. With the complicity of Dr Turbot and the nurse, he was being allowed to go in half an hour before the official time. Now feeling better about sugar, he put two lumps in his coffee, then closed the box carefully and put the elastic band back round it.

At eight thirty, the nurse discreetly opened the door to him. Léo was waiting, sitting up in an armchair, and already dressed. Dr Turbot had given permission for her to go home today. It had been arranged for Brigadier Blériot to pick her up, accompanied by Fleg.

'You haven't come just for the pleasure of seeing me, have you, commissaire? But I'm being very rude,' she reproved herself. 'It was you who got me taken to hospital and stayed by me, and it was you who arranged this special doctor. Where does he practise?'

'In Fleury.'

'Turbot even told me you combed my hair. You really are nice.'

We are nice people, Adamsberg recalled, visualising the faces of the Vendermot children, two fair and two dark, and it was almost true.

Adamsberg had ordered Dr Turbot above all not to mention Émeri's arrest to Léo. He wanted her testimony to be entirely without influence.

'Yes, it's true, Léo. I want to know.'

'Louis,' she whispered, 'it was my little Louis.'

'You mean Émeri?'

'Yes.'

'Are you all right, Léo?'

'Yes.'

'What happened? With the sugar? Because that's what you said to me, Léo. You said Eylau, the name of the battle, then you said Fleg, and then sugar.'

'Did I? I don't remember. When was that?'

'A day or so after you were attacked.'

'No, I don't remember that. But yes, he did have a problem with sugar. And ten days earlier, I'd been to St Antony's Chapel and I hadn't seen anything.'

'That was before Herbier went missing.'

'Yes. And the day I met you, while I was waiting for Fleg, I saw all these little white papers on the ground by the tree trunk. I hid them under the leaves because they were litter, and I counted least six. Next morning, I thought about them again. There's never anyone on the Chemin de Bonneval, you know that. So I thought it odd someone would have been around when Herbier was getting himself killed. And I only know one man who eats six lumps of sugar at a time. And doesn't crumple up the wrappers. It's Louis. He sometimes has an attack, you know the sort, and he has to take sugar quickly. Next day, I wondered if Louis had been along there before, looking for the body in the forest, but if so, he hadn't said anything and, even more surprisingly, he hadn't found it. I was curious, so I called him again. You wouldn't have a cigar about you, would you, commissaire? It's ages since I had a smoke.'

'I've got a half-smoked cigarette.'

'That'll do.'

Adamsberg opened the window and gave Léo the cigarette and a light.

'Thank you,' said Léo, inhaling. 'Louis said he'd come over. But when he arrived, he hurled himself at me. I don't know why, I don't understand.'

'He's the Ordebec killer, Léo.'

'He killed Herbier, you mean?'

'Herbier and others.'

Léo took a long drag on the cigarette, which shook a little.

'Louis, my little Louis?'

'Yes. We'll have time to talk about it this evening, if you let me stay for supper. I'll do the cooking.'

'It would be nice to have some soup with plenty of pepper. They don't put pepper in here.'

'Right you are. But tell me, why did you say "Eylau", not "Louis"?'

'It was his nickname when he was a little boy,' said Léo with that faraway look that accompanies a memory rising up from the past. 'It was his father who gave it to him, when he had a toy drum, but it was probably meant to make him think of a career in the army. And it stuck to him until he was five: the little drummer boy of Eylau, Little Eylau. Did I really call him that?'

At roughly the same time, the Clermont-Brasseur affair was hitting the news-stands, provoking much scandal. Questions were asked about whether the brothers had been protected in the aftermath of the crime. But the queries didn't last. Nor was much attention paid to the arrest of young Mohamed. All the flurry wouldn't last long. In a few days, the affair would be arousing little comment then forgotten, as Hippo would have been if he'd fallen into the well.

Adamsberg, with mixed feelings of shock, disillusion and abstraction, was listening to the news on Léo's dusty little radio. He'd done the shopping, and liquidised some vegetable soup – a light meal suitable for one returning from hospital. Although he thought Léo would probably have preferred a more solid or indeed rich meal. If he was not much mistaken the evening would end with cigars and Calva. Adamsberg left the radio and lit a fire in the grate to welcome her. The hot weather had ended along with the career of the killer and, after its trials, Ordebec was returning to its usual cool temperature.

LVII

OVER A MONTH LATER, ON A WEDNESDAY, DANGLARD TOOK DELIVERY at the squad headquarters of a solid wooden case with two handles, carefully packaged and brought by special carrier. He put it through the X-ray machine, which revealed it as a rectangular object packed between wooden slats and surrounded by shavings. He carefully lifted it up and put it on Adamsberg's desk. Danglard had not forgotten. He looked avidly at the object, stroked the rough outer surface of the case, but hesitated to open it. The idea that a canvas from the School of Clouet was lying a few inches away from him plunged him into a state of high excitement.

He intercepted Adamsberg.

'Parcel for you in your office.'

'Right, Danglard.'

'I think it's the Clouet.'

'The what?'

'The Valleray's painting. School of Clouet, the jewel, the gem, the consolation.'

'Right, Danglard,' repeated Adamsberg, noticing that sweat had broken out strangely on the commandant's suddenly blushing face. Danglard had no doubt been anxiously awaiting this for some time. He himself had completely forgotten about it since the scene in the library.

'When did it get here?'

'Two hours ago.'

'I was visiting Tuilot, Julien. He's got them doing level 2 crossword competitions now.'

Adamsberg opened the case, a bit roughly, then started to take out the wood shavings in fistfuls, to Danglard's anguish.

'Don't for god's sake damage it. You don't realise.'

Yes, it was the promised picture. Adamsberg placed it in Danglard's hands, which had stretched out instinctively, and smiled in imitation of the real happiness which illuminated the commandant's features. For the first time since he had taken him off to fight the army of Ghost Riders.

'I'm going to entrust it to you, Danglard.'

'No!' cried Danglard in panic.

'Yes. I'm a peasant, a mountain dweller and cloud shoveller, an ignoramus, as Émeri always said. And it's true. Keep it for me, it'll be much happier and much better cared for with you. It ought to be with you, and look, it jumped into your arms.'

Danglard looked down at the canvas, unable to speak, and Adamsberg presumed he was on the verge of tears. It was Danglard's capacity for emotion that took him up to heights Adamsberg never reached, as well as to the shame of the station platform of Cérenay.

Besides the picture – and Adamsberg was aware that this was a priceless gift – the Comte de Valleray sent him an invitation to his wedding to Léone Marie Pommereau, five weeks later in Ordebec Church. On his wall calendar, Adamsberg ringed the date with blue felt pen, sending a kiss to his old Léo. He would not forget to inform the doctor in his 'place at Fleury', but it was unthinkable that even with the powers of the Comte de Valleray he should be allowed to be present at the festivities for the woman he had resuscitated. Such powers are only to be found in fortresses like that of the Clermonts, where the rathole the commissaire had opened was being blocked up again, irreversibly, with the help of thousands of devoted hands, wiping out acts of infamy, complicities and trails of gunpowder.

Another three weeks and five days went past before Hellebaud the pigeon reappeared one morning on Adamsberg's kitchen windowsill. He was warmly welcomed and it was a lively visit. The bird pecked up some seed from the hands of Zerk and Adamsberg, flew round the table a few times and told them the story of his life in many cooings. An hour later, he flew off again, followed by the blank and thoughtful eyes of Adamsberg and his son.

Author's Note

Many references to the story of Gauchelin, the priest of Bonneval who encountered Hellequin and his ghostly cavalcade, can be found on the Internet. The ancient texts cited in this novel are taken from Claude Lecouteux, *Fantômes et revenants au Moyen Age*, Image editions, Paris, 1986.

Translator's Note

There are two police forces in France, the gendarmerie and the Police Nationale, both controlled by the Ministry of the Interior. The gendarmerie, military in origin and normally in uniform, polices the countryside and small towns (fewer than 20,000 inhabitants). In this book, the little town of Ordebec has a station manned by a capitaine and a lower-ranking brigadier. The Police Nationale, operating in larger towns and cities, is the organisation which would employ Adamsberg's Serious Crime Squad. The military ranks now applied there too do not exactly map on to British or American equivalents. As a commissaire, Adamsberg is roughly the opposite number of a British supertendent, and his colleagues' ranks in descending order are: commandant, lieutenant, and brigadier. In this book, his squad is exceptionally called in to investigate events in Ordebec at the request of the local gendarmes.